ANNIE MURRAY

Birmingham Blitz

PAN BOOKS

First published 1998 by Pan Books

This edition published 2010 by Pan Books
an imprint of Pan Macmillan,
20 New Wharf Road, London N1 9RR
Associated companies throughout the world
www.panmacmillan.com

ISBN 978-1-5098-8172-7

1 3 5 7 9 8 6 4 2

A CIP catalogue record for this book is available from
the British Library.

Typeset by SetSystems Ltd, Saffron Walden, Essex
Printed and bound by CPI Group (UK) Ltd, Croydon, CR0 4YY

Visit **www.panmacmillan.com** to read more about all our books
and to buy them. You will also find features, author interviews and
news of any author events, and you can sign up for e-newsletters
so that you're always first to hear about our new releases.

Birmingham Blitz

ANNIE MURRAY was born in Berkshire and read English at St John's College, Oxford. Her first Birmingham novel, *Birmingham Rose*, hit *The Times* bestseller list when it was published in 1995. She has subsequently written thirteen other successful novels, including, most recently, *A Hopscotch Summer* and *Soldier Girl*. Annie Murray has four children and lives in Reading.

For Mum and Dad,
with love and gratitude

ACKNOWLEDGEMENTS

Special thanks are due to the Birmingham people who generously gave their time to talk to me about 'their war': Elsie Ashmore and Nancy Holmes for their hospitality and frankness, Doris Burke who was a star and prepared to answer any number of daft questions, Rose and Jack Hall with whom I spent a great afternoon (Jack makes the best chips in Birmingham, if not the world), and Eric Langston for his welcome and his memories. A particular thank you also to Joe Mattiello who made himself available at unexpected moments and was a rich vein of information, and to my parents, George and Jackie Summers, who have frequently cast their minds back fifty or more years at a few seconds' notice.

Thanks also to Martin Parsons at Reading University, to Dr Rob Perks, Oral History Curator at the National Sound Archive, to Tony Doe and Concept Creative Productions.

There are a great many excellent books available about the Home Front during World War II and I drew on a variety of them, but none deserves mention more than Angus Calder's comprehensive and humane book *The People's War*. Thanks also go to Birmingham's Tindal Memory Writing Group which convened to produce *Writing It Down Before It's All Gone*, edited by Alan Mahar, which is a repeated source of inspiration.

NOTE TO THE READER

This story was originally conceived round the concept of the new and powerful influence of radio during the Second World War. Each chapter was prefaced by part of a contemporary song which in some way reflected its contents. Regrettably, because of the extremely high copyright costs of reproducing quotations from songs, these have had to be omitted from the finished book. However, readers who are familiar with the lyrics of the time might like to supply a suitable song for themselves as they go along.

A little happiness, a little sorrow,
May be awaiting you tomorrow –
That's what life is made of anyhow.

A little tearfulness a little laughter
And not a care for what comes after
There's nothing to be afraid of anyhow.

For the world rolls on the same old way
Just as night comes after day
And none of us can have a say about it,

So make the most of every minute
And get your sixty seconds in it,
'Cos that's what life is made of anyhow.

Ray Noble
(That's What Life is Made of)

August 1939

'Mom?'

Silence.

'MOM!'

'What?' That was her 'what the hell do you want *now*?' voice.

'Come up quick. It's Lola. She's dead.'

A pause from downstairs. We never usually called her Lola. Granny, Nan, filthy-old-cow, depending on who was talking, who listening. I couldn't call her Granny today somehow, not now she'd gone.

'Hang on a tick – let me put this on the gas. Genie? Sure she's not having you on?'

God Almighty. 'I'll ask her shall I? Lola? You dead, or what?'

'Don't be so cheeky.' I heard her footsteps across the back room. Then nothing. Above the mantel there was an oval mirror with a green frame, faded pink flowers stencilled round it. I realized she'd stopped, actually stopped to look at her reflection, her pale face which looked gaunt and scooped out under the high cheek-bones, thin brown hair twisted in a knot at the back, wisps of it always working out of the pins.

She dragged herself up the stairs eventually, muttering, the martyr as usual. 'She would go on a Sat'dy morning when no one's around and your dad's off playing soldiers. As if I haven't got enough on my plate.

1

What're we going to do? Oh!' She clapped her hand over her nose at the door.

'She must've messed herself,' I said.

'As if I couldn't tell. In this heat too!'

She hadn't messed like that before as a rule. Not the full works. Just wet the bed, my bed where I'd had to sleep with her every night for three years, pressed up against the bugs on the wall waiting for it, the wet and stink and it seeping across, warm first, then cold.

Not taking her eyes off Lola, Mom backed over and flung open the window with one hand. We could hear kids playing out the back next door. Then she crept forward, face all screwed up, on tiptoe as if she thought Lola was going to explode or jump up and dance a polka. She bent over the bed, keeping her hand on her nose. Long, pointy nose like a pixie, my mom.

Lola's hands were lying outside the covers. They'd barely looked like hands for a long while. Had a hard life. They were red like mutton chops, the knuckles tight and swollen, and she used to nurse them in her lap when they throbbed. Mom picked one up like she would a dead rat (except she never would pick up a dead rat, she'd get me to do it), her face still looking as if someone'd forced a cup of castor oil down her.

'She's not breathing.' One hand was still pegged to her nose, the other groping about round Lola's wrist. 'She's gone.' Dropped the hand and let it fall back on the bed. Finally she loosed her nose, staring at Lola's grey old face. '*Shame.* Looks quite peaceful now, don't she? You'll have to clean her up, Genie, before we get her laid out. Can't let her be seen in that state, can we?' She was over at the door by now. 'I couldn't do it. It'd make me bad.'

*

So I washed my dead granny that baking hot afternoon. You have to do your duty to the dead, even though she was smelly and vicious and I hated her. She had disgusting habits. Taking snuff was one of them and she only had two hankies which I always got the job of washing out. They looked as if a dog had sicked on them and I could never get them any cleaner. She sniffed louder than water going down the plughole and gobbed into the fireplace, she soaked me in urine nearly every night and talked a load of gibberish. I'd kneel down in front of her to roll her stockings up her sickly white legs with the bacon-burn marks up them from sitting close to the fire all her life, the smell of wee rising off her. Sometimes she'd slap me, hard as she could round the face. Brought tears to my eyes. She'd squawk, 'Bitch! Common little bitch!' and I knew she meant Mom because she always reckoned Mom wasn't good enough for her darling babby Victor, her youngest and best. Mom wouldn't lift a finger for her so long as I was around to do it.

She was still wearing her corset, the colour of old cement, with bits of whalebone sticking out all over the place. I pushed her over on one side which was an effort because I wasn't much of a size, and skinny with it, and she was heavy for such a scrawny old bird. Shoving my shoulder against her, I managed to get her unlaced. She was trying to roll back on me all the time, with me gagging at the stink. I took off her lisle stockings, the interlock vest and bloomers and saw all the brown mess between her legs and up her back and in her scraggy little mound of hair down there.

While I was going over her with a rag and a pail of water (cold – Mom said, 'What's the use in wasting gas, she's dead, isn't she?') I thought, what would she have looked like when she was fifteen? And how with a name

3

like Lola Mavis she ought to have been in a circus act instead of working factories the length and breadth of Birmingham.

I bent down to squeeze out the rag in the water that looked like stewed tea but didn't smell at all like it, trying not to drip any on my frock.

'Oh my God!' I said, straightening up. My heart was pounding like a mad thing and sweat pricked under my arms because I'd have sworn on my own life she moved and I was out of that room and down the stairs as if my bloomers were on fire.

'Mom – she moved. She's not dead. I saw her titties going up and down!'

'*No.*' Her hand halted a wooden spoon in the air. 'You're seeing things!'

But we both tiptoed up the stairs and peeped into that room, not knowing what we were scared of except we'd both have screamed like billy-o if there'd been one tiny flicker of movement from her. All we could see were the grimy old soles of Lola's feet and the soiled sheet in a heap on the floor and the enamel bucket and there wasn't a sound as we moved closer. She lay quite, quite still.

We stood by the bed and suddenly Mom was tittering away like the Laughing Policeman and set me off. I thought this was a bit of all right, Mom being nice to me, us laughing as if we couldn't stop. But we did stop, very sudden, because we saw Lola's eyes had slid half open and she was watching the pair of us like an old parrot.

'For God's sake get her eyes closed,' Mom said, disgusted. 'I'll fetch you a couple of pennies.'

I pushed Lola's eyes closed and laid a penny and a ha'penny on top, which was all she could find. I covered her, pulling an old sheet up over her twisted feet, the wasted belly which had turned out twelve children, three dead, nine living, her papery old bosoms and her mean, crumpled face. I thought how a dead body isn't just the person who's left it a few minutes ago but a shrine to everyone they've ever been. And I also thought thank God I can have the bed to myself instead of perching on the edge waiting for the deluge.

There was a deluge then, because outside it started to rain like hell and the sky was so low it nearly scraped the rooftops. It felt like a promise of something, like God saying yes, I'll give you a chance, kid. Now you can make things right in your family. Now you can be happy.

Mom chose to name me Eugenie Victoria Josephine Mary Watkins (I don't suppose Dad had any say in the matter). At my christening at St Paul's Church in 1924, he leaned over my pram, a father for the first time, and I imagine his round face pink with pride.

'Look at her,' he said, chucking my cheek. 'She'll go far.'

Nanny Rawson, my other grandmother, stood just behind him, commented, 'With a gobful of names like that she'll need to.'

I don't know how far he thought I was going, but by 1939 none of us had got further than Brunswick Road, Balsall Heath, where we had a back door as well as a front and our very own flush toilet in the garden. I lived with my mom, my dad who was a bus driver, my little brother Eric, seven years younger (Mom's 'other mistake' as she kindly called him), and Mom's brother, Uncle Len. And Lola of course, up until now.

Nanny Rawson lived nearly half a mile away in Highgate, and Len stopped at home with her up until Mom's sister, my auntie Lil, had to move back in there with her kids and Len came to live with us. He wasn't quite the full shilling, Uncle Len. No one'd say why, so I took it for granted he must've been born that way. He was an enormous bloke. Didn't just come into a room, he took up half of it. He was all right. Sweet natured, and loved to hear people laugh. Not that living with Mom and Dad was ideal on that score.

He came to us a few months after Lola'd arrived, so our terraced house started to get crowded. Lola and I had had a room each. Mine was the little one at the end and Eric slept in with Mom and Dad at the front. But when Len arrived everything had to be juggled round.

'Eric'll stay in with us,' Mom decreed. She didn't object to Eric down at the foot of their bed on his mattress. I suppose someone else in the room helped keep Dad off her. 'And you'll have to bunk up with Lola at the end.'

'With Lola! But Mom – there's no room for another bed in there.'

'You won't need another bed. The one you've got now's three-quarter size. You'll have to share. It'll only be for a bit. She can't last much longer.'

This was appalling news. Lola was revolting enough round the house, but to have to share my bed with her! Being an innocent twelve-year-old, I protested, 'Well, why can't I share with Len?'

Mom glowered at me. 'Don't talk so silly. Len's a grown man and he needs a decent room to himself. And besides,' as she was turning away, 'he's not without a few funny habits.'

Typical of her, that was. Never explained things.

6

'Don't run backwards!' she'd shout at me when I was younger and capering along the pavement. 'I know someone who died doing that.'

I found out about Len's funny habits all too quickly. I barged into his room one day and there he was, kneeling on the floor in front of the chamber pot, unbuttoned, with his willy clenched in his hand, except it wasn't like a willy any more. More like a policeman's truncheon. He didn't even notice me, he had this grin on his moon face and whatever he was doing I could see he was enjoying it. I knew I'd best not say anything to Mom. I carried on sharing with Lola and kept out of Len's bedroom.

Len was no trouble though. I was puzzled to notice Mom'd do anything for him, because she certainly didn't display that attitude to anyone else, not even her pal Stella, and you can at least choose your friends. Len just sat about or went for little walks round the local streets. He played tip-cat and football with Eric and me. He looked through Eric's comics, *Desperate Dan* and *Hotspur*. He sat in the pub and laughed if someone else was laughing, and people were mostly kind to him. He never had a job in those days. Jobs were hard enough to come by for anyone. I grew ever so fond of him. He was more like a big, soft brother to me than a grown up man.

Dad couldn't make a fuss about him moving in because he had Lola there already, transforming Mom into one of the saints and martyrs even though I did most of the skivvying. He liked Len. Besides, he wasn't the sort to make a fuss. Quiet man, my dad. He didn't get up and bang on about anything much. Mom could've got away with murder, and often did. Emotional murder. Poison darts kept flying his way – 'Victor, you're useless, hopeless, no good to anyone . . .'

She made it quite clear to Eric and me that pregnancy and birth had been the greatest trials of her life and that to compensate her for the ordeal of bringing us into existence we had to bother her as little as we could manage. We'd been through the ploys of trying to get her attention by loudness, naughtiness and breaking things, and nothing had worked for long, so we had to learn to put up with it and shift for ourselves.

Mom had days sometimes when she couldn't even seem to move herself, just sat in a chair staring at the walls. Life weighted her to the floor. She was literally bored stiff. Bored with my dad, my solid, reliable dad, who had not an ounce of lightness or fun in him but was all a husband and father should be – except whatever it was she wanted him to be. I know she never loved him – not even when they first got married. Lil always said Mom married him to keep up with her pal Stella.

When I used to hear them talking, Stella and Mom, about their lives, Mom'd say, 'And then of course I went and married Victor.' The way she said it it might as well have been, 'And then I died.'

A lot of women didn't expect more than they got, but she did. She was romantic and full of dreams. I reckon on those bad days, when her face was strung tight and her hair never came out of a scarf and she smoked and snapped and sighed all day, she was looking at her life those last twelve, thirteen, fourteen years and thinking, 'What a waste.'

For Eric and me there was Nanny Rawson. She was always there and always, after a fashion, pleased to see us. When Mom sat listless in her chair and said, 'Oh go out and do summat with yourselves,' we'd often as not shoot up the Moseley Road to our nan's, me holding Eric's little hand to keep him off the horse road. Nanny

Rawson'd give us a piece with jam if she had any and let us play out in the yard with the neighbour's kids. We'd stay until it was nearly time for bed. When we got home, sometimes Mom had cooked for us. Sometimes she was still sitting in her chair, the same cup of cold tea balanced on the arm.

Course, all the family were at Lola's funeral in their glory. Dad got back from his camp with the Territorials two days earlier. He joined the TA a year before, after the Munich crisis, which I suppose made him feel useful and got him out of the house one evening a week after a shift on the buses, and some weekends. Must have been restful for him. They were training him up as a signalman.

Life was barely worth living in our house the morning we buried Lola. Mom had given Dad hell ever since Lola passed on because he hadn't been there.

'I couldn't help it, Doreen,' he snapped at her finally. He must have been feeling guilty enough already. 'But I had to go. The way things are there's going to be a war – soon.'

'There's not going to be a war,' Mom sneered. 'They won't let it happen.' She looked suddenly frightened. 'They won't, will they?'

She'd been up since crack of dawn, a scarf round her curlers, cutting bread for sandwiches, eggs bobbling noisily in a pan of water. Good job it was only sandwiches because she wasn't the world's greatest cook. She got everything too dry or too wet and finished it off by burning it. Her rock cakes spread out into black coins of sponge, charred sultanas bulging out.

'Who's coming then?' I asked.

Mom sniffed. 'Don't know for sure. But some of *them*'ll most likely turn up.'

'Them' were some of Dad's long lost relatives, and she was going to show them what was what. Dad's brothers and sisters were all scattered about, some in Birmingham, some wider still. We weren't sure where and we never saw any of them. But Mom was determined that she was a cut above whoever might turn up so it was out with a tin of salmon and the house had to be spotless.

The coffin was in the front room taking up most of the space between the whatnot in the window with an aspidistra on the top in a brass pot, leaves snagging on the window nets, and the little china cabinet at the back end of the room. The chairs had been pushed to one side, and dead flies dusted out of the vases. Mom liked to keep the front room a bit special so we spent most of our time in the back round the table.

Thing about my mom was, she had dreams of everything all kippers and curtains out on one of the new estates. She'd say names like 'Glebe Farm, Weoley Castle, Fox Hollies' with a special look in her eye, sort of tasting them on her tongue. New houses with bathrooms and neat little gardens front and back. But she wouldn't go. It wasn't Dad stopping her. And we weren't half as hard up as some of the neighbours. Balsall Heath, just a couple of miles south of the middle of Birmingham, may not have been her first choice, but she could at least feel she'd gone up in the world because she had a back and a front room and a patch of garden, and she had a set of willow pattern china off the Bull Ring when many a household in the street were still drinking out of jam jars. And in the end she needed another kind of security – she'd never move too far from her mom, Nanny Rawson, in her back-house in Highgate.

It was Nan who'd arranged everything for Lola: the plot in Lodge Hill Cemetery, registering the death, the hearse. Mom had one of her times of deciding she couldn't cope. But she was the one in charge today, pinner over her nightdress, dispensing orders. The house filled up with shouting.

'Doreen – I need a shirt collar . . .' Dad didn't tend to move when he needed anything, just sat tight and hoped it would appear.

'Here!' she hollered up the stairs from the back room. Could bawl like a fishwife she could, when she forgot she was trying to be respectable. She had a collar in one hand, loaf under the other arm, the top half buttered. 'It's starched.' Course it was. I'm surprised she didn't starch his underpants.

'Genie – I want you out scrubbing the front step before you think about getting dressed up. Eric—' thwack—'get your hands off. Look – the table's all smears now!'

'I daint mean to,' Eric snivelled, clutching his smarting ear.

'Genie – just get him out of here. Keep out of my way. And Lenny, sit down, will you? You're getting me all mithered. At least you're ready – even if it is hours before time.'

Len launched himself backwards into a chair so the cushion would've groaned if it were capable. His clothes were too tight and none of us had had any breakfast, but Len still had the grin stuck on his face that had been there since Monday when he got his first ever job, aged twenty-nine. He was going to pack shells at the Austin works, travel out on the bus, the lot, and he was so pleased with himself he'd hardly been able to sit still since.

'You'd best go in the garden for a bit,' I advised Eric. 'I've got to scrub the step.'

'Can't I come and watch you, Genie?'

'All right. If you have to.'

I completed my chore in the morning sunlight, made hazier by all the smoke from the factory chimneys. The smell of manure rose from the horse road and there was a whiff in the air of something chemical. Eric stood leaning against the front wall, sniffing and idly scuffing his shoes against the brickwork.

'You'd better pack that in,' I said, 'or you won't half get it.'

Then I was allowed to get changed. I had one decent dress which Mom had knocked up on her old Vesta machine. First time she'd made me anything. It was a pale blue shirtwaister, and I wore it with a pair of white button-up shoes which were scuffed grey round the toe-tips and pinched at the sides, but I could at least still get them on. I felt awkward in that dress. That was partly because Mom had managed to get the waist too high. And I suppose I didn't think of myself as a girl – not a proper one, like my friend Teresa, and other girls who liked to dress up. I was so skinny, Dad used to say, 'We could use you as a pull-through for a rifle' – elbows and knees sticking out and my socks would never stay up. I was supposed to be a woman by now, getting 'bosoms' and acting grown up. After all, I was out at work. But it was all a flaming nuisance, to my mind. Your monthly coming on, rags chafing in your knickers. I didn't half wish I was a boy sometimes.

Downstairs in the back room I peeped in the oval

12

mirror. My face looked back at me from the yellow glass, big grey eyes almost too big as my face was so thin and delicate, pointy nose, though not sticking out as far as Mom's. My straight, straight brown hair was parted in the middle and hung thick over my shoulders. Auntie Lil used to say I was prettier than my mom. She may've said that just to rile Mom of course. I gave myself a smile which brought out my dimple, like a little pool by the right side of my mouth.

Dad emerged from the stairs and said, 'You look a picture, Genie. Be nice to see you doll yourself up more often.' I went pink. Dad seemed to be having trouble turning his head. Must've been the starch in that collar.

Mom'd been fussing on the way. 'Victor, your tie's not straight. Genie, you take Len into church and make sure he behaves himself. Eric, for pity's sake stop sniffing.' Poor Eric. Very snotty, my little brother. Whatever the time of year there was always a reservoir of green up his nose.

They were all waiting outside St Paul's Church in their Sunday best, a line of desperately polished shoes, and coats even though it was the middle of summer, giving off a smell of mothballs. Nanny Rawson had on a navy straw hat and her mud-coloured coat which she'd bought off a lady second-hand, saying you could get away with brown on any occasion. She was a wide lady, walked rocking from foot to foot the way you might shift a full barrel of beer. She had an ulcer on her right leg so it was thickly bandaged, and round, muscular calves as if someone had dropped a couple of cricket balls down inside her legs. To match her hair she had a bit of a black moustache, which is more than my grandad had. Bald as a pig's bladder he was. But of course he'd been dead ten years by 1939.

There were a group of four people in shabby clothes and down-at-heel shoes who I thought looked ever so old, and when Dad went to them, red in the face, sweat on his forehead, I realized these were some of the uncles and an auntie we never saw. He shook each of their hands or slapped their shoulders, said, 'Awright are you?' and couldn't seem to think of anything else to say. Mom was looking down her nose at them, and they shifted about on their feet and looked embarrassed. I went and shook hands too, and one of the men looked nice and kissed me, and they said, 'Hello Eugenie,' the woman with a sarky note in her voice. I don't think she was my proper auntie. She just married someone.

Lil was there with her kids. She had a wide black hat on with a brim which we'd never seen before. Mom sidled up to her nodding her head like a chicken at the hat. 'Cashed in your pawn ticket in time, did you?'

Dad was saying, '*Doreen*,' pulling her arm. 'Remember who we're burying today, please.'

'I'm hardly likely to forget, Victor,' brushing his hand off. 'Since I was the one left to deal with it all while you were off playing soldiers.'

Dad's cherub face was all pink now, his voice trembling. 'How many times do I have to tell you, the Territorial Army does not play soldiers. Don't you realize just how serious . . .'

Lil started putting her threepence ha'penny in too, her lovely face puckered with annoyance. In a stage whisper she started off, 'Don't forget, you stuck up cow, that some of us do a job of – Patsy!' She broke into a yell, catching sight of him leaping gravestones like a goat. 'Get here – now!' That was our Lil for you. Scarcely ever got through a whole sentence without having to bawl out one of the kids.

'Pack it in, the lot of you,' Nan hissed at them. 'They're staring at us.' She tilted the straw hat towards the aunt and uncles whose eyes were fixed on us. 'Doreen – go in,' Nan commanded, still through her teeth. 'And see if you can keep your gob shut.'

'Come along, Eric.' Mom flounced off in her mauve and white frock, yanking Eric along in his huge short trousers which reached well below his knobbly knees.

Dad seemed flustered, not knowing who to sit with, and ended up following me in with Len. I took Len's hand. 'Come on – I'll look after you.'

He came with me like a little kid. No one wanted to sit in the actual front row so we filed into the second lot of pews. Len's knees were touching the back of the pew in front, his enormous thighs pressed against mine. It wasn't that he was a fat man, he was just built on a huge scale. He kept looking round at me, pulling faces and grinning.

'S'nice this, Genie, in't it?' I think he liked the candles and the coloured glass. He pointed to his fly buttons and said loudly, 'What if I need to go?'

'You just tell me,' I whispered. 'I'll take you out. Try and keep your voice down, Len.'

He heard Cathleen, Lil's three-year-old, laughing behind us, so he started laughing too – hor hor hor – hell of a noise, shoulders going up and down.

'Len.' I gripped his arm, nervously. 'You're not s'posed to be laughing. Lola's in that coffin up there.' I pointed at it, flowers on top, the lot.

'In there?' He pointed a massive finger.

I nodded. 'She's dead – remember?'

15

But that set him off even worse and I had to start getting cross and say, 'Now Len, stop it. You mustn't.'

Along our pew Mom was frowning across at Eric for pulling snot up his nose too loudly. Then there was a bawl from behind. Cathleen must've pulled Tom's hair and made him whimper and Lil had smacked him one low down on the leg hoping no one'd see. He blarted even louder and Cathleen was grinning away to herself under those angelic blond curls, the mardy little cow. Nanny Rawson, next to the aisle in our pew, swivelled round and gave them all the eye from under that hat.

A train rattled past at the back of the church. At last the Reverend started in on his prayers. 'We brought nothing into this world and it is certain we carry nothing out . . .'

I started to feel sorry for old Lola now I couldn't smell her. Dad was a bit upset and blew his nose a lot. He'd tried to do his best for her. After all, she was his mom, even if she was a miserable old bitch. He was forever telling us it was just her age. She wasn't always like that. Mom'd say, 'Oh yes she flaming well was.'

But I sat there and thought what a rotten life she must've had. Terrible poverty they lived in when her kids were small. A slum house, not even attic-high, two up, one down on the yard, with nine children in the house and never enough to go round. Didn't make her a kind person. Her husband did his best, from what Dad said, but he was a bit of a waster. My father was her little ray of sunshine. Bright at school and had always held down a job. The other kids drifted away and mostly stayed away.

I looked across at the coffin as we stood up and started in on 'Abide With Me'. I thought about her old

16

wasted body in there. How she'd climb out of bed very quick and pull her clothes up to sit on the chamber pot. Sometimes I'd get a glimpse of something hanging down there, like an egg, white and glistening. She'd sit for an age, grunting and cursing, willing urine to flow the way you will a late train to come. Sometimes she'd put her hand up her, try and push it back and relieve herself, and she'd give a moan. Soon as she lay down again it'd all come in a rush and I'd be clinging to the edge of the mattress trying to keep as far from her as I could, almost crying at the smell.

Poor old Lola. Thank God she'd gone.

'I hope they don't notice I've eked the salmon out with milk,' Mom whispered, stirring the teapot in the kitchen at the back. 'Here, take these through, will you Genie?'

I carried the sandwiches to the front room, Mom's willing slave as ever. Willing because I'd have done anything for her if only she'd be glad I existed. She was being quite pally-pally with me today because she needed my help.

Everyone was crushed into the front room except Lil, who'd taken the kids out to let off steam in the garden. Eric and Little Patsy, a year his junior, were brawling on the grass like puppies.

It went all right, just about. Dad's brothers and sister were either silent or very very jolly and the uncles loosened their threadbare ties, asked each other for a light and stood about smoking and sweating. There wasn't the room to sit down. The auntie spent a lot of time peering in Mom's china cabinet. They ate all they could and went out saying, 'We'll have to do this again,' but all knowing the truth was that it'd be at the next funeral, and departed even more awkward than when they arrived.

So that left our family with the curling egg sandwiches and nubs of Madeira cake to get on in our usual affectionate way. I stuck with Len and brought him more helpings of food because he could eat for ever, his mouth churning away like a mincer.

Lil had brought the kids back in. She was a stunner, our Lil, and like a flypaper to men. Like Nanny Rawson she looked as though she had a touch of the tar-brush: she had tresses of black hair, almond-shaped brown eyes and olive skin, and today she'd got a dab of colour on her lips. Before she had the kids she sometimes used to put curl papers in her hair, and it hung in shiny black snakes down her back. Wild as the wind she was then, all high heels and make up. She worked as a french polisher in a toy factory, on gun handles and little carpet sweepers.

Mom'd always been jealous of her. Lil's looks of course, for a start, even though she was worn to the bone nowadays with the kids. Lil was chosen as the May Queen when they were kids at school and Mom's never forgiven her for that. But I think another part of her jealousy was Lil moving back in with our nan after her husband died. Well, I say died. Patrick Heaney was his name. Cheerful Big Patsy. Mom never liked him. Doesn't like the Irish full stop, and his other crime was to make Lil happy. Patsy got into a fight one night – more of a friendly by all accounts – but the other bloke knocked him over on the kerb and he had a nasty bang on the head. He was never the same after. Turned to the booze, had fits, couldn't get out of bed of a morning.

Next thing was they were dragging him out of the canal. It was a shame. Lil was in pieces. But at least while he was alive she really had something with Big Patsy that Mom'd never had. You could see it in their eyes. She'd sit in his lap, even after Little Patsy was born. Popped out a couple of kids in as many years.

But she couldn't cope on her own, what with holding down a job and the kids and their third child Cathleen being only a titty-babby. Poor Lil.

Cathleen sat on Lil's lap and started pulling at her waves of black hair.

'Leave off, will you?' Lil snapped. 'Never get a second to yourself with kids, do you? Can't even fart in peace.'

'Give 'er 'ere,' Nan said. She took the little girl on to her enormous lap and bounced her until she squealed.

Lil sat back, tired as usual. Her mouth turned down more nowadays. 'How about another cuppa tea, Dor, now that lot've gone?'

'You know where the kettle is,' Mom said with her usual charm.

'I'll get it.' I went to the kitchen and made tea, not that I expected any thanks for it, and when I got back they were arguing. Mom and Lil that is. Len was shuffling a pack of cards. He never played anything, just shuffled. He and Dad usually just sat waiting for the wenches to burn themselves out.

Our nan had a look in her eye I didn't quite like. She was sat forward. Cathleen had got down and was on the floor waving her legs in the air, showing off her bloomers.

'Because,' Nan was saying, 'it's the practice run Sat'dy, ain't it?'

19

'I'm not sending my kids nowhere,' Lil said, scraping at egg on Tom's face with her nails. 'Whatever Adolf bloody Hitler's planning.'

Hitler this, Hitler that, all we ever heard nowadays. I put the tray down, pushing plates aside. Everyone was keyed up about the thought of war war war.

'Your mom'll need you at 'ome,' Nanny Rawson said to me. 'You can look after your dad.'

'Why?' Lil looked at Mom. In a nasty tone she demanded, 'Where're you off to then?'

'With Eric.'

Eric looked from one to the other of them, mouth full of cake and a hopeless expression on his face. He knew he wasn't going to get a say.

'You mean you're sending him? To live with complete strangers?' Lil was on her high horse. She caught hold of Cathleen and cuddled her tight, doing her best impression of the Virgin Mary.

'That's what we're supposed to be doing, isn't it? Or d'you want your kids bombed and gassed like they say they will be?'

'But just sending him off . . . Poor little thing.' Eric looked about as depressed as anyone would be faced with the choice of bombing and gassing or being sent away to live heaven only knew where. 'Anyhow,' Lil said. 'You don't need to go to the practice. Not as if you're going with him, is it?'

Mom was silent for a split second. Everyone stared at her. She stuck her chin out. 'I thought I'd go.'

Dad sat up then. News to him, obviously. 'But Doreen . . .'

Nan was scandalized. 'You mean go off – leave Victor and Genie?'

'Not for good. I thought I could just deliver him. Have a look over where he's going.'

'But you're not allowed,' Lil argued. 'I'd be allowed to go, with Cathleen so young, but you're not – not unless you're a helper or you're . . .' Lil looked ever so suspicious all of a sudden.

Mom stared back at her, brazen, nose in the air.

'You're never going to tell them . . .' Lil started laughing a real nasty laugh. 'Oh I get it. Well it wouldn't be the first time, would it? After all, you were "expecting" when you got Victor to marry you, weren't you? Longest pregnancy on record that one. What was it? Fifteen months?'

Dad had gone nearly purple in the face, to the roots of his hair. Mom stabbed her knife into the last piece of Madeira cake as if she wanted to kill something. 'You bloody little bitch.' I thought she was going to slap Lil but Nanny Rawson was on her feet pushing them apart.

'That's enough from the pair of you.' She stood with her arms outstretched between them.

'She only said she was pregnant so she could beat Stella to the altar!'

'Well at least I've still got a husband – I'm not dragging my kids up in the slums.'

'But you don't give a monkey's about sending Eric off to live with Christ only knows who . . .'

'That's why I'm saying I'm expecting you silly cow – so I can get on the train with him . . .'

I went and sat by Eric, who no one seemed to have given a moment's thought to.

'Take no notice,' I said, putting my arm round him.

'Is she going to send me away?' He had tears in his eyes. 'Where am I going?'

'Somewhere nice I expect. In the country. See the cows and sheep. It'll be all right,' I told him, though I hadn't the foggiest whether it would or not. 'Here – want a game of snap?'

Eric nodded, picture of misery.

'Right, now sit yourselves down,' our Nan was saying. 'As a mark of respect to Lola, since we 'aven't seen much of that yet, we'll 'ave a song.'

'I'm not singing with her,' Mom said.

'That's what you think.' Nan got her squeeze box out from the corner and sat with it on her lap, legs apart, skirt pulling tight across her knees.

'She's wearing red bloomers,' Eric whispered to me, distracted for a moment.

'Doreen, Lil, stand up. You sing along too, Len,' Nan urged him.

I got the cards off Len and played with Eric, and Dad sighed with relief that they'd all stopped carrying on and the two loving sisters started on a song. Nan was fantastic on the accordion. She'd picked it up off her dad and she could play the piano too. Just about anything you asked in the way of songs. A gift that, that ran in the family until it got to me, apparently. Mom could have a go too, given the chance. She, Lil and Nanny Rawson all had good strong voices. People called them the Andrews Sisters, and they did a turn in the pub now and again. Times when they sang were mostly the only occasions when they weren't arguing.

So they stood in our front room with the sunlight fading outside and Dad lighting one fag after another to calm his nerves. They sang 'The Rose of Picardy' and 'Ta-ra-ra-boom-de-ay', blending their voices, and then that new song, 'The Lambeth Walk' everyone was mad about. Lil looked so pretty and not tired suddenly, Nan's face was softer than usual and Len was swaying from side to side in his chair, face split by a smile, in heaven.

Mom looked almost happy while the music was going on. I saw Dad watching her and there were tears in his eyes. Shook me a bit, that. I wondered whether he was thinking about Lola, or about the fact that he might soon have to go away, or whether he was wondering the same as I was: why Mom couldn't find it in her to be happier with him – with all of us.

Come the end of that week we were in for a surprise. I was working in a pawn shop in Highgate, which disgusted Mom, but it was one of the best jobs I'd had so far. That week, as we stood in the little shop on the Moseley Road, we watched a crowd filling sandbags to shore up the factories opposite. Every day there were changes. That Friday I walked home after work and saw the last evening rays catching the bloated shape of a barrage balloon, a silky light coming from it. Some people, Mom among them, were still saying, 'Oh there's not going to be a war.' But if there was to be no war, what was all this for? Digging trenches in the parks, blackout curtains downstairs, and sending the kids away.

We'd had the gas masks months. One day when I got home Mom'd said in a grim voice, 'Look what's arrived.' There was a pile of boxes by the door. The masks were most off-putting. They looked a bit of a joke with their mouse faces until you put one on. When I pulled it over my face it was so tight, and the smell of rubber made you heave. The leaflets told us there'd be wardens round with rattles if we had a gas attack.

'I couldn't wear that,' Mom said, shuddering. 'Make me sick that would.'

Dad, standing in shirtsleeves at the door, remarked, 'I don't s'pose being gassed'd make you feel all that marvellous neither.'

I didn't really understand about war. Everyone was forever on about 'the Last One' but I wasn't born till nearly six years after it finished. All I knew was that everyone was living on their nerves. Mom was on at Dad because he might have to go away. 'What did you have to go and join the TA for? Other men of your age aren't being called up. How d'you think I'm going to manage without you here?' she'd wail. Tears turned on as well. There was a feeling about, excited and deadly serious at the same time, building up like the tension in a dog waiting to spring.

When I walked through the front door that evening I knew something was different. It was quiet, much more so than usual, but I could hear a voice in the back room. A man's voice. Posh. I didn't know who it was. I pushed the door open and before I'd had a chance even to open my mouth they all said, 'Ssssh!' without even looking at me. There they were, all sat round the table: Mom, Dad, Eric, Len. And in the middle of the table, shiny and new and absolutely gorgeous, there she was.

'Blimey! Whose—? What—? Whose is it?'

'Sssssh,' they said again. Len was making gleeful sounds, bouncing up and down in his seat.

The man's voice went on for a moment longer, then music started to trickle out into the room. I tiptoed closer and stared. It was a beautiful thing, almost a couple of feet long, encased in veneered wood with a dark grain across it as if it had been washed by the sea. On one half of the front was the speaker, the overlaid wood cut into a sunburst. On the other half, set into a metal surround, was the dial, with little ebony knobs underneath it. Out from it, louder now, were coming the sounds of violins and trumpets and other instruments all pitching in together, and it gave me a queer feeling. Made me want to cry suddenly though I didn't know why. Even Len went quiet.

I didn't get any sense out of anyone until Mom got up to put the kettle on.

'So – whose is it?'

'Len's. He bought it. First wage packet.' She moved her mouth close to my ear. 'We made up the extra for him – saw he had enough.' Her little brother. The one person in the world she'd kill to protect.

'Is that yours then, Len?' He looked as if he was going to burst, head nodding up and down like crazy.

'Pleased as punch he is,' Dad said. As if he needed to.

I squeezed Len's shoulder. 'Aren't you lucky? It's really smashing.'

Next day, Mom dragged Eric off to school for his evacuation rehearsal. The schools opened specially, even though it was the summer holidays. Mom had put away her ideas of being able to wangle a passage with him now it had dawned on her that Dad might have to go sooner than she'd realized. Eric had to go off with a small holdall for his clothes and a little bag for his 'iron rations' and his gas mask.

It was a peaceful morning in one way. Dad sat and read the *Sports Argus* and we didn't clear away breakfast for a good hour. Len settled himself down by his wireless and kept twiddling the dial, catching torn up bits of sound until he heard something he fancied.

I was supposed to be cooking lunch, but I sat down for a bit too, feeling that without Mom around I could leave my hair loose and straggly and no one would tick me off for the grubby stains on my frock. I stretched my legs out in front of me, seeing how skinny and pale they looked, and wished I didn't have a figure like a clothes-horse. But all the time worries about Eric kept flickering through my mind and I had a queasy ball of tension inside me. I thought about my family all being split up and suddenly they didn't seem so bad any more and I wanted things to stay as they were.

'Dad?'

'Mm?'

'If there's a war will you have to go straight away?'

He laid the paper down in his lap and looked ahead. Outside someone was having a fire and rags of smoke kept drifting past the window. 'Could be any time now, love.'

'Oh.' The music carried on quietly behind us.

Dad turned his head to look at me. 'I know I'm not all your mother would want . . .' He couldn't seem to finish that bit. 'You will look after her for me, won't you?'

I nodded and he looked away again. 'You're a good wench.'

That morning, while we were waiting and wondering, I heard a singer who was to become one of my favourites. Her voice came from the wireless strong and dark as gravy browning. We sat quite still while she was singing. The second she'd finished, Len pointed at the wireless and said, 'Gloria.'

'What you on about, Len? They said her name was Anne Shelton.'

He shook his head hard and pointed again. 'Gloria.'

I realized he meant the wireless itself, and I saw how

much it suited her. Glorious Gloria. From then on she was never known as anything but Gloria.

One Wednesday night we were all listening to *Band Waggon*, all in stitches at Arthur Askey, Len laughing at us laughing – hor hor hor – out of his belly. We had Gloria turned up high and I thought she was the best thing that had ever happened because before that I never ever remember us all sitting laughing together. Even Mom looked happy, and I saw Dad watching her, all hopeful.

And then she stopped. Right in the middle of it, no more Gloria. Len was out of his chair, wild at the knobs. 'Gloria . . . Gloria . . .' Not listening to Mom, who was trying to say, 'Lenny, it's OK, it's just the accumulator . . .'

Len sank back on his chair and blubbed, fat slugs of tears rolling from his eyes and his shoulders shaking as if there was an earthquake. 'Gloria . . . Gloria!'

'LEN!' Mom bawled down his ear. 'GLORIA WILL BE ALL RIGHT. WE NEED TO TOP UP HER ACCUMULATOR!' To the rest of us, she said, 'Listen to me. *Gloria*. Getting as bad as he is.'

She got through to him in the end and he stopped crying, but his face was dismal. He spent the rest of the evening with Gloria in his lap, lying across his thighs as if she was an injured cat.

I took the accumulator in on my way to work the next day. There was a cycle shop on Stoney Lane would top them up for you. I'd never given much thought to what was in them before, but I soon found out because the aroma of spilt acid in that shop made my eyes water. It was eating into the floor.

'You got a spare?' the bloke asked.

We hadn't, though I thought we'd better get one so's not to have this performance every time.

'I'll be back for it after work,' I told him.

So, come the evening I handed over threepence, and it would have been worth a shilling just to see Len's face when I walked in with it. Gloria was on again straight away in time for *The Six O'Clock News*.

Those last days of August we still waited and waited. It was like being held under water.

The groups of people gossiping in Nan's shop were saying, 'Let's get it over with if it's coming. Just let us know one way or the other.'

It was a time full of instructions. Leaflets through the door, the papers, and of course Gloria, who took our hands and led us into the war, giving out advice and information as we went. Hearing the voices which came from her was like someone sat right there in the back room with you. And she gave us relief from it, letting our minds slip away into plays and stories and songs.

The newspapers were different. On 31 August Dad brought home the *Birmingham Mail*. There was the banner across the front, stark in black and white:

EVACUATION TOMORROW ... BRITAIN AWAITS
HITLER'S REPLY.

September 1939

'Genie? can I come in with you?'

It was before dawn. I could just see Eric's outline in the doorway of my room.

'What's up?'

He came silently up to my bed. 'She's sending me away, ain't she?'

I pulled the bed open. 'Here – hop in.'

'Ain't she?' His toes were chilly against my leg.

'She thinks it's for the best. You don't want that nasty man Hitler dropping bombs on you, do you, Eric?'

His tousled head moved from side to side against my chest. I put my arms round him, scrawny little bit that he was, and pulled the sheet close round us.

'Little Patsy's not going.'

'But the Spinis are – Francesca and Giovanna and Tony – even Luke.' My friend Teresa's brothers and sisters.

'They'll all be together . . . I'll be all on my own.'

'You never know – you might be able to go with them.'

But he was already crying, snuffling like a kitten, a hand pressing on one of my titties, such as I had.

'Don't wanna go. I don't wanna.'

'Now Eric – it won't be for long,' I kept telling

him. 'It'll be for the best. Mom only wants the best for you.'

I lay holding him, hoping that was the truth.

Mom stood by the open back door with a packet of Players, blowing smoke across our thin strip of garden. I went out to use the privy. There were cobwebs under the roof, cut out squares of the *Gazette* on a string, and no seat. I sat on the cold white enamel feeling a breeze under the door. When I came out, a bird was singing. A thin mesh of cloud covered the sky but the air was growing warm. It was about six-thirty.

Mom stood with one arm wrapped round the waist of her cotton nightdress, her bit of stomach pushing out from under it, other hand holding the cigarette in front of her face. Her skin looked pasty, nose shiny with night sweat. She was often like that, miles away, but this time her expression was drawn and frightened. I didn't even think she'd seen me, until she said, 'What're we going to do?'

I stared at her. I was angry at her for sending Eric away, and angrier because I knew she was right: there was going to be a war and none of us knew what would happen, and we were all confused and frightened.

'How d'you mean?'

'I don't know if I'm doing the right thing.'

You're the mom, I thought, not me. What you asking me for?

'Mrs Spini's got four to send,' I said, stepping past her.

'Thought she wasn't going to.'

'Changed her mind.'

'Typical.' Tutting. 'Italians.'

30

I filled the teapot. Mom turned, slit-eyed, smoke unfurling from her nose. 'I'm only doing what I'm told, you know Genie.' She pointed in, towards Gloria. 'She – I mean they – say that's what we've got to do. This is an evacuation area. So we're s'posed to evacuate.'

'Well that's all right then, isn' it?'

'What are you looking at me like that for then?'

'I don't know.' I could feel the tears coming on. I turned away.

We heard my dad coming down. The stair door pushed open into the back room.

'It's right, in't it Victor?'

'What is?' He was stood there in his shirt and underpants.

'Sending Eric out of harm's way.'

Dad looked in some amazement into Mom's pinched, foxy face and saw that for the first time any of us could remember she was actually asking his advice. He pulled his shoulders back and stroked the reddish stubble on his chin. 'I should say so. If that's what they're saying.'

'Where is he, anyhow?'

'In my bed. Still asleep. He came in in the night, crying.'

'Shame.' Mom stubbed out her cigarette, grey ash dirtying a white saucer. 'Better get him up. It's an early start.' She went to the bread bin and fished out the stub end of a loaf. 'I'll make him a piece. He'll need summat on his stomach.'

Eric had to leave as soon as he'd had breakfast. His little bag and his gas mask stood forlornly in the hall. He clung to me, bawling his eyes out, and I was in tears myself. Hadn't thought how much I'd miss him, even though he'd been stuck to me like my shadow all his life. There'd be no more Eric sneaking out after school with jam jars to sell for a ha'penny each, or driving us mad with that clattering go-cart of his with the back wheel falling off. No more walks to Cannon Hill Park to 'get him from under my feet' with a stale crust for the ducks. He suddenly seemed the most precious person I knew, my baby brother.

'Can't you come with me, sis?' he sobbed, already in his little gaberdine coat.

'I've got to get to work, Eric. Mom'll look after you. We'll see you soon.' Someone had their hands round my throat. 'Won't be for long.'

Mom didn't say much, couldn't. I did my best to hide most of my tears until they were away down the road. I stood waving him off, him turning, cap on his head, silver streaks of dried tears on his cheeks and new ones coming. He was twisting round, trying to wave, right the way to the corner. Then they were gone.

I had a proper cry then, upstairs. Dad had gone out the back. I suppose he was upset too. After, I blew my nose, pulled myself together and hurried to work. I thought of Eric all the way there, wondering where he'd end up, what it was like outside Birmingham, and what an unknown family somewhere would make of the arrival of my snotty-nosed brother, Eric Rudolph Valentino Watkins.

Palmer's was on the Moseley Road, its golden balls hanging outside. It was a dark little shop and stank a bit inside of course, of frowsty clothes and camphor, of the gas lamp that was kept burning most of the time so we could see to write out the tickets, and of Mr Palmer's fags.

He was already in when I got there. He was ever so old – seemed it to me – fifty-something at least, with half-moon glasses, a paunchy stomach and grey hair greased flat to his head. The whites of his eyes had gone yellow, maybe from smoking, like his fingers. He was a shrewd operator, Mr Palmer, but well capable of kindness.

'Ready for the Friday rush, Genie?' he said as I walked in, shivering in the dank shop in my cotton dress.

I liked Fridays. Payday – everyone coming to redeem the Sunday outfits they'd pawned on Monday for a bit of extra to see them through the week, and many would stop for a chat. We'd see them all back in the next Monday.

''Ere I am again,' one lady used to say. 'In out, in out, quick as me old man on a Sat'dy night.' Took me a minute or two to work out what she was on about.

'You get busy then,' Mr Palmer said. He was half way through a fag and didn't seem to be planning on shifting himself. I started tidying bits and bobs, dusting the crocks. He'd told me he'd never seen the place so organized before I came along.

That was my trouble with jobs. If I wasn't kept on the run I got bored. And not just a bit yawning bored, but screaming and running round the room sort of bored. I'd done all sorts: sticking Bo-Peep stickers on babies' cots, taking calls for a taxi firm where I got so fed up I gave the windows a going over in my spare time . . . Soon as it got too slow my head filled with fog and my legs went heavy as brass weights. That was when it was time to look for something else.

As I was tidying I heard a click, and a voice said, '... we're on number twelve platform at Waterloo Station...'

My head jerked up. 'A wireless!'

Mr Palmer nodded, pleased with himself. It was at the end of the counter, a little box with a curved top and nothing like as grand as Gloria, but the reception was quite clear.

'Thought I'd bring it in,' he said, through a cloud of blue smoke. 'Didn't want to miss anything. Funny times these.'

'... the train's in,' the voice was saying, 'and the children are just arriving ... the tiny tots in front ... they're all merry and bright, we haven't had a single child crying and I think they're all looking forward to this little adventure ... The whistle goes, the children are looking out ... and in a moment this train moves out to an unknown destination ...' We heard the sound of the train chugging hard and loud, finally dying away. I thought of Eric sobbing his little heart out. Was he the only child in England not 'merry and bright'?

'You all right?' Mr Palmer asked. He twizzled the knob and the wireless went off.

I started to fill up a bit then. 'It's my brother Eric. He's eight. He's gone today.'

Mr Palmer tutted and shook his head. 'Terrible,' he said. 'They said they had it all sorted out the last time. Mind you, wench, it's for the best. They say this one'll start with bombing. If my kids were young I'd want 'em right out of it. Anyhow—' he winked at me— 'they reckon if anything happens it'll be finished by Christmas.'

The rush started, with all the Sunday best going out again, as if it was going to be just any old normal weekend. Then we heard Mrs Wiles coming. She lived round the corner on Balsall Heath Road and she'd bring in bundles for the neighbours. You could hear her coming from half way up the road, pushing the rottenest old wheelbarrow you've ever seen.

Mr Palmer turned to give me a wink. 'Oh – 'ere we go.'

The first we saw of her was her behind because she turned and shoved the door with it, too hard, so it flew open and the bell almost turned itself over ringing. She pulled the barrow down over the step with a loud 'thunk' so I wondered if that would be its last time, and stood blinking for a second or two, in her old man's cloth cap, a sacking apron and man's boots tied with string. She can't have been much different in age from my nan, but her face looked like an old potato.

'Mrs Johnson wants two shilling for this,' she said, picking up Mrs Johnson's bundle of washing.

Mr Palmer looked her in the eye over his glasses. 'One and nine.'

'Two shilling. She wants two shilling.'

'One and nine.'

Every week it was the same, and the look she gave him, I was laughing that much bent over the counter that I could barely write out the tickets.

'Oh you bloody fool,' she said, screwing up her leathery face. 'Oh, you old miser.'

They went through this with every bundle on the barrow. She counted and recounted the coins Mr Palmer gave her, and pushed them into a little pouch which she had tucked into her waistband.

This was all part of the normal performance. But what wasn't part of it was that this week she looked a lot more agitated than usual, couldn't seem to find her waist at all and was pulling at her long skirt as if she thought something might drop out of it. Then she started making funny noises like a guinea pig. Mr Palmer glanced anxiously at me.

'You all right, Mrs Wiles?' He pulled up the flap in the counter to get through and then just stood there while Mrs Wiles suddenly clutched at her chest, fingers clenched and head back pulling the chicken skin under her chin tight, and then dropped to the floor, pawn tickets fluttering from her.

'Oh Lor',' Mr Palmer said, looking down at her. 'Genie – what do we do?'

'Her pulse.' I ducked under too and knelt by Mrs Wiles's slumped body. 'I'll feel for her pulse. You go and get help.'

Mr Palmer charged out of the shop, probably faster than he'd moved in thirty years, and I found myself alone once again with a dead old lady. Because she was dead. I felt the faint pulse flicker, then disappear in her wrist. I folded her hands together over her chest, except one of them kept dropping off. Other customers started coming in.

'What's Mrs Wiles doing down there?' the first woman asked.

'She's dead.' My knees were shaking.

'Oh you poor kid! Did she just . . .? Where's Reg Palmer?'

I shrugged. 'Gone to get help.'

By the time Mr Palmer came back with Mrs Palmer, who was fat and usually jolly but not at the moment as someone'd just died, there was quite a crowd in the shop, waiting with their tickets and standing round the walls because Mrs Wiles was taking up such a lot of the floor.

'Her son's coming,' Mrs Palmer said after tutting. 'He's arranging transport. In the meantime . . .'

Since we couldn't leave Mrs Wiles where she was, the Palmers and I stowed her behind the counter. Mrs P found an old sheet on a shelf.

'No one'll be wanting that back now,' someone remarked.

Course, there was barely room to move behind there, and I had to work with one foot on either side of her legs.

When things had settled down a bit Mr Palmer said, 'Oi – it's news time.' It was ten-thirty. He switched on the wireless.

The customers in the shop stood stock still as we heard it. Afterwards, everyone was coming in with their lips all in position as they got through the door to say, 'Have you heard? I suppose you'll have heard by now?' It was on everyone's face. 'They've gone into Poland. The Germans have invaded Poland. We're for it now.' One lady was crying. Her son was twenty and she hadn't forgotten the last war, lost two brothers.

What about my dad? I wondered. The air crackled with goings on, with nerves. I knew everything was changing and everyone thought it was very serious, that the kerbstones on the Moseley Road had been painted black and white for the blackout, that my brother had been taken from us.

It wasn't until the afternoon that Carl Wiles turned up to pick up his mom, and then not with very good grace. I saw Mrs Wiles carted out to his van like a sack of onions. I wondered if anyone had ever really loved her. And I thought, surely, surely there's got to be more to existence than slaving your fingers to the bone all

37

your life and then dropping dead in a pawn shop and no one really caring whether you do or not?

The thought of Mom in a soggy heap was too much for me straight after work so I went to my nan's, which felt just as much like home. I knew I could tell her about Mrs Wiles passing on in front of me and she'd listen.

Belgrave Road was a wide, main street sloping down from the Moseley Road to the Bristol Road. Nan lived almost at the top, had done for years, in one of the yards down an entry behind the shops. As you went down the hill the houses gradually got bigger and bigger and at the bottom end there were some really posh ones. Nanny Rawson started her working life in one of those, in service to a family called the Spiegels, soon after the turn of the century. She didn't get paid in money, they gave her bits of clothes and food instead. She'd lived in three different houses in Belgrave Road, and, as Mom was forever reminding us, Nan brought up her three surviving children at about the same level of poverty as everyone else in the back-to-back courts of houses. Poor as grinding poor back then, after the Great War, not knowing from one day to the next if my grandad would be in work or out of it, drunk or sober. Their clothes shop was the heap tipped out in the yard by the rag and bone man.

'We couldn't shop three days ahead in them days,' Mom'd say (oh, here we go). 'It was hand to mouth. Your grandad was out of work and your nan in the factory, until she got that shop . . . You got an ounce of jam at a time in a cup, if you was lucky. Your nan was up in the brew'us at five in the morning doing other people's washing to make ends meet.' Mom'd never forget it, scrubbing at the top of shoes with barely any soles on them, never knowing a full stomach, coats on the bed and the house lousy and falling down round their ears. Nan had struggled to give her kids better and Mom knew to hold on tight to what she'd got.

The road was full of the smell of hops from Dare's Brewery and the whiff of sawn wood from the timber merchant's down opposite Hick Street. On the corner stood the Belgrave Hotel, and Nan's huckster's shop was across the road with a cobbled entry running along the side of it which ran into the yard. The shop's windows had advertisements stuck to them for Brasso, Cadbury's, Vimto and such a collection of others that you could hardly see in or out. Her house, which backed on to the shop, was attic-high – three floors, one room on each, and in the downstairs you could walk through the scullery, lift up a little wooden counter and you were in the shop.

I was almost there when Nan's shop door flew open, bell jangling like mad, and two girls tumbled out shrieking and spitting like cats. One had a heap of blond hair and long, spindly legs pushed into a pair of ankle-wobbling high black patent heels. The other had crimpy red hair and a skin-tight skirt, scarlet with big white polka dots, and showing a mass of mottled leg.

'You mardy old bitch!' the blonde yelled into the shop at the top of her lungs. As she did so, she caught her heel in the brick pavement and fell over backwards, white legs waving. 'Now look what you've made me do, you fucking cow!'

The redhead was helping her up. 'You wanna watch it – we can have you seen to, grandma . . .'

Nanny Rawson loomed in the doorway, enormous in her flowery pinner crossed over at the back, face grimmer than a storm at sea. Bandaged leg or no, she was out of that door in a jiffy, giving the redhead a whopping clout round the face that nearly floored her. The girl set up a train-whistle shriek, as much from wounded pride as from pain, which brought people out of the shops to stare and grin.

'All right, Edith?' someone shouted. 'That's right – you give 'em one!' Nanny Rawson ignored them.

'Get this straight,' she barked at the girls. 'You may be Morgan's latest tarts but while you're in my shop you behave like proper 'uman beings and keep a civil tongue in your 'eads. Don't come in 'ere showing off to me. And if you want to come through and up my stairs—'

'They ain't your stairs, they're Morgan's,' the redhead retorted, hand pressed to her cheek. 'And there's bugger all you can do about it. 'Cept move of course, and do everyone a favour.'

Nan bunched her hand into a fist and the redhead quailed. 'Don't hit me again!' she pleaded, backing off.

The blonde had got to her feet by this time. Now I was closer I saw she had pale, pitted skin, thickly caked in powder, and can't have been that much older than me. If she'd been thinking of having another go at Nan she changed her mind, knowing she'd more than met her match, and turned on me instead. 'And what d'you think you're gawping at, you nosy little bitch?'

Nanny Rawson suddenly saw me too, and she didn't like her family getting involved with Morgan and his women. She rounded on the girls. 'Get inside there quick. For my own state of health I'm going to forget I ever saw you.' As they teetered back in through the door she shouted after them, 'Coming to him two at a time. It's disgusting!' There was a cheer from the bystanders which Nanny Rawson, on her dignity, completely ignored.

Her run-ins with the landlord Morgan and his endless parade of 'young trollops' had been going on since she started renting the place nigh on sixteen years ago, and she and Morgan, a scrawny, over-sexed weasel of a man, were growing old together. When Nan first got the shop she was desperate to keep the lease and was beholden to Morgan for keeping the rent low. Now she'd been here this long she wasn't going anywhere for anyone and Morgan knew he'd never get a better tenant. It had developed into a contest – who could hold out there the longest. But the fact that the only way to get to the upstairs was through the shop meant that Nan had had her nose rubbed in his preoccupations week in, week out, and even after all this time there was no chance of her accepting it.

As soon as the girls disappeared it was as if nothing had happened. Suddenly her face was full of doom. Hitler. Poland.

'What you doing 'ere?' she demanded.

'Come to see you, what else?'

'You don't look too good – seen your mother, 'ave you?'

'No. Why?'

She jerked her head towards the door. 'You'd best come in.'

Nan's shop had seemed like a magic palace to me when I was a kid. You couldn't see across the room much better than you could through the windows, there was that much stuff in there. She sold everything you could think of: sweets, kids' corduroy trousers, balls of string, gas mantles, mendits for pots and pans, paraffin, safety pins, scrubbing brushes. There were glass-fronted wooden cabinets where I used to bend down and breathe on the glass, see my ghostly eyes disappear into mist. Inside, rows of little wooden drawers held all sorts of bits and bobs, spools of cotton, hooks and eyes, ribbons. There were flypapers, brushes and paraffin lamps from the ceiling, and shelves round the sides and across the middle.

Nan folded her arms and stared at me. 'You'd best get home. Doreen'll need you. It's your dad. Soon as the news came out this morning they started calling up the territorials – 'e's already gone.'

'Gone?' I couldn't understand her for a minute. 'Where?'

'Into the army, Genie.' She softened, seeing the shock on my face. It was all too much in one day. Eric, Mrs Wiles, and now this. 'He's not far away. He'll be back to see you. Come on—' She led me by the shoulder, through the back into the house. 'Your mother'll cope while you have a cup of tea. It's just as much of a shock for you as for 'er, though no doubt she won't see it that way.'

I sat by the kitchen table which was scrubbed almost white. Nan's house was always immaculate, even with Lil's kids living there. She still prepared all her food on the old blackleaded range which gleamed with Zebo polish. She rocked round the table from foot to foot, rattling spoons, taking the teapot to empty the dregs in the drain outside. I looked at her handsome, tired face. Always here, Nan was. Always had been, with her hair, still good and dark now, pinned up at the back. She'd always been the one who looked after everyone: Doreen this, Len that, Lil the other. Slow old Len always here, round her, until he came to us. And now she was half bringing up the next generation.

I watched her pour the tea into two straight, white cups. There was shouting from the yard outside, getting louder, rising to shrieks. The sound of women bitching. Nan eyed the window and tutted. 'Mary and Clarys again.'

'You all right, Nan?'

'As I'll ever be.'

I went and looked out of the door into the yard. Two of Nan's neighbours, Mary and Clarys, were up the far end by the brewhouse, Mary with her red hair, hands on her hips, giving Clarys a couple of fishwifey earsful. Little Patsy, Tom and Cathleen had been playing round the gas lamp with another child. Usually there'd have been a whole gang of them out there. They'd stopped to watch, Tom, my favourite, swinging round the lamp by one straight arm.

'Wonder what's got into them two,' I said.

'Be summat to do with Mary's kids again,' Nan said. 'Right 'andful they are.'

The bell rang in the shop. Nan stood still, teapot in hand, listening as the door was pushed carefully shut. There were furtive footsteps on the front stairs. Morgan had arrived. His life was strung between his mom, who he lived with over his ironmonger's shop in Aston, and his bolt-hole here. Nan carried on with what she was doing, which nowadays was exactly what she would have done if Morgan was in the same room. It was the girls who could still get under her skin, but Morgan, so far as she was concerned, was invisible, like a tiny speck of dirt. He crept in and out with an ingratiating smile on his face, and what was left of his streaks of greasy hair brushed over so they lay across his head like something fished out of a river.

I sat back down and within minutes we heard Lil.

43

'Awright, awright,' she was saying to the kids. 'Let me at least get in through the sodding door.'

'I see them two are at it again,' she said, flinging herself down on the horsehair sofa, in the worn cotton dress she wore to work at Chad Valley Toys. She put a hand over her eyes. 'She wants to keep them kids in order she does. My head's fit to split.'

Nan handed her a cup of tea and stood in front of her, hands on hips. 'You having second thoughts?' There was silence. ''Bout sending the kids?'

'No I'm not!' Lil sat upright quick as a flash, then winced at the pain in her head. 'I'm not having anyone else lay a finger on them. Sending the poor little mites off to fend for themselves.'

At that moment the three 'poor little mites' roared in through the door at full volume. 'Mom! Mom! – what's to eat? We're starving!'

'Out!' Lil yelled over the top of them. 'Stop "Momming" me when I've only just got in. You can push off out of 'ere till your nan says tea's ready!'

The room emptied again. The voices had quietened down outside but Lil's boys started drumming a stick on the miskin-lids down the end of the yard. Lil groaned, then sat up and drank her tea, pulling pins out of her hair so that hanks of it hung round her face.

'That foreman won't leave me alone again. I'm sick to the back teeth of it.' Lil was forever moaning about men chasing her. It was such a nuisance, the way they wouldn't leave her alone . . . None of us believed a word. She loved every minute of it.

Nan ignored her. 'Victor's gone you know. Dor was up here earlier in a state. Called 'im up straight away.'

Lil stared back at her. 'Bejaysus.' She often said that. It was one of Patsy's sayings and she clung to it. 'I

44

didn't think it'd be so soon. They haven't said there's going to be a war yet. Not for sure.'

'Looks mighty like it though.'

'Poland,' Lil said with scorn. She lit a fag and sat back. 'Where the hell is Poland anyhow?'

Nan sat on the edge of her chair, sipping tea. 'I've cleared out the cellar.'

'What for?'

'What d'you think for? I'm not going out in those public shelters with just anyone. There's not much space down there but we can fit and it'll have to do. I've given it a scrub.'

'Charming. Reducing us to sitting in the cellar.'

'Want some bread and scrape, Genie?' Nan said.

'No, I'm all right, ta. Nan?'

'What, love?'

I told her about Mrs Wiles.

'Well, what a thing,' she said. 'I thought you was looking a bit shook up. Poor old dear.'

'Shame.' Lil took a drag on her cigarette. 'Be much nicer to die in Lewis's, wouldn't it?'

'Better not tell Doreen,' Nan said. 'She'll only say that's what you get for working in a pawn shop up 'ere.' Mom put on a show of thinking people in Highgate were common, which was rich considering she grew up there herself. When I got the job I didn't tell her for days.

'You'd better be moving on,' Nan said to me. 'Got to see to this blackout palaver tonight. Your mother never got it done for the practice, did she? She won't want all that on 'er own.'

'She's all right – it's light yet,' Lil said. She seemed to be coming round a bit now she'd got some tea inside her. 'Eric get off all right, did he?'

I nodded, miserable at the thought. Lil sat forward, her old sweet self for a moment. 'You'll miss him, won't you Genie love? But he'll be all right. He's a good boy.' She smiled at me prettily. 'You'll have to come round and see my lot when you want some company.'

I found Mom in tears of course, with Len taking not the blindest bit of notice. It wasn't that he lacked sensitivity. He'd most likely just given up by now. Soon as he got in from work he usually sat down by Gloria without even washing his hands unless we nagged him, and that was that.

'My boy!' Mom was carrying on behind her hanky. There was no sign of tea on the go. 'My poor little Eric. How will we ever know if they're looking after him properly?'

I felt impatient, although all day I'd had nothing but the same thought in my mind. 'Oh, I expect he'll have a grand time,' I said bitterly. 'Forget we exist.'

'But that's what I'm worried about!' Mom wailed. She flung herself up out of her chair, dabbing at her red eyes. 'First I've got no son, and now I haven't even got a husband!' She clicked the stair door open and disappeared upstairs, slamming it behind her.

'She's crying,' Len remarked.

'You don't say, Lenny.'

I was really fed up with her. Sometimes I'd have liked to be the one who could flounce about and cry and behave like a child. I got sick of being a mother to my own mom. I wanted someone to sit down and put their arm round me while I cried because my dad and my brother had gone away.

'I s'pose this means I'm cooking tea, does it?' I

snapped at Len, since he was the only person left to snap at, though I got no answer anyway.

There was liver in the kitchen. I started chopping onions. Len fiddled with Gloria until music came streaming from her. I felt a bit better. Len beamed. 'S'nice this, Genie, in't it?'

There was a voice kept coming on as I was cooking, saying we had to retune the wireless. Len was taking no notice, didn't understand.

I wiped my hands and went over. 'Len, the man says we've got to turn the knob to a different number.' Len stared blankly at me. I went and fiddled with Gloria's dial and Len got a bit agitated.

Just as I was dishing up, this voice said, 'This is the BBC Home Service.' I'd just called Mom down and we looked at each other expecting something else to happen.

'The what?' Mom shrugged and stepped over to look at herself in the mirror – 'What a sight' – then, as the light was waning outside, went round the windows, pulling all the black curtains she'd made. 'This should've been done earlier,' she said accusingly, pulling the ordinary curtains over them. 'I'll have to do upstairs tomorrow. Well this *is* going to be jolly I can see. Feels like the middle of winter.'

My liver and onions wasn't out of this world, though no worse than Mom would've managed, but she still turned her nose up at it.

'Gravy's lumpy. And how did you get the liver so hard?'

We waited, tensed up as the nine o'clock bulletin came on, but there was nothing new, nothing definite, except that Australia had said she'd support the Allies if war broke out.

'Who are the Allies?' I asked.

'Us of course.'

When we turned Gloria off, finally, to go up to bed, it was eerily quiet. There wasn't a sound from outside. Wasn't something supposed to be happening?

'I wonder what Victor's doing,' Mom said, turning all soggy again. 'How could he do it to me?'

Saturday 2 September. The day of waiting.

It had been a golden afternoon, the city's dark bowl lit by autumn sun. Two blokes whitewashing the entrance to an ARP post whistled at me on the way home. The balloons sailed in the sky, tugging gently on their lines.

What's up now? I wondered, stepping in from work that evening. The house was quiet again but I could hear music in the distance. They were out in the garden, Gloria too, on a paving slab with her accumulator. Someone was playing 'Somewhere Over the Rainbow' on the organ with twiddly bits.

At the end of the garden, next to the wizened lilac tree, its mauve flowers now brown, stood Mom, Len and Mr Tailor from two houses along. They were all looking at a big, grey loop of corrugated iron and two other flat bits which were leant up against the fence. The Anderson shelter had arrived.

''Ullo Genie!' Len boomed across at me. The others didn't seem to notice if I was there or not.

Mom was all worked up. 'Isn't this just the limit?' She lit one cigarette from the stub end of another and sucked on it like a sherbet dip. 'Isn't it just like Victor to go away the day before the shelter gets here. How am I ever going to cope with all this?'

'Look, love, you're awright – I've said I'll do it,' Mr Tailor said. He was always the philosopher, Mr Tailor. Maybe because he had a grown up son whose testicles had never come down. Nan said with something like that in the family there was no point in getting worked up about anything else. He'd most likely be there on his own deathbed in the same grey braces saying, 'Yer awright, bab – things'll look better in the morning.'

'I'll sort it out for you, soon as I've finished my own. I'm not going anywhere, am I? Too long in the tooth for that caper. Look – you just have to dig down and put this bit in the ground—' He pointed to the big curved bit which I saw was two sheets of metal bolted together at the top. 'Then you put the soil back over the top, these bits are the front and back, and Bob's your uncle.'

Len had already got the spade and was all for starting off.

'He could do it if I show him,' Mr Tailor went on. 'Big strong lad.'

Mom was hugging her waist. I could see the shape of the Players packet in the pocket of her pinner. 'Looks more like a dog kennel. I certainly don't fancy sitting out in that of a night.'

'It's tougher than it looks,' Mr Tailor said, slapping his thick, hairy hand on the side of it. 'I'll come and give Len a hand finishing it tomorrow – how's that?'

Mom nodded. 'Look, I've got to get in and finish these flaming blinds. Been queuing half the morning for the material . . .'

The organ music which had gone on and on stopped suddenly. 'Sssh,' I said. 'Listen!'

We walked back over the toasted daisies and stood round Gloria.

'This is the BBC Home Service ... Here is the six o'clock news ...'

Everyone stood still. Mr Tailor raised one hand in the air, flat as if he was pushing against an invisible wall.

The government had given a final ultimatum to Hitler. Withdraw from Poland or we declare war. They'd given him until the next morning.

When it was over, another voice said, 'This is Sandy MacPherson joining you again on the BBC organ ...'

'Not again,' Mom said. 'That bloke must be exhausted. He's been stuck on that flaming organ all day.' As she disappeared into the house she added, 'Why does that Hitler have to do everything on the weekend?'

The sun went down slowly, though not slowly enough for Mom, who was still toiling away on the Vesta, the reel of black cotton flying round on the top, cursing to herself.

Without being told, I picked up the idea pretty quick that I was cooking tea. I saw there was a rabbit hanging by its hind legs in the pantry. Mom said Mr Tailor had got it somewhere. Don't ask, sort of thing. 'That's for dinner tomorrow,' she said. 'Do summat with eggs tonight.'

When I'd got the spuds on, I went and stood out in the garden. Len was working like mad digging out turf and soil, dry though it was. He was droning some kind of tune and he didn't look back or see me.

I took my shoes off, felt the wiry grass under my feet and wondered what it'd be like to live in the country with nothing but grass and trees. I wondered about Eric. The street was so quiet. Usually it was full of kids playing, in the gardens and out the front.

And I thought this evening was like no other I'd ever known. Not even the night I left school when I knew I

50

was going to a job next week and everything else would be the same, not like Christmas Eve, even though there was the same sort of quiet. Everything was shifting, you could feel it all around you, those balloons filling in the sky. No one had a clue what was going to happen tomorrow.

I didn't know whether to be excited or frightened.

Mom still didn't manage to black out the whole house by sundown. 'Cotton kept breaking,' she complained. She wasn't very good at sewing either.

We ate scrambled egg and potatoes. Len ate astonishing heaps of mash. It was a queer feeling sitting there with the windows all muffled. Made you feel cut off, as if you were in prison. And Mom decided for reasons of her own that we had to have the windows tight shut as well and nearly suffocated the lot of us.

None of us could settle to anything. Mom said she couldn't stand the sight of any more sewing. So we sat round Gloria and listened in. She was our contact with the outside world: Sandy MacPherson, records, news. Parliament had sat in emergency session. Len slouched, picking his nose.

'Don't, Len!' Mom scolded.

We sang along with 'We'll Gather Violets in the Spring' and 'Stay Young and Beautiful, If You Want to Be Loved.'

We wondered what tomorrow would bring. There was a storm in the night and I barely slept.

The Prime Minister was due to speak at eleven-fifteen. Mom was in the front at her machine again, tickety-tick, and I, who seemed to be cook for the duration, was stuck at the sink. Len was out digging, the ground softened by the rain.

It dried out to a perfect, calm morning, though the air was humid. I could hear church bells early on, then they stopped.

Our dinner was going to be late.

'I can't touch that thing,' Mom said, pointing at the rabbit, its legs rigid against the door. 'Make me bad, that would. You'll have to skin it, Genie – we'll have stew this afternoon.'

What a treat. Didn't she always find me the best jobs?

I spread an old *Sports Argus* on the kitchen table. There were a couple of knives that needed sharpening and the kitchen scissors. It was a wild, brown rabbit with a white belly, and heavier than I expected. Its back legs were tied with string and it was sticky with a smear of blood where I touched it on one side. Its eyes looked like rotten grapes.

Before I got started I went and switched Gloria on and heard a band playing.

'What time is it?' Mom called through.

'Five to eleven.'

There was a ring of blood like lipstick round the rabbit's mouth. The ears felt very cold and there was a pong coming off it like fermented fruit.

It was a hell of a job to get the head off. Our knives sunk in deeper and deeper but wouldn't break the pelt. In the end I snipped at the neck with the scissors, but it took so long it made me feel panicky, as if I was fighting with it.

The news came on on the hour. There was a knock at the front door.

'Get that, will you Genie?'

'Can't – I'm all in a mess.'

I heard her sigh, like she always did if I asked her to do anything. Peeping into the hall I saw Molly and Gladys Bender from across the road. I knew Mom'd be thinking, oh my God. They both stood there with big grins on their faces, each of them the size of a gasometer, still in their pinners. Gladys was Molly's mom and by far the sharper of the two. They lived together and both did charring and you almost never saw them without a pinner or an overall. They both wore glasses and both had their hair marcelled and probably had done since it was fashionable sometime round the year I was born. Molly looked the image of Gladys except that Gladys, being twenty years older, had hair that wasn't exactly grey, but dusty looking, and Molly's cheeks weren't full of red wormy veins.

They were beaming away like a couple of mad March hares. 'We was wondering,' Gladys said in her blaring voice, 'Mr Tailor said there's to be an announcement – only, we haven't got a wireless . . .'

So all Mom could really say was, 'Why don't you come in then?' and called to me, 'Genie – get the kettle on, love.'

Love? That was a sign we had company.

'Don't mind Genie,' Mom said. 'She's doing our dinner.'

I caught a whiff of Molly and Gladys. There were grey smudges down their pinners and they always reeked of disinfectant and Brasso and sweat. Especially sweat, but it was always mixed in with all these cleaning fluids and polish. They sat down, filling the two chairs. Molly craned to see out to the garden.

'Oooh,' she said. 'Your Len's busy, in't he? We could do with borrowing him.'

They chattered away to Mom, who was as polite as she could manage. I got into the rabbit by snipping up from under its tail with the scissors – tricky with me being left-handed – along the soft white belly. With the first cut a round hole appeared like a little brown mouth and the smell whooshed up and hit me. Lola. I opened it up and there was a pool of muck inside, and round it, holding everything in, a glassy film of pink, grey and white, tinged with yellow. The kettle whispered on the stove. It was ten past.

'Shall I call Len in for you?' Molly asked eagerly.

'You stay put,' Gladys bossed her.

I called down the garden. Len dropped the spade and loped up to the house. I don't know if he knew why he was hurrying but he'd caught the atmosphere, something in my voice. He stamped his feet on the step outside.

'It's all right – nothing yet.'

I pushed my knife into the thin, tough film of the rabbit's insides. There was blood everywhere suddenly. Soft jelly shapes slumped into my hand, cold trails of gut like pink necklaces, rounded bits with webs of yellow fat on them, green of half-digested grass when I pulled on its stomach and it tore. I knew which bit the liver was, rich with blood, four rubbery petals like a black violet.

When I'd got everything out it had gone quiet next door. Nice of them to call me, I thought, washing my hands. Mom, Molly, Gladys, Len and I all stood or sat round, everyone's eyes fixed on Gloria.

'I am speaking to you from the Cabinet Room at Number Ten Downing Street,' the Prime Minister said. Words we'd never forget. The announcement of war.

'Now that we have resolved to finish it, I know you will play your part with calmness and with courage.'

When Mr Chamberlain had finished they played the National Anthem. Molly and Gladys struggled grunting to their feet. Then church bells pealed from Gloria, filling the room. We drank tea. None of us spoke for a time. No one knew what to say. Molly and Gladys weren't grinning any more.

'So it's finally happened,' Mom said at last. 'Len – you'd better go out and finish off. Mr Tailor's coming later.'

Len wasn't listening and nor was Molly, because they were staring hard at each other as if they'd never seen one another before, with great big soppy smiles on their faces. He walked backwards out of the room, tripping up the step into the kitchen.

'I'll have to watch him,' Mom said when Molly and Gladys had departed, thanking us endlessly. 'He may be soft in the head but he's all man, our Len.'

'I know,' I said.

Her head whipped round. 'What d'you mean, you know?'

I finally finished the rabbit, pulling back the skin from over the front legs like peeling a shirt off. The inside of the pelt was shiny and covered with hundreds of wiggly red veins like Gladys's cheeks. When I got the skin off it looked small and helpless like a new-born babby. Tasted all right though, come three o'clock, with a few onions.

We waited for the peril that was supposed to fall from the clouds. That's when people started staring up at the sky, heads back, eyes narrowed. The night war was declared I went out into the garden after it was dark. Mom was despondent because they'd announced in the afternoon that all the cinemas were going to close.

'Life's not going to be worth living!' she kept on. I wanted to get out of our muffled rooms.

I leapt out of the back door closing it as fast as I could so's not to spill any light. I walked down the garden. It was dark as a bear's behind out there. Everything was quiet, deathly quiet I thought, really eerie.

At the bottom of the garden I could just make out the hunched shape of the Anderson which Mr Tailor had put in for us that afternoon. Len had heaped the soil back on top. It was odd seeing it there. A web of searchlights danced in the city sky, but down in the garden you could barely see a hand in front of your face. No lights from the street, the houses, the cars. Nothing.

I stumbled on a hummock of grass. Then there was a sound. Must've been a twig scraping the fence but it set me thinking, and my heart was off thudding away.

No one knew when the Germans would come. We'd expected them down the street straight away. Maybe they were here already. Was that what I'd heard, someone moving about in the garden next door? Or maybe there was someone in the Anderson ... Someone just behind me with a gun ...

Panic seized me tight by the throat and I was across that scrap of lawn and struggling with the door handle so mithered I could hardly get it open. I landed panting in the kitchen.

'What's got into you?' Mom called through. There was a laugh in her voice.

*

One Sunday in the middle of September Mom was having one of her wet lettuce sessions. Lunch had been cooked by yours truly (I was getting a lot of practice). I'd done a piece of chine and Mom said, 'This isn't up to much, Genie. How d'you manage to make such a mess of it?'

So I said, 'Cook it yourself next time if you're so fussy.' She slapped me for that, hard, at the top of my arm. Sod you too, I thought.

I knew what was wrong though. Partly the feeling of anticlimax.

'You only have to strike a match out there at night and someone jumps on you,' Mom moaned. 'But there's nothing cowing well happening, is there?' You could tell she was under strain when her language started slipping.

Earlier in the week Dad had come home to tell us that his short period in Hall Green was finished and that they were being transferred for training outside Birmingham. He didn't know where. Before he went, suddenly younger-looking in his uniform, I saw Mom go to him, and they held one another. He stroked her hair and she clung to him.

'I can't stand it,' she sobbed into his chest. 'Can't stand being here on my own. I won't be able to cope.'

'You've got Genie,' Dad said. 'I'm sorry, love. I hadn't realized it would all be so soon.'

She seemed to have more respect for him now he had an army uniform on. And I hadn't seen Mom and Dad cuddling before, not ever. Made me cry too. And then Dad did something he'd not done since I was a tiny kid. He came and took me in his arms too and I saw there were tears in his big grey eyes.

'Goodbye, Genie love. Eh, there's a girl, don't cry

now. You're going to help your mom out, aren't you? I s'pect I'll be back before we know it.'

Len was starting to blub too, watching us all, and Dad gave his shoulder a squeeze and then he was gone. I dried my tears. Didn't like crying in front of Mom. It didn't feel right.

She'd been all right up until Sunday. Even though we had a letter from Eric:

Dear Mom,
    Ime well and I hope you are to. And Genie and Dad and Len. I was at one ladys and now Ime at annother. Shes qite nice. Shes got cats.
    Love Eric.

It was from Maidenhead. Mom sniffled a bit when she read it – 'Not much of a letter, is it?' – but then carried herself along being busy and was quite cheerful. She even had a mad cleaning session and the house was spotless. But finally she fell over the edge into gloom and sitting for hours in chairs without her shoes on.

So I left, and went to see my pal Teresa. She'd always been my best pal, ever since we were kiddies, although we were never at the same school. The Spini kids traipsed all the way over to the Catholic School in Bordesley Street. Teresa, who was always up to something the rest of the time, could dress up demure as a china doll on a Sunday with a white ribbon in her hair and go off to Mass at St Michael's with Vera's – Mrs Spini's – family, who all lived in the streets of 'Little Italy' behind Moor Street Station. It was like stepping right into Italy down there, with them all speaking Italian and cooking with garlic. I used to go with Teresa and see her granny sometimes. Nonna Amelia was a wispy old lady with bowed legs and no teeth who always wore black and spoke hardly any English. She used to suck and suck on sugared almonds from home and spit the nuts out because she couldn't chew them.

They had a back-house in a yard just along from my nan's, though not behind the shop as they'd tiled that part white like a hospital and turned it into their little ice-cream factory. The door of the house was almost always open, summer or winter, and usually there were kids spilling in and out. When I got there I could see the back of Micky, Teresa's dad, sat at the table in his shirtsleeves. He wore belts, not braces like my dad. I could hear their voices, loud, in Italian.

'Genie!' Teresa called, spotting me. Soon as I got there they switched to talking in English.

Their house was much like any other in area inside, with a couple of small differences. Near the door was a black and white engraving ('my photograph' as Vera called it) of Jesus, and over the mantel hung a tile, in a thin wooden frame. On its deep blue glaze was a handpainted figure of the Madonna and child, and beneath, the words AVE MARIA. I'd asked Teresa about it once, years ago.

'My nan in Italy gave it to Dad before he came here,' she said. 'She didn't want him to go, and she gave it to him as she kissed him goodbye. She said "If your own mother can't watch over you, remember that the mother of God is always near to catch you when you fall."' Micky had never seen his mother again after walking out with that lovingly wrapped tile at the age of twenty.

'Anyway,' Teresa'd said. 'He met Mom his second day in Birmingham, so someone was looking out for him.'

Teresa pulled a chair out for me at the table between her and Micky.

' 'Bout time,' she said. 'We haven't seen you in ages.'

'Some of us work for a living you know.' Now I was at the pawn shop I worked most Saturdays. 'No time for gadding into town to try on hats in C&A. Come to think of it that might be a good reason for moving on!' I glanced nervously at Micky. You never quite knew what mood he was going to be in.

He frowned. 'I thought you were at that pie factory?'

'I was – for a week. There was this bloke opposite me with a great long dewdrop in 'is nose. I reckon there was more snot than meat in some of them pies. One week of that and I was off.'

The others groaned and laughed, even Stevie, Teresa's older brother who was usually either in a daydream about shiny new Lagondas or being a self-righteous pain in the neck. I saw Teresa looking nervously at her father for his reaction and I wondered if I'd walked into the middle of something. 'You wouldn't want your seat getting too warm anywhere, would you?'

'I have to be kept busy.'

'You've practically done the lot already!' Teresa said. She sounded envious, and her eyes strayed once more over to Micky. He was holding a hunk of bread in his strong hands, pulling off pellets and half throwing them into his mouth.

I looked round the table. 'It's quiet, isn't it?' And then wished I hadn't said the one thing they were all most likely trying not to think about. Vera's eyes turned to pools of misery.

But God, it was quiet. Normally when I went in there eight pairs of dark brown eyes turned to look at me, but now the four younger ones were missing and I felt the loss almost as if they were my own brothers and sisters. In terms of noise you barely noticed Eric being gone because he was such a mouse most of the time. Micky and Stevie weren't all that vocal, but those Spini women were LOUD. Even Giovanna at seven had a voice on her like a foghorn, and Teresa was about the noisiest of the lot. Great blast of a voice and sandpaper-rough as if she'd smoked forty a day since birth.

'I can hardly look at Teresa in that dress for wondering how they are and what they're doing.' Vera's homely face was crumpling.

The dress was crimson with a white lace collar and Vera had made three to match, so other Sundays Francesca and Giovanna had been turned out in theirs too, matching and all lovely with their dark hair, Teresa's long and loosely tied back, Francesca with plaits and Giovanna's in a pert, swinging ponytail.

'Will they be able to go to Mass where they've gone?' I asked.

Tears started running down Vera's cheeks. She shook her head and shrugged. 'Don't know, love. I told Francesca to ask, but with them down Wales . . . Don't know that they're all that keen on Catholics down there. I can't stand thinking about it. At least they've been kept in twos – Francesca's got Luki, and Tony and Giovanna are together. I s'pose I should be thankful for that.'

'They'll be all right, Mom,' Teresa said, putting her hand on her mother's plump arm. She was such a happy woman usually. You'd see her in the shop even in the depths of winter, blowing on her hands to keep warm, songs billowing white out of her mouth. And she hugged and kissed those kids like no one had ever done to me in my life.

61

'I don't know why I sent them,' she went on. 'Nothing's happening. Only I kept on thinking about what they did bombing Spain and I thought it'd be the same here. Every day I have to stop myself going to fetch them back.'

'No good thinking like that,' Micky said more gently. 'The war's only just started and we don't know what's coming. Francesca'll see they're all right. She's nearly grown up now.'

I looked at Micky timidly. He was a moody so-and-so – tough as anything on his kids, though he'd barely ever said a harsh word to me. 'How's the Fire Service, Mr Spini?' I asked.

'Dad 'ad a bit of a shock this week, didn't you?' Teresa said cautiously.

We waited for a split second to see the reaction. And Micky's face broke into a grin, as did Stevie's. 'Oh God yes, the jump!' He blew smoke at the ceiling, smoothed a hand over his wiry black curls. He'd done his first two weeks in the Auxiliary Fire Service. 'They got us doing sheet jumps. That means you 'ave to go up the drill tower in the station. Everyone else is standing at the bottom holding out a sheet to catch you. If you're holding it you have to brace yourself to take the weight.' He clenched his fists, the hairy backs of his hands turned towards the floor. 'So you're up the top of the tower, sitting on this window-sill and the instructor's told you "Don't jump off, just step off." You're thinking Christ Almighty—'

'Micky!' Vera interrupted, eyes fierce.

'Sorry. But I was, I can tell you. I was thinking to myself, that's not a sheet down there, it's a pocket handkerchief.'

'So you jumped?'

'Didn't have no choice. My insides followed me down about five minutes later!'

'You should just thank your stars you don't have to jump out of aeroplanes!' Vera said.

'Well at least they have a parachute!' We all laughed at his head-shaking indignation.

Vera got up, clearing dishes already wiped clean with bread, scraping bones and wrinkles of fish skin on to the top one. She was not a tall woman, but rounded and comfortable, and Teresa looked very like her, although Vera Spini's long hair was blond – out of a bottle Mom said – but it suited her, even though her eyebrows were jet black.

Already it was half way through the afternoon. They could make meals last an age, the Spinis. Eating was a pastime as well as a necessity. Sometimes, Sundays, they were all still sitting round the table at four o'clock, spinning the meal on into cups of tea.

'Who wants ice cream?' Vera called from the scullery.

'Oooh!' I said. 'Yes please!'

'I didn't need to ask you, did I?' She smiled, bringing the basin of homemade ice cream to the table. 'You'd eat it until it came out of your ears.' She leaned forward and pulled my cheek affectionately between her finger and thumb.

'Only my ice cream,' Micky teased.

Vera faced him indignantly, hands on her shapely hips. '*My* ice cream? Listen to him. Who makes all the ice cream around here Micky, eh? Whose family has been making ice cream for three generations?'

'Yours, my darlin'.' Micky looked mock humble.

'I should think so.' Vera dug in the spoon. 'We had a few punnets of strawberries over so I put them in too.'

That set my mouth watering. Vera's mom and dad,

the Scattolis, were part of the community from Sora in the middle of Italy, one of the ice-cream families, and you came across Scattoli ice-cream cycles all over town. When Vera married Micky, a newcomer and a southerner, the family accepted him and helped set them up in their own shop. Old Poppa Scattoli gave his blessing not only on the marriage, but also on their using the family's ice-cream recipe for another string to the Spinis' business bow – provided they used the Scattoli name.

The ice cream was delicious. I was just sitting there relaxing, thinking how nice it was to be eating food that might've been made by angels, in a proper family with a mom and dad there and no rows, when Teresa had to go and say, 'I wish I could get a job.'

Micky's eyes swivelled round to her angrily and Vera and Stevie sighed. Teresa always had a way of offering the red rag straight to the bull. You didn't argue with Micky – except Teresa did – and the Spinis' ding-dongs had a way of blowing up on you sudden and harsh as a summer storm.

'We need you here,' Micky decreed, jabbing a stubby finger towards her. 'And first you got to learn 'ow to behave yourself before you go anywhere out of my sight on your own.'

'I am behaving myself.' Teresa was on the boil already, voice booming. 'He was a customer. I was only talking to him. What's wrong with that?'

'Talking to him!' Micky's voice was mocking. He sat back, waving one thick, hairy arm, his Brummie accent laid over his Italian one. 'You think you're just talking but I can see what he's doing with his eyes. And what you're doing with yours too. You make yourself cheap, girl, behaving like that. You give him ideas about yourself. If I see you doing that again . . .'

He stopped because for once he couldn't think of anything to say and Teresa stared back brazenly. She never went out anywhere, except to Mass, and she knew she was an asset in the shop. The customers loved her, listening to their moans, her big laugh ringing down the road behind them.

'Don't keep on, Micky,' Vera interrupted. 'You've said enough already.'

'But she don't take any bloody notice!' Micky roared. 'What do you want – eh? You got no respect!'

'You got my respect,' Teresa bawled. 'But how come it's always me?' She pointed at Stevie, who was watching her across the table with his heavy-lidded eyes. 'You don't say anything when he's going about with that lunatic Fausto. Or is it awright now to invite a mad man into the family and one who still thinks he's a Blackshirt as well – eh?'

'You've got Fausto wrong,' Stevie said with contempt.

Micky waved the air dismissively. 'The boy's a hot-head, a fool . . .'

'It's not fair!'

'Teresa!' It was Vera's turn to try and calm her down.

'But I'm sick of it! The men in this family do just what they like and expect us to stay at home and wait on them hand and foot.' She pushed her chair back and marched off outside, saying, 'It's like a prison here . . .'

Micky slammed his spoon down and left as well. I thought he was going after her but we saw him move past the window and head for the street.

Vera sighed. 'When will Teresa ever learn to keep her mouth shut?'

*

Teresa and I sat out on the back step, frocks over our knees.

'I s'pect Dad's gone over Park Street to the pub. I really hate him sometimes.' She squinted up at the sky. 'Wish they'd come if they're coming. We could do with a bit of action round here.'

'You're awful,' I said. 'Any rate, I didn't think that was the kind of action you were interested in nowadays.'

She stuck her tongue out at me as far as it would go.

'Come on then, tell us. Who is 'e?'

Teresa stuck a finger urgently against her lips and peeped round the door. Vera was washing up, had said Stevie should help so he was wiping, with his altar boy face on.

'Come over here.' Teresa pulled me to my feet and over towards the brewhouse and we stood with our faces to the wall. Her whisper tickled my ear.

'He keeps coming in the shop – from that sheet metal place opposite Frank Street. I'm sure he's taken a fancy to me.' Even at this distance she kept looking back nervously at the house. Micky and Vera thought Teresa was far too young to be thinking about boys.

Although we'd left school we were still treated as kids, weren't allowed out dancing, nothing like that. Teresa was barely allowed to set foot outside by herself. But the boys went for her. It wasn't that she was pretty exactly. She was shorter than me, small and round, whereas I was bony and boyish; she had Vera's looks, a snub nose, and her complexion wasn't all that marvellous. But what she had was a lot of life and a lot of laughs in her. And what's more she was ripe and ready to be swept off her feet, even though she was innocent as a day-old child, and looked it in that Sunday dress.

'He keeps coming in – I've never known anyone buy

so many apples – 'cept he comes and gets them one by one!' She burst into her infectious giggle. 'Ooh, sometimes I feel like taking off just anywhere, just for a bit of excitement!'

'So he's Prince Charming then, is he?' I couldn't help sounding sarky.

'He's all right. Nice enough. Bit skinny. I like 'em with a bit more brawn on them than that!'

'Brawn or brains – make your choice.'

'And he's got this great big Adam's apple – wobbles around when he's talking as if he's got a plum stuck down his throat ...' The giggle turned into her loud, exuberant laugh. 'No, I'm being unkind. He's got a nice way with him. Oi – what's up with you?'

'Nothing.'

'Don't just say nothing—' She elbowed me but I pulled away, staring stubbornly across the yard. From the top-floor windows the Spinis' bedding was hanging out to air as usual, an Italian habit the neighbours still weren't sure about.

'B for Boys. B for Boring.'

'Well, you wanted to know!'

'Yeah, and you told me,' I snapped, crosser with myself than her because I was mucking up the afternoon. But God she didn't half go on. I wanted her to be happy – she was my best pal. But I wanted her all to myself as well. She was so restless and impatient. Even now she was tapping her feet against the grey bricks as if she wanted to be off and none of us were good enough for her.

'I don't know what you're always moaning about—'

'Who says I'm moaning?' she interrupted my outburst.

'If I had a family like yours I'd think I was in clover. You should try living with my lot.'

'Oh don't you start getting on your 'igh 'orse with me!' Teresa's temper had a shorter fuse than a banger on fireworks night. 'You're not the one stuck in the shop and minding little kiddies all the time . . .'

'Nor are you now, 'cause they're not here, are they?'

'And your dad doesn't come down on you like a ton of bricks every time you even open your mouth to talk to a boy . . .'

I was getting ready to say that's because he never noticed anything much I did but she was getting well warmed up now. 'Family this, family that. You can't get away from them ever – and if it's not them it's the sodding church.'

'Well how come Stevie doesn't mind?'

She made a big, irritated puffing sound through her lips. 'Because Stevie's pain in the backside little Stevie. He's like a policeman round the place and all he ever thinks about are cars and football.'

She relented and looked round at me. 'All I want's a bit of excitement. We'll be pals whatever. Boys don't make any difference.'

'I know,' I said, face all red.

Just then we heard footsteps charging along the entry. The Spinis' yard was a 'double knack' which meant there were two ways in, and there was an entry running along by the brewhouse. When I saw who it was my face blushed to my ears. Walt Eccles, Stevie's pal. I was scared stiff every time I saw Walt, by the way my knees turned wobbly and my heart went like the clappers and my insides churned with frightened, helpless adoration. An adoration I'd rather have jumped from the spire of St Martin's than let him know about. After all, Walt was two years older than us, which seemed like centuries, and why should he be interested in a gangly scarecrow like me?

The sun shone on his shock of gold hair and there was the usual cheeky grin on his freckled face as he came panting up to us, looking gorgeous.

'In a bit of a rush, are we?' I said, tart as I could manage, while Teresa smiled sweetly at him, as she would at anything in trousers.

Walt gave me his best ingratiating smile which filled me brimming over with panic. 'Nice to see you too,' he said. 'How're you then?'

'None the better for seeing you.'

He pulled a face at me. 'See you're full of charm as ever. Stevie in?'

'Somewhere,' Teresa said, waving into the house.

A moment later the two of them came out, off up to the park to kick a ball around. The blush rose in my face again, and I turned crossly to the wall. Teresa was giving me a really close, squinty look.

'You're sweet on 'im, aren't you?' Her face was full of devilment.

'I'm not!'

'Oh yes you are!' she bawled in her big husky voice, and jumped about triumphantly clapping her hands. Luckily the yard was quiet. 'Genie's sweet on Walt. Genie likes boys after all!'

I went all tight inside. Only half joking I pushed her up against the wall of the brewhouse, gripping her shoulders.

'One word to Stevie, or *anyone*,' I said between my teeth, 'and you won't live to see another day. And that's a promise.'

We were bored with the so-called war already. Every night we sat round the wireless, windows blacked, waiting. Mom hadn't been to the pictures for three weeks. It was Bore War. Sitzkrieg instead of Blitzkrieg. We wanted something to happen, and not just in the Atlantic. Something we could see.

Gloria kept handing out announcements. Keep off the streets. Carry your gas mask as at all times, etc. In fact recently she'd been a bit of a bore herself.

The proper programmes were back on now at least. *Band Waggon* now on a Saturday night, Len with his cup and saucer jigging about as they sang, 'Come and make a trip upon the Band Waggon – skiddeley-boom,' until Mom'd say, 'For goodness' sake give me your Bournvita, Lenny. It'll be in your lap, else.'

She was still low. Blackout, no pictures, supposedly in charge of the house, the uncertainty of it all getting on her nerves. Said she was scared to be out at night. Her so-called pal Stella had moved across town with her husband and hadn't troubled herself to come back and visit so she wasn't around to have a moan to. Mom did crack her face at Tommy Handley sometimes.

One evening she got out of her chair and said, 'I've had enough of this. There aren't going to be any air raids. Let's have the last of the light before we all die of asphyxiation, never mind the flaming bombs.'

She threw open the blackout curtains and the waning light lapped across the room. We all took in a deep breath, thought something would happen. Nothing did.

The weeks passed. Poland surrendered. We clung to the music and wondered what was happening. We waited.

October 1939

'Well, that's that,' Mom announced. 'I'm not stopping in like this. I've had more than enough already.'

Mr Churchill had just announced that the war would last three years. How he knew that we didn't understand, but something about him made you believe it. And that did it for Mom.

'There's no knowing when your father'll be home for good.' That thought seemed to rouse her out of the depressed stupor into which she'd kept dipping.

Lil had just moved jobs, though she hadn't escaped the factory. She was learning welding at Parkinson Cowan, in overalls and with a snood over her hair, and kept on about how useful she was being to the war effort and humanity in general despite having three young children. She put on a good show of being irritated by a new set of admirers.

Mom decided that for the first time in fifteen years she'd get herself employed. She fixed herself up with a job on the telephone exchange, second shift of the day.

'But Mom – you'll have to come back from town on the bus late at night. You won't even go out as it is now.'

Apparently this didn't matter. 'I'll just have to manage.' She was excited all of a sudden, cheeks pink. 'You'll have to stop in and keep Len company.'

This was all quite a turn about for the woman who'd

refused even to go up to our nan's of an evening because she was too scared to come back in the blackout.

'I could be knocked down in the street and robbed,' she'd kept saying. 'There's a lot of it about you know.'

'So who's going to cook? And shop and clean?'

'Genie!' She laughed, looking back over her shoulder at her reflection in the mirror. 'You sound like an old woman. We'll get by. I'll be home mornings, and you know what to do by now, don't you? It's not as if we've got your father to feed.'

On the strength of the vast fortune she was about to earn she went out and kitted herself up with a couple of frocks and a pair of shoes with T-bars and a chunk of heel, and started on her new working life. The rest of us, who'd been at it for some time with no red carpet laid out, had to stand aside.

She went off at dinnertime, hair knotted low in her neck, in one of her new dresses and her small black bag over one arm, and came home at about half ten at night off the bus. She was full of it. The work, the people. It was fast, busy. And she was needed suddenly.

'They even have special gas masks for us with a little microphone at the side so we can carry on working.' She laughed. 'After all, in a gas attack the telephones would be essential.'

I could just imagine her putting on a posh telephone voice. She stood more upright now, strutted about as if she owned the place, and didn't sit in chairs and stare at nothing any more. Nor, from the first day, did it seem to cross her mind that there was such a thing as housework to be done.

I decided to have a go at something else myself. I was getting restless with all this change around me, and I needed a job which allowed me to start early and finish

72

early, what with the shopping and cooking to do and often washing thrown in as well. Mom was at home all morning but she was barely ever up until gone eleven. She needed the time to recover, she said.

There was a job going at a firm in Cheapside called Commercial Loose Leaf. I walked through the sand-bagged entrance up a gloomy staircase smelling of glue, to a cluttered little office above the shop floor. The gaffer was a middle-aged man with a tired, worried-looking face, thin hair and blue eyes like a little boy's.

'D'you know your numbers properly?' he asked.

'Oh yes,' I said airily. 'I was good at arithmetic at school.' Once again I showed my certificate and reference from the school.

He just glanced at them, not really interested. 'Just so long as you can count.' He gave me a quick look up and down. 'Table hand. You can start Monday.'

Well, that job nearly did me in. The company produced trade books and ledgers. To start with they put me to collating piles of paper covered with print about technical things I couldn't make head or tail of. The second week I was put on numbering. So this was the reason I needed to be able to count. The blue-tinged papers were all numbered by hand. You had to concentrate enough doing it so's you didn't lose your place and that meant you couldn't talk to anyone, but it didn't take up anything like the whole of your mind. The second night I dreamed of nothing but numbers.

We got used to a new routine at home. Suddenly we were a family where everyone had a job. I was working from eight in the morning until half past four. So after work I'd walk home and pick up any shopping on the way. Len came in soon after from Longbridge, so muggins here would cook the meal and wash up (Len wiping) and we'd sit in the rest of the evening until Mom came in. Occasionally Teresa would come down to keep us company.

'You're the one person who cheers me up,' I told her one night. 'It's an endless round of drudgery otherwise, and no one notices what I've done anyway.'

'Why don't you say something to your mom?' Teresa said, not being one to sit down under anything.

I shrugged. 'She'll only play the martyr. She's got her head so high in the clouds I don't think she even notices the rest of us exist any more.'

Teresa sat back with her legs stretched out, playing with a lock of her hair. 'You'll make someone a lovely wife,' she teased. 'With a flock of kids.'

I scowled. 'I'm not getting married. Not ever. I'm going to work as hard as I can and get rich and buy a cottage in a field next to a river, where there's no chimneys and no factories and no people, and I'm going to live there on my own for the rest of my life and grow flowers. Well – Len could come too if he wants.'

'Oh, I want to get married,' Teresa said. 'I think it's sad seeing a woman left on the shelf.'

'Sure you're talking about marriage and not just a white dress and a veil?'

'Oh Genie! You're such a flaming misery you are!' She laughed, exasperated.

'I just think you're better off on your own. I mean, look at my family. Who'd want to get hitched after seeing them lot?'

'Lil had a decent husband.'

'Yes, but what's the good of a decent husband if he's just going to throw himself in the canal?'

74

Teresa found this mighty hilarious for some reason. 'Genie, you're awful you are!' She sat up again. 'Guess what?' Then she was off again, giggling so much she set Len off and then I started laughing too, which came as a relief, although in the end none of us knew what the hell we were laughing about.

'My love life is about to begin,' she got out in the end.

'No,' I said. 'Not him? The Adam's apple?'

'That's the one,' Teresa managed to get out between guffaws of laughter. 'We're going out for a walk – Sunday. In Highgate Park.'

My eyes widened. 'Does your mom know?'

Teresa shook her head. 'I'll tell them I'm coming to yours.'

'But that's lies! How many Hail Marys is that, Teresa?' It wasn't like her to tell fibs, even if she was a bit wild.

'It is not as if we're going to do anything. Not real mortal sins or anything.'

'What's a mortal sin?'

'Having a babby when you're not married and killing someone and – you know, bad things. But I just want summat to happen. Some excitement. I get sick of being under Mom and Dad's noses all the time. Anyway, his name's Jack and he's seventeen.'

Determined not to look impressed I said, 'Well keep me posted. Don't go giving sweets to any strange men. And Teresa – don't make me lie for you.'

Why did I do it? I asked myself, cheeks aflame at the memory. Something made me. Something called living in hope. I'd been at Commercial Loose Leaf for a couple of weeks. Already I was half mad with boredom. We needed something for our tea and I had to shop on the way home. Sausages would be easiest for Len and me. Mom had a meal in the works canteen.

I went home via Belgrave Road, along to Harris's the butchers where Walt worked. It was a detour, but it made perfect sense to go there, didn't it? Because after, I could pop in and see my nan.

Walt was standing behind the counter in his striped, bloodstained apron, a pencil behind one ear, bright red against the shorn gold of his hair. I could see through the window that most of the stock had gone by this time of day. I walked into the tiled shop, my feet almost silent on the sawdust-covered floor, though the bell on the door gave me away with a loud tinkle. Walt was sharpening a knife and whistling as if he had not a care in the world.

'Can I help you, madam?' He half caught sight of me, then looked up properly, his freckly face spreading into a grin. The grin was laced with mischief that at first I was too blind to see. ''Allo, Genie! What're you doing here?'

'Come for a pound of sausage, what d'you think?' I said, my cheeks pinking up, to my extreme annoyance. 'This is a butcher's if I'm not mistaken.'

I didn't know exactly why I was like that whenever I saw Walt, but I couldn't help myself. I lay in bed thinking about him, daydreamed about him for a proportion of my time that I would rather die than admit, but I simply couldn't let him know I liked him. I wasn't going to set myself up for being kicked in the teeth. What I was too stupid to realize was that he could see it as clear as day.

'I was only asking,' he said, pretending to be hurt.

'Sausage? There's a few left.' As he was weighing them out he said, 'Seen Teresa?'

'No I 'aven't. Not in a week. Don't get time for anything, do I, what with Mom working, Len working . . .'

Walt flung the sausages into the scale with a flourish, eyes fixed on the needle, which swayed back and forth. 'Just over,' he said. 'Seeing as I know you. How's the new job then?'

I gave him a sideways look. 'If you're looking for a new exciting life, don't go to Commercial Loose Leaf.'

Walt grinned again. 'Don't go on. You're making me jealous.'

As I handed over the money he closed his fingers over mine and held them. I managed to look into his eyes. 'You'd be nearer Jamaica Row there, wouldn't you?' he said.

It was true. We were a stone's throw from the meat market where I could easily have chosen to shop if I'd wanted. Feeling his warm hand on mine I blushed like mad and realized that was exactly what Walt had been aiming for.

I yanked my hand away. 'I'm allowed to shop where I want, aren't I? I've come up here to see my nan. If that's all right with you.'

I flounced out of the shop. Half way along the road I stopped, cursing. I'd taken off without the sausages. I stood there for almost a minute trying to decide what to do. I had to go back. I was going to look a right idiot whatever I did. Summoning what dignity I could, I pushed the shop door open. Walt stood there with my bag of sausages held out in one hand, with the kind of teasing smile on his face that made me want to curl up somewhere dark and never come out. I couldn't look him in the eyes. I grabbed the sausages, said 'Ta' in a sarky voice, and took off to the door as fast as I could.

'Genie.' His voice was soft suddenly, sweet, with a kind of longing in it.

I turned back, my pulse speeding up, and for one split second my silly little heart told me Walt'd been hiding his feelings. I was special to him . . . As I looked round at him he must have seen it, my need and hope spraying out like sparks across the room.

And he was grinning, a mean, triumphant smile which made me shrink and buckle up inside. 'You still haven't got your change.'

I snatched the tuppence from him, dropped the sausages, had to fumble to pick them up and finally slammed out of the shop, cheeks ablaze.

'Bye bye beautiful,' he shouted, his mocking laughter following me along the pavement.

'You bastard, Walt Eccles,' I fumed, storming along the street. I was in too much of a state even to go and see my nan.

Life was peaceful in its way without Mom around. Len'd roll up his sleeves and get a fire going in the grate after work while I got the tea and we'd listen to Henry Hall or some other show. Then *The Nine O'Clock News*, after that old 'Jairmany calling, Jairmany calling' Lord Haw-Haw. He gave me the creeps at first, just the sound of his voice, but then we all just used to listen for the daft things he came out with. Then there'd be music and I'd do mending or tidying or hand washing – whatever else was needed – until Mom came in like the conquering hero and we'd have a cuppa with bread and butter. Then bed. That was our day, every day.

One night while Len and I sat waiting we heard the front door open and Mom's voice, high and animated in a way I'd almost never heard it before.

'Goodnight then – and thanks ever so much!'

The door slammed shut. She was in the hall taking her coat off and humming to herself. I went to look and she turned round and smiled at me. Which was all pretty unusual. She was unknotting a woollen scarf from round her neck.

'Brr, s'getting cold out nights now. Awright?' she said. 'Everything OK?'

'Who was that at the door?'

'Oh . . .' She kept her tone casual, hanging the scarf on the hook behind the door. 'He's a copper – seen me home a couple of times off the bus after I said I was scared in the blackout. He's very helpful.'

'That's nice.' I stood watching her, her lit up expression. I'd seen my own face in the mirror not long before, pale, with dark grooves under my eyes from exhaustion like an old woman. I felt wrung out and lonely, and I wanted her to look after me and be my mom.

'Got the kettle on? Hallo, Lenny love.' He nodded amiably at her. I went and lit the gas. Mom stood by the hearth, back to the fire. She rubbed her hands, started telling us about the 'girls' at work, jokes, things that'd happened. I sank into a chair. 'Aren't you making tea?' she asked eventually.

'I'm tired out. Can't you make it?'

Her eyes narrowed. She looked spiteful. 'You're tired? Huh. I get in from work in the middle of the night and you tell me you're the one who's tired.'

I was near to tears with weariness. After all, who was running this house with no help or thanks from anyone?

Sometimes I wish she'd just go, then there'd be just me and Len. Things were all right until she came home. But I wasn't going to show how miserable I felt in front of her.

She sank down by the fire in a martyred fashion and twiddled bits of her hair round her fingers as I got up to make the tea.

'Mrs Spini does the house and the shop,' I said. 'Always has.'

'I've got quite enough on my plate with your father and Eric away,' she snapped. 'Vera Spini.' She put all her energy into that sneer. 'Hair out of a bottle.' The way she said it dyeing your hair might have been crime of the century.

Then she turned plaintive again. 'It takes getting used to going back to work again and working shifts. I think I deserve all the help I can get.'

November 1939

Strikes me it's about time someone told Teresa the facts of life, I thought to myself. And who else is going to take the trouble but me?

Teresa was one of those girls who could give men the wrong idea. Too friendly, too vivacious, too downright appealing, but with barely the first idea of what it was all about, for all her talk of mortal sins. Of course most of us girls were innocent as morning dew until we strayed into marriage or trouble, but what with the trollops coming and going I'd long started asking questions, and Lil made it her business to get a few things straight with me when I left school.

'Your mother'll never be able to bring herself to do it,' she said. 'God knows, she spends enough time with her head stuck in a pile of sand as it is. But you ought to know, Genie. The factory's no place for an innocent kid like you. Specially with your pretty face.'

We were in Nan's house. Lil had chased the kids out to play.

'You're 'aving me on!' I said when she explained. 'Not with his willy!' My mouth hung open for minutes after.

Lil's cheeks went rose pink all of a sudden. 'I know it don't look much of a thing as a rule, but when they come on to you and get the least bit excited, it . . .' She gave me a vivid demonstration with her index finger. 'That's how they put the babbies inside.'

I sat there goggling at her. Her brown eyes smiled mischievously. I had so many questions I couldn't think what to ask first. 'But doesn't it feel – *funny* – them doing that?'

'Feels a bit funny at first of course. But you get used to it. Can be ever so nice . . .' Her face took on a dreamy look. I got the definite feeling this was something she liked talking about. 'Best feeling on earth at times, that's if you love 'im. But Genie . . .' She leaned forward solemnly and lowered her voice to a whisper. 'What I'm saying is, you don't want to do it with any old dog who comes along. Keep yourself nice for someone special. And make sure 'e's going to marry you before your knickers get below your knees.'

'Lil!'

'I'm giving you good advice, Genie, believe me. It's not nice to be a tart, and anyhow, you don't know quite where else they've been dipping it if they're that way inclined.'

Things were beginning to make a bit of sense, quite apart from the trollops. Len, for a start. That enigmatic smile that used to come over Big Patsy's face when Lil sat on his lap. And Lil was right. I couldn't for the life of me imagine Mom coming out with any of this information. For a second I thought of Walt and blushed to the roots of my hair.

Since, according to Lil, men were only after One Thing, I thought it was time Teresa knew. Which she didn't, I was sure. Her Mom and Dad treated her as a child and she was still safe in the bosom of home – or so they thought. Course they didn't know she was walking out late some Sunday afternoons now with Mr Sheet

Metal, supports-the-Villa Jack, using me as her alibi. Lil had given me such a vivid account of the male sex drive that I thought Teresa was in immediate danger of losing her virtue in Highgate Park.

I went to the Spinis' in the middle of Sunday afternoon when I guessed the marathon meal would be over. In any case, with only half of them there the heart had gone out of it. Only Vera and Teresa were in and Vera was sat at the table touching up the roots of her hair from the bottle of peroxide which Mom had been right about.

'Micky's pumping water out of air raid shelters,' Vera said, squinting at the little oblong mirror. Her dark eyebrows looked startling set against the bleached-out hair. 'That's all they seem to have to do in the Fire Brigade. S'pose I shouldn't be complaining though, should I?'

Teresa had on her red dress from Mass and she'd dolled up her hair with a matching red bow. 'We were just going out, weren't we?' she said, looking meaningfully at me.

'S'pose so.' I didn't take too kindly to being treated as a decoy in place of some bloke.

'What're you doing here?' she hissed at me as soon as we were in the street. 'You know I'm meeting Jack.'

'All right, all right, I'm not going to forget, am I, the way you keep on?' Jack this, Jack that. The minute he'd come along he'd become far more important than I was. I didn't seem to be important to anyone nowadays.

We cut past the closely packed lines of houses and factories along Stanhope Street.

'Don't walk so fast.'

'I'll be late. I told him half past three.'

'But I've got summat to tell you.'

I suddenly felt like the guardian of Teresa's virginity, my imagination running riot about what she and Jack were getting up to.

'Hang on a tick.' She pulled me into an entry. 'Hold these for me a minute.' I found I was holding a handful of pins.

'What the hell are these for?'

Skilfully Teresa made a thick tuck in the red skirt, pinning it up round her bit by bit and shortening the drop of the church-length dress by a good six inches.

'You can't go around like that!' I laughed at her. 'You'll get them sticking in you!'

'Wanna bet?' She did her coat up round her with a grin, hiding the clumsy lump of material. 'There. That's better. Come on.' She pulled me along the road again. 'What you got to tell me?'

Once I'd blurted it out Teresa stood stock still on the pavement and just stared at me, brown eyes popping. I thought for a horrible moment she was going to come out with something like, 'Oh Genie, how could you think I didn't know? Jack's already had his evil way with me and I'm expecting twins . . .'

Instead of which she erupted into her huge laugh, bending backwards, then leaning forward doubled up. I ended up in stitches too just watching her. People were staring.

'Oh no!' she cried when she could speak. 'No, that can't be right, Genie. Where in hell did you get that from? That's the most horrible idea I've ever come across!' And she was off again, tittering away. 'You don't half come up with some barmy notions, you do.'

'But it's true!' I insisted. 'How else d'you think . . .?'

She moved closer, aware of ears flapping along the

street. 'A man kisses you a special way and then the Holy Spirit gives you a babby. That's what really happens. Come on,' she said, stepping out again. 'He'll be waiting. You keep out of sight, eh?'

'Charming.' I was stung by jealousy again. 'Don't believe me then. I just hope you don't live to regret it.'

'All he's ever tried to do is hold my hand,' she said smugly, disappearing round the corner. 'Which is more than anyone does for you.'

'I've got more bloody sense, that's why!' I felt like tearing her eyes out, the stupid cow.

Her voice floated round to me, mocking. '*Ciao*, Genie.'

I peeped round the corner. Standing by the gate to the park, waiting for her, was one of the tallest, gangliest blokes I'd ever seen. His hair was curly and a bright carroty red as if his head was on fire. I couldn't spot the Adam's apple, but it would've been hard to miss the great big daffy grin on his face as Teresa walked up to him. She'd forgotten all about me, that was for sure.

When I couldn't stand any more of Commercial Loose Leaf I got myself another new job in a little factory in Conybere Street, staining bunk beds which they made for the forces and the shelters. It was a small, dark place, all one room. On one wall there was a poster in big red letters which read: 'FREEDOM IS IN PERIL. DEFEND IT WITH ALL YOUR MIGHT. YOUR COURAGE, YOUR CHEERFULNESS, YOUR RESOLUTION WILL BRING US VICTORY.'

On one side a few fellers were knocking up the beds, then they came to us to be stained before the webbing was put on. It wasn't too bad. If it ever got a bit slack I went round and swept up or kept my hand in cleaning windows again.

'I've cleaned that many factory windows,' I told them, 'I'm starting to think I ought to set up in business as a window cleaner.'

'You're like greased bloody lightning you are,' one of the lads said to me. He had black curly hair, uneven grey eyes and his name was Jimmy. 'Don't you ever let up?'

'No,' I said. 'Not if I can help it. Gets boring. I like to be on the go.'

'I can see that.' He kept watching me dashing about, throwing me the odd wink.

The other girl working with me, a stodgy blonde called Shirley, said, ''E fancies you. See how 'e keeps on looking over here? You're in there, you know.'

'In there? What's that s'posed to mean?'

Shirley looked at me pityingly. 'Don't you want a bloke? I'd do anything to 'ave a bloke of my own.'

It was odd the way she said it. She might just as well have said she'd do anything to have a dog, a budgie, a house ... But I can't say I wasn't flattered by his attention. I pulled the belt tight round my overall and kept my hair brushed. I couldn't help thinking about what Lil had said about men and their willies. But then I'd go and look at a real live man – let alone these boys around me – and I couldn't quite put the two together. I thought maybe Lil was having me on after all. It really was beyond imagining.

Every week we had a letter from Dad, who was down south, somewhere with a funny name. He said he'd started off being billeted in a barn with rats running round his head of a night, the food was abominable and he seemed to spend most of his life digging – trenches, latrines, holes . . .

He said he missed us and hoped he'd be back for Christmas, though the war showed no more sign of being over than it did of getting going.

Mom seemed a bit shaken by this news. 'It's funny, isn't it?' she said. 'Feels as if he's been away such a long time. I've got sort of used to it. As if he was never here.'

Eric wrote every so often and told us not a lot except that he was all right and Mrs Spenser was a very nice lady, and thanked us for the letters we sent him.

'Can he come home at Christmas, Mom?' I asked. 'We can't just leave him down there – not then.'

'Oh, I should think so,' she said vaguely. I had this feeling when I talked to Mom nowadays that most of her mind was out to graze somewhere else.

'Couldn't he stay home? Lots of other kids have - come back. There's nothing happening, is there?'

'What?' Her attention snapped back to me. 'Oh no – I don't think so, Genie. Not while there's any danger of bombs. I mean, they keep telling us to leave the children where they are. And in any case, there's no one at home to look after him, is there?'

I didn't dare ask why she couldn't just give up work. Was it that the country needed her or that she was enjoying herself far too much? After all, as she'd kept reminding us one way or another, we'd been getting in her way for the past fifteen years.

One night after work I got so fed up with doing bits of hand washing, and had a bit of extra energy for once, so I stoked a fire with slack under the copper and had a good go at it, pounding it with the dolly. When it came to mangling it I called Len to come in the kitchen and give me a hand. We just fitted into the room and he turned the handle for me.

'Things all right at work?' I asked him. 'You managing still?'

'Yes,' he said in his slow, thick voice. 'I like it. S'nice.'

'Good.' I pulled a snake of wet washing from the wooden rollers of the mangle. 'I'm glad you're happy, Len.'

He nodded enthusiastically, looking across at me, his eyes always appealing, somehow innocent. 'You OK, Genie?'

'Oh . . .' I sighed. 'Yes. I'm OK, Len. Ta.'

There were shirts and underclothes, the lot, draped all round the room by the time Mom got in. We heard the front door and felt its opening jar all the other doors in the house.

'Come on through,' I heard her say.

Len and I looked at each other. Her voice was so smooth, soapy bubbles of charm floating from it.

I saw the shock in her face as she came into the back, catching sight of her drawers hung out to dry by the fire. But she recovered herself quickly. Over her shoulder I could see his face – dark brown hair, swarthy, handsome and young – quite a bit younger than her actually. The shoulder of a copper's uniform. He was looking nervous.

'This is Bob,' Mom started babbling. 'He's just popping in for a bit. He's been very kind and escorted me home from the bus a few times and his shift's finished so I thought a cup of tea was the least we could do.' She gave a tinkly laugh. 'This is my brother, Len. Shake hands, Len.'

Len said, ''Ullo,' and did as he was told, dwarfing Bob's hand in his. Bob coughed and nodded at him.

Now he'd got himself into the room I could see he wasn't much taller than Mom, with a stocky, muscular body.

'Len's not quite – you know . . .' Mom was saying. She slid over that one. 'And this is my daughter, Eugenie. I had her when I was very young of course. Much too young,' she threw in quickly.

'Eighteen,' I added, pretending to be helpful. 'And I'm fifteen.' Mom glowered at me. PC Bob nodded again, even more nervously.

'Genie,' Mom said between her teeth. She gave a little jerk of her head. 'The washing – couldn't you just . . . Until we've finished . . .?'

'I've just hung it all out,' I said stubbornly. 'I've spent the whole evening doing it.' My hostility wasn't lost on her. 'You could go in the front.'

'It's icy cold in there.'

'Never mind,' PC Bob said quickly. He gave a stupid little laugh. 'I take people as I find them in my job. And I have got a family of my own, after all.'

'Bob's got two kiddies,' Mom said, seeing him to a chair. She turned up the gaslight, peeling back the shadows. 'Kettle on, Genie?'

'No.'

She clenched her teeth again. 'D'you think you could put it on?'

We all drank tea while Len and I sat quiet and Mom chattered on about her job, my job and about Eric being away. She didn't talk about Dad. I watched her. She was like another person from the one we saw every day – alight, talkative, a bit breathless.

I had a good look at PC Bob. He knew I was staring at him but he couldn't do much about it. It's not that I dislike people on sight as a general rule, but I couldn't stand him. I could sense it with them. What was between them. And I didn't like it.

He didn't say much. Smiled in the right places when Mom laughed. He had a heavy-set face and dark, mournful eyes which hardly ever looked anywhere but at her. I knew she could feel it, that stare. I'm not sure he was more than half listening to what she was saying, and she was making less and less sense because of the charge his look had set up in the room. His eyes travelled over her as she talked. I think they were a sludgy grey but it was hard to tell in the gaslight. I wanted to get up and shout stop it. Stop staring at her like that. He was following her shape and she talked all the more as if to fight off the magnetic intensity of those eyes.

When he'd drunk up and left, at last, the force of his presence left a hole in the room, like the sudden silence when we switched Gloria off for the night.

Mom was in a dither, cheeks flushed. 'You didn't have to be so short, Genie,' she said. 'All he came for was a cup of tea.'

'Just make sure the house is tidy when I come in,' Mom instructed me at least once a day. 'Just in case.'

And he was soon back.

I made tea and sat watching them. No one was saying anything much and all you could hear were spoons in the cups and the fire shifting. Mom looked down at the peg rug by the hearth, at her feet, then up at Bob. He was sat forward on the edge of his chair in his dark uniform, sipping the tea, giving Mom soulful looks. When their eyes met she giggled.

God Almighty.

'What about some music?' Mom said in the end. 'No Gloria tonight, Len?'

'I told him to turn her off when we heard you come in,' I said.

'Oh, there was no need.'

PC Bob was giving a quizzical sort of frown. 'Gloria?'

'Our wireless.' Mom tittered again. I'd never seen anything like the way she was behaving. 'Len calls her Gloria. Go on Lenny – switch her on.'

Len lumbered to his feet and in a second there was music, something soft, violins. Bob sat there dutifully for a few minutes, pushing the fingertips of each hand against the other.

'Better be off home,' he said. At last. He put his cup on the floor.

'Oh yes.' Mom was sparkly still. 'Back to your little family. Never let you loose for long, do they?'

They both went into the hall, snickering like a couple of monkeys. It went quiet for a moment. I wondered what they were doing. I thought about walking through to the front just to annoy them, but then I heard her letting him out.

When she came back she saw me staring sullenly at her. Oblivious to this, she gave me a wide smile. 'He's such a nice man, isn't he?'

A week later when she was due home from work, I left Len shuffling a pack of cards in the back with Gloria on, and went to the front room. I left it dark, pulled back the corner of the blackout curtain and slid the window open just a crack. There were no lights in the road of course and I knew I shouldn't be able to see them coming from far. But the room was very dark as well, and my eyes were settling to it.

Not many minutes later I heard them. I couldn't make out the shape of them in the sooty darkness, but I could see the burning tips of two cigarettes, and I knew Mom's tone. Their voices were low and I couldn't make out any words at first.

They came and stood on the front step and I was scared stiff they'd see me or notice the open window. I felt it must be plain as daylight I was there. But even if they could have spotted anything much out in the cold damp of the evening, the only thing they were interested in seeing was each other. They came and leaned up against the window where I was sitting. Mom perched on the sill, so if I'd wanted I could have pushed my fingers through the slit and touched her coat.

'Least we don't have to worry what the neighbours are thinking in this,' she said, giggling.

Silence. Kissing. The blood pounded in my ears.

'Bob . . .' Her voice was wheedling now. 'You are going to be able to sort out your shifts, aren't you?'

'For this week,' he said, impatient. His mind was on other things. 'What about your kid? She giving any trouble?' His voice was a low growl. There was something hypnotic about it.

'Nah – she hasn't got a clue about anything. Anyroad – we said you'd got a family, didn't we?'

'Oh yeah.' He thought that was very amusing apparently. 'My family. My two kids! Come on Dor—'

Mom said 'Oooh' and gave a little squeal. Then it went quiet and I knew they were kissing again. After a bit Bob pulled away, giving an impatient sigh. 'I need more than this, Doreen. I can't wait for ever, you know.'

'Oh, I don't care what anyone thinks!' Mom

squeaked at him. 'I know I shouldn't, but I want it too – if only there was a way we could get on our own . . .'

Silence.

'You do love me, don't you Bob?'

Lord above, I didn't want to hear any more of this. I let the curtain drop, reminding myself I'd have to come back later to shut the window.

I was all tight and squirmy inside. As I sat with Len, waiting for her to come in, I thought of my poor old dad in a barn full of rats, of the way he looked at Mom, always wanting, always hopeful.

Cow! I thought to myself. You horrible selfish cow. I felt like killing her.

I didn't say anything. I started to think I was the only sensible person left around the place, what with Mom and PC Bob and Teresa going doolally over Aston Villa Jack and telling fibs to her mom and dad.

'Len,' I said to him one evening, 'at least I've got you. You've got more common sense than the rest of them put together.'

'Yeah.' Len swayed and grinned. 'You and me, Genie. You and me.'

The winter set in and our days of limbo crawled past. Work, work, work, was all life consisted of now. All day painting woodstain on the rough bunks with Jimmy the Joiner, as I called him, winking away at me across the small factory floor as he bashed the frames of the bunks together. I started smiling back. What the hell.

Then there were the evenings of enthralling drudgery and Mom fluttering in late, her brains gone AWOL for the duration. The war was still not showing any signs of getting off the ground so far as we were concerned, but we still had to live with all the disadvantages: creeping about in the dark, staying in, and food costing a bomb.

The only thing that cheered me up in the evenings now was Gloria, and when Nanny Rawson and Lil paid us an occasional visit, usually on Mom's day off. The kids'd erupt into our house, glad of a bit of extra space round them, and I'd always try and have something nice laid on for them – a bit of cake or some sweets, with the best one saved for my soft, brown-eyed Tom. Nan'd bring her squeeze box and we'd sit round the back room and drink endless cups of tea and talk about how much better things were 'before the war' – barely three months ago.

At the end of the month they came, full of news.

'Have you heard, Dor?' our nan said, plonking the accordion down on the table. 'There's bombs gone off in town.'

'Oh Lor,' Mom said with the kettle in her hand. 'Has it started? Are they over here?'

'They reckon it was the IRA again,' Nanny Rawson said. 'Blew a couple of phone boxes to bits. No one killed I don't think.'

'That's just what we need, isn't it?' Mom was climbing up on her high horse already. 'Them coming over here making trouble.'

Oh no, not the Irish again. That usually set Lil off and then they'd be at each other's throats ... But Lil wasn't even listening. Sometimes, especially when she was feeling low, she went off into another world. She was pulling the kids' boots off to dry by the fire. Cathleen was moaning on about something. Patsy'd brought a comic with him.

''Orrible night out,' Lil said absent-mindedly. Her face was pale with exhaustion, the dark hair scraped back. She struggled with the knots in Tom's laces, and I knelt down beside her and worked on the other foot.

'We're in for a hard winter I reckon,' our nan said.

'Got your torch?' Mom stood watching in her pinner, hands on hips.

'Course.' Lil sounded impatient. 'It's like looking up a bear's arse out there. And the flaming paper got wet through.'

Torches and the batteries to go with them were like gold dust. Nowadays you could use a torch so long as the light was dulled down with a sheet of tissue paper. Lil laid the crumpled sheet of paper on the tiles by the fire to dry out.

'We had about three people following us down the Moseley Road, all in a line.' Nan laughed. 'Just for one bleeding little torch.' She was wiping the accordion down. 'That won't've done it much good. Still – it's had worse in its time. Come on – let's have a cuppa before we get started.'

Mom beat me to the kitchen. She seemed mighty eager to please. Guilty conscience, I thought.

She came back in again with a few Rich Tea on a plate, and offered them round, hovering round her sister like Nurse Cavell. 'How're you bearing up, Lil?'

Lil looked round at Mom as if she'd just been spoken to by some barmy person. 'Awright, ta. What's got into you?'

Mom couldn't hide it, try as she might. The new look, the glow, the vivacity. She was lighter altogether. 'I wouldn't mind a bit of whatever it is you're on,' Lil said wearily. 'Patsy – leave Tom alone.'

'Here.' I pulled out a bag of aniseed balls. 'This'll

keep you lot quiet for a bit.' The kids' cheeks soon had satisfying bulges.

'Ta, Genie,' Lil said, then announced out of the blue, 'Any rate – I've put my name down for a council 'ouse. I'm sick to death of living in a rabbit warren. I want the kids to breathe in some clean air for a change.'

'But how'll you cope if you get one?' Mom asked, with a snidy edge to her voice. Glebe Farm, Turves Green, Weoley Castle . . . Was Lil going to get the little dream house Mom had always fancied? 'You couldn't cope last time.'

Lil stuck her chin out. 'I was in a state, what with Patsy's – accident. And Cathleen was only a babby. Not long now and she'll be at school. I'll cope. I'll just have to, won't I?'

'Well, that'll remain to be seen.'

'Doreen,' Nan said, warning.

Mom, remembering she was the perfect hostess all of a sudden, poured tea, spooned in the condensed milk and offered round biscuits which the kids had to take the aniseed balls out of their mouths to eat, the red outsides already sucked white. Len chomped away, eating two biscuits at once.

'Ah – nectar!' Nan smiled, sipping the tea. 'That's better. Let's 'ave a bit of a sing-song now.'

Patsy lay by the fire with his comic and we fished out a few of my old crayons for Cathleen to scribble on some paper.

'You come and sit with me, Tom,' I said. Stuck between an elder brother and his temperamental baby sister I could see he was always hungry for affection. He came readily to sit on my knee.

'That's it – you go to Genie, she'll look after you,' Nanny Rawson said, sitting forward on her chair and settling the accordion on her knees. She smiled across at me as I hugged Tom tight, her dark brows lifting. 'Hey, Genie—' She frowned suddenly. 'You look all in. Is she sickening for summat, Dor? She's as thin as a stick, and ever so pale. Don't you think she looks peaky?'

Mom looked at me properly for the first time in weeks. Tears came into my eyes and my cheeks burned red. 'You're awright, aren't you Genie?'

I glowered back at her over Tom's head. If I was exhausted she ought to know the reason perfectly well, the way she was carrying on.

'You ought to take better care of her,' Lil said. 'After all, it's not as if you've got any others to worry about now, is it?' That was another of Lil's hobby-horses – she'd got more kids, more problems. I waited for the fight to begin but, to my amazement, Mom said cheerfully. 'Oh, she's all right. Just needs a bit of sun on her face like the rest of us, that's all. Come on, Lil – I feel like a real good sing tonight.'

They sang the rest of the evening away with their strong voices. It was a miracle because we got through that night without a fight, even though the fuse was lit more than once. Cathleen fell asleep on the floor among the crayons while they were singing 'When They Begin the Beguine', and Tom dozed on my lap. All the old favourites which Nan could pump out with an ease that never failed to impress me, never once looking down at her fingers.

I watched Mom as we went through 'An Apple for the Teacher', walking her feet on the spot in time with the music and snapping her slim fingers. Tonight she looked so vivacious, almost prettier than Lil. There was a spark in her eyes so that somehow you didn't notice the hard angles of her face. I thought of Dad watching her with that 'Love me – please' look in his eyes. And I knew it was only through his going away that she'd been able to come to life again, come out from under it all, the years of wife and mother and nothing else and not really wanting it. Maybe she really couldn't help herself. But neither could I help my deep, burning anger at seeing her so carefree, so disloyal.

December 1939

It was evening and I was lying talking to Teresa up in the 'girls'' bedroom in their house which she now had to herself. There were two beds in there and nothing else – the big one which Francesca and Giovanna shared and Teresa's next to the wall. We had a bed each to lie across as we talked. Teresa's hair was loose, laid out in a dark swathe one side of her head.

'You shouldn't tell fibs to your mom and dad like you do,' I said to her. 'They've always been so good to you.' The Spinis would've been broken-hearted if they knew Teresa was deceiving them. Both of them looked so worn and tired at the moment.

'But they'd stop me seeing Jack. Dad's a bully. You just can't see it.'

'He's strict all right, but . . .'

Teresa half sat up. 'He's not just strict. He's not fair. Like last week – it was Nonna Spini's anniversary, my nan in Italy. We all had to go to Mass because that was the day she died and none of us have even met her. And he belted me one because I said I didn't want to go. And it's only because he feels guilty because he always said he'd go back to Italy and see her and he never did.' She lay down again with a thump. 'He just pushes things on us that are nothing to do with us.'

I sighed. We'd been having a bit of a laugh until she

got on to the inevitable Jack. She leaned over to me, tight-faced. 'You'd better not tell 'em.'

'Don't worry – I won't.'

Teresa was changing. I felt old and disappointed, as if such childhood as I'd had was dead and buried overnight. Even though the war had barely affected us in terms of fighting, we had all changed. It was as if we'd had a layer of something scraped off us and we acted more on our impulses than we used to. I watched my mom and my friend and felt like a disapproving old spinster.

Teresa couldn't talk enough about Jack. She was droning on about him again, leaning up on one elbow. 'He's ever so good looking when you get up close – lovely eyes. And so grown up. He's got a real cigarette lighter and he likes football. It's a great game, you know. He said he might take me to see the Villa play one day.'

'For God's sake, Teresa, you hate football!'

'I don't. It's just I've never had the chance to see it played properly – that's what Jack says. He says—'

'I couldn't care less what he says!' I exploded at her. 'It's all a bloody waste of time. Boyfriends. Getting married. All of it. It's stupid.' I found myself nearly in tears.

'You're just jealous.'

I hated her. I wanted to smack her smug face. 'Well, bugger you, Teresa. That's all I can say.' I climbed down from the bed. 'I'm off.'

I ran downstairs and shot through the room where Micky and Vera were sat by the table.

'Hey!' Micky said, as I was going to open the door. He was leaning forward on a chair pushed back from the table, cleaning his boots. Vera sat across from him

100

with a darning mushroom pushed into a stocking, squinting in the gaslight. 'Going already?' he said. 'You just got here. Stay for a cuppa tea with us, eh? Kettle's on.'

I shook my head, choked up inside, looking down at the floor. I couldn't open the door and I couldn't speak.

Micky stood up. 'Genie? Hey darlin' – what you unhappy about?' At that, I burst into tears. Micky stood there at a loss and Vera came quickly over to me, making comforting noises, and pulled me into her arms, pressing my head against her soft body.

'Come on – you can tell your Auntie Vera. What's got into you? You and Teresa had a bit of an argument?'

I couldn't tell them. Not about Mom and Bob or Teresa and Jack, and how I was feeling inside. I was too ashamed. And I felt so silly blarting in front of Micky. When I looked across at him though, I saw such unexpected kindness in his eyes. But I just nodded, let them think it was just over me and Teresa squabbling.

'Teresa!' Micky shouted upstairs grimly. '*Vieni qui – subito*!' Teresa clattered down the stairs right quick. 'What you said to Genie to make her cry like this?' He turned to me. 'She's got a terrible temper on her, you know. You should take no notice.'

I was beginning to feel really stupid about this and I didn't want to get Teresa into trouble, but I just couldn't stop crying now I'd started, blubbering away like a little kid. Vera looked really concerned.

'You feeling all right?' She looked down into my face with her dark eyes, which made me want to cry again. 'Not sickening for summat, are you?'

Teresa was looking pretty scared. I suppose she thought I might've given the game away about Jack, but

101

it soon became clear to her that I hadn't. 'Come on, Genie,' she said. 'What's got into you? I hardly said a word,' she told her father. 'Honest.'

The three of them all gathered round staring at me, so I felt obliged to cheer up and start smiling just to stop them looking so blooming worried. Vera fed me a cup of tea with a heap of sugar in it and Teresa kissed me. 'Pals?' she said.

I sniffed, nodded. 'Yep.' And felt a bit better.

As Christmas drew nearer I thought, at least Dad'll be home. Maybe he'll be able to knock some sense into Mom. Not literally of course. He was never violent. I just thought him being there might bring her to her senses. Can't really imagine what made me think that but I had to have something to cling to.

That day the week before Christmas had started off badly in the first place. I was already feeling run down, so much that even Mom noticed enough to say, 'What's up with you?'

At work a couple of days before, a whopping splinter speared into the thumb of my left hand. I thought I'd got it out, but found my hand swelling up enormously.

'That's a full-blown whitlow,' Mom told me. 'Looks bad that.' I'd made a linseed poultice to try and bring it on but my thumb was still throbbing like mad, felt about ten times bigger than it should have done and was making me turn feverish and light-headed.

Breakfast time wasn't improved by a letter arriving from Eric's foster mother, Mrs Spenser. I watched Mom read it. The letter had got her out of bed unusually early.

Behind her Gloria was pumping out *Up in the*

Morning Early, a new exercise to music programme. Mom's face was stony.

'. . . across . . .' the woman's voice chirped on. '. . . to the side . . . the left arm . . .'

'The cow!' Mom erupted, reaching the end. 'Who the hell does she think she is, telling me what to do about my own son? The nerve!' I took the letter off her.

'I have told Eric that you require him to be sent home for the Christmas holiday,' Mrs Spenser had written. 'I felt obliged to do so, naturally, but to be frank with you I am not sure that moving him again at this stage would be advisable. Eric seems most reluctant to go through the process of uprooting himself again, and I wonder whether it would not be better to surrender your own desires on this occasion and let him remain here until it is deemed safe for him to return to you permanently.

'I shall, of course, abide by your final decision.'

' "Require him to be sent . . ." I ask you.' Mom ranted on for a bit about Eileen Spenser: stuck up, condescending bitch, and a few other choice terms. Then the doubts sneaked in.

'Eric wouldn't not want to come home, would he?' Her face looked pinched and anxious. 'This is his home. Not with some woman in Maidenhead.' She was pacing around our little room. 'Of course he wants to come back. Doesn't he, Genie?'

'Course he does,' I said, feeling, in my sick state, as if the inside of my head was lunging around. I couldn't believe Eric wouldn't want to see us, even though it sounded as though he had a cushy number down there with this Mrs Spenser.

'I'll write and tell her what's what,' Mom said,

searching for a pen to do just that. All she could find was the wooden handle of one of my old dip pens from school with no nib and no ink.

Work didn't go too well. I couldn't use my left hand so tried to hold the brush with my right and I was slow and clumsy. I tried to keep busy, keep my mind off the pain, and crack jokes with the lads in the factory, but even Shirley noticed I wasn't myself. 'You sure you're awright?' she kept saying, and I thought how it was strange that everything Shirley said sounded like a moan.

Come dinnertime I was feeling rotten. I went to stand up from my work place and the next thing I knew I was on a chair with my head between my knees and people fluffing round me. My right ear was hurting me now as well. Must've caught it when I went down.

'You'd best get 'ome,' Jimmy was saying, his face topped by black curly hair, swaying in front of me as I tried to focus again.

'You've gone green,' Shirley complained.

I groaned, sick and dizzy.

The gaffer said I should get off as well. It was a while before I cooled down and the inside of my head stopped throbbing and swimming about. After that I went cold and shivery.

I headed out into an overcast, freezing afternoon, hugging my hand up against my chest as if it was a kitten needing protection. It felt so swollen and sore I'd have screamed if anyone had tried to touch it. I cut through on to Belgrave Road and up to my nan's, thinking that if I came over faint again I could at least go in there for a rest. I thought about home, about curling up under the blanket on a chair with a hot cup of tea and the wireless on. The house to myself. Bliss.

And then I saw them, across the road. By the

doorway of Harris's, where of course I couldn't help my wretched eyes turning. They were standing just outside, Walt leaning one elbow up against the glass and her facing him sideways on. Some girl. She had copper-coloured hair, a sweet pretty face with an upturned nose, and was laughing away at something he'd said, the cow. He was smiling, talking, liked her a lot, I could tell.

He had to go and catch sight of me across the road, and in that split second I saw a vicious smile sneak across his face. He moved deliberately closer to the girl and shouted across at me, 'Awright, are you Genie? Nothing I can get for you today then?'

The girl frowned up at him, hearing the taunting in his voice. Yes, you just be warned, I thought.

'Found a better class of shop, ta,' I shouted back, then pulled my collar up round my face with my good arm and hurried past with my nose in the air and Walt's mocking laugh again to speed me along.

It gave me new strength to get home. All the way I was saying to myself, you're so stupid. You're such a stupid little cow, Genie. Why would Walt be interested in you? You've no looks like that other girl and you can't open your mouth to him without coming out with something tart or horrible. You deserve everything you've got. And after all, you don't care anyway, do you?'

But as soon as I was in the house I couldn't pretend any more and the tears came. I couldn't even find the crocheted rug I'd dreamed of sitting under. I sat in the cold back room hugging my throbbing hand and Janet, my old worn-faced rag doll I hadn't touched in years, feeling frozen and ill and as sorry for myself as it's possible to feel.

The next two days disappeared down a long dark

pipe full of confusion. Tossing from side to side in bed, conscious of nothing much except the agony in my hand and arm and unable to lie in certain positions because it hurt so much. Sometimes I knew there were people in the room. Len bringing me drinks of Beefex cubes which I sometimes drank and sometimes not. Mom's face, her voice – 'Genie? Can you hear me?' – trying to get me to take a spoonful of some stuff or other. Nanny Rawson knitting by the side of my bed on the hard chair, knowing her mainly by the rough black wool of her sleeve or her singing. A patchwork of dreams, cooking smells, bits of talk: Walt, the girl, 'bomb . . . IRA . . . doorway of Lewis's . . . mess . . . Eric . . . Victor . . .' Walt, *her*, that girl . . . Christmas carols and band music coming from Gloria downstairs. The lumps in the hot mattress swelled under me into molehills.

By the time I could sit up and eat oxtail soup and hold a cup of tea myself, Eric was there perched on my bed.

'You look bigger!' I told him.

'I get lots to eat. She's got chickens and a vegetable patch. And I got a nice comfy bed and she uses table napkins. And you don't have to go down the garden to spend a penny.'

He'd also grown a couple of new teeth since he left.

'Sounds a bit of all right then.' I noticed Eric was talking a bit different, putting his aitches on. 'You glad to be back?'

Eric looked down at the old blanket with a bleak expression and shrugged. Then he met my eyes and managed a bit of a smile. 'Yes. S'pose so.'

'Aren't you pleased to see me?'

He'd gone stiff and shy.

'Come on – come 'ere.' I pushed the soup bowl aside

and gave Eric a cuddle which he submitted to. He wasn't just skin and bone any more.

'Cor, Genie,' he said, pulling away. 'You don't half pong, you do.'

'Oh.' I was hurt. 'Well I've been stuck here for a bit.'

'You been bad?'

'I had a bad hand.' I pointed to the dressing on my thumb. 'It's getting better.'

'Mrs Spenser says, whatever happens, there's no excuse for not keeping clean.'

'Oh. Does she?'

Eric was looking round my room as if he'd never seen it before. I had a bedstead, an old rickety cupboard and a chest of drawers, a mirror that hung on the wall by a nail and a couple of old squares of carpet on the floor. Suddenly he got up and started kicking the chest of drawers with his boots, hard, until he splintered the front of the bottom drawer. 'Cheap!' he shouted. 'Everything's cheap and old and rotten.' His face was red and furious.

I started crying but he took no notice, just stood there with his fists clenched.

Eventually I said, 'Dad's coming home Sat'dy.'

Eric looked at me for a second, then turned and ran back downstairs.

Mom managed to wangle herself some time off work the night before Dad came home.

'I'm having an evening out,' she said, touching up her hair in front of the mirror in the back room. She had it hanging loose at the back and pinned up in a roll away from each side of her face at the front. 'Wish the dratted mirror was bigger.' She had to go right up to it to peer

107

down and see if her dress looked all right. 'You'll be OK, won't you Genie? You got Eric for company now.' She was putting lipstick on, so it was mostly the vowels we heard.

I sat watching: Len was peeling spuds at the table and Eric was playing Shove Ha'penny, nudging at me to join in. Apart from his outburst to me, he'd just been quiet since he got home and Mom hadn't seemed to notice any difference in him.

'This is one of the things you don't want me to tell Dad about then, is it?'

She whipped round and gave me a really nasty look, eyes like slits. Then she tried to soften her expression. 'Now Genie, there's no need to be like that. It's just better if you don't say anything about Bob – your father'll only go and get the wrong idea.'

'Will he?'

She stared hard at me. 'Bob's just a pal of mine. Someone to have a chat to – bit of company. I'll just have to hope he doesn't . . .' She jerked her head in Len's direction but he was well taken up with his potatoes.

Come seven o'clock Bob arrived, in a suit this time, not his uniform, five o'clock shadow shaved off and a hanky dangling from his breast pocket. Smoothy bastard, I thought.

'D'you tell your wife you're on a late shift then?' I asked him. I wasn't going to act polite to him. He should've known better. They both should.

'Genie!' Mom snarled. 'Not in front of Eric. Say you're sorry.'

I didn't say anything, just walked off into the kitchen. 'Come on,' Bob said. 'Let's get out of here. Bringing your gas mask?'

'Nah,' Mom said. 'No point, is there?'

When they'd gone Eric said, 'Who's he then?'

'Just someone Mom knows. They go out sometimes. He's a copper.'

'Bob,' Len said.

'That's right, Len. Now let's just forget about them, shall we?'

'Mrs Spenser says—'

'Will you shut up about that cowing Mrs Spenser!' I yelled at Eric, finding my hand raised ready to hit him. He cowered in front of me which made me feel even worse.

We passed the evening, ate our meal, had Gloria on. I played games with Eric, trying to make up to him. Make him want to be my brother again. Come nine I put him to bed and waited for Len to go. I wanted to have a good wash and brush up for the next day with Dad coming home, especially after Eric's charming comment, but I wasn't going to do it with them about. I still couldn't find the yellow and green crocheted rug which I wanted to put on Eric's bed. Normally it was kept folded over the back of a chair.

I heated up two kettles full of water on the stove and filled a basin. The house was very quiet except for the clock ticking on the mantel. I switched Gloria back on low, so as not to disturb the others.

I wanted to wash my hair, which was limp and greasy and smelt sour as I hadn't washed it since before I was ill. I thought of Mom's rainwater bucket outside. Why shouldn't I have nice hair as well? God knows, I had little enough time to spend on my looks.

I opened the back door and let a wide slice of light fall on the garden, trying to see the bucket. Blackout – what blackout? Couldn't see it. I stepped outside. It was a freezing night. The air almost cut your face and I could see stars clear as anything. The bucket was down by the privy, but when I found it of course the water inside was frozen solid. Just my luck. I'd have to use the water I'd already got.

Then I heard the noise. It didn't scare me. Wasn't that sort of sound. It was a giggle and it was coming out of the Anderson. I crept down there and stood outside, breathing very light little breaths. There wasn't much to hear. Long bits of silence, whispering, then a burst of giggling. Mom's giggling. I'd heard enough. Shaking with anger, I went back to the house. I thought of bolting the side gate on the outside to spite them but I didn't want them traipsing through the house with me about to strip off.

Bugger the both of you, I cursed to myself, tipping water wildly over my hair. At that moment I hated the whole world.

'Long film was it?' I asked Mom next morning.

She'd stayed in bed late and came down yawning. She gave me a startled look, hearing the hate in my voice. 'We went dancing. At the . . .' She trailed off. Couldn't think of a porky-pie fast enough. 'It was really lovely.'

When I said nothing and just kept looking at her, she said between her teeth, 'If you dare breathe a word . . .'

When Dad got home she was all over him. Poor Dad was as pleased as punch. Thought she'd missed him so bad she'd decided she loved him after all.

He'd even brought a box of eggs from the farm where he was billeted.

'You brought those all the way back on the train?' Mom laughed. 'That's just like you, Victor – and look, only one broken.'

'Lovely and fresh too,' Dad said. 'Laid this morning I expect.'

When he saw our dad, Eric showed the first real signs of positive emotion we'd seen since he got back. Dad squatted down and Eric flung himself into his arms, face against the scratchy khaki uniform.

'That's a lad,' Dad said. After a moment he held Eric away from him and looked at him. 'You're bolting! Must have grown six inches since I last saw you!'

'It's the country. Mrs Spenser seems to be looking after him a treat,' Mom said smoothly.

'We'll play some football while I'm at home, shall we?' He gave Eric a playful punch. They'd never played football together before. Eric's face was a picture, lifted with delight. Dad looked younger and thinner in the face, with more life in him than I'd remembered. He looked over Eric's shoulder. 'Genie, you're growing up too.'

Shy suddenly, I went to be taken in his arms. Relief seeped through me and even my anger with Mom stopped bubbling and lay calm and still. Everyone was back. We could now at least pretend things were normal, that we were a proper family again.

'Here – I've got summat for you.' Dad pulled a little folded piece of paper from a pocket of his kitbag. 'Not much, but I thought they'd suit you.'

Inside were three ribbons, red, white and blue.

'Patriotic too,' Mom gushed. 'What d'you say, Genie?'

'Thanks Dad, they're smashing.' And they were. I

was so chuffed, not just with the gift but because he'd thought of me. A smile worked its way across my face and settled there.

'We're having Christmas here,' Mom said. 'Our mom and Lil and the kids can come over. We'll make a real celebration of it.'

Dad put his arm round her. 'That's my wench. It's good to be back where I belong.'

The Spini household was alight with celebration. The kids were home!

'And they're not going back, neither,' Vera vowed from behind one of the lines of washing strung across the tiny room due to the rain outside. 'Never again.' She poked her head out from behind a row of the damp children's clothes which she'd washed as soon as they arrived home. Her face looked shaken out and softer, the tension gone from it. 'Whatever happens, if anything ever does the rate we're going, at least we'll all be together.'

The tiny back-house seemed to have shrunk even further now it was full of children, all bigger than they had been when they left. The two younger ones, Giovanna and Luke, who was now nearly five, came home and settled in as if they'd never left it. Francesca, who was twelve, was glad to be back with Teresa and her mom and dad, although she seemed more moody and far more grown up than before. It was Tony who was finding it hardest to settle back.

'He keeps saying the house is too small,' Vera said dismally. 'The family he went to had a rabbit hutch not much smaller than our house.'

'He'll be OK – give him a chance,' Micky said. He

was happy now, sat at the table in the heart of the family, all his kids around him. 'Another three months and he won't remember he was ever there.' He gave Giovanna's cheek a playful pinch. 'Who's my beautiful girl, eh?' And she went pink and said, 'Gerroff, Dad!' the little ponytail swinging at the back.

It was Christmas Eve and I'd brought a few sweets for the Spini kids. They were all home after the rush in the shop, customers clearing the shelves of Brussels and chestnuts and potatoes. There wasn't room for a tree, but Francesca, who was now used to being in charge, was organizing the younger kids, making streamers, so they were up to their ears in strips of paper and flour and water paste at the table and squabbling over the scissors. Luke was sat on the floor smearing paste down his legs as if he was embalming himself. They fell on the sweets, jelly babies and fruit drops – 'Cor – thanks Genie!' through hardworking mouths.

Stevie was hooking bits of holly over the mantel, adorning a picture he'd got hold of of a shiny Lagonda. There wasn't room for Teresa and me to sit so we stood around watching. Vera was stirring pots on the stove and the room smelt of stew and was steamy with boiling spuds.

'What about a bit round here?' Stevie said to Micky, pointing to his Italian tile.

'Yes – go on. Put it there, put it everywhere!' Micky waved his hands, ready today to decorate his house, his life, everything.

Vera gave us all a cup of Tizer. Teresa was in a good mood too.

'Must be lovely having Eric and your dad home,' she said. 'Proper family again.'

'Ummm – 'tis,' I said. I hadn't told her about Mom

and Bob of course. I just couldn't. Even if I'd wanted to she hadn't had much time for listening lately.

Amid the chaos I whispered, 'How's Jack?'

Teresa's face clouded over for a second. 'OK – I think.'

'Haven't you seen him?'

'He's busy.'

'Take a hint then. He's had enough of you.'

'That's just like you, ain't it?' She managed to snarl in a whisper, which isn't easy. 'Making me think the worst. I knew you were jealous.'

'I'm not,' I lied. 'I just don't want to see you get your feelings hurt.'

'They won't be,' she said haughtily. 'I know what I'm doing.'

'You reckon?'

'Oi – you two aren't falling out, are you?' Vera scolded. 'You staying to have a bite with us, Genie? There'll be enough.'

'Can't, Mrs Spini, thanks very much. Got too much to do at home.' In fact that brought me up sharp. 'Blimey. I've got to go.'

All the family kissed me and wished me a happy Christmas. Vera pushed a small packet into my hand.

'That's for you, love. You deserve a little summat. And these are for the family.'

She sent me off with a bag of fruit and a warm happiness fizzing inside me.

That night I tucked Eric up in bed. Now I was better he was sharing my bed, which I didn't mind at all. I quite liked it. After all, he wasn't Lola. I sat on the bed beside him.

'Look – I've put you this old stocking here for Daddy Christmas.' I laid it at the foot of the bed. I was puzzled he hadn't asked for one. Last year he'd been on about it for days. 'You need to get to sleep quick – he won't come if he knows you're awake.'

'There's no such thing as Father Christmas,' Eric retorted. 'Mrs Spenser says. She says it's just a story made up by grown ups and I'm too old for it now.'

'Mrs Spenser's got a lot to say for 'erself, hasn't she?' I snapped. Then I was sorry and patted him. 'You just get to sleep and see what happens.' There wasn't much to put in it but I'd gathered up a few bits and pieces.

As Eric dozed off to sleep I sat there feeling very low in myself. Damn you, Mrs Spenser, I thought, for nothing like the first time. Even if my childhood seemed to have long vanished, I'd still wanted to share what was left of his. To have something pretty and magical and more than real life to believe in. Reindeer on the roof and bells and a white world when it wasn't really snowing. I still half believed in it all myself. But now even that was gone.

Mom did us proud over Christmas. She put on such a good show that even I was lulled into forgetting what a deceiver she was. She adorned the house with a tree in the front room, mistletoe (of all things) in the doorway of the back room so Dad kept bashing his head on it, and tinsel all along the mantel, which Len loved. He kept going and stroking it.

We had turkey and trimmings. Len and I sat and peeled spuds, scraped carrots and put criss-crosses on the stalks of sprouts. Mom took over the main cooking for once and did her best to get it all the right consistency and a colour other than black. She filled the turkey's behind with sage and onion and the craw with a cooking apple. She was like another person, bright and chirpy and singing carols along with Gloria and the rest of us, stirring the gravy, pink-cheeked and happy looking. Dad was allowed to go in the kitchen and put his arm round her waist. I watched from the back room.

'Love you, Dor. You know that, don't you?' This, by Dad's standards, was an outburst fit to be put on stage.

She said, 'Oh Victor,' in a half-reproachful voice but she turned and kissed him and he touched her hair.

Before lunch Nanny Rawson and Lil brought the kids over and they all came in singing, 'Ding Dong Merrily on High' out of time with each other and laughing, and Patsy was shouting with excitement. Tom came straight over to me. Nan had brought her accordion. She had a bad chest but was cheerful. Eric seemed happy enough to see his cousins.

'You're looking very pleased with yourself,' Lil said to Mom, and she didn't sound spiteful about it for once.

Mom was feeling so well disposed to the world in general that she even invited Gladys and Molly over after dinner to listen to the concert on the wireless put on for the boys in France. They had taken their pinners off and wore flower-print dresses in the same material and had dabs of rouge on their cheeks.

'This is ever so kind of you,' they kept saying. They'd brought over cake with a scattering of dried fruit and a little packet of butterscotch.

Molly made a beeline for Len who was sat at the table and plonked herself down right next to him, smiling away like mad. Most of the butterscotch went by Molly's hand straight into his mouth, which was definitely the way to Len's heart.

It was grey and cold outside but cosy in the house. We listened to the concert, opened our few presents and drank ruby port, the scraped turkey bones still jutting up on the table. Vera's present to me was a pretty hairslide, Mom had talc from Dad and there were chocolates. Gracie Fields was singing 'The Biggest Aspidistra in the World' as Gladys fell asleep in the armchair with her legs apart. Molly barely took her eyes off her until she was letting out little snores. Then she shifted her chair even closer to Len's, giggling and peeping round into his eyes. Their two hands crept together and lay there like ham joints on the pale blue tablecloth. Mom pretended not to notice. Molly slipped the last square of butterscotch into Len's mouth.

Dad was due to leave in the New Year. It'd been a happy week, the happiest I could remember in a long time, since way before the war ever started. Lots of singing and talking and people being nice to each other. I kept trying to forget it was a lie. That the glow on Mom's face was put there by a stocky copper called Bob several years younger than both her and my dad.

On New Year's Eve we joined in 'Auld Lang Syne' along with the people singing on Gloria. We listened to the King's stumbling voice: 'I said to the man who stood at the gate of the year, "Give me a light that I may tread safely into the unknown." And he replied, "Go out into the darkness and put your hand into the hand of God. That shall be to you better than light and safer than a known way."'

We looked over the year's dark rim into the unknown of 1940.

January 1940

Once Christmas was over we came down to earth with a crash. Dad had to go and so, apparently, did Eric.

'D'you want to go back to Mrs Spenser?' I asked him.

Mom was watching us like a hawk. 'He's got to go, there's no two ways about it. "Leave the children where they are." That's what they're saying.' For a moment she squatted down next to Eric and looked into his face. 'You do understand, don't you love? It's for your own safety. It's not 'cause we don't want you. I wish you could stay.'

Fortunately I had the wisdom to keep my mouth shut about the Spinis. 'But d'you *want* to go?' I asked again.

Eric shrugged. 'Dunno.'

'Oh Eric, spit it out!' I nudged his arm impatiently. 'You must know whether you want to or not.'

'Don't mind going,' Eric said. 'Mrs Spenser's all right.'

'I've told you,' Mom snapped, straightening up again. 'He's going.'

Ten whole days of Bob deprivation had left her nerves properly frayed. The sugary act she'd managed for Dad was beginning to wear off too and she was being short and snidy with him again. Now Christmas was over there was nothing to look forward to but being

118

back where we were with more work, more blackout, more drudgery. Mom at least had a grand reunion with Bob to look forward to, so she was better off than the rest of us.

Dad knew he was bound for France and he was a bit emotional. I didn't see Mom shed any tears for him, although she was smoking her fags end to end the morning he went. He set off very early so he could take Eric on the way and meet the dreaded Mrs Spenser. So the two of them got togged up, Dad in his uniform, which suddenly made him stand up straighter, his kitbag over one shoulder, and Eric as before with the gaberdine, little case and gas mask. Mom and I weren't yet dressed.

Dad came and gave me a big tender hug and I felt like bawling and saying, don't go because everything's going to be terrible once you've gone. But I didn't, I just hugged him back and swallowed on the lump in my throat as I felt his newly shaven cheek against mine. He stroked my head like I'd seen him do Mom's. 'Tara, Genie,' he said, looking into my eyes, and I saw his were watery. Then he hugged me again. 'Be a good girl now.'

All I managed to get out was, 'Bye Dad.'

Eric clung to me and I tried to talk in a normal voice, still sounding as if I had a bad cold. 'Be a good boy for Mrs Spenser, won't you? I s'pect you'll be 'ome again in no time.'

Len gave Eric a bear-hug and Mom, Len and I stood out the front as the two of them walked off down the street into the pale dawn, hand in hand, Eric swinging the gas mask from its string. At the corner they turned and waved a last time.

Mom let out a big breath, said, 'So . . .' and went indoors.

That very evening Bob was round again. Must've

been psychic. Later on in the night I had a dream about the pie factory and the bloke with the leaking nose. In my dream, Bob had fallen into a gigantic mincing machine and scraps of blue uniform kept turning up, pressed tightly into the pies. I woke feeling quite happy the next morning.

Teresa managed to tear herself away from Jack long enough to come with me into town one Saturday. Big of her.

'It's blooming freezing, isn't it?' she said as we cut down Bradford Street to the Bull Ring. She pulled the collar of her old blue coat close round her. Our cheeks were pink and raw.

'S'going to snow. Gloria said.'

The sky looked grey and full.

'Jack said too.'

'Oh well – must be true then.'

'Cheeky cow.' She decided not to take offence, which made a welcome change. 'Here, what you going to get? I'm going to Woollies to buy a lipstick.'

'Lipstick?' I'd had in mind some new knickers from off a stall in the Bull Ring. 'You can't wear that!'

'Who says?'

'You'll look like a tart. What'll your mom say?'

'She won't see. I'll put it on when I'm out. Jack can kiss it off again.'

'Yeeurgh! Thought you said you got babbies if you kissed.'

'Hasn't happened so far,' Teresa said smugly. 'Anyhow – I've decided you were probably right about what really happens. Now I've got a bit more – experience.' She went ever so red in the face all of a sudden.

'What experience?'

'Never you mind.' Her cheeks aflame.

'You *haven't*, have you?'

She was shaking her head like anything. 'Course not. It's just—' She put her mouth by my ear. 'Once when we were having a kiss and cuddle he pulled me close and I could feel it there against me. As if it was waiting.'

'So what did you do?'

'Nothing! What d'you take me for?' We both got the giggles a bit then. We turned up past St Martin's Church.

'When are you going to let me meet wonder boy then?' I practically had to shout over the din in the Bull Ring.

'Oh – sometime,' she said, casual like. 'Don't want him running off with you, do I? You and your big soulful eyes.'

I was still recovering from this remark as we made our way through the bustling and pushing and shoving in Spiceal Street. There was a tight bunch of people round a bloke stood on a box who was throwing socks into the crowd.

'Here y'go – three pair a shilling. I'm practically giving 'em away. Don't for God's sake wear 'em and then bring 'em back, will yer?' Lots of laughter and repartee from the crowd. There was the usual collection of people hanging round the statue of Nelson and someone playing a trumpet, a melancholy sound, and all the stalls of fruit and veg and cheap clothes and crocks and some people getting a bit scratchy with the crowds round them. There were some uniforms mingling in with the rest, on their way up and down to the station, and kids crying and stallholders yelling and smoke from cigarettes curling into your face on the freezing air. The sky was so dark and heavy that some of the stalls already had naphtha flares burning on them.

We went to Woolworth's, catching whiffs of fish from the market next door. Teresa bought herself a sixpenny lipstick called 'Lady Scarlet' and put some on straight away.

'It does make you look like a tart.'

'Ta very much.' She preened in front of a little round mirror in the shop. 'I just want to grow up. I'm fed up of being treated like a kid.'

I sighed and she looked round. 'What's up with you?'

'I wish I was a kid still. A little tiny babby who doesn't know about anything.'

Teresa saw my downcast face. 'D'you want to do your bit of shopping?'

'Nah. Shan't bother.' Couldn't face the idea of buying camiknickers now somehow.

'Let's go to the Mikado then – have ourselves a cake?'

On the way round there we passed one of the emergency water tanks ready for all the fires this war was supposed to set off. Some clever dick had stuck signs on saying 'NO BATHING NO FISHING'.

The Mikado was a lovely café and was packed as usual. It was a big place with an upstairs, did lunches and teas, and the windows full of cakes invited you in. You walked into a warm, fuggy atmosphere of steam and the sweet smell of all sorts of cakes, people with bulging cheeks wiping cream from their lips with rough little paper napkins, and cups and saucers chinking.

Teresa and I took our trays upstairs after we'd passed through the agony of choosing a cake. This was just before things were rationed and we'd come to appreciate it even more later. What to have? Chelsea buns you could unroll into a long, currant-spotted strip, flaky

Eccles cakes dark inside, chocolate éclairs squirting cream at every bite? I settled for a cream doughnut and Teresa had a custard slice which erupted with yellow gooiness every time she stuck the dainty little fork into it.

We hung our coats on a proper coatstand and took a table by the window, looking out over the Saturday bustle of Birmingham's Martineau Street. Everywhere people were milling about with bags of shopping.

Teresa and I grew drunk on the sweetness of the cakes and got the giggles. I tried to forget everything at home and we sat and laughed and reminisced. Teresa was her old jolly pre-Jack self, and I looked at her dancing eyes and lipsticky mouth which had faded in the onslaught of custard and thought, she really is my best pal and that'll never change. And I was in a quite good mood until suddenly Teresa said, 'Seen Walt?'

'No.' I couldn't help sounding sulky. 'Why would I have done? You're the one whose brother's pally with him, not me.' I slammed my fork down too hard on the tea-plate and a lady stared at me.

'Come on, Genie. You know you like Walt. You're your own worst enemy, you are. You're not going to like this but I'm going to say it—'

'He's walking out with another girl. I know, ta.'

'How?'

'Seen 'em.' I kept my eyes fixed on my plate.

'Oh Genie.' Teresa was all sympathetic in a superior 'I'm so lucky to have gorgeous Jack but poor old you' sort of way which got right under my skin. She leaned forward. 'She's not reliable that one. I've heard things about her.'

'So what, anyhow,' I said savagely.

'He does like you, you know he does.' Teresa was

grinding on at me. 'If you didn't do everything you could to put him off. Why can't you be nice to him instead of eating him alive every time he speaks to you?'

'I don't like him now anyway. He's a pig.'

'How come then?'

I wasn't going to tell her about him making a fool of me. Twice.

'What's her name?'

'Lisa.'

'Bully for her.'

'Well you asked.'

I didn't want to know any more. Didn't want to think about it any more either. The afternoon was spoilt.

'Fancy going to C&A?' Teresa said when she'd drained her teacup.

I shook my head, staring at the endless movement of people outside. As my eyes focused on the faces, I noticed one shambling along who was nearly a head taller than everyone else, gangly, head aflame with red curly hair.

'Isn't that . . .' I said, before I had time to think.

'Who?' Teresa craned her neck, following the direction where I'd been looking. I saw her eyes widen. 'It is,' she said. I could hear the hurt in her voice. 'It's Jack.' Her cheeks went red, clashing with the fading lipstick. 'He told me he had to work this afternoon. Was doing an extra shift. That's why I came . . .'

'With me?' I finished for her, pushing back my chair. 'Well thanks a lot, Teresa. It's always nice to feel second best to some carrot-top who doesn't give a monkey's about you in any case.'

She was peering round the window-frame, following him as he disappeared. 'Was he with anyone? Did you see?'

'No, I didn't as a matter of fact. But it proves one thing. You can trust your beloved Jack about as far as you can spit.'

'It's just a misunderstanding,' Teresa said, lower lip trembling. 'Course it is. He wouldn't lie to me. Not Jack.'

But I couldn't help a guilty feeling of triumph at the sight of Teresa's crumpling face.

Next time I saw her of course, Jack had wormed his way out of it. Fibs? Him? Downright porky-pies? No – it had slipped his mind, he wasn't working after all, and being a model son he had to run some urgent errands for his mom.

His devoted, starry-eyed girl told me this in all seriousness, face ashine. 'I knew it'd all be all right! He's explained everything.'

'Teresa,' I said, 'if you'll believe that, you'll believe anything.'

The thing I hadn't told Teresa was that I did have an admirer in Jimmy the Joiner.

I paid him a bit more attention. Smiled sometimes. After all, I wanted someone to want me. In fact I pretty desperately wanted someone to want me. Number one on the list would have been my own mother. But I wasn't going to show it or go begging for it from anyone. I managed, me. I could cope. Didn't need anyone. That's what I wanted to say to everyone. Scared the life out of me, all that wobbliness every time I saw Walt. And the terrible stabbing jealousy when I saw him with Lisa or whatever the hell her name was. I didn't dare think what would happen if I gave in to feelings like that. But Jimmy was different. Apart from the fact he wasn't unpleasant as such, I had nothing in the way of actual attraction towards him at all. Except for being a bit flattered. It gave me a warm, stroked sensation that anyone was taking an interest.

Since I didn't feel anything except a helping of curiosity, I wasn't worried enough to be nasty to him. In fact I started to get a thrill saying 'Hello Jimmy' when I came into work and seeing I had the power to make a red flush spread over his pale, underfed-looking face.

'Rationing starts today,' Mom said, though I could hardly have missed the fact since Gloria had been on and on about it. The week's ration was to be: bacon, 4 oz.; butter, 4 oz.; sugar, 12 oz. We were already registered with all the right people. Thank heavens we were with another butcher and not Harris's, I thought with a shudder. Didn't need my nose rubbed in it.

'We'll have to make sure we don't have that Molly over every five minutes, living off our ration,' Mom said. She was ironing at the table. Now there was an unusual sight. I should've had a photographer in. 'She seems to be coming over here a lot.'

She didn't know the half of it. Molly was over just about every evening when Mom was out at the telephone exchange. She seemed to have got out of Gladys's clutches, and instead of being dragged into premature old age had decided to *live*. The dabs of rouge got thicker. She brought boiled sweets. She had a cousin worked over at Cadbury's and got her cheap chocolate so she brought that along as well and saved all the best bits for Len, even some with nuts in. Once Len was home from work he and Molly parked themselves in front of Gloria for the evening, enormous in their chairs, sucking and champing away on barley sugars and Dairy Milk with serene smiles on their faces. They never said much to each other. Barely a word in fact. Whatever was on, they listened. *The Nine O'Clock News*, they tuned into Haw-Haw, concerts, records, *ITMA*. They cheered the house up no end, chuckling away when anyone laughed on the wireless, Molly's titties heaving up and down. I thought how their dimensions suited each other.

And Gloria had just given us a new treat: the Forces Programme which was put on for the lads in France, but we could tune into it at home as well. I wondered if Dad'd hear it and felt cheered by the thought that he might. It was like a link with him. Gloria's music was the one thing that could lift my spirits on these chill, dreary days. All those bandleaders, their music like shiny sparkling trails through the house, making you want to sing, to move your body – Geraldo, Joe Loss, Ray Noble, Glenn Miller. I was in love with them all, though I had no idea whether any of them looked like the Hunchback of Notre Dame. And my Anne Shelton, and the Mills Brothers with those sweet, melancholy voices. I wanted to be tucked into bed by 'Goodnight Sweetheart' and dance till I was drunk on happiness to 'In the Mood'. They did what they did for me, for Len, for Molly, and for countless other people. They made life worth living.

It started snowing. I say snowing. It was snow such as I'd never seen in my life before. Heaps and swathes and layers and banks of it clogging up the town and blown across the parks. The old'uns were all saying, 'Can't remember snow like this since . . .' – though each of them seemed to recall a different date. Gloria said it was turning into the worst winter for forty-five years. Everything was muffled and the sky seemed to sink lower as if it was creaking under the weight of it all. Buses, already crawling along in the handicap of the blackout, were now going so slowly they were almost going backwards. Everyone was even friendlier than usual and Mom had to buy herself a new pair of boots to get to and from work.

'Feels safer somehow, doesn't it?' Mom said, when the snow had been falling for some time. 'As if they couldn't get at us with all this wrapped round.' She stood staring out of the back window.

'It's so cold though.' I was crouched by the fire, turning this way and that to try and feel the warmth on every bit of me. 'I was frozen in bed last night. Where's that crocheted blanket of Nan's gone?'

Mom picked up her bag and started fiddling inside it. 'What blanket?'

'You know. The yellow one.'

Mom shrugged and made a show of checking through her coins. 'It's so flaming dark on the bus you can't see what change they're giving you . . . Maybe Len's got it.'

Since Len had already gone I couldn't ask him, but there was no sign of it on his bed.

'That strip of baize we had in the front room's gone too,' I told her.

Mom frowned. 'D'you think that Molly's light-fingered?'

'No, I don't.' The thought hadn't crossed my mind.

It was hard to imagine Molly being light-anythinged. 'I s'pose it'll turn up.'

One night Len and Molly started kissing. After some sign between the two of them which I must have missed, Len knelt down on the floor in front of her. Molly spread her legs apart to let him come near and they locked their lips together. And that was that. For ages. I was ever so embarrassed. Seeing people kissing like that's enough to make you jump out of a window even from the top floor, and they didn't care whether I was there or not. They didn't even notice.

But what could I do? Len had his eyes shut and Molly's brawny hands were clamped behind his back, so I went into the kitchen and did the washing up. Mom would've had a fit if she'd known about them. But then who was she to complain? Everyone else seemed to be at it, so why shouldn't Molly and Len have a go, even if they were both as thick as butter? So I just left them to it.

When I crept back in later Molly was sitting on Len's lap. She beamed at me, her red face pressed against Len's, and he was in some sort of dreamy trance as well.

'Awright, Genie?' Molly said. 'Don't mind us, will you?'

'D'you want a cuppa tea?'

'Ooh yes,' Molly gasped, as if she'd just run ten times round the block. She lurched off of Len's knee. 'I made a few biscuits – 'ere.'

She handed me a paper bag containing four crumbly biscuits. 'Two for Lenny,' she said, planting herself opposite him.

Soon after there was a loud hammering at the front. The three of us looked at each other.

'Stay in your own chairs,' I said, running to answer it.

Lil was in a right state. Her coat collar was pulled up round her throat and her hair and shoulders sparkled with snow.

'It's taken me a bleeding age to get here,' she panted, steaming in past me. When we got into the back her eyes looked darting and scared. 'It's your nan. She had a fall earlier and they've taken her up the hospital. She's done summat to her leg. Where's Doreen?'

'Work.'

'Course. I'd forgotten you're on your own every evening.' She nodded at Molly. 'Len – our mom's hurt her leg. Fell on the ice.' She spoke slowly so he'd take it all in. Molly made some sympathetic noises and then, surprisingly, seeing she'd be in the way, took herself off home.

'I'll wait and tell Doreen,' Lil said.

It was ten o'clock. 'She should be half an hour or so.'

Lil went and stood by the fire. 'Jaysus, my legs are shaking.' After a moment she burst into tears and sank into a chair. 'I've never seen Mom like that,' she sobbed. 'She was on the corner of Moseley Road. She'd been to see Mrs Briggs – the one who's got pleurisy – and she fell on the way back. When they came to get me she was lying there making this horrible noise. I can't get it out of my mind. It was the pain – she sounded like a dog whimpering. Someone from the hotel got her an ambulance and it took ages and ages to come. Mom went quiet and I thought she was dead.'

I went and knelt down by Lil and watched her,

130

wondering if I should take her hand. I was scared. Len sat, looking stunned.

'It's all right.' Lil looked quickly across at him. 'She's not dead. She'll be OK. She's done summat to her knee. But when they put her on the stretcher to go in the ambulance, someone shone a torch in her face and she looked so old and her eyes were full of fear. I've never seen her like that before.'

She was sobbing even harder now. I felt so sorry for her and for our nan I nearly started crying myself. I went and poured her a cup of tea. She hadn't even taken her coat off and was still hunched up in its grey, prickly warmth.

'You said Nan's going to be all right, didn't you?' I asked cautiously. I felt very young suddenly. I wasn't exactly sure what was up with Lil but I put it down to shock. Len leaned forward and took her hand and Lil suddenly threw herself into his arms, laying her head on his big strong chest.

'I hate being on my own,' she cried in a desolate voice. 'I want my Patsy back. I want him so bad. Why did he have to do it?' She tried to say a few more things that got lost in sobs and gulps. Len rocked her back and forth. 'I can't stand it,' Lil said. 'I can't go on. I need someone to be with. I hate sleeping in a lonely bed every night and doing all the worrying for all of us on my own. It's too much, day after day. How'm I going to manage now?'

When she'd calmed down a bit I said, 'Who's with the kids?'

'Mary, from next door.' That was a sign of how bad things were if she'd entrusted her kids to Mary Flanagan.

Lil suddenly seemed to lose all the energy that had

131

driven her here in such a state. She sniffed, sat quiet back in her chair and drank her tea. But it was still all going round in her mind because after a while she said, 'Mom won't be able to manage. I'll have to give up work and run the shop.' She sighed. 'I hate that bloody factory, but I'm making better money now than I've ever done in my life.'

'Or I could,' I said. It sounded like a nice idea to me. There was no point in suggesting my own dear mother. I knew that just wasn't going to happen.

'I can't move out now,' Lil said gloomily, only half hearing me. 'Not even if they offer me a council house. I'll be stuck in Belgrave Road for ever.'

'No you won't. Nan'll get better.'

Lil looked at me, dark eyes filling again. 'When she was laid there in the road I saw what it'd be like without her at home. And I thought how she's had it hard, what with me coming back to live and Len ... And Doreen and me not getting on. I wanted to make it up to her. She's been a good mom to us ...' And she was off again.

The mantel clock said ten twenty-five. 'Mom'll be in soon,' I said, desperately.

But she wasn't. We all sat and waited. Lil was tapping her foot on the tiles round the hearth. By a quarter to eleven I had this nasty suspicion turning round in my mind.

'Probably the weather,' I said.

Ten more minutes passed and I was getting in a panic. How could she, tonight of all nights? She had to be somewhere with PC Bob, but I couldn't tell Lil that because the most God Almighty amount of shit would hit the fan if she was to find out about that, specially the state she was in tonight. I sat tensed with terror at the thought of hearing the front door and Mom, in her flirty voice, asking Bob in for a drink.

Once it reached ten past eleven Lil stood up. 'I'll have to go and let Mary get home. What the hell's happened to her? Is she often this late?'

'Oh, sometimes she is,' I said quickly, praying Len wasn't going to say anything.

'Will you be all right?'

'We'll be OK, just as normal,' I said. I was nearly laughing with relief that Lil was going. 'I'll tell her, soon as she gets in.'

When I opened the door to let Lil out Mom was standing on the other side of it with a kind of smirk on her face which she wiped off right quick when she saw us.

'What's the matter? What're you doing here?'

When Lil told her, Mom was about as upset and flustered as she deserved to be. We all stood crushed into the hall.

'I'll go straight up the hospital and see her tomorrow,' Mom said. She hadn't taken her coat off either.

'Visiting's afternoons,' Lil told her in a chilly voice.

'Oh – well, Genie can go after work, can't you love?'

I was going anyhow. Didn't need her sending me.

Lil disappeared along the road, her muffled torch playing on the icy ground. I shut the door carefully and turned round and stared at Mom. She had guilt not just written, but carved in massive gullies all over her face.

Eventually, with a shrug, she said, 'We just went out for a drink.'

I kept staring really hard at her eyes. How could she? How could she?'

'What, Genie?' Her face went all sharp and spiteful.

'I didn't know, did I? How could I know what was going to happen? Don't barge past me like that . . .'

I'd heard enough of her already.

'I have too much of your cheek sometimes . . .' she shouted up after me.

I didn't say another word. Just went up and shivered myself to sleep in bed wishing to God I could have a new life, new family, new everything.

The next morning brought a blue sky without blemish, grey clouds wiped away and the sun brilliant on the snow. Before Mom was up I opened the back door and went out. From the kitchen to the privy the snow had been well stamped down by us tramping back and forth. No one, so far as I knew, should have walked on the thick pie crust of snow towards the bottom of the garden where the Anderson sat smooth and rounded as an igloo. But of course I found footprints, not filled in by any night snow, leading from the side gate to and from the shelter. Two sets. I followed them, pressing my feet into the bigger ones with their rugged prints. Round the door of the shelter it'd all been stamped down. There was a cleft in the snow at the edge of the roof as if someone had rested their hand there.

I pulled the door away and looked inside. In the confined space a piece of thick canvas had been laid out to cover the frozen floor. On top of it were a Tilley lamp, a variety of covers and materials: a thick grey blanket I'd never seen before, the strip of green baize, a couple of pillows and the yellow, orange and green crocheted blanket of Nan's which had long been missing from the back room.

February 1940

Life got a bit better after that because Lil took up my offer and I said goodbye to Jimmy the Joiner and Shirl, and went to look after my nan and help run her shop.

She was properly laid up and Lil was earning better money than me. I was happy. Nan let me come and go as I needed to. She understood about Mom. Not Mom and Bob of course – I hadn't said a word to anyone about that. Just about the way Mom used me.

'She don't deserve you,' she said to me, laid back on the horsehair sofa with her leg, rigid in its plaster cast, stuck out in front of her. She'd done some horrible thing to her knee.

'Summat to do with cart-lidge they said up the 'ospital. They say it'll take weeks to heal. Flaming nuisance.'

It'd knocked the stuffing out of her. Her face looked thinner and more lined. Sometimes I found her asleep, head lolling back on the sofa, which was unheard of for her as a rule. But she was always on her dignity. She'd never come down in her nightclothes. When I arrived in the morning she was always dressed. I suppose she must have hoisted herself up off the bed to put her dress on, rolling a stocking up her good leg – good except for the ulcer dressings. She always sat and pinned up her hair.

'I've taken to coming downstairs on my backside,' she said. 'I'm not up to hopping at my age.'

I looked after her as if she was a queen, which she was in my eyes, as she'd never been anything but good to me. I wasn't the only one who thought so – the neighbours drifted in and out of the back door like flies, wanting to know if she needed anything. Hot-tempered, red-headed Mary Flanagan came almost every hour trailing an assortment of her seven kids behind her. She'd tried evacuating them once but they'd all come home.

'You awright there, Edith?' she'd say. 'You shout me if you need anything.'

And in the shop it was always, 'How's Mrs Rawson?' and then they'd say, 'I bet she's glad of your 'elp, bab. I couldn't borrow you for a bit, could I?'

'You're golden,' Nan said to me sometimes, watching me work. I scrubbed her quarry tiles on my hands and knees. I blackleaded the grate, did her washing in the brewhouse when it was our turn, and hung it steaming across the freezing yard. I cooked for her, I ran errands, I scuttled back and forth to the shop whenever we heard the click of the door opening and the bell ringing out.

I felt grown up. I'd just turned sixteen after all, even if that hadn't been much of an event. I served in the shop. I sorted stock, arranging jars of sherbet lemons and throat drops – there were still sweets to be had then – and bars of Lifebuoy and blue Reckitt's powder in packets and piles of enamel buckets. It was peaceful in there most of the time, except once or twice a week when Morgan made his forays through to the upstairs with a selection of trollops in tow. Once the girls arrived there were bangs and squeaks of the floor and giggles and thumps from the bug-ridden rooms upstairs. It was no good suggesting to Nan that she move. There was a time when I just didn't understand this attitude. But it was so much part of the fabric of life at her house I barely gave it a thought now. There was Nan, and there was Morgan. That's how it was. Nan would roll her eyes to the ceiling and tut a bit at the louder noises, but we mostly just had to ignore them. Besides, people being the nosy so-and-sos they are, the trollops were surprisingly good for business.

I adopted Nan's policy towards Morgan, that he was like a mote of dirt passing through, unseen under my nose. That is until he started coming in a bit early – before his girls – and fixing his pale eyes on my chest.

'Allo my dear,' he'd say, wiping his sweaty forehead with a hanky. The strips of hair hung down like pondweed. 'You are growing up fast, aren't you?'

'Nan, he keeps talking to me,' I reported.

'Right,' she said.

Next time he turned up, sneaking in and pussyfooting about instead of going upstairs, grinning at me with yellow smoker's teeth, Nan's voice roared through from the back.

'You filthy bastard, Morgan!' He actually jumped. It had more impact her being invisible, like God's voice out of a cave. 'You as much as speak to my granddaughter again and I'll 'ave your bollocks twisted round the back of your neck!'

'No offence intended, my dear,' Morgan said to me, retreating hurriedly to the stairs.

I kept the place immaculate, took people's money or filled in the strap book so they could pay later. I checked with Nan. She knew them all and trusted most of them. She'd been known to land a punch on the jaw for bad debts. I tore round the place like a whirlwind and I loved it. I was doing it for my nan and I could decide what I wanted to do and when and do it as fast as I liked. I had a fierce mixture of anger and love inside me and I was like a fury.

Sometimes Cathleen trailed round after me, or Nan tried to keep her amused. There were the other kids to deal with when they got home from school. They came and sat by the hearth, hands blue from the cold walk home, and I gave them each a cup of tea and cut them a piece to eat so they were in a good mood by the time Lil got home. I got high marks from Lil because I saved her a lot of chores.

Nan was none too happy though. She wasn't fed up with me, who she couldn't find enough praise for, but because sitting about on her backside wasn't exactly her style. She tried to teach Cathleen to knit but the kid was too young and flew into a tantrum and was happier with a bag of clothes pegs. But Nanny Rawson was bored, so I asked Len if he'd be very very kind and let her borrow Gloria for a bit while she was poorly? It took a bit of persuasion of course, because Gloria was meat and drink to him. But he did love his mom, and in the end he nodded his heavy head when I said we could all have our tea over at Nan's of an evening so he could hear Gloria too.

One morning I trudged over to Nan's through the slush, water seeping into my old boots, carrying Gloria, with the accumulator hanging from one arm in a hessian bag. Nearly flaming killed me. I had to stop every few yards to rest because my muscles were aching so bad, balancing Gloria on people's front walls and switching the accumulator from arm to arm.

I was standing by St Paul's churchyard with Gloria resting on the wall when a voice said, 'Need a hand?'

I nearly dropped the thing.

'Er – oh, hello,' I said. 'Yeah. Ta.'

Walt took Gloria off me with ease and the accumulator suddenly felt light as a sparrow on its own. I rubbed my arms as we set off.

'Where you off to with this?'

'My nan's.'

'I 'eard about her accident. She bad?'

'She'll be all right. Bust up her knee. She's fed up not being able to get about.'

'I'll bet. You brought this to cheer 'er up?'

Why the hell was he being so chummy all of a sudden?

'It's Len's – my uncle. I nearly 'ad to put a gun to 'is head to get 'im to borrow it 'er.'

I gave a laugh, to show I could be light and joke. He was nothing to me now. I didn't care. I'd seen Walt in his true colours, putting me down the way he did, and now he was walking out with that Lisa girl I found it perfectly easy to be civil to him and show I didn't care. I wasn't out to waste my affection on someone who'd taunt me and put me down. That'd be a sign of things to come all right. So talking was easy all of a sudden. Walt was even laughing at my jokes as we walked to Nan's house.

When we got to the shop I said, 'All right, Walt, ta. This'll do.'

'Might as well take it in for you,' he said. 'Not much further is it, and I can't put it down in the wet.'

But he stopped me before we went in.

'Genie—' He was the one blushing now. 'We got off on the wrong foot, didn't we? I was wondering. D'you fancy going to the pictures – with me?'

I could feel my face taking on a wide-eyed innocent look. 'But Walt, you've got a girl to walk out with. Lisa, ain't it?'

Walt looked at the ground, embarrassed. 'Not any more. I'd rather go with you.'

Oh, would you now.

'Sorry. I can't go out. Mom's working evenings and I'm busy.'

'What about a Sat'dy matinée?'

'No ta,' I said, ever so politely. 'To be truthful I wouldn't go out with you if you were the last man on earth.'

He decided to stop helping me after that.

Nan of course was up and dressed. She was amazed. 'Is that Len's wireless?'

I nodded, a smile spreading ear to ear. She looked ever so pleased and I knew I'd done something good. 'He said you could have it while you was laid up. I'll set it up, shall I?'

Between us we wired it to the accumulator and Gloria was off, jollying the place along no end. Nan cheered up straight away. 'Isn't it marvellous?'

By the end of the day, during which Gloria was barely switched off, Nan said, 'I think me and Lil ought to see about getting one of these.' She nodded at the kids who were sat next to *Children's Hour* sucking bulls' eyes. 'And it doesn't 'alf keep them quiet.'

I was tingling from more than one sense of triumph.

Soon after, I popped into the Spinis' one dinnertime and walked slap bang into a family row. The Spini family's disputes had two things which outdid even the most ferocious yard fights in the area: one was fluency, the other was volume.

I could hear it coming when I stepped out the front of Nan's, voices all the way down the street, and there was a gaggle of people gawping in the Spinis' doorway to watch the fun. Their rows seemed to work better in Italian, so none of us could understand a word, and even if we could the four of them were all yelling at once.

I went and pushed through the nosy parkers until I was just inside. Vera was holding her ground on one side, arms waving in the direction of Micky, who was wagging an infuriated finger mainly in the direction of a box heaped with turnips, and I couldn't tell who he was actually shouting at. Stevie, in a white apron, his sleeves rolled up, was framed by the back door leading into the ice-cream-making room where he had presumably been interrupted churning the 'Scattoli's Outstanding Ices'. He, like the others, was shouting and wore a heavy scowl, although that wasn't unusual.

Close by was the tall young man with a drooping black moustache, a nose curved and slender as a knife blade, who Teresa had such scorn for. Fausto Pirelli. He was watching, wearing a superior kind of expression, saying nothing.

And in the middle of them all stood Teresa, between two sacks of carrots as if they were protecting her, like sandbags, from the blast coming from all around. But she was doing her fair share of shouting too.

They must have found out about Jack, I thought, and I wasn't quite as sorry as I should've been.

But no. Teresa was off again, hair hanging down, hand out in front, slapping at the air with the back of her hand. In the midst of all the Eyetie I heard the words 'war effort'.

Suddenly catching sight of me standing there, she yelled in English, 'Ask Genie, since you think she's such a model daughter. Go on, tell 'em, Genie. She goes out to work in factories and there's no trouble. Nothing. All the time you treat me like a child and I'm sick to death of it. Sick of it!'

The row suddenly switched into English. 'We just want to protect you,' Vera said. She didn't seem on the boil as much as Micky and Stevie, who were doing their injured male pride bit. 'We want to keep the family together.'

'Well that didn't stop you sending the kids half way across the country, did it? You soon did that when you decided it was the right thing. So what's wrong with me just going out to get a job up the road somewhere?'

'No one's going anywhere unless I say so,' Micky decreed. His face was thunderous. 'I'm not having you going off behind my back. You stay here, you work here and that's an end of it – finish.' He swiped his hand across as if cutting his own throat and made as if to walk off, but found the door blocked by all the gawping passers-by, so he turned and had another go. 'That's the trouble with you young people. You got no respect for your families now. You got to keep respect – do as you're told.'

'You're stupid, Teresa,' Stevie started up. 'You're being selfish. You should act more responsible instead of being so childish.'

'I'm not childish!' Teresa shrieked at him, arms waving. 'I'm just sick of you all running my life for me. "Teresa you can't go here . . ." "Teresa you've got to do this . . ." And anyway, Stevie, what's all this got to do with you? Why don't you shut your trap and take your bloody ice-cream cart out? It'll give us all a rest.' She waved an arm at Fausto Pirelli. 'And take Mussolini here with you!'

That did it, they were all off then, Fausto too, who

was totally enraged all of a sudden, and no one could get a word in edgewise for minutes at a time.

Then, in a tiny chink of quiet, Teresa said, 'But they've given me the job!'

'Tell them you can't do it—'

'Go on – let 'er get a job,' some woman shouted from the doorway. 'It's all for the war effort.' No one took the blindest bit of notice of her.

I could see they were going to start off all over again. This one could go on for hours. So I pushed my way out and slipped back to Nan's, their voices following me down the street.

'What happened?' I asked Teresa, tiptoeing back in later.

'My daughter, she wants to just go,' Vera said, one hand scooping through the air like a plane taking off.

'She got her own way – as usual,' Stevie said, grumpy sod that he was.

Teresa put her thumb up and grinned. 'I'm going to have a go. It's Green's, over in Sparkbrook, making army uniforms.'

'You'll be kept busy then.'

She waited till Stevie had moved out of earshot, then hissed at me, 'The factory's right by Jack's house.'

'Oh,' I said. 'Bully for it.'

Jimmy the Joiner walked back into my life one freezing Saturday with a ring of the shop bell. I ran through, ducking under the dividing counter, and there were Jimmy and Shirl.

'Genie!' Shirl greeted me as if I was her long lost, best ever pal, and I found I was really pleased to see her. I'd quite missed her voice droning on down my ear.

Jimmy was giving me a shy smile and his squiffy eyes were warm and friendly. I wasn't sorry to see him either. 'We thought we'd come and see how you was getting on,' he said. 'T'ain't the same at work without you, Genie.'

This was gratifying to hear. 'Come through and meet my nan,' I said.

Nan was friendly, as she was to people she expected to approve of. 'Sorry I can't get up and do anything for you,' she said. 'It's not me at all, sitting about like this.'

'Oh no, you must rest,' Shirl said.

Shirl's pale hair was soft and curly and she had thick pink lips and enormous blue eyes. Everything about her was round, her behind, the shape of her legs, her cheeks, her big heavy titties. She was another of those that made me feel scraggy and boyish. But there was something very comforting about Shirl. Cathleen was hovering by her and Nan seemed to feel it at once.

'Come and sit by me,' she said to her. 'Genie'll make us a nice cuppa tea.'

'Lovely place you've got 'ere, Mrs Rawson,' Shirl said in the sort of voice most people put on to tell you someone's died. Nan knew perfectly well her house was just like thousands of other back-houses, if perhaps more spick and span, but she seemed chuffed all the same.

Jimmy sat quiet. He'd hardly taken his eyes off me since they arrived. I kept looking at him out of the corner of my eye, not sure whether I liked him or not. There was something awkward about him, his very pale skin, dark hair curling at his white neck, and when he looked at you he almost squinted in a way which made my flesh creep a bit. But on the other hand I'd seen worse. And he'd come specially to see me, and not many people ever did that.

'She's a good girl, our Genie,' Nan said, nodding across at me as I lit the gas. 'She's been a right little gem to me.'

'We miss her,' Shirl said, taking Cathleen up on to her lap and stroking her plump hands. 'It's not the same at the factory without her buzzing about.'

They sat and drank tea while Nan gave Shirl a blow-by-blow account of the fall, the doctors, the hospital where she'd spent four days.

''E said 'e didn't like the look of my knee at all,' she was going on. ''E said, "I shall 'ave to consult with my colleague." Those are the exact words he used.' Shirl gave every sign of loving it all, and cuddled Cathleen. I could picture Shirl with loads of kids.

Jimmy kept sneaking looks at me. Once he winked and I smiled back. Yes, he was all right Jimmy was, I thought. I'd missed his attention.

Outside in the yard when they were going, Cathleen still clung to Shirl's hand.

'Jimmy's got something to ask you, Genie,' Shirl said.

Jimmy shuffled his feet. 'D'you fancy coming out with me, Genie?' Then, thinking he'd been a bit short, he added a quick, 'To the pictures or a walk or summat?'

I thought about Walt. Stuff Walt.

'I would, Jimmy,' I said. 'Only it's hard for me to get away, what with my nan and my uncle and my mom.'

His face dropped.

'You two go,' Shirl said. 'I'll come and sit with your nan Sat'dy afternoon, that's if she's no objection. And I can play with little Cathleen here.' She pinched Cathleen's cheek. 'I'd like that. We got on ever so well.'

145

We consulted Nan and she looked pleased. 'It's time Genie 'ad a bit of life of her own for a change.' She turned a sterner eye on Jimmy. 'As long as you both know 'ow to behave yourselves.'

Next week Jimmy and I walked down the Cannon Hill Park. I wore my best green winter frock and huddled in my coat. Truth to tell I wasn't feeling at my best. I had a cold and a blocked nose and it had been an effort to come out. But I decided to think positive, to like Jimmy's loping walk and his voice, which came out sounding deeper than you'd expect from the size of him.

Almost as soon as we were on our own he grabbed my hand, which took me aback. Bit pushy, I thought, when he'd always seemed a timid sort before. But he turned and smiled at me and said, 'Don't mind, do you? I've been wanting to hold your hand ever since I first saw you.'

Course, if someone says something like that you don't resist, do you? And it was a nice feeling, special, having someone close. His hands were warm even in the cold. The snow was thawing slowly and there was wet everywhere.

'You're ever so pretty, Genie.'

'Me?' I laughed, pleased as punch. Sometimes I just wanted to be a proper girl. 'Go on. I'm not.'

'You are. Your eyes are like – like – well, they're – nice. And the way you get that dimple when you smile.'

We walked round watching the ducks on the small lake. The park stretched wide around us, sloping down to the swimming baths at the bottom, full of leaves now, and chunks of ice. It was a shock to see green again after all the days of white. There were still hard mounds of

146

snow with grey crusts on top melting slowly down the slope.

Jimmy told me he had four sisters and a brother and his mom was deaf, had to lip read.

'What about your dad?'

'Oh . . .' he said, almost as if he'd forgotten about him. 'He's reserved occupation – Heath's, the foundry.'

'Mine's away,' I said, suddenly proud. 'In France.'

'Wish mine was,' Jimmy said with feeling. 'He's a bugger – pardon me.'

I wasn't sure what to say to that. There are such a variety of ways of being a bugger and I wasn't sure I wanted to know the particulars.

And Jimmy said, 'I don't want to talk about 'im. What d'you like doing best?'

I had to think hard about that one. 'I don't seem to get the chance to do anything much these days. I like going to see my friend Teresa. When she's got the time,' I added gloomily.

'I like football.'

Oh Gawd, not another one. 'You don't support the Villa, do you, by any chance?'

'Nah – never. Blues.'

That was something, although whether he was going to carry on about Aston Villa or Birmingham City wouldn't make much odds to my passing out with boredom in the long run.

When he got me up by the trees at the quiet, top end of the park, he caught hold of me and kissed me like I'd seen Len and Molly doing. I had a bit of trouble with that because I didn't think to breathe in before he started and my nose was all stuffed up. His big slimy tongue popped into my mouth and he was sucking away at my lips and I found myself thinking Jaysus – like Lil would

147

have said – is this right, us getting on to kissing so quick? I couldn't do anything back except cling on to his shoulders struggling for breath as he pushed his body against me. In the end I had to pull away and take in a big gasp, which Jimmy took to mean I was so overcome with emotion I couldn't stand any more. Which was pretty near the truth, only not quite how he thought.

When I turned round again after fixing some sort of smile on my face, he was giving me a grin brimming over with triumph. 'You're my girl now, Genie.'

Len was coming to Nan's straight from work now, early evening, so I could cook for all of us with Lil, and get it all over in one go. It also meant he could have a good old listen to Gloria before we had to go home. It was much nicer this way, sharing some of the chores with Lil. She was being as nice as pie to me as I gave her so much help with the kids, dunking them in the tin bath by the fire for her once a week, clearing up the mess after and keeping them entertained. She taught me a few tricks to help the cooking go better, like taking the custard off the heat to start stirring it so it didn't heave up into lumps like it usually did. Mom never told me anything useful like that even though she'd once worked in the Bird's factory in Digbeth, and you'd think she'd at least have picked up how to make the stuff.

That night we had stew with loads of dumplings. Lil showed me how to make them really nice with suet. We all squeezed round the table, except for Nan who couldn't get her leg under it. It was cosy with the fire and Gloria and the dim gaslight and we all ate hungrily.

'Feels a bit like Christmas, doesn't it?' Nan said. 'Shame Doreen's not here as well.'

My eyes met Lil's. We couldn't bring ourselves to agree with Nan on that one. My feelings of fury at the way Mom was carrying on had grown worse and worse.

Len and I walked home together after, holding hands for safety: the street was so dark and it was beginning to freeze again. We had our torch but didn't bother carrying the gas masks any more.

'I'm glad you're here, Len,' I said. 'I'd be scared stiff else.' He was so big and slow and solid.

One hint of sound from outside our house brought Molly to her door. 'You're back then?' she called across the street.

Couldn't really disagree with her there. Sometimes it got on my nerves a bit, her pouncing on us like that. But you couldn't dislike Molly. She was inoffensive and as generous as she could afford to be. And she made Len happy.

'Doesn't Gladys mind?' I asked as she came over. I was struggling to find my key in the dark.

I just saw Molly put a finger to her lips, rather coyly. 'She's asleep. Didn't see me go.'

As I went to the front door I heard a faint knocking noise from the side of the house. There was a breeze and the entry gate was unfastened. Anger twisted in me, and dread.

'You go in,' I said to Len and Molly, unlocking the door. 'I'm just going to shut the side gate.'

They weren't listening to me anyway, so wrapped up were they in each other.

I tiptoed down the little alley between our house and the next into the back garden and slid across the wet grass. I knew it. Noises from the Anderson. Even more blatant noises than before. It was horrible. Molly and Len, Jimmy, now this. Something exploded inside me.

I pelted back round and in through the front door, steaming in past Len and Molly who were in each other's arms but still alert enough to look round in amazement at me.

'Len!' I commanded him from the kitchen. 'Get in 'ere a minute.'

I had an enamel pail in the sink, the tap full on so water was rushing into it at the full strength of the old plumbing. Len stood watching. When it was three-quarters full I dumped it on the floor in front of him.

'I want you to do a piddle in there. The biggest one you can manage.'

Nice thing about Len was, he never asked questions. Just unbuttoned his flies and obliged, with Molly watching, eyes on stalks, over his shoulder.

I flung open the back door and stomped down the garden, leaning well over to one side to balance the pail. On the way I stopped and scraped what dirt I could from the top of the flower bed, hurting my hands on the icy ground, and chucked that in too.

From inside the Anderson I could still hear loud, indecent sounds. They wouldn't have noticed if the whole bloody Luftwaffe had come over that night.

I could barely see a thing but it was so small I couldn't possibly have missed. I yanked the front aside and sloshed the bucket of wee-wee stew in on top of them.

'Bob's your sodding uncle!' I yelled. And left them in a wet, shrieking, effing and blinding heap inside.

Mom's rage knew no bounds. To begin with. She called me every name under the sun, once PC Bob had dripped off down the road refusing to stay another moment to be treated like this, etc. etc.

'You *stu-u-upid*—' she screeched, dragging the word out long, '—selfish, evil little cow!' She was shivering in the back room, lank strips of hair hanging on her shoulders and her red dress daubed with soil, clinging to her. 'I wish I'd never – never even *seen* you in my whole life. I'm cowing frozen – and Bob could catch his death . . .'

'There was wee in there as well.' Thought it best to tell her. Otherwise she'd never know, would she?

'WHAT?'

She'd stormed into the house without even noticing Molly sprawled on top of Len in one of the chairs, the top buttons of her dress undone. They hadn't wasted any time. Molly strugged to her feet like an upturned beetle and skedaddled, right quick.

'Who in the hell d'you think you are?' Mom ranted on. Quite a bit of pacing up and down the room went on, except being such a small room any pacing turned more into pigeon stepping. 'Interfering. Passing judgement. What's Bob going to think, me having a daughter like you?' She was working herself up. 'He might never come back and it'll be all your fault.'

'GOOD!' I shouted. 'I hope he dies. I hope he catches pneumonia or falls under a bloody bus. He shouldn't be here at all. He's not my dad, and you shouldn't be carrying on behind Dad's back. You're a disgusting tart, that's what you are.'

That was when she started hitting me, the bitch, stinging slaps round my face again and again until Len had the wit to grab her arms and stop her. I bit my lip until it bled. I wasn't going to cry for her. I hated her.

151

It was she who burst into tears then, sobbing and snivelling and carrying on while Len and I just stood there staring at her. I put my hands to my smarting cheeks and my heart was completely hardened towards her.

Until suddenly she said, 'You don't understand, Genie.' She looked up, sharp face all raspberry blotches, appealing to me. For the first time trying to tell me something she truly felt. 'You don't know what it's like to find someone you can really love. To be lifted out of years of feeling dead and buried, and scared stiff you might lose it again. You've seen how he looks at me. I've never in my life been wanted like that before – ever.' She was sobbing again at the thought of it.

'Dad wants you.'

She looked down and I knew she was ashamed. 'But I don't want him. God knows, I've tried. I just don't. He makes me feel buried up to the neck. Always has.'

I started crying then. Didn't know where it came from, all of it. Frightened Mom a bit I think, the way I howled. Scared me too. It was like a pain pushed down so far I didn't know it was there, all gushing out. I didn't want to hate her. She was my mom. Your mom's the one person you can't hate or it eats you inside. She's like the North Star and you always need that right direction.

And for once she forgot herself and put her arms round me, and I sobbed and bawled and couldn't stop. Len came and hugged the both of us together like a gorilla.

'I'm sorry, Genie,' Mom said in the middle of it. I could feel her tears dropping on the top of my head. 'I can't help it. I just can't help myself.'

152

March 1940

My Dear Doreen and family,

Well at least the weather's warming up slowly and we wake with the birds now – they've started singing at last! We can still see clouds of our breath on the air first thing too. Roll on spring proper. So now my only complaints are that I still haven't found a pair of boots that fit properly and that I wish I could be at home with you. We're still here waiting to find out what proper soldiering, as the lads call it, is all about.

One new thing – they've issued us with special day passes to go into——. I went, Saturday, with Dickie, the pal I told you about who comes from Stechford. It was an experience. Very smart and pretty with flowers at the windows and people sit out and drink on the pavements. We tried some of the wine they sell. It's some rough stuff – I'd rather have a pint of Ansells!

I've read so many books since we've been here. The lads pass them round. Otherwise it's card sharping and letters. Thank Genie for the chocolate – a proper taste of home. How is Gloria doing? The wireless in our billet stops us feeling too blue. Today I heard Vera Lynn singing 'Somewhere in France with You' and it made me pick up my pen to tell you, my Dor, how much I miss you.

Glad to hear Edith's knee is on the mend. I'll write again soon. In the meantime, try and keep in good spirits, won't you?

Your loving husband, Victor.

I liked letters from Dad, knowing he was safe and hearing about new places he'd been. Mom always read the letters of course, but she'd put them down on the table without a word. After, she'd be scratchy and short for a bit.

Bob stayed away for a week after our little set-to. Don't know whether she told him to or whether he was in a huff or scared I might go for him with the carving knife. Whatever the reason, he kept his distance and all was rosy. We had Gloria back – Nanny Rawson and Lil had bought a little set of their own – and Mom was being extra specially nice to me. She ran me up a new dress on her machine and it actually fitted me. It was navy with white polka dots and a little matching scarf to go in the neck. She visited our nan twice a week. She even did some cleaning. I found her up early one morning sweeping out the back room.

'I know I've been a bit neglectful, Genie,' she said a couple of days after our fight. 'And your nan says you've been a proper treasure to her.' She even brought me up tea in bed, which was an unheard of luxury. Suddenly I felt like someone's daughter.

One morning she sat on the edge of my bed, her hair loose, and said with a coy little smile, 'So who's the lad courting you, Genie?'

Can't say I'd thought of it as courting exactly. But Mom was trying to be my friend and I wasn't getting much change out of Teresa nowadays.

'His name's Jimmy Davis. He was at the factory in Conybere Street.'

'Nice then, is he?'

''E's all right.'

'Bring him home to meet me, Genie.'

As I nodded she put her head on one side so her hair fell in a fine, straight sheet. 'You're not getting up to anything you oughtn't, are you?'

What a question. 'No,' I said, thinking, no more than anyone else round here anyhow. Jimmy was keen on kissing. Ever so keen.

'What about Len and Molly?' she asked suddenly.

'What about them?'

'Are they behaving themselves? I don't want any trouble on my hands from them two.'

'They're all right.' She may have been my pal all of a sudden but I wasn't going to go and spoil things for Len. 'They keep each other company in the evenings.'

'So long as that's all they're doing.'

'Mom?'

She raised her eyebrows.

'Is Bob ever coming back?'

'Genie – I've told you.' She gave a big sigh. 'I love Bob. He loves me.'

'But what about my dad?' My voice turned squeaky and tearful. 'What're you going to do?' It felt as if the world was falling apart.

She got up and went over to the window, stood with her back to me in her white nightdress. 'I don't know. Can't seem to think about it. I keep hoping it'll just sort itself out, one way or another.'

I was crying quietly behind her. 'But what about when Dad comes home?'

'I've told you—' She turned to me again, half angry but near tears herself. 'I don't know, do I? This has never happened to me before. Don't think I don't feel badly about your father. He's a good man and he don't deserve it, I know. But I can't throw away what I've found. Bob's come along and I feel as if he's saved me – saved my life.'

''E hasn't really got a wife and kiddies, has 'e?'

'No.' She at least looked ashamed of this lie. 'He hasn't.'

I pushed my face down into the prickly blanket, hugging my knees, rocking back and forth. 'I want my dad. I want him home. I want things to be all right again.'

She sat by me, even stroked my back. 'I'm sorry, Genie,' she said eventually. 'But Bob's the man I love.'

After his short bout of quarantine, Bob was back and I was faced with an offensive of charm.

'Hello Genie,' he said when he first came back one Saturday morning, his tone sounding as if I, not Mom, was his long lost love. He produced a bunch of daffs from behind his back like a conjuror with a rabbit. 'These are for you. To make friends.' He stuck a really sick-making smile on his brawny face.

'You'd better give them to Mom. Flowers make me sneeze.' I flung the bright yellow blooms on the table as if they were dog muck.

Bob clenched his teeth but he didn't say anything. He stood in the back room with his hands in his trouser pockets. I didn't remember inviting him in but he seemed to be there anyhow.

'All right are you, Len?' he said in the stupid, jolly

voice people seemed to think they'd got to put on with Lenny just because he was a bit simple, as if he needed humouring. Len grinned obligingly. But then Len'd have grinned at Adolf Hitler if he'd happened to pop in. He was like that. Bob turned round and about, jingled coins in the pockets of his loud checked suit. I stood watching him, po-faced.

He tried again: 'That's a right pretty frock you're got on there, Genie.' Then he coughed. 'Very nice.' I glowered at him. 'Your mom knows I'm here then, does she?'

'No.'

'How about telling her then? There's a good girl.'

'Mom!' I yelled up the stairs without shifting myself. '*He*'s here.'

She looked ever so nervous when she came down. She had her hair up and was wearing a pretty, tight dress which hugged her waist and her small bosoms. Bob's eyes swept up and down, devouring her, dirty sod.

'I've got to go,' I said. Nan was expecting me.

'We'll all have to go out together one day, won't we Bob?' Mom said brightly. 'To the pictures or something. Get to know each other better. You'd like that, wouldn't you Genie?'

I didn't even bother answering that one.

Teresa was rather full of herself. Working outside the family business had turned her head.

'Don't know what you see in it,' I told her, since for the moment I was finding more freedom working in my family's business than out of it. 'Clocking on, and at someone's beck and call every minute of the day.'

157

'Yes, but it feels like a real job. And I feel as if I've grown up.'

'And you get to see Jack? When am I going to meet lover boy then?'

Teresa hesitated. Even with her olive skin she blushed easily. 'Yes – I see Jack,' she said, very offhand.

What was going on here then? 'I thought that's just what you wanted?'

'I did – do. Only . . .' In her eyes I could suddenly see a funny little gleam. 'Oh Genie – there's the most gorgeous feller at the factory. It's mostly girls there of course – but he brings all the supplies in and he's forever stopping for a chat. Specially with me.' I could well imagine. I could hear Teresa's wonderful, life-giving laugh echoing out across the factory floor.

'But Teresa, I thought Jack was the be all and end all, your one and only—'

'Oh, I'm still walking out with Jack,' she said hastily. 'Only I can't help liking Clem. He's got the most beautiful green eyes.'

Oh yes, green eyes? I didn't believe in green eyes. I mean I couldn't put my hand on my heart and say I'd ever in my life seen anyone whose eyes were truly green.

I was hanging on to what I had with Jimmy. Which wasn't much. But I needed someone. Truth was, after his opening outburst of affection and that first breathless kiss Jimmy hadn't poured out much in the way of feelings. In fact he never said very much at all.

A typical date with Jimmy went like this. We usually went out on a Saturday. Shirl came to be with our nan, even though Nan was better and hobbling about with a stick.

Jimmy and I would meet, him grinning away in anticipation. He'd take my hand and sometimes we'd go to a matinée at the Carlton, or if it was fine we'd walk in the park. And I'd try to get him to talk. I told him my nan was better.

'Oh well – that's good.' End of that conversation.

'I might look for another job soon.'

'Oh ah.'

Another attempt. 'D'you still like me, Jimmy?'

'Course. Wouldn't be 'ere else, would I?'

I was even forced to ask about football. Problem was, we just hadn't got anything to say to each other. Was this something I was supposed to mind, I wondered? I thought about married people I knew. Mom and Dad had never had a lot in the way of conversation, other than what was needed to get by. Lil and Patsy had at least had a laugh together. But what I wanted to know was, was this the very best you could expect? I'd hoped for something a bit more like being friends with Teresa. Getting on, feeling the warmth and excitement of seeing her, laughing together. Was it normal to find your mind wandering when a man kissed you and to be thinking up a shopping list in your head, or wondering why it was Jimmy's mouth often tasted just a bit of rhubarb when it wasn't even in season?

After he thought we'd indulged in enough pleasantries, Jimmy set to with the real business of the date so far as he was concerned. It'd be back of the cinema as the picture flickered on high above us (I'd try to twist into a position so I could at least watch it as well, over his shoulder). Or in the park, or a doorway on the Stratford Road monkey run while near us, girls snatched handkerchieves out of the boys' breast pockets – you name it, Jimmy took his chances. Blimey, the hours I spent locked, more than half bored, in Jimmy's grasp. Sometimes he got bold and tried to worm his fingers into my coat, inside my dress, but I wasn't having that.

'Oi – you can get out of there.'

He'd give me a sheepish grin and those lips would come close again. So far none of it was like Lil said. Certainly not the best, dreamiest feeling in the world. Frankly I'd rather've had a more tasty sort of gobstopper like a bag of Brazil nut toffees. Except that he was there and he wanted me and kept coming back for more.

Maybe I'm not normal, I thought. Teresa seemed to get a lot more of a thrill out of a man than I did. Perhaps all my housewifery and careworn life and all that was going on at home had made me old too soon?

Bob, like the proverbial rash, was back with a vengeance. Our house was nothing short of a knocking shop and it was getting me right down. First of the evening shift was Len and Molly. They didn't seem to be pushing the boat right to its full limits with sex, but having those two snogging in front of me half the evening was a disturbing enough sight. Didn't know where to put myself. If we'd had a proper coal shed I'd have gone and sat in it.

I did as many things to distract them as I could. I got them playing rummy, gave them things to eat, made endless cups of tea, switched Gloria on. I was cooking our meals back at our house by now, but sometimes I went out to my nan's, prepared to brave the walk back later through the black streets rather than face the canoodlings of Len and his Moll. After all, he was thirty now. I was just in the way.

Second shift, on nights they could manage it, were

the other two love birds. Now they'd moved into the house, the Anderson shelter not being the ideal place to carry on a romance, particularly because as the ground was no longer frozen it was sometimes ankle deep in water. I saw the first signs of trouble when the crocheted blanket appeared again, folded over the back of a chair like it had always been before.

Thing was, Mom was still being uncannily nice to me. She did the ironing and brought me the odd treat when she could: sweets or bits of clothes, some new black shoes with a bow on the strap. I knew perfectly well it was hush money, bribes to keep me sweet, but at the same time I couldn't bear to lose it. The price was knowing she took Bob up to my father's bed while I sat and cried downstairs and Len, alone by this time of night, comforted me.

'S'all right Genie, s'all right.'

'It's not sodding well all right,' I'd sob, cringing in myself at the slightest sound from upstairs. But they were quite quiet, I'll grant them. Len and I put Gloria on loud as we dared and tried to drown out even the slightest sign that they were there. I did a lot of that in those days – blocking things out, closing my eyes, my ears and my very heart.

Some nights when I thought Bob was coming, sickly sweet as he was to me these days, I just stayed over at Nan's and slept on the prickly horsehair sofa by the dying heat from the range and the ticking of her clock.

It didn't take Nan long to catch on. 'I'm not a fool, you know, Genie. What's going on with Doreen?'

I couldn't meet her eyes. 'Nothing, Nan.'

She sat quiet for a minute, the stick resting by her leg, her breathing loud, wheezy on her chest. 'Is she carrying on behind your dad's back?'

I couldn't tell her a real lie. Not Nan. I just sat there, wanting to die of shame.

'Genie?'

'She's got a – friend.'

'Thought so. She'd been like a bitch on heat since Christmas. I noticed it then but I gave her the benefit of the doubt.' Nan pursed her lips, face grim. 'Selfish little cow. Always been the same when it came to riding roughshod over everyone else.' The extent of her anger took me by surprise.

I was relieved Nan knew, but frightened to death at the same time. Mom'd never forgive me for letting it slip and if she found out I'd lose her again, just when we were getting on so well.

'She says . . .' I began timidly. 'She's never been happy with my dad.'

'Happy? *Happy*.' She turned the word round and about like someone looking for the chip at the edge of a saucer. 'You show me someone who thinks they are happy. A marriage is a marriage and that's that. Wasting time dwelling on whether you're happy or not is a sure way into trouble.'

I looked at her tough, lined face. Mom had told me that Grandpa Rawson used to bash her about till sometimes her face was almost unrecognizable. I wasn't sure whether her missing teeth had dropped out with each child born or whether they'd been knocked from her gums by his fist. He didn't restrain himself any better when she was carrying a child. She'd miscarried two on account of his violence. But even when she managed to lease the shop, when she had more money and could've got shot of him, she carried on, steadfast, in a marriage she'd chosen. 'Where would leaving 'im have got me?' And then he died. If there was anyone,

Mom always said, who deserved heart failure, old man Rawson was the one.

'Don't say anything to 'er, will you?' I begged. 'Not at the moment. Things are all right really.'

'Are they?' Nan's voice was sarky as it ever got. 'So what're you doing sleeping here on my couch?'

I saw Teresa now and then. I wasn't sure about the latest of what she was up to and at the moment I didn't really care. I presumed she was thinking up all the backhand ways she could manage to meet Jack or Clem or whoever the hell it was. Good sodding luck to her.

One night though, she came round to Nan's.

'I was hoping you was still here.' She looked a bit down. 'Fancy coming to ours for a bit?'

I suppose I wasn't very gracious greeting her. My mind was back in Balsall Heath, wondering anxiously what might be going on in our house.

'You go on,' Nanny Rawson said. She was standing ironing at the table which was swathed in an old, singed blanket. 'Do you good to have some young company.'

At the Spinis' I found Teresa's Dad in a bad state. He was downstairs, in a chair by the hearth, but his face was very pale, his skin clammy, and he seemed only able to talk in a whisper. Opposite him sat Fausto Pirelli, the young man who'd been in the shop that day they were all yelling at each other. His shadow fell on the wall beside him, nose like a hawk's beak. He was talking, on and on in Italian in a soft, earnest voice, with a frown on his face. Micky seemed agitated, kept trying to interrupt, but when he tried to speak it ended in a bout of agonized coughing.

Vera, standing by Micky's chair, looked worried to

death as well, and exhausted. 'Micky was called to a factory fire yesterday,' she whispered to me. 'It was over Bordesley way, some chemical place, and he said the fumes and smoke were evil – choked him. He only just managed to get out. It's done something terrible to his chest.' Her eyes filled with tears. 'I hate seeing him like this. Micky.' She leaned down and touched his hand, 'please go to bed.'

'Later,' he managed to say, trying to smile at her, and indicating with an angry nod of his head that the other man was still talking. The anger was directed at him.

'Fausto,' Vera implored the man, and the rest was in Italian, but I could see she was begging him to go, to let Micky rest. He flapped his hand impatiently at her, saying, '*Subito, subito* . . . straight away,' and not moving.

The smaller children were in bed but Stevie and Francesca were at the table, not doing anything but listening and watching. Stevie's eyes were absolutely intent on Fausto's face.

'Brew up, Teresa,' Vera ordered quietly. I could see how tense she was.

'What's going on?' I asked, following her into the scullery.

'That stupid idiot.' She jerked her head. 'His family comes from the same place as Dad's in Italy. They're talking about what's happening there – Mussolini . . . Fausto still reckons he's a Blackshirt, even though he can't find many to agree with him. They don't like all that round here. He doesn't even really know what it means – he's all hot air. But Stevie looks up to him – thinks it's big talk. Fausto hasn't got a father of his own, he's dead, so Dad feels responsible for him. He's worried he's going to get into trouble.'

'Trouble?'

Teresa shrugged. She seemed distracted, stood with the empty kettle in her hand as if she couldn't think what to do with it, so I took it off her and went out across the yard to fill it and set it on the gas.

'You worried about him?'

'Who?'

'Your dad.'

'Yes – but the doctor said he should be all right. Needs time to let his lungs clear again. It's not that, it's – Jack found out about me and Clem.'

'What was there to find out about you and Clem?'

Teresa looked down at the floor in shame, face hidden by her dark hair. 'We started to get a bit keen on each other and I went out with him a couple of times. And with Jack living so close to the factory and that, I knew I was going to have to tell him and he was so angry and said he never wanted to see me again.'

'Well what d'you expect? Anyway, that's all right, isn't it, if it's Clem you want to see.'

'But I don't know if I like Clem very much any more. He's ever so cocky.' She sounded very sorry for herself. 'And I'm going to end up with nobody.'

A wave of great weariness came over me. What a load of stupid rubbish it was. All of it. Men, women, girls, boys, love, romance. It was all a silly story put out at the pictures and in sixpenny romances to make us think such things were possible and then cast us in the deepest blue depression when we were brought nose up against real life.

'Oh Teresa,' I said. 'For God's sake just pull yourself together.'

I went out and sat with Vera Spini, watching Fausto

as he talked on urgently. He seemed very strange, as if something was burning him up inside. And I listened to Vera's worries, which at least had some proper substance to them, leaving Teresa to sulk in the scullery.

April 1940

The spring was here with all its usual fevers enhanced, worse luck for me. And then the Flanagans' roof fell in, two houses away from Nanny Rawson's. I was out with Mary Flanagan, hanging out my nan's washing and basking in a little thread of sun which had managed to reach in and light up the far side of the yard. One minute there was the Flanagans' house, large as life, in tightly squeezed back-to-back line. The next, there was a massive great crash and glass shattering and, for what seemed an age afterwards, things groaned and shuddered, tinkled, smashed and finally settled, and sworls of thick dust rose up choking us. Minutes later, when the dust finally sifted down out of the air, we could see through to the street outside and there were people standing looking. My washing, needless to say, was black again.

'Jesus, Mary and fecking Joseph!' Mary was gasping over and over. 'My house – will you look what's happened to my house!'

Then panic set in. 'Where's Geraldine?' Mary laid her hands on each of the other two of her small children who were still at home, reassuring herself. 'Eamonn, where was Geraldine? Was she in the house now, was she?' She was screaming at the boy, shaking him. There was plaster and dust all over her red hair.

All the neighbours were out of their houses. They

stood round, numbed. No one seemed able to move. The thought that six-year-old Geraldine might be trapped under the weight of the house was too terrible to take in. Then people started saying 'What about Mr and Mrs Griffin?' and everyone wondered whether the elderly couple who lived in the front-house had been crushed under it, until Mr and Mrs Griffin were spotted out in the street with a crowd round them.

A small bang was heard from the end of the yard and Geraldine, a child with hair as bright a red as Mary's, emerged unconcerned from the privy saying, 'Mom, what was that noise?'

Mary dashed to her and whacked her one soundly round the ear. 'You eejit of a girl! What did you think you were doing in there? Sure I thought you were dead.' She clutched the bewildered girl against her great big chest, clinging to her while Geraldine bawled from the walloping she'd had. 'Where's our house gone, Mom?' she sobbed over Mary's shoulder.

Mary stood up again slowly and turned to face the fact that she had seven children, a husband away in the RAF and no house. The slum houses in that area were built back in Queen Victoria's day to give the worker bees who manned the factories a place to live, or at least exist. They were jerry built – the state of some of them was so bad it defied description – and Mary's, after the harsh winter, the weight of the snow and then the thaw, not to mention the landlord swiping slates off the roof every time the rent was overdue, had finally given up the ghost.

Mary was silent now and deathly white in the face. As everyone in the yard normally did in a crisis, she turned to my nan.

'Edith – what in the name of heaven am I going to do?'

Nan hobbled over and took command. 'For a start what you'll have to do is go to the Corporation and get on the list for another house. With seven kids they'll have to get summat sorted out for you. In the meantime . . .' She looked round the yard with the kind of expression on her face no one would dare disagree with, even Mary's next-door neighbour and sparring partner, Clarys. 'We'll all make sure you're all right, won't we?' There were nods, some more doubtful than others. 'We can fit some of you in,' Nanny Rawson went on.

Where on earth? I was thinking, listening to my nan setting example by what I thought of as rash promises.

By the evening it was sorted out. Lil's kids stayed on in Nan's attic bedroom. Nan persuaded Lil to move in with her and freed up the second bedroom for Mary Flanagan and her two youngest kids. Geraldine and one of the lads were taken in by another neighbour, the other kids by a third. And so, the teeming yard at the back of Belgrave Road, already overcrowded, ramshackle and insanitary, managed to redistribute itself with one less house to go round. The only person driven completely barmy by it was my auntie Lil, who already thought her own kids quite enough to cope with, ta very much, without having extras foisted on us.

'How about a trip to the Lickeys?' Jimmy said, and at the time I couldn't think of anything better. It was a gorgeous spring, the skies powder blue, sun warm, any last nip on the air long gone now, and the trees uncurling their leaves to the spring air looked like a miracle after the winter we'd had. Even the yard behind our nan's seemed a less drab place with sunlight streaming off the newly washed windows.

Course, just as the world seemed the most precious and lovely the spring can make it, Hitler's troops started to move across Denmark into Norway and we sat round Gloria waiting to hear the latest. In the newsreaders' solemn voices we heard names which were strange on our lips, ones we'd never heard before – Narvik, Trondheim – bringing the world in on us. You could feel suspense in the air.

Jimmy and I rode the 62 bus out to the Lickeys. The Lickey Hills are a beautiful, wooded ridge on the south edge of Birmingham where the trams and buses terminated after the long, tree-lined swoop along the Bristol Road. This was the place where hordes of factory-pale, work-weary Brummies would congregate on holidays and weekends to escape the claustrophobic closeness of the city's walls and alleys, to feel they were in the country and picnic with the sun on their faces if they were lucky.

Jimmy started trying to kiss me on the bus.

'Oh, gerroff, will you,' I said irritably. 'Not in front of all these people.'

Jimmy leered at me. Love, or at least a shortlived infatuation, is blind, I thought. His wonky eyes had given him charm and appeal at first. Now they looked as if they were squinting at me all the time, full of unwelcome lust.

'No one's looking.' There were loads of kids on the bus which kept stopping to pick up more passengers until it was crammed full. People were clinging to each other in the aisle and there were shrieks of laughter when we swung round a corner.

'I don't care. You should behave yourself when there's people about.'

'What – so I don't 'ave to when we're on our own?'

'Don't you ever think about anything else?'

It was well warm enough for my summer frock and Jimmy only had on trousers and a grey shirt that had once been white. We had a bag with bread and butter and cake, apples and a few lumps of cheese and bottles filled with cooling tea. I was excited. A trip to the Lickeys was a really special day out.

We passed through Northfield, Longbridge, to the terminus at Rednal where the bus disgorged us all. Mothers in hats yelling at gaggles of kids, all with too much to carry, headed off in excitement for the paths to Lickey Hill or Cofton Wood.

I'd have liked to go to the park with its ornamental pool, swans riding their reflections in the glassy water, and peaceful, dreamy paths and flowers. But no. Jimmy had other plans. Grabbing my hand, he said, 'Come on – let's get shot of all this lot, shall we?' and dragged me off to the tracks that led off through the woods. It wasn't that difficult to get away from the other day trippers. The Lickeys had paths winding all across them and through the trees. Many of the families out for the day walked as short a distance as possible and settled on the grassy hillside with a sweeping view of the surrounding counties, picnicking and lazing while their kids played round them, and hardly shifted all day.

Truth to tell, I was already wishing I could have come on my own. I could feel coming over me the bored restlessness I felt more and more with Jimmy, making me want to tear about shrieking or thump someone, preferably him.

'Come on.' I pointed to a place on the grass with

rings of families in view. 'This is a nice spot. Let's have our picnic here, eh?'

'Nah.' Jimmy pulled me on further and further, into the woods. 'Don't want to be surrounded by people, do we? This way . . .'

He dragged me right out to the edge of the place somewhere, finding a spot in the woods which no one else apparently thought was the great beauty spot of the Lickey Hills because no one else was there. It was pleasant enough, light darting in through the leaves, never still, and leafmould and twigs on the ground. But it wasn't exactly the scenic view I had in mind. And I knew what he wanted. God, I was fed up at the thought of wasting a day in the Lickeys stuck to the end of Jimmy's lips.

'Now I've got you all to myself, 'aven't I?' He chuckled. 'Come 'ere . . .'

I saw those lips coming towards me again, a light stubble on the white skin above them.

'Will you just lay off and let me eat my dinner in peace,' I snapped.

'Well, you're not much company, are you?'

'Can't you think about summat else for a change? Or don't you have anything else in your head at all?'

'What I've got's all 'ere,' he said, patting his crotch.

'So I've sodding well gathered.' I shifted away from him and opened the packet of sandwiches. Boredom perched on me like a gigantic bird. I wished Teresa was here. Not that she was better at the moment, but with a bit of work you could get her mind off men.

At least he let me eat for a bit.

'Find you were hungry after all, did you?'

Jimmy grinned. 'Nice cake of your nan's.'

'She's a good cook.'

'My mom's cooking's terrible.'

'So's mine.'

We laughed together. He was talking to me, which made a change.

'I bet yours has never cooked a hen with the feathers on like mine did once.'

'She never! What the hell'd she do that for?'

'She was the worse for it – the drink, you know.'

'She drink a bit then, does she?'

'Yep. Don't blame her. If I was married to a bastard like my dad I'd get kalied all the time as well.'

'What's he like then?'

Jimmy dug a dirty thumbnail into his apple. 'Our mom relies on him, see, not being able to 'ear. And he treats her like the lowest form of life. Brought the clap 'ome to her once – never been the same since, she 'asn't. She was expecting a kid at the time too. She lost that one.' Jimmy took a big bite of the apple. 'If he died I'd cheer.'

I watched him, glad at least to feel something for him again, even if it was only sorry. Some fellow feeling. And I was hoping at last here was someone who would understand what was on my mind.

'My mom . . .' It was costing me to speak and I wasn't even sure he was listening. 'She's going with another bloke. Brings him to our house. I hate him.'

Jimmy said nothing, just munched on the apple.

'It's horrible, isn't it?' I persevered, watching his pale face.

Jimmy hurled the apple core away over into the trees. 'Come on. Let's do it.'

'What?'

'The whole thing. Fucking. Properly.'

'Jimmy!' The very word gave me the heebie-jeebies. It sounded so *rude*. 'You don't use words like that.'

He was shuffling closer to me. 'Sorry.'

'Should think you are. It's not nice.' I was sitting clenched up tight, knees against my chest.

Jimmy slunk his arm round my back. 'What d'you want me to say instead?'

'Something nice and romantic. Say how you feel about me.'

'Well, you're all right, you are. I've told you. I like you, Genie.'

'But d'you feel anything more than that? D'you love me, Jimmy?' It felt important that he did, that it wasn't just One Thing he was after.

His face loomed closer. 'Yeah, OK Genie. I love you. Now give us a kiss.'

I gave a big sigh. What price affection. He kissed me for some time, then undid a couple of the buttons on the front of my dress and wriggled his fingers inside.

'Don't,' I tried to say, but he wasn't having it. He squeezed until I squeaked with pain. I was mortified. Didn't want his hand down my dress. His eyes had started rolling about and he looked so queer with his white face close to me and his body rocking up and down beside me as if he had a horse under him.

There's got to be more to it than this. Lil hadn't had those dreamy eyes on her just for this. And how long'd we got to sit here doing it for? What a complete waste of the afternoon when we could've been out in the sun. And then I started thinking about home, Mom and Bob doing this. I felt sick.

Jimmy started fumbling about in his clothes. ''Ere,' he said, ''ave a feel of this. This is 'ow much I want you.'

174

He yanked at my hand, rubbed it against him.

'No!' I said, pulling away. It felt hot and sticky. 'Don't be dirty.'

He scowled. 'All right then. If you're going to be like that, we'll do it another way.'

Hands on my shoulders, he shoved me back so my head was in a pile of leaves and twigs. He pulled my dress up and got his hand down my knickers, poking around hard and clumsily. Lying along me, half on, half off, he ground his body up and down, faster and faster. It didn't take long. He tensed up, eyes squeezed shut, hurting me with his hand and I called out in pain.

When he got off, my blue dress was all wet and sticky.

'You pig,' I said. 'You horrible, disgusting pig.'

'Go on.' He half turned away, buttoning himself up again. 'That's what you wanted. Next time I'll give it to you proper.'

I felt very cold suddenly, and shivery, sat huddled up, clutching my knees tight. The world was a nasty mean place.

'Let's go. You wanted a walk, didn't you? Bit of sun on your face?'

I spread out the skirt of my dress, all gluey and wrinkled. 'What's my mom going to say?'

Casually, Jimmy picked up one of the stera bottles we'd brought our tea in. It was a third full still, and he poured the rest of it in my lap. The blood-warm tea seeped through and trickled between my thighs.

'There y'are. Now she'll never know the difference, will she?'

*

'There's no need for you to keep my nan company no more,' I told Shirl. 'I'm not going to be seeing Jimmy again.'

'Oh.' The smile dropped off Shirl's face but I was too wrapped up in my own mortification to take in how downcast she looked.

'Got fed up of 'im, 'ave you? Thought you would. Not got a lot going on upstairs, 'as 'e?'

I shook my head.

'So – you don't need me round then? I mean I don't mind . . .'

'No,' I said, very short with her. 'There's no need to put yourself out any more.'

She took me at my word and walked out of our lives again. I didn't give it a lot of thought then because it was absolute mayhem up at Nan's, with Lil's lot and the Flanagans roaring in and out. Nan was getting better. She was taking over from me again day by day and I knew I'd soon be booted back out into the working world. She bore the Flanagans with her usual stoicism – 'The Corporation'll sort them out a place soon enough.'

But it was Lil who was doing her nut. The price of fags had gone up by a ha'penny a packet, the government was behind the factories to up production (especially aircraft – Len was on extra long shifts) and to cap it all the house was nearly full to bursting.

'Your life's never your own,' she moaned regularly. 'At work you don't have time to turn round hardly and when I get home I can't see across the room for mad bloody kids.'

And the Flanagans were wild. After all, we only had two of them, but the mess they made was indescribable. The boys were bedwetters, so there were smelly sheets to be dealt with every day, dirty clothes left in heaps, Patsy, Tom and Cathleen's things all turned upside down and scattered round the place, and the constant noise of them charging in and out. Mary seemed helpless to control them, try as she might. How the hell did she cope normally? we wondered. They started to make Lil's kids look like angels with haloes.

It was getting Lil down and I felt sorry for her. She was growing sourer by the day and I thought she deserved better.

I went to see Vera Spini one day. The shop was quiet and she was out the back making ice cream, her face sagging with exhaustion. She wore a white cap on her head to keep her hair out of the way.

'Let me help, Mrs Spini,' I said, going to the churning handle.

They boiled the ice-cream mixture in the copper until it was like custard, which stood overnight covered with muslin cloths to keep any flies out. The next day it'd go in the churning machine, a long cylinder which was kept cool by electricity. There were blades inside to turn it round and it got paler and paler yellow, smelling sweet and turning into food from heaven when you were used to lumpy tapioca.

'How's Mr Spini?'

'Not too good.' She stopped turning and pulled the cap off. Her pale hair was dark at the roots as if it was planted in soil. 'He hasn't managed to do anything much for the past two weeks. I'm ever so worried about him, Genie.'

She wiped her dry, workworn hands on a cloth and

tried to force a smile. I'd never seen her do that before. Not force it. But there were no songs on her lips today, no hymns or Santa Lucia.

'Here, come and see him. He'll be glad to have a bit of company.'

'Me?'

Vera looked at me in surprise. 'Course. He'd love to see you. He's got a real soft spot for you, Genie. Always has had.'

This was news to me all right and it didn't stop me feeling scared. I'd hardly ever seen Micky without Teresa around.

'Stevie!' Vera shouted into the yard. 'Come up front for a bit, will you? I'll not be long.'

In the house, Micky was sitting by the fire huddled in his coat, watching Luke push an old wooden horse with rough little wheels along the floor. His body looked thinner, his face was drawn and sick looking and he had several days' worth of greying stubble on his cheeks. There was a newspaper on the table and a cup with tea dregs in it.

'Genie!' He really did look pleased to see me and I felt warmed by it. In fact he looked nothing like as stern as usual. 'Come and have a sit down with me. I'm stuck here, useless to everyone at the moment.'

'You're telling me,' Vera mocked him.

'Feeling any better, Mr Spini?' I asked, perching on the edge of a chair by the table.

'A bit.' He ran a hand over his wavy, pepper and salt hair and nodded insistently at his wife. 'I do. She don't believe me. Makes you think though. I don't know what was in that smoke but it nearly did for me, I tell you.' And he was off, coughing again. He didn't sound well, whatever he said.

178

Vera stayed long enough to brew up a pot of tea, sugaring a cup for Micky and placing it tenderly on the table beside him before going back to the shop.

'You got time to sit for a bit?' Micky asked.

I nodded.

'It's very nice. Long time since you sat and had a chat. Now you're a working girl.' He laughed, then coughed. I couldn't say I ever remembered sitting having a chat before, but I wasn't going to argue. But what in heaven were we going to talk about?

'You OK, Genie? Everything all right at home?'

'Yes,' I lied.

He looked into my eyes with his dark ones for a moment then stared at the back of the door which Vera had closed for once.

'I've been sat here all this time – so I've been thinking. Never get the time on a normal day.' He stopped. I waited for him to keep talking, not sure if I was meant to ask, and then I saw he was struggling to keep from coughing.

'I remembered something from when I was a little boy in Italy – about seven or eight. I had a special place for myself. No one else knew about it.' He stirred the tea and took a sip, slurping it. 'Of course everyone knew about it – but no one except me knew it was special. Our village was outside Castellamare, and the church where we said Mass was high on the cliff and the land round it looked out over the water – that's the Mediterranean Sea. Beautiful blue it is. There were a few trees on that piece of land and one was an olive tree with a very old, twisted trunk where I used to go and sit. It was at the far end, away from the church, so the old ladies who came in and out to clean the church or say their rosary couldn't see I was there. I used to feel the trunk of the tree behind my back and the land in front of it sort of dipped down towards the sea. There'd be salamanders – little lizards – running up the tree and there were crickets in the grass. You ever heard the noise crickets make, Genie?'

I shook my head.

'The grass was a dry, wiry kind that scratched at the back of your legs. Sometimes I sat there as long as an hour, hoping no bigger boys would come and find me. The sky was always blue – that's how I remember it, and you could smell salt on the wind. And because I was alone and all I could see was sea and grass and sky it gave me room for all these dreams to pass through my head. I felt very big sitting up there, as if I owned all the world and I could do anything I wanted.'

He laughed again suddenly as if he'd said something daft, because he never talked like this normally. Certainly wouldn't have done to his own kids. The laugh ended in a long bout of coughing and his lungs sounded as if they were half full of liquid. Each breath was a strain for air and his face went red. Luke stared up at him. When it'd passed he said, 'D'you have a place like that, Genie?'

I shook my head. 'There's no room for that here, is there?'

Micky tapped his head with one thick finger. 'There is in here.'

I thought of my house all for me, by the river with fields and trees and flowers. 'I s'pose I do then, yes. Only it's not real.'

'It don't matter. When I want to dream of something outside all these houses so close together I can go back to my tree. So you're looking at a crazy bloke who spends his morning sitting under a tree thousands of

180

miles away!' He seemed embarrassed now, after saying all that. Luke jumped up and pulled at his father's leg and Micky lifted him up on to his lap, Luke watching him with a finger in his mouth.

Seeing the newspaper on the table, Micky picked it up and handed it to me. 'Here – another good reason for sitting under a tree.'

It was the *Mirror*. With a black-rimmed nail, Micky pointed to one column:

> There are more than twenty thousand Italians in Great Britain. The . . . Italian is an indigestible unit of population . . .
>
> Even the peaceful, law-abiding proprietor of the back street coffee shop bounces into a patriotic frenzy at the sound of Mussolini's name . . .

'In Italy we have the *Fascio*,' Micky explained. 'The Fascist Party, pretty much like the German Nazis. So they think that because we are Italian we must support Mussolini . . . I can't think of anyone now who is a supporter – well, except young Pirelli, or he likes to think so anyhow . . .' Micky shook his head.

I read the last part of the newspaper column: 'We are nicely honeycombed with little cells of potential betrayal.'

'But what does it mean?'

He must have seen the worry on my face because he reached over and patted my arm. 'I hope it don't mean nothing. I've been here far too long to worry about.

'Come and see me again if you get time, eh?' he said, as I got up to leave. 'I'll be on my feet soon. Oh – and by the way, Genie. Teresa. She getting up to anything she shouldn't be?'

I shook my head, panic stricken. Why did people have to keep asking me such blooming awkward questions?

'Not that I know of.'

He looked into my eyes for a moment, then smiled. 'All right, love. Thanks for coming to see me.'

I wanted to say something nice but couldn't think of anything. In fact what I really wanted to do was go and put my arms round him for being kind, for making me feel special. I didn't do it, but I knew I'd never see Micky Spini in the same way again.

'Tara,' was all I said. 'Hope you get better soon.'

Mary Flanagan's kids were not the easiest to get to bed. I'd thought of Mary as someone intimidating, forever yelling and carrying on, until she moved in with my nan and I saw her trying to control her kids. It was pitiful.

One night when I was round there the tension of having two families living under one roof was reaching breaking point and although the Corporation had promised to rehouse Mary 'at the earliest possible opportunity' so far there was no date.

'Get up there and stay where I put you or you'll be feeling my hand across you again,' Mary was bawling up the stairs in her deep, throaty voice for about the tenth time. Downstairs I was trying to deal with the devastation the kids had caused while they were still up.

Lil sat on the couch chewing her nails as if she'd like to gnash someone's head off. I could tell she was bubbling inside like a boiler about to explode. She was a stickler for getting her own kids to bed in good time, and once they were there, that was where they stayed, and no messing.

Not long after, despite Mary's threats and pleas and bribes, we could still hear feet padding back and forth upstairs, then the clattering and squeaking of the bed-frame as the two boys bounced on and off it like little rubber acrobats.

Nan and I exchanged glances in the scullery.

Lil suddenly snapped. 'Christ Almighty, would you listen to them! They'll be waking Cathleen again if they carry on like that. What's the matter with them? Why the hell can't you get them to do as they're told? They're like bloody animals.'

'I'm doing my best,' Mary snapped from the bottom of the stairs. 'Don't you talk about my kids like that. Eamonn, Colm – I'm coming up to give you a hiding so I am!'

'They're unsettled,' Nanny Rawson said. She was washing up, I was wiping. 'Poor kids've been split up. They're not used to it.'

'I don't bloody well care.' Lil was on her feet, brown eyes darkened further with fury. 'I've had enough of it. If they come to live in our house they should do as they're told. We want some peace, no sodding kids running round the place all evening. Some of us have a job of work to do as well you know!'

Suddenly there were wails from upstairs. 'That's it!' Lil exploded. 'That's Cathleen. Move, will you.' She pushed past Mary who was at the foot of the stairs. 'They've really done it now.'

'Don't you touch my kids!' Mary spat at Lil's back, following her up the stairs.

'I wouldn't touch your poxy kids if they were the last ones on earth. I'm going to see to mine now they've cowing well gone and woken her up.' But as she passed through the boys' room we heard her bawl at them,

'GET INTO BED AND STAY THERE YOU LITTLE BASTARDS' at the top of her voice as she went up to Cathleen.

We could hear Cathleen's weary, half-awake screams downstairs, and it took Lil some time to get her settled again. Eventually she came back down, but the Flanagan boys were still up there tripping the light fantastic with Mary yelling helplessly at them.

'At least Cathleen's gone off again,' Lil said through clenched teeth. 'I just can't stand any more of this, I really can't. Come on, Genie, I'll take you home.'

'It's hardly even dark,' I protested. 'I'll be all right.' My mind was doing gambols over and over, trying to think what time it was and what exactly might be going on at home.

'It's only nine.' Lil glanced at the clock. 'I can take you along and sit with you for a while. Have a bit of peace out of this madhouse.' Lil was already walking out into the spring evening.

'Just drop me at the door,' I said. 'I'll be all right – really. I've walked back much later than this.'

'Do I smell or summat? I've told you – I'll come and keep you company. See Len. Wait till her in there's got her act together.'

My mind was racing madly ahead. What the hell were we going to find if Molly was over at our house? And then I remembered. How could I have forgotten? They wouldn't even be there. Len and Molly had gone to the pictures – big excitement – and wouldn't be back until after ten. Thank you sweet Jesus.

Lil was carrying on down my ear, sorry for herself, her voice hardly changing tone. Moan tone. 'I'm that tired I can hardly get about these days. If it's not work it's the kids. Sometimes I ask myself why I go on with it all. Why I don't just go and do the same as Patsy did and jump into the canal?'

'Don't say that. You don't mean it, do you Lil?'

'I do. Some days I really do. I mean what's there ever going to be for me now? My life's over. Only you can't do a thing like that to your kids, can you?'

I didn't blame her really. Only I was so relieved, after those moments of outright panic, to think the house would be empty when we got back, I was almost ready to dance down the road.

'Things'll get better, Auntie Lil. You'll get a nice new house and move out – have a garden for the kids.'

'At the rate Mary's getting hers it'll be the turn of the century before they find me one,' she said despondently. 'And I'll be dead by then anyway.'

The house was dark. Blacked out of course, but there were no lights on inside when I opened the front door, finding myself grinning like an idiot with relief.

'Come on in,' I said. 'I'll put the kettle on.'

'Doreen got anything stronger? Drop of port?'

'Dunno. I'll look.'

I lit the gaslight in the back room with a spill and found a tipple for Lil. I'd put the kettle on as well and was trying to poke some life into the fire when we heard it from upstairs. Clear and loud and horribly unmistakable.

'Jesus,' Lil said. 'What the . . .?'

I couldn't answer her. I went straight to a chair, pushed my burning face into it and pulled the cushion over my head as my mother's cries upstairs reached fever pitch. Knees tucked up on the worn seat of the chair, I curled tight into the smallest speck I could manage.

But Lil was at me, poking my back.

'Genie . . . Lift your head up. Genie!' She yanked me out of the chair by one arm. I wouldn't look at her, just covered my face with my hands, squinting out between my fingers. Lil hissed at me. 'Who is that up there?'

'It's Mom.' What an admission, my mom behaving like that.

'I know. I can hear that much. But who the hell is that with her?'

'Bob.'

'Who's Bob when he's at home?'

'A copper.'

Lil mouthed air like a fish. 'Well how long's this been going on?'

I shrugged. Couldn't think. I couldn't think of anything. The noise had calmed down upstairs.

'The little bitch.' Lil advanced on the door to the stairs.

'Lil no, don't! You can't!' But it was like shouting into an avalanche.

My legs were trembling so much as she stomped upstairs that I had to sit down, waiting for all hell to break loose above me. I kept thinking over and over, what are they doing here? They're not supposed to be here. How could they do this? How could they?

The fight Mom and Lil had that night outdid anything I could ever remember before. Lil was fit to burst with outrage, righteous indignation, fury at being related to such an obvious trollopy bitch of a sister and, though she'd never have admitted it, pure, grass-green jealousy. And Mom – also outrage at being burst in upon while she lay stark naked in candlelight, her head lifting in panic off Bob's King Kong hairy chest when she heard feet on the stairs. And anger and mortification at being caught in the act of complete, undeniable adultery.

The shouting, sobbing, cursing, slapping and recriminations went on and on. Some time, at about the eye of the storm, Bob slunk downstairs, half dressed in socks, drawers and shirt, looking like an ape in clothes. He pulled on the other bits, the trousers, jacket, even tie, as I sat crying. His shoes came flying down the stairs on the force of Lil shouting, 'Take these with you, you filthy bastard, and don't ever come back!'

Bob never said a word to me. Didn't even look at me. He let himself out and left them to it.

May 1940

It was soon after that Mom started being sick. Course, not having had a babby myself, the sight of someone heaving over a bucket every morning didn't automatically make me suspicious.

'My cooking's not that bad, is it?' I said to her.

All I got in reply was a lot of groaning. Some mornings she'd say finally, 'Oooh, I can't go to work in this state. I feel terrible.' And she'd crawl back up to bed and stay there until the middle of the afternoon. She did a lot of crying as well. A real lot.

I started to get worried. 'Shall I get our nan?'

'No!' She found the strength to push herself up on one elbow. 'Don't you dare say a word to anyone. D'you hear?'

'But you look terrible.'

She did too – face greeny white and clammy, hair in greasy strips. The room smelled stale and sweaty.

'I'll be better in a while. Just get me some water, and don't breathe a word to anyone.'

By the evening she'd dress and come downstairs, unsteady on her feet, eat a little bit and sit, silent most of the time. This went on for days. The time that for the rest of us was really the beginning of the war almost passed her by. Suddenly Gloria's news bulletins were once more the most important notches on which we hung our day. We listened in to *The Nine O'Clock*

News in the evening like religious fanatics, shutting up anyone who dared open their mouth to interrupt.

Hitler invaded the Netherlands. More names of places we'd never heard of. More realization that there was a world out there where things were happening. Bombs fell somewhere outside Canterbury. And Mr Churchill became Prime Minister. I liked him. Nearly everyone did, I think, with his way with words. Made you feel carried along and full of strength, not like the others, all muttering away.

'We have before us,' he said, 'an ordeal of the most grievous kind.'

But he made you feel noble, chosen in some way to do it, as if the fate of the world rested on us, each of us. Even Lil, the great sceptic, was impressed. ''E makes you feel it might all be worth it, doesn't 'e?'

Life was beginning to gleam a bit brighter for Lil. Or at least it was going to revert back to what it was before. Mary Flanagan and her kids were to be rehoused in Stanley Street.

'A front-house too, if you please!' Lil said. But she didn't really care whether the Flanagans were being moved into Buckingham Palace so long as they were well out of her hair.

Mom finally admitted one morning, between bouts of sickness, that she was going to have a babby. She was crying when she told me.

'I can't keep it to myself any more, Genie. You're my daughter' (she'd noticed!) 'and I've got to tell someone.' She lay back weakly sobbing into the pillow.

I was right out of my depth here. 'Is it – er . . . is it Bob's babby?'

'Course it's Bob's!' she wailed. 'How many men d'you think I've been with the past few months?'

189

I felt sorry for her. I did, really. Because I knew she didn't find having babbies any joy, and to cap it all this one was a little bastard and it wouldn't take the neighbours long to work that out for themselves.

'Are you going to tell 'im?'

Mom sobbed even louder. I sat down on the bed and touched her shoulder. 'D'you want a cuppa tea?'

'No, I don't want a cuppa tea! How's that going to help anything?' Then she softened. 'Sorry, Genie. No ta.' She looked bleakly across at the window. I saw dots of white light in her eyes. 'I want to tell him. I want everything to be all right – for him to want it. But after what happened . . .'

Since the Big Fight with Lil, neither she nor Bob had been near the place. 'I'm scared he won't ever want to see me now . . .' And off she went all over again.

'D'you want me to find 'im for you? Where does he live?'

'You can't go to his house,' she said, wiping her eyes. 'He still lives with his mom and her sister, and he says they're both proper tartars. Look, he works at Moseley Police Station – if you could take a note?'

The note said, 'I've got to see you. D.' I made a detour on the way to my nan's, going to Moseley first.

That night we heard the Germans had bombed Rotterdam. Everyone thought thousands and thousands of people had died, the doom-laden faces were back in my nan's shop – 'We'll be next' – and everyone started dusting off their gas masks again. Len had to take a cactus in a pot out of his and we sent him off with it again every morning. It was a shock. It was near, and getting nearer. The Dutch capitulated and the next thing was they were moving into France, into Belgium, Antwerp, Liège, Brussels, names falling like ninepins.

'They're saying at work,' Lil told us, 'that all the Germans've got to do is fly over. Some of 'em might even be here already. You got to be careful who you talk to.'

Straight away I had a mad, beautiful daydream that 'Uncle Bob' was really a Fifth Columnist spying for the Nazis who would soon be unveiled as the traitor he was, humiliated and tortured in public, then strung up in the Bull Ring to meet as slow and agonizing a death as possible.

Shame life isn't that simple. When he finally turned up I let him in, still in his uniform.

'Awright, Genie?' He was very short with me, pushed past into the hall. We'd had no warning of him coming. Len was still at work at one of his endless shifts at Austin Aero. Luckily Mom was up and dressed and had managed to get some soup down her. She was wearing an old dress, and had dragged a comb through her hair. I didn't get a chance to warn her, what with old Charmschool barging in like that. I heard her say 'Bob!' startled. She struggled weakly to stand up and held on to the back of the chair, smiling so sweetly at him, really trying hard.

'What d'you want?' I couldn't quite make out his tone. It wasn't angry or abrupt, more cautious and slippery.

'I er, didn't get a chance to say sorry. About what happened. My sister . . .' She gave a little laugh. 'Can't ever get away from your family, can you? One way or another?'

Bob didn't look particularly amused. 'Is that it? I haven't got a lot of time tonight.'

'Bob, please.' Mom's eyes filled with tears. 'Don't be like that. It was our fault. We shouldn't have been there

191

– not then. Genie wasn't to know ... Look, Bob, stop—' He was starting to turn away. 'I've summat to tell you. Genie – leave us alone, will you? There's a good girl.'

I went upstairs, feeling sick at everything that was happening. I didn't want PC Bob anywhere within shouting distance of our house.

It didn't take her long to tell him. Didn't take him long to get to the front door either. Within minutes I heard it slam, and Mom's howls of despair from downstairs. I found her lying along the hall on her front, arms stretched out as if she was heaving on an invisible rope, trying to pull Bob back.

'Oh please, *please* ...' she moaned, until the words gave out to sobs with no sound coming at all.

Then there was a great banging on the door. I stepped over Mom. There was Molly, a big grin on her pork pink face. 'Is Lenny in yet?'

'No, he sodding well isn't!' I yelled at her, guilty for it before I'd even finished. 'Sorry, Molly. No, he'll be back later tonight.'

Molly peered in between my legs at Mom's head on the floor behind me. 'Everything all right, is it Genie?'

'No, Molly, it's not,' I said savagely, and slammed the door in her simple face.

'Nan, there's summat you're going to have to know.'

Mom told me to tell her and Auntie Lil, because she couldn't face doing it herself. I told our nan first. Didn't want Lil there ranting and raving.

We had a few quiet moments in the shop. Nan was

sorting through sugar coupons. She looked round at me. I could see she was sort of steeling herself for something she half dreaded already.

'It's Mom. She's expecting.' My cheeks were aching hot. I couldn't look Nan in the eye. 'The babby's Bob's.'

Nan bent her head and pushed the coupons into her battered tin cashbox, her fingers working fast and nervously. I watched her strong profile, dark hair swept round, half covering her ears. 'Nan?'

'What?'

'Did you hear me?'

She bent to push the cashbox under the worm-riddled counter. 'I may be a lot of things, Genie, but I'm not deaf.'

'I just thought you'd say something.'

Nan stood up. She looked tired. 'What d'you want me to say? That she's a fool? That she's throwing away a perfectly good marriage? Your father may not be a Rudolph Valentino if that's what she was after, but 'e's been a good husband to her. 'E's a worker. 'E's never laid a finger on 'er and 'e's looked after you and seen you all right. What more does she want?' She passed a hand back over her forehead. 'I don't know.'

She let herself through into the house at the back. I heard her moving the kettle on the range and wondered where it was Nanny Rawson kept her feelings about all the horrible things that happened. She must have had a hump hidden somewhere where she could store and absorb them like a camel.

I followed her through. 'Mom's bound to ask what you said.'

Nan didn't even turn to look at me. 'No point in me

193

killing the messenger is there? Tell 'er she knows where 'er family are. We ain't going nowhere.'

'Is there any news, love?'

Vera had run up to Nan's shop in a pair of battered old slippers for a packet of fags.

'I didn't know you smoked.'

'I do today.' She bought matches too and lit up straight away.

'The last letter we had was all wiggly,' I told her. 'He said he was writing in the wireless truck while they were moving along. Said he'd seen German planes dropping bombs and a great big crater where they'd blown up a farmhouse.'

Vera grimaced. I wasn't sure if it was at what I'd said or the cigarette. 'I bet your mom's worried ain't she, poor thing? If there's anything I can do to help . . .?'

'Ta.' I couldn't think of anything at all I could say about Mom's state of mind at that moment. When Dad's letter came she cried and cried.

'Poor Victor. My poor Victor.' Tears of remorse. She'd almost forgotten he existed over the past months and now she could see he wasn't so bad after all.

I changed the subject quickly. 'Mr Spini any better?'

'He's awright – it's taking time.' Vera shrugged. 'Teresa's the one who's trouble – always wanting to be somewhere else away from us. She doesn't do as she's told and she makes Micky furious.' Vera was starting to wave her arms. 'We don't know what she's getting up to. She won't listen to us. She and Micky had a set-to the other night because he tried to make her stay in and she disobeyed him. If he was in better health she'd've more than felt his hand across her.' She sighed heavily.

'As if there ain't enough to worry about. What she needs is to find a Catholic boy like her – one of the lads from St Michael's. Mixed marriages only cause trouble.'

'Oh, I'm sure she's not thinking of getting married!' I laughed. Vera's mind always ran on to the worst possible. Teresa marrying a Protestant!

She smiled suddenly, sheepish. 'You think I'm stupid. But she don't tell us what she's doing or where she is. It's not right. I wish she could be more grown up and sensible like you, Genie. D'you think you could have a word with her?'

Mom was managing to pull herself together by dinner-time these days, have a bit to eat and get to work.

'The babby won't show for a bit yet, so I'm not going to get asked any awkward questions. If I don't get out I'll only sit here feeling sorry for myself.' This came as a bit of a surprise to me because I'd thought that was exactly what she would do. What with Bob taking off and his bun in the oven I thought she'd be about ready for the canal herself. But after a few days of pure misery while she mourned her rejection by PC Bob and leaned on me as if I was an iron doorstop, she became almost cheerful. I was baffled. She started going on about my dad.

'I've never given Victor enough credit for what he's given all of us,' she said one evening. 'He's been a good husband and father – not like some. And he's given me you and Eric. It's time I acted like a proper wife to him.'

I was so relieved she wasn't in the depths of despair at this point that I didn't think to ask her what she imagined Dad was going to say when he came home to find this little cuckoo in the nest. Surely she wasn't going to con him again with one of her record pregnancies?

Lil, who'd already had her say in no uncertain terms, came to the conclusion that that was exactly what she was going to do. 'He was here December,' she said in her sarky voice. 'And the babby's due about next December. So it'll be a good three months shorter than the first time, any rate. Poor old Victor, he must love her, God help 'im.'

'Well don't you go interfering,' Nanny Rawson told her. 'We've enough trouble already without you letting fresh air in your gob out of place.'

In the meantime, I got myself a new job. Nanny was recovered, barring a stiff knee. 'You want to get out and earn yourself some more wages,' she said. 'I'm all right 'ere now.'

Lewis Broadbent's foundry was an old family firm with a good reputation in the back streets of Highgate. In peacetime they made brass plumbers' ware – taps and sink bases, washers and screws, but for the war effort the firm had gone over to making caps for shells and petrol cans, and other small parts.

A middle-aged woman called Doris with jet-black hair and watery brown eyes showed me round the factory, which was hot from the furnaces where they heated the brass, and noisy with the clank of metal and the chunking of the pressing machines.

I was taken on in the warehouse at the back as a checker. It was a wide, not very well lit area with rows of women working at long tables. Doris slotted me into a work place at the end of a table and showed me how to look over the parts, searching them for mistakes or rough bits.

'See this one—' She showed me the inside of a petrol cap. 'The thread's not taken properly. You'd never be able to screw that up.'

After checking, we had to wrap the parts in tissue paper and a layer of brown paper and string and pack them in tea chests to go to other factories needing the parts.

It kept me busy enough, that did. We were all working flat out and quite honestly it was nice to get away from my family for a bit. I began to see Teresa's point. Out in the warehouse I was almost the babby of the place. There was just one other girl anywhere near my age, a year older, very pert, called Nancy. She had little freckles on her nose and auburn eyebrows plucked to a thin line. The other women were mom's age and older. They treated me very well and looked after me in a motherly way. In between chat about the job I learned about their families, those with good husbands and bad, those with none at all, who was in a reserved occupation, who'd signed up, and about their children, mothers-in-law, landlords. And about the Broadbent family who owned the factory. Everyone seemed agreed that Lewis Broadbent was second only to God, that his wife Betty was a scheming hypochondriac, his two daughters no better than they ought to be and his son, who was in the RAF, had the sun shining out of various bits of his anatomy. Nancy went silly at the very mention of Joe Broadbent's name.

''E's all set to take over the factory when this lot's over,' one of the women said, waving her hand over the petrol caps as if they were the war itself.

''E's got no airs and graces though, Joe, has 'e? Comes in and knuckles down to any job 'e's given. Knows how the place works backwards.'

'You'd hardly believe 'e was related to the two sisters, would you?' Nancy said bitchily.

'Ooh, she's got her eye on 'im all right,' someone teased and Nancy looked round coyly.

'Just hope they look after 'im in the airforce . . .'

The talk turned, and then one of them said to me, 'You got yourself a nice fella, 'ave you, Genie?'

I shook my head, not looking up.

'Go on – why not?'

'Don't tease her – she's only young yet,' a voice said.

I thought with a pang of Jimmy, and of Walt. I'd messed up my chances good and proper with both of them. Oh well, I thought, giving a shrug inside myself. So what. Who cared anyway?

When it came to Dunkirk it was everyone's news, everyone's war suddenly, and for those last days of May no one could talk or think of anything else. Gloria was on for every news bulletin whenever anyone was in. Mom, still sick, was in a shocking state.

One evening when it was all going on, Auntie Lil turned up. She came to bury the hatchet and not, for once, in the back of Mom's head.

'You still bad, Dor?' she asked, sweet as jam.

Mom was sitting writing to Eric, and Lil's sympathy sent her all weepy. 'I've not been into work I feel that terrible.' Her appearance had gone all to pieces. She was gaunt, her skin the colour of porridge.

'Come on now,' Lil said. 'Genie and I'll help you, won't we love?' She pushed Mom back down into a chair. 'You need some company – get Stella over for a chat.'

'She don't care. Never seen her for dust – some friend that one,' Mom said despondently.

'Never mind. You just stay there and we'll see to everything.'

'I thought you hated me!' Mom sobbed.

'What's done can't be undone,' Lil said. 'Here – I brought you a bottle of stout for later. Buck you up.'

Lil was a busy sort. Spun round the place doing housework as if it was a race. She'd always been like that. Patsy and Tom, who'd come down with her, were out in the garden playing in the evening sun. Before I could blink hardly, Lil had brewed up tea, dusted and tidied downstairs, rinsed and hung out a bucket full of washing and was all for setting in on the cooking.

I watched her as I worked on carrots and parsnips for our tea, her sleek body bending and straightening in the garden as she pegged out, shouting to the boys now and then. Her life had been the same for so long, I thought, and wondered if it'd ever be any different for her, for any of us.

'How is Eric?' she called to Mom as she came in with the empty washpail.

'He's all right.' We could hear the emotion in Mom's voice. She was never more than a breath away from tears these days. They seeped up into her eyes at the mention of all sorts of things: Dad, Eric, the babby, the war, going to work, sometimes even the thought of getting up in the morning. 'He doesn't write much. That Mrs Spenser's got her claws into him – Victor said when he took Eric down there she had ever such a nice house and she nearly jumped on Eric as if he was her own.' She gave a little wail. 'It's not right. I feel as if I've lost him.'

Lil pulled a grim face at me and went in to her. 'Never mind,' she soothed. 'You know he's safe, and at least he's happy where he is. You've no worries on that score.'

'But he shouldn't be happy – he doesn't belong there. You wouldn't send yours off, would you?'

I took them another cup of tea, then retreated into the kitchen. Patsy and Tom were playing down round the Anderson which was now sprouted over with dandelions. Some had already gone to seed and the boys were blowing dandelion clocks. I had a peculiar feeling for a minute which was so strange it took me a while to work out what it was. I was happy. Just for a little flash of time. Seeing the boys there looking carefree like kids should be in the last of the sunshine on these calm, clearcut days of spring, and Auntie Lil here and people being nice to one another.

But then I heard Lil say, 'What are you going to do, sis?' and the little spark of harmony which lit those few seconds was snuffed out because Mom was crying again and trying to speak and Lil was saying, 'Ssh . . . ssh . . . there.'

'I've been so bad,' Mom was pouring out to her. 'Such a fool. But I loved him. Really loved him, and I've never had it before like that, you know . . . But he never loved me. Not really, properly. It was all a lie . . .'

'Yes.' Lil's voice was desolate. She knew only too well what it was to be left alone. 'He was using you, sis.'

'I want to get back to what we had – me and Victor. I mean it wasn't all I've ever wanted but it was good enough. If I lose that I'll have nothing.'

'But Doreen, the babby. It's not just going to go away.'

I held still in the kitchen listening.

'No, but . . .' I heard her hesitate. 'He might be away ages and the babby'll be born in seven months. I could hand it over. There's people would take it off me – adopt it. And he'd never know. Nothing would have changed then, would it?'

'Doreen!' Lil was dreadfully shocked. 'You can't go on like that, deceiving him. He's your husband!'

'But what else can I do?'

'The truth'll find you out, Dor. The neighbours aren't blind and deaf, are they? Some bloody busybody's bound to say summat even if it ain't out of spite – although the chances are it will be. What about Gladys and Molly for a start? They've not enough sense between them to keep their mouths shut. You're just going to have to tell him the truth.'

'No. Oh no, I couldn't do that!'

I pictured Dad's face if he knew, the twisted hurt in it, and she must've seen it the same way.

We heard Len at the door then and they had to stop talking.

'Awright Len?' Lil said. 'Been at it since the crack of dawn, have you?'

I heard Len making pleased-sounding noises. Then a click and Gloria was on. There was news due. 'Ssssh,' everyone said.

The Germans had reached the Channel coast. The British Expeditionary Force as well as Belgian and French troops were surrounded in a small pocket of ground inland from Dunkirk.

The days as we waited were so beautiful. So lovely it hurt. It looked all wrong for disaster and dread and knowing great calamities were happening somewhere far away. By 24 May the BEF was completely cut off. Those of us who had people there could think of nothing else. What was happening to my father? Were they safe? What was going to happen next? Even for those who could look at the thing less personally, the fact was, the Germans were only twenty or so miles away from the south coast, looking at us across a tiny vein of water.

Over that weekend, when they began the evacuation of Dunkirk, the skies were clear and lovely and people watered their vegetable patches and sunned themselves in the park, wore cotton frocks and held cricket matches. That was the oddest part of the whole thing, trying to hold together in your mind that these things were happening in the same world.

The nights were horrible, broken, patched with bad dreams, and waking it hit you, thoughts coming in a rush – 'Oh God, oh no!' – like black water filling a drain.

On the Monday the Belgians capitulated. They were bringing troops out of France by the thousand every day. Mom was in such a state of agitation she scarcely knew where to put herself. She managed to carry on working most days, which helped keep her mind occupied. But at home she paced the floor, couldn't keep still.

'I feel as if I'm going mad,' she cried. 'I wish they'd get it all over with. This waiting's worse than anything.'

She'd got all the options worked out by now with the clear-cut selfishness of a true survivor.

'If he gets killed I'm going to be a widow on my own. And if he comes back he's going to find out about the babby and everything'll be ruined anyway. He can't come home now. He just can't!'

June 1940

There was no other conversation in those days. Nothing else on anyone's lips. Walking home from work I'd hear the muffled sounds of wireless sets through open windows. The women at the factory were marvellous to me. 'Any news, Genie?' every day. Ever so kind. ''Ow's your mother?' People who saw Mom thought she was jumpy with sleeplessness on Dad's behalf, desperate for him back. I couldn't tell them it wasn't quite like that.

I loved being at work, away from her. She wasn't feeling well still, wasn't sleeping. 'What if Victor comes back? What if he doesn't?' I found it a strain being with her when I was in a state of nervous exhaustion myself. I felt sick almost all the time.

We all sweated it out. The weather was boiling. Every day Mom shrunk a bit thinner. She carried on confiding in Lil and I'd never seen them so close. As for Len, we barely saw him. When he wasn't at the Austin he was off somewhere with Molly. Nanny Rawson was a pillar of strength as ever.

'Come over to ours and have a sing-song,' she insisted to Mom. 'Take your mind off it.'

'Oh no, I couldn't,' Mom said. 'Not singing. Not now.'

'You should,' Nan said. 'Works wonders for you.' She and Lil still played in some of the pubs round and about.

I went anyway, and sat singing with Nan and Lil on an evening that felt like the middle of summer with the door open so some of the neighbours stood round in the yard and chimed in with us. And Nanny was right, a bit of 'Knees up Mother Brown' and other old favourites did take your mind elsewhere for a bit.

But we were still being swept along with the fleets of Dunkirk. All the little vessels, fishing smacks, tramps, paddle steamers, shrimpers and tugs that had gone to support the naval ships and channel steamers to get the boys home. It made you nearly boil with pride inside. Made defeat seem like victory, although really now we were right up against it and we knew it clear as anything. But all I wanted to know then was, are they bringing my dad? I was praying all the time, 'Please God, please . . .'

They started trickling home. Gloria told us how in the Kent gardens along the railway, people stood waving them back. By 4 June the evacuation was over. They'd done all they could and the Germans were getting too close. No more ships were going.

When the men started coming in from the coast, there were heroic stories about their welcome, the programmes of washing and feeding and entertaining them all. We heard of arrivals in Birmingham. We waited and waited, Mom like someone preparing to be fired from a cannon.

'Mom asked if there's anything you need?' Teresa said when she appeared on our doorstep.

It was my mom's day off from work and she was slouched in an old dress with a pinner over the top and her hair all over the place. Teresa looked really taken aback at the sight of her, and seeing Teresa, Mom straightened up and tried to pull herself together. 'Nothing you can do,' she said. 'Waiting's the only thing – ta.'

Teresa, in contrast to Mom, was looking lovely. The sun had only to come out for her skin to light up brown and the days had been tropical. She had on a bright yellow dress with big orange flowers dotted across it and her black hair was hanging loose.

'You look nice,' Mom told her. 'Haven't seen you in ages.' She had to pretend with Teresa. It seemed to do her good, having to act like the pining, faithful wife. 'Sorry I'm such a mess. Got other things on my mind.'

'You must be ever so worried, Mrs Watkins,' Teresa said, sitting down opposite her, dark eyes full of concern.

'Oh I am,' Mom was saying demurely. 'But we're still hoping. There's more coming back all the time.'

She was being a model Person Taking It Well. 'How's your job?' she asked Teresa.

'Boring. Wouldn't mind a change to tell you the truth. Stevie says it serves me right.'

Stevie would, I thought.

Teresa told us about some of the antics they got up to to liven the place up. Her voice rang round our house. Must've shocked the walls. They weren't used to happy sounds.

'Hope you don't mind me having a laugh, Mrs Watkins,' Teresa said.

'No, you go on,' Mom urged. 'Good for us to hear you.'

When Len came back he joined in at the sound of her. Said that after tea he was going out with Molly.

Teresa being there kept Mom together all evening.

We ate boiled beef and spring cabbage – 'Hope you don't mind our sort of cooking,' Mom said – listened to Gloria's music and news bulletins and talked and joked. Teresa even made Mom laugh with her infectious energy. After dark, Len came in looking pleased with himself. Mom gave me a look full of meaning and I tried to ignore her.

'Where've you been, Lenny?' she asked him.

'Out,' was all she got in reply, while he twiddled Gloria's knobs as he had no doubt just been twiddling Molly's.

Teresa ended up staying over. 'Mom'll know where I am.' It was like the old days, before Lola, when she used to come and sleep the night, weekends sometimes, when there was no school the next morning. The more we'd been together that night the more I felt we could be close again. She hadn't even mentioned blokes all evening. But there was this great lie and pretence going on in front of her and it made me really uncomfortable.

She bunked up with me on the bed in my room. It took her ages to get ready. I lay down in my thin white nightdress, watching her. She peeled off the sunny yellow dress and laid it over the chair. Underneath she had on a cotton petticoat, old but still surprisingly white, or it seemed so in the candlelight, and her skin looked dark against it. She stood facing me, using my hairbursh to brush her hair forward, first over one shoulder, then the other, then holding it up luxuriously with two hands and letting it fall down her back, bosoms lifting as she raised her arms. Her body tapered down to narrow hips. She smiled at me, eyes dotted with little candles, and laughed her chesty laugh. She's beautiful, I thought. Not pretty, but beautiful.

206

'Haven't done this for a long time, have we?'

I shook my head, shy of her suddenly. She looked so grown up.

'Hope I'll fit in.'

'You will. You're nothing like the size of Lola. Here—' I pulled the covers back.

She half lay in bed, leaning over on one elbow to blow out the candle on the chair beside her, hair falling forward. It was very dark then, with the windows blacked out. I couldn't even see her outline, only feel the warmth of her next to me. I smiled in the dark.

'I feel like a little kid again,' she said.

'Just what I was thinking.'

I wouldn't want to be though, would you? A kid I mean. Not for anything.'

I was still wondering about this when she said, 'Sorry I behaved like such an idiot over Jack.'

'And Clem.'

'All right. And Clem then.'

'S'all right.'

'Genie? What about Walt – d'you still like him?'

'Haven't seen him.'

'But if you did?'

'No.'

'Never mind, there'll be someone.'

I thought about Jimmy, his body pushing down on mine. The tea hadn't all come out of my dress and Mom had been livid.

'I don't think I care all that much.'

'We just haven't met anyone good enough for us.'

'That must be it. Anyway, there's always us. Pals?'

'Pals.' After a moment she said, 'Your mom's being ever so brave. If it was my dad away I can't imagine how Mom'd cope. Or me.'

'It's a case of having to.'

'Course. All the same, I think you lot are tougher than us. All too emotional, Italians.'

I couldn't lie to her any more, not being there so close to her. And I wanted to stop feeling so alone. But my heart was pounding so hard at the thought of bringing it all out that I couldn't speak and I was shaking.

'What's up with you?' Teresa said.

'I want to tell you summat . . .' Then I was crying so much I couldn't get it out.

Teresa turned on her side and wrapped her arms round me and I hugged her back, feeling her full chest against my skinny body. She felt lovely. She kissed my cheek and I kissed her too.

'Go on – you can tell Teresa. What's got you worked up into this state all of a sudden?'

'It's Mom. None of it's how it looks. She doesn't really want my dad back because she's having a babby and it's not his.' I told her all about it then, spilt it out, about Bob coming to our house in the winter and how he took to his heels as soon as he knew she was expecting. 'Mom's scared about my dad coming home and him finding out. She's been in a state for ages . . .'

'I'm not surprised,' Teresa said. 'Oh my God, Genie, that's terrible. Your poor, poor dad.'

'Promise you won't say anything to anyone,' I begged her. 'I shouldn't be telling you really, only I couldn't help it. You won't, will you?'

'Of course not. On my life.'

She let me cry myself out and eventually we settled down to sleep, with her curled round behind my back. She felt warm and comforting and she wasn't bossing me, wasn't after anything like Jimmy. Lying there with her was the best, warmest feeling I'd had in a long time.

I was at work the morning Mom saw a man in army uniform move into view in front of our window, then stop, looking up at the house. Her legs turned to jelly. She was sure at once it was Dad. 'Even though I could see it wasn't,' she said later. 'I couldn't move. I was convinced it was him. I mean who else would it be? But he was the wrong height and everything.'

Another person stepped into the picture, a neighbour, who spoke to the man, who then came to our front door. Mom opened it, shaking. She saw a face with thick black eyebrows and a grubby khaki uniform.

'Are you Doreen Watkins?' To her nodding he announced, 'My name's Dickie Carter. Army pal of your 'usband's.'

Mom asked him in, gibbering questions. She made tea and sandwiches.

'Didn't know if I'd find him 'ere,' Dickie said. 'We promised each other, whoever got home first, we'd go and see each other's missis and let 'em know.' He ate the bread ravenously. 'I ain't got back over to my missis yet but I sent a message, and she knows I'm on my way.'

'So – Victor's coming home?' Mom asked. Dickie must have seen a white, stricken face in front of him.

He nodded, chewing away. 'Last time I saw 'im 'e was about a mile from the beach. Not far at all. But see, it was chaos at the time – pandemonium. All sorts of stuff blocking the road, lorries and that, things going off all round us . . .' Dickie carefully didn't give us all the details he might have done about the bodies of men and horses in the road. We heard about that later. 'Any rate, I never saw 'im after that. Thing was though, we was so close. We 'ad to walk a couple of miles along the beach. Bloody 'ard going across that soft sand and we was all in after the miles we'd come already. There were lines of blokes everywhere so it'd have been easy to miss 'im. Somehow we never caught up with each other again. I reckon 'e'd've got to a boat though. Not much doubt about it. There was all sorts of stuff coming in to get us out.'

'You haven't see him though – over here?'

'No, I ain't, but that don't mean 'e's not 'ere. There's blokes being sent about all over the place. I came through Reading but 'e could've gone anywhere else. But I reckon 'e'll be back.'

When he'd eaten and drunk as much as was on offer, Dickie set off to go back to his missis. 'Don't you worry, Mrs Watkins,' he told Mom. ''E'll turn up sooner or later.'

'I don't understand it, Genie,' Mom said to me. 'If he was back over here, he'd've got a message to us, wouldn't he? Or written a letter. He was always writing letters.'

She was like a Jumping Jack. The slightest sound and she was at the front door to see if it was him coming. There was nothing could be done to set her mind at rest. She didn't turn up for work again and they were already getting browned off with her being so irregular. She was a bag of nerves. Seeing Dickie, a real live returner from Dunkirk, she was now convinced Dad must be on his way.

When I got home from Broadbent's and heard the news I was excited. I wanted my dad home, whatever mess Mom had got herself in. I wanted him fair and square. By the time I got in she'd obviously been at the port bottle and wasn't quite steady on her feet.

'I can't stand this waiting,' she said. Her cheeks were an unnatural, shiny pink.

'Let's go to Nan's.' I couldn't cope with her here on my own all evening.

'What if he comes back when we're out?'

'He'll guess where we are. It's got to be better than just sitting here.'

On the way she insisted on calling in at the Outdoor for ale. 'Mom and Lil'd like a drink I s'pect,' she said.

Nanny Rawson and Lil were all agog hearing about the appearance of Dickie Carter. Another Dunkirk survivor had come home to Belgrave Road, everyone crowding round to hear the tale he had to tell, and we were still waiting for our family hero. Mom had to repeat the details at least three times.

'Is Uncle Victor coming home then?' Tom asked.

'We hope so,' I said.

Mom was already the worse for drink by the time we got there and she kept on tipping it back as the evening wore on. Nanny Rawson was full of an indignant tale about an unusual customer she'd had in the shop that day. She sat with her stocky legs stretched out, leaning down to rub her injured knee as she spoke.

'She stopped outside in a great big car. Come in 'ere with five pound wanting to buy up all the sugar. Told me she came from Henley-in-Arden if you please.' Nan laughed. 'Voice like a glass chandelier.'

'D'you give it to her?' Lil asked.

'Hadn't a lot to give her. But she was prepared to pay well over the odds.' Nan shook her head, laughing suddenly. 'She was wearing a fox fur stole. Beautiful it

211

was. Must have wondered where the 'ell she'd found herself when she came in 'ere.'

'The nerve though,' Lil said. 'They think they can just buy anything, some of 'em.'

Mom was knocking back the beer and Len was eyeing up Nanny's little wireless set. 'Can we 'ave it on?' he said hopefully. It may not've been Gloria, but in his eyes it was better than nothing.

'No,' Nan said. 'We'll make our own music tonight. Lil and I did a spot down at the Eagle last night and it cheered us up no end. Run up and get my squeeze box, Patsy. Otherwise we'll forget how to do it.'

Patsy clomped up the bare wood of the stairs in his heavy Mail charity boots and hairy socks to Nan's bedroom where she kept the squeeze box. We all sat round, the house seeming almost spacious now there were no Flanagans hurtling about. Tom sat close to me on the couch, Lil next to us with Cathleen asleep across her lap, looking angelic enough now her eyes were closed. Len joined in the singing with unpredictable shouts. All Nan's old favourites.

'I wish you could come and live with us, Auntie Genie,' Tom said to me. 'Here – d'you want to see my marbles? I swapped 'em with Wilf at school.'

'Go on then.'

Tom showed me five scratched marbles. He was pleased as anything. 'He collects cards so I give him the ones I had off Auntie Doreen.'

Mom gave her cigarette cards to Tom now Eric wasn't here. Mrs Spenser was paying for Eric to have piano lessons. He lived in another world.

I cuddled Tom to me as Nan's fingers leapt across the keys of her squeeze box, oom-pa-pa, oom-pa-pa.

Mom got up, said she was going to the lav. Her face

212

was sickly white and she couldn't walk in a straight line. Lil was saying, 'Steady on, Dor. How much've you had tonight?'

She got as far as the door and leaned up against it, faint, saying, 'You'd better get me a bucket,' but it was too late and she was bent over pouring her guts up into the yard, making little moaning sounds in between.

Lil and Nan got her inside and sat her on the couch with a bowl.

'Len!' Nanny ordered. 'Get a bucket of water and wash down the yard.'

'What's the matter with Auntie Doreen?' Tom asked me, and at the same time Lil was on at me saying, 'How much did she have before you came out?'

'I dunno exactly,' I said. 'She had a bit of port I think.'

'More than a bit by the looks of it.' Mom was lying back on the couch now, head lolling.

'I'll make her a cuppa tea,' Nan said. 'The state she's in I don't know as you'll get her home tonight.' She went over and put the kettle on the heat. We could hear Len sloshing water about outside.

Clarys' face appeared round the door. 'Everything awright, is it Edith? Only I saw Doreen looking ever so poorly.'

Lil marched over to the door. 'Everything's tickety-boo, ta, and if it wasn't, you poking your nose in wouldn't make it any better, would it, so why don't you just go in and get on with your knitting?'

Clarys retreated in a huff.

'No call to be so rude,' Nan said, spooning tea. 'We've still got to live with her tomorrow.'

'Nosy bitch,' Lil was muttering.

Len came back in and switched the wireless on as if

to say he deserved it after that charming job. Music streamed out. Glenn Miller, 'In the Mood'. Mom was asleep, snoring. I was ashamed of her.

'She been bad again this week?' Nanny asked me.

I nodded.

'She's bound to be, what with the babby and the worry,' Lil said. 'And if Victor's coming home any minute . . .'

'She's not going to be able to keep it in the family much longer,' Nan said, advancing on Mom with a cup of black tea. 'She always shows early.'

'Let her sleep it off,' Lil suggested. 'She can stay here.'

'She needs summat on her stomach.'

I felt frightened watching my nan sit Mom up, saw her flop as if she was dead, head rolling forwards, unable to open her eyes.

'Give us a hand.'

Lil went over as well. Patsy, Tom and I stood watching, the other side of the table. Lil held Mom's head as Nanny tried to force some of the tea down her. She spluttered and dribbled and murmured, 'Hot.' Eventually, after tipping tea into the saucer and back a few times, they got her to drink some before she subsided back on to the couch. She looked terrible. I felt tears come into my eyes. My life felt like a mirror that had been shattered. I just wanted my dad to come back and make everything all right.

No sign of him. It was a terrible week. The women at Broadbent's tutted round me, and about me.

No one spoke the worst but I knew they were

thinking it. If he's not home by now he must be dead. Surely. It couldn't have taken this long?

At home the strain of living with Mom took its toll. She was falling to pieces and I wasn't far from it myself.

'It's not knowing,' she sobbed one evening. 'I just can't stand not knowing whether he's alive or dead. I just want to get it over with one way or the other. But they'd tell me if he was dead, wouldn't they? There'd be a letter or a telegraph.'

I still clung to my hope that he was alive, maybe in hospital.

She couldn't get through the days without drinking. She still managed to get to work – slept it off in the morning. But as soon as she was home she'd go straight to it. She started on what she had in the house – that bottle of port. But it wasn't long before that was gone and she had to buy more, gin this time, downing it quick, with tears, not pleasure. But at least she was still drinking it nicely then, out of a glass. She'd say, 'Oh – that's better,' and plonk herself down, half gone with drink and tiredness, and just sit there until it was time for bed.

It was a lonely life, even with the kindness of the women at work, of the Spinis. Len was barely ever in in the evenings now, either because of work or Molly. He'd slope in and have his meal, and on these warm, sultry evenings he and Molly took off until after dark. Never said where. They must have gone and walked in the parks, gas masks and all. I found myself missing Len's presence even though it was a relief not having him and Molly in the house together.

I was left with Gloria for company. *Hi Gang! Garrison Theatre*, *Band Waggon*. Without them I might have gone off my head in those days when part of my mind was always listening for a bang at the front door, for Dad's voice in the hall.

But it didn't come. Still didn't come.

A few little notices started to appear in the *Birmingham Mail*. They tore at your heart. Did anyone have information about . . . ? Know the whereabouts of . . . ? People's sons, brothers, husbands, who had not, as hoped, walked in off a train from the coast and Dunkirk. Mom put one in. It was peculiar seeing his name, Victor James Watkins, in the paper like that. As if he was just another name, nothing to do with us.

While we were waiting, a whole new lot of trouble broke out. On 10 June, Italy declared war on Hitler's side and suddenly no one was supposed to like Italians any more. The papers had already stirred that one up, as Micky had shown me. Now the headlines were screaming, 'INTERN THE LOT!'

I went straight to see them that evening. The house was full of people, the older ones sitting on the available chairs, the others all standing round. Vera's family, except for her mom, two other elderly men, a woman with thick black hair swept back in a bun, her arm round Vera's shoulder, and some younger men including Fausto Pirelli. All the talk was in Italian. Bottles of Micky's wine and tumblers stood on the table.

'You all right, Genie?' Teresa asked.

I nodded.

Vera took my hand for a moment and squeezed it. Her face looked strained. 'Any news?'

The other woman was watching me, her dark face serious. 'Her father's missing in France,' Vera told her.

The woman tutted, shaking her head. 'A terrible thing – I 'ope you have better news soon, darlin'. Don't lose 'ope. You must always have 'ope.'

It was hot and airless in the room. Normally they'd have kept the door open but that night it was closed, maybe because they felt safer that way. The air was full of cigarette smoke and loud talk. Stevie was over by Micky looking solemn and grown up. Teresa and I stood by the door.

'Should I go?' I whispered to her.

'No, course not. You're all right.' She put her mouth closer to my ear. 'They're worried. They think people will be arrested.'

'But there's no one here who'd do any harm, surely?'

She shrugged. 'Even today at work someone made a nasty remark about my name. I suppose I'm Italian now whether I like it or not.' She sounded bewildered more than upset.

Suddenly Fausto leaned over the table, raising one of the thick glasses half full of red wine. His sharp-featured face looked quite bonkers, I thought, eyes blazing with fanaticism and the effects of the drink. The men round him, Micky included, all started shouting at him at once, telling him, so far as I could make out, to shut up.

But Fausto wasn't going to shut up. He lifted the glass even higher, slopping some of the wine on the head of a bloke sitting next to him. '*Viva l'Italia!*' he shouted. '*Viva il Duce!*'

Two of the younger men, one an uncle of Teresa's, moved in and took Fausto by the shoulders, forcing him towards the door.

'What did he say?' I hissed at Teresa.

'Long live Mussolini,' she said without turning her head, too busy watching what was going on. 'Dad's not going to have that. Fausto's such a bloody idiot. Doesn't spare a thought for anyone else.'

Micky pushed his chair back and stood up. He talked so well with his hands that I didn't need to understand the rest. Get him out of my house. Out. Now. D'you want to get us all arrested?

Fausto was led out of the house by two of the men. As they stumbled past the window we could see his mouth was still going.

That night, Teresa told me, there was a loud hammering on the Spinis' door. Micky went down, pulling on his trousers. The rest of them listened, frightened, at the top of the stairs.

'Micky?' It was a neighbour. ''Fraid you got some trouble out the front, mate. Someone's broke your windows.'

They all went out, except Giovanna and Luke who stayed asleep, and stood in the street in their night-clothes staring at the shattered front window of the shop, the big hole in the glass with jagged splinters round it. Stevie was cursing, Francesca crying. Vera stood with her hands on Tony's shoulders in silence.

'We should have stayed in the Quarter,' she said, shaking. 'Then at least we'd all have been together.'

Micky didn't say much, just kept running his hand through his hair.

'It might have been someone trying to break in?' Teresa suggested. 'Or kids?'

'No. We know why it is.' Micky's voice was quiet, but angry. 'I don't know what to think. I suppose we get it glazed again tomorrow. But maybe now this is going to happen every night? We're in the wrong camp, even if we have spent most of our lives here. We're the enemy all of a sudden.'

There were to be no more church bells. No more of the usual pattern of chimes across the Sunday city. Only if we were invaded. That was to be the warning.

The Germans were closing in round Paris. It was over a week now since the evacuation of Dunkirk ended and we hadn't heard anything. Our newspaper clipping about Dad was starting to go yellow at the edges.

Mom was having to wear her loosest clothes already, though she could still easily get by as not being pregnant. But being a skinny woman she did show early. She put her hand to her stomach a lot. Her face was permanently sullen and sulky as if life had cheated her. Of everything.

The day after Italy declared war, she went out into the garden in the evening. She'd only had one glass of port so far. That performance at Nanny Rawson's had brought her up a bit sharp. 'I'll have to watch myself.' I went out and found Mom staring at the sky, the last bronze light on 'our' barrage balloon. From inside we could hear Gloria playing 'When You Wish upon a Star'. Mom was standing sideways on to me and I thought I could see the little bulge of the baby growing inside her.

'Victor's dead.'

I didn't say anything. I didn't want to hear those words.

'He's dead. I know he is.' She whipped round. 'Genie – whatever am I going to do?'

We stood there, both in agony, but not touching each

219

other. I wanted my dad so badly, wanted the solid, sensible bit of our family. Mom blew about like a feather and I couldn't trust or rely on her. Everything was breaking up. No Dad, no Eric, and now she was going to bring a babby into the house whose father I could murder with a smile.

'At least he'll never know,' she said, all wrapped up in herself as usual. 'He'll've died thinking I was a good wife to him. I can keep Bob's babby.' Then, voice going high, she went on, 'But how on earth am I going to manage? We'll have no money, and another babby and no man to look after us . . .' That old bogeyman poverty, the cold, aching, eking-out struggle she remembered from her childhood, leered up over her shoulder.

'You've got me, Mom. I can earn money now, don't forget. And Lenny.'

She squatted down on the grass suddenly, hands over her eyes, head bent. 'I've messed up everything, Genie. Every single thing I've ever done I've made a mess of it.'

'Mom . . .'

She didn't look up.

'He might not be dead . . .' I still hoped that, prayed it. Until we had some sign or letter we'd never properly believe it.

She got up suddenly without another word and went into the house as if someone had called. They had. The gin bottle.

On the Wednesday that week, in the evening, the police moved into Park Street, Bartholomew Street and the others which made up Birmingham's Little Italy, arresting a man from every house and carting them off to the police station. Among them was Vera's elder brother, Teresa's uncle Matt Scattoli.

'They thought it was a bit of a joke at first,' Teresa told me. 'Some of the lads anyway. A group of 'em went down there all full of themselves and the police said if they didn't get off home they'd arrest them as well.'

'Have they let them go now?' I asked.

'Oh no. No one knows what's happening. They haven't got themselves sorted out.'

'Well what about your dad?'

'God knows. They haven't come down our way. He's in the Fire Service, Mom keeps saying. What would they want to arrest him for?'

The Germans moved into Paris and the French surrendered. The newsreader's voice was very sombre, seeming to come out of a big echoing silence behind him. After the news they played trumpets.

The heat and breathless calm made the atmosphere electric. Waiting. Rumours all the time. They've landed on the coast at Margate! No – they hadn't. Planes overhead! They were ours. Leaflets came fluttering through our doors again, 'Don't give the invader anything'. Strangers were remarked on, even invented. Previously normal behaviour seemed suspect and all sorts of tales spread based on hearsay. They might parachute in dressed as nuns. Look out for hairy-knuckled nuns!

Even the newsreaders started telling you who they were. 'This is the — o'clock news, and this is Frank Phillips [or Stuart Hibbard or Alvar Liddell] reading it.'

The rumour-mongering reached such a pitch that the government released a whole collection of posters to try and keep us quiet: 'Careless Talk Costs Lives'. This was our turn now. Us. We were next in line now the French had gone. Would we have Germans marching down our street, kicking down our door with their jackboots?

Lil said, once France had fallen, 'Well at least we know what we're up against now.'

But we didn't. Not really. That was the trouble, and our imaginations were on fire.

'Have some dinner with us, Genie – there's enough,' Vera said.

It was Sunday and the Spinis were all squeezed round the table as usual, except for Stevie who was out with the ice-cream cart. Mom was at work, trying to redeem herself by turning up regularly, and so was Len, so I'd come looking for company.

The door to the yard was open and it was quiet, everyone in having dinner. I could see the tap across the way, shining drops falling fast into the blocked drain. The Spinis' yard always stank of drains.

Micky Spini seemed relaxed enough, his health improving by inches. He sat at the table in his shirt-sleeves, in one of his quiet moods, just staring ahead at the table as if he had things on his mind. He smiled at me though, when I came in. Vera had cooked beef, pink in the middle, liver-coloured at the edges, and there were potatoes and peas. It was nice to be in a proper family again with a dad, and a mom who could see further than the bottom of a glass.

'Sorry to hear about your windows,' I said to Micky. 'You had any more trouble?'

He shook his head. 'Not so far.' They kept talking about Uncle Matt and the others still held by the police. Everyone was edgy.

'No news, Genie?' Vera said to me as usual.

'Mom doesn't think he's coming back. He'd've come by now if he was coming, wouldn't he?'

Vera stared at me wide-eyed and tried to make comforting noises but I could see she'd been thinking the same. What else was there to think?

'What about Eric?'

'He still writes. Sometimes. Seems to like it down there. His handwriting's come on a treat.' I sniffed and Teresa reached across and squeezed my hand. 'Can't see him wanting to come home after all she's done for him down there.'

'Course he will!' Vera said indignantly. 'Home's home. You're his family. Not Mrs Whateverhernameis down there.'

I didn't contradict her but I wasn't sure any more. About anything.

'And how's your mother bearing up?' This was always Vera's conversation. Family concerns. She knew Mom hadn't got any time for her but close family ties were what she'd been brought up on.

Teresa's eyes met mine. I couldn't tell Vera about Mom's other predicament. She was kind all right, but sins were sins and she wouldn't have had any cotter with what Mom had been up to.

She brought in ice cream flavoured with vanilla pods.

'It's made with unsalted margarine. There's nowhere near enough butter about.'

'It's not the same,' Teresa said. 'Doesn't have the creaminess.'

'No, it's OK. You're imagining it,' Micky said, sliding it over his tongue.

'I'm not. D'you think I can't tell!'

Already the argument was growing heated. Micky splayed his stubby hands, palms up. 'You put two plates side by side. You'd never be able to tell the difference.'

'I can't tell the difference,' Francesca said.

'You see?'

'She doesn't know!' Teresa was shouting by now. 'She can't tell if she's eating lemon drops or bulls' eyes. She's got no sense of taste at all!'

All the kids were tasting now, making their own comments at full volume. Personally I thought Teresa was right but decided to keep my trap shut about it.

'My tongue must be more sensitive,' Teresa said. 'It tastes of margarine. It tastes cheap.'

'Cheap!' This caused uproar. One of the Spinis' full-blast ding-dongs was just getting warmed up, Luke banging his bowl on the table since he couldn't manage anything loud enough with his mouth to enter the competition.

'What d'you think, Genie?'

'I can't remember what it used to taste like,' I was saying, when we all realized there was a shadow across the doorway. Two shadows. Men in dark suits with bowler hats. One red-faced and fat, everything about him round, even his nose, the other tall and gangly. Laurel and Hardy to a tee. But their faces weren't anything to laugh at at all. Their coming slashed into the afternoon. The shouting switched off.

Micky stood up, nervously rubbing his hands on his trousers. 'Can I help you?'

Without being invited they stepped in, and looked

round the tiny room at the ice-cream-smeared faces of the children and at the Spinis' tidy few belongings: the shelf with their remaining bits of chipped crockery that weren't on the table, the worn pieces of brocade draped over the mantel, Vera's 'photograph' of Jesus. They wore sneers on their faces. Considering how hot it was they had ever such a lot on, and the fat one's face was perspiring. It seemed a long time before anyone spoke again and it all felt bad before they'd even opened their mouths.

Eventually the fat one said, 'Are you Michele Spini?'

Micky nodded.

'I am instructed to arrest you under Regulation 18B as an enemy alien to this country.'

Vera let out a gasp and put her hand over her mouth.

'But for God's sake, I've been here eighteen years!' Micky protested. 'My wife was born here, and my children. I'm in the Fire Service.' The agitation started him coughing again.

'That's as may be. But you haven't been here *twenty* years or more, have you?' The thin man stood up very straight and recited pompously, 'We are given leave to take into custody anyone believed likely to endanger the safety of the realm.'

The two of them went to Micky and took him by the arms. 'So let's not waste any time about it, eh?'

'No!' Vera cried, standing in front of them, barring the way. 'You can't do this. It's all wrong! You've already arrested all the wrong people. My husband loves this country. He'd fight if he was the right age. You're making a mistake.'

'Vera,' Micky said quietly. 'It'll be all right. We'll get it sorted out.'

'You've been consorting with known members of the Italian *Fascio*,' the thin one said. He pronounced it '*Fasho*'. 'We have Mr Fausto Pirelli in custody already.'

I heard Teresa make an explosive noise of outrage.

'But it's Sunday today,' Vera carried on. 'You can't arrest him on a Sunday!'

'I'm afraid we can, Mrs Spini,' the fat one said. He nodded at his colleague as if they were about to set off and then said, 'Norman, we haven't searched the house.'

'Ah yes,' said the one called Norman. 'The house.'

Vera sank to a chair as they released Micky and started going through their few possessions. The fat one went and peered up the stairs.

'You ain't going up there!' Vera said. 'There's nothing there.'

'Is that so?' Next thing was his fat arse climbing up to Micky and Vera's room, feet clomping on the floor above. Vera covered her face with her hands.

The thin one was pulling drawers open and shut, and yanked one so hard that it came out and fell on the floor. The side fell off the drawer and Micky and Vera's small collection of papers slid out in a heap. Giovanna started to cry and set Luke off. Teresa picked him up and cuddled him on her lap and Giovanna ran to her mother. Tony sat staring.

'Hoi,' Micky called out. 'Watch what you're doing. What you looking for anyhow?'

'We'll know when we've found it,' the thin one called Norman said. He had squatted down and was rifling through the papers, a look of disgust on his face.

Teresa suddenly erupted from behind the table, still holding Luke in her arms.

'What the hell d'you think you're *doing*?' she bawled at him. Luke was so startled he stopped crying for a moment. 'Coming here, scaring our family, breaking things and insulting us. Who the bleeding 'ell d'you think you are?'

Micky hurriedly laid a hand on her arm. 'Teresa, be quiet. Now!' he ordered, the exertion making him cough again.

'D'you know why he's coughing like that?' The man just stared at her with a flat expression. 'He was in a fire, trying to save a factory, and his chest'll never be the same again. How many times've you done summat like that, eh? You smug bastards. He'd die for this country my dad would. And yes, we do know Fausto Pirelli – he's an ignorant jumped up little shite with a bleeding great chip on his shoulder and anything he thinks or does is nothing to do with us. So why don't you just get out of our house and leave us alone? We haven't done anything.'

The fat man appeared from the stairs. What with Teresa yelling and the kids bawling the racket was getting pretty overwhelming.

'What on earth's going on?'

Teresa turned on him. 'Satisfied now you've had a good nose round, are you?'

'Can't someone shut this wop tart up?' the fat one said and I saw the blood of fury pump into Teresa's cheeks. He jerked his head at the other policeman. 'Come on. Let's get out of here. Mr Spini—' They went and caught him by the arms again. 'You'll be coming with us.'

'No!' Teresa roared. 'No – you can't do this!' Vera watched helplessly. Teresa shoved Luke at her and went to her father, gripping his arm.

Micky's face was grey. He spoke calmly. 'Teresa, *cara*, it's a mistake. I'll go with them and get it cleared up.'

'What – like all their other mistakes?' Teresa retorted. I heard the strain of tears in her voice but she wasn't going to let herself go in front of them.

They ignored her and started to take Micky from the house. He turned his head at the door. 'Don't worry, Vera. It'll be OK.'

We saw them as they took him past the window, his ashen face turned down towards the ground.

Churchill said this was going to be our finest hour, but it didn't feel like my finest hour at all. It felt like the worst time of my entire life.

My mom was only just holding together and I was strung between her and the Spinis. Stevie had returned home to find his father gone and went straight down to the cop-shop only to be banged up as well. They'd be able to see them in a day or two, Vera was told.

A week passed. Vera and Teresa were down at the police station in Steelhouse Lane every day. Eventually they were allowed one visit and they saw Micky, Stevie and Uncle Matteo for a few minutes. None of them had a clue what was happening. Vera said they were all trying to be cheerful, but no one would tell them anything. She was getting more distraught by the day.

Then she found out they'd been moved and they wouldn't say where. The house swarmed with Italians, many in the same position, others offering sympathy or just coming for a nose. Vera was up and down to her mom's. Her eyes were sunken with lack of sleep and she looked as if she'd lost pounds in days.

Teresa gave up her job and came home. 'Mom needs me – and the little 'uns.' So she was back among the fruit and veg, keeping up an amazingly cheery front with the regulars who didn't desert them because they were Italians and suddenly on the wrong side of the war. And I saw a new Teresa, one who was even stronger than I'd thought. Her face looked as sleepless as Vera's, but she pinned her hair back, dressed as nicely as she could and accepted everyone's sympathy.

'They've got to find out sooner or later that Dad shouldn't be there,' she said. 'We've got to keep going for 'is sake.'

She gave me strength. I had to do the same for my own dad. And I noticed a new gentleness about the place. Not just the Spinis. It's not just nostalgia talking to say this. It was nearly everyone. People cared more about each other now we were all in trouble. They'd go out of their way, do anything for you. Even Mom managed to think about Vera and what she must be feeling.

'What the hell are they playing at? That Micky Spini may be an Eyetie but what harm's he ever done to anyone?'

On 22 June the French signed the German Armistice. Mr Churchill expressed grief and amazement. The impossible was happening. The hot spring days passed agonizingly slowly.

Sometimes of an evening when I'd done all the chores I couldn't stand to be near Mom, her sitting there lifeless, half in a stupor, as if the world had already ended. I'd go up and lie on my bed, on the rough blanket, and look out at the light evening, the barrage balloon's silver tail. I often thought back to a year ago when everyone was home, squabbling, it's true, and looking daggers. But remembering it from where we were now, even with Lola there it had been normal. Blessedly normal.

I had to hold onto my dreams like Mom used to cling to the stories of the picture shows she saw. Mr Churchill said that if we could stand up to Hitler and beat him our lives would move forwards into 'broad sunlit uplands'. I liked the sound of them, those broad, sunlit uplands. They stretched out in my mind covered in golden corn and poppies and yellow and white flowers, with a warm breeze blowing and bare legs and the sweet, sweet smell of the fields.

July 1940

I heard the news over the factory wireless.

'Oh my God!' I was stuck to the floor like a statue.

'What's eating you?' Nancy snapped. Her voice was always tart as vinegar when she spoke to me and I could never make out why. What'd I done? 'Bunch of Nazis and wops,' she went on. 'Good riddance to them, I say.'

I was too upset to pay too much attention to Nancy. The appalling news was sinking in. The Germans had torpedoed a ship called the *Arandora Star* and sunk it off the coast of Ireland. The vessel had been carrying 1,500 German and Italian internees bound for Canada, and it looked as if an awful lot of them had drowned. Vera and her family still had no news, not of Micky, nor Stevie, nor Uncle Matt. For all we knew they could have been on that ship.

'What's up, Genie?' Doris leaned round me. 'There's surely no one of yours on there?'

'I don't know.' I was numb just then. 'That's the trouble. Could be.' I struggled to keep my eyes on the screw pitches of the brass caps in front of me.

Doris and the others were making sympathetic noises.

'Poor kid,' I heard someone say. 'Another thing to cope with.'

'While you don't know there's still hope,' Doris's deep voice came to me.

'Didn't know you was one for mixing with Nazis

and wops,' Nancy said. Now she'd picked on that phrase she was obviously keen to work it to death. 'Did you, girls?'

'Shut your trap, Nance,' someone said.

Nancy gave them her coyest smile, which was designed to melt hearts, and I felt like slapping her one. I turned on her. 'What do you know about it, you ignorant little bitch? Just you watch what you're saying.' I marched round to her side of the table. 'You're talking about my best pal. One more word out of you and my nails'll be making a pretty pattern on your face. Got it?'

'Did you 'ear that?' Nancy turned in exaggerated outrage to the others.

'You asked for every word of it, Nance,' Doris said. 'So just shut it, eh?' The others agreed with her. None of them liked Nancy, despite her pretty looks and winning ways. Didn't take anyone long to work out she was as two-sided as a half-crown.

'You'd better pack it in the lot of you,' another voice said from down the far end. 'Mr Broadbent's about today and you don't want him 'earing this carry on, do you?'

We certainly didn't. I went back to work, picking up each bit of moulded brass, trying to check it as thoroughly as I could. Mr Broadbent was a kind, straight man and I'd do the very best for him I could. When I glanced up I could see Nancy looking hate at me along the table, her auburn curls pushing out from under the snood we had to wear. Even in the dull light from the grimy factory windows I could see she had rouge on her white cheeks, and her thin, heavily plucked eyebrows made her face look wrong somehow – cheap, like one of Morgan's trollops. I saved that insult up for the next time I might need it and gave her my best 'and bugger you too' look down the long table.

If I could have kept my attention on all the most horrible insults I could think of to hurl at Nancy it would have been much the better for me. But I spent the day in the most agonizing state of mind, imagining terrible things. I kept seeing Micky and Stevie and Theresa's jolly Uncle Matt struggling in the waves, sinking down and down until they were lying on the bottom of the seabed but somehow never dead, always alive, peering helplessly up into the murky water.

After work it was still warm and sunny. I found Teresa packing up the shop for the day. She was wearing the orange dress with the splashes of yellow on it. Without saying anything I picked up one of the boxes from outside and carried it inside for her and together we gathered up the empty crates on which they arranged the pyramids of fruit.

When we'd finished both of us straightened up and I looked into her stricken face. She was holding on tight, I could tell. She couldn't seem to speak. After a moment she shrugged despairingly.

'Oh Teresa – come 'ere.'

We stood in each other's arms and Teresa held me very tight as I did her, our cheeks pressed together.

'We don't know they were on that boat,' she said fiercely. She squeezed me to make the point more strongly. 'We've got to believe they're not – till we know for sure. But we haven't heard from them . . .'

I saw her pull her mind away from that thought.

'You're brave, Teresa. Much braver than me.'

She shook her head. 'Not brave. It's just, if we think of the other, of what might've happened, we can't go on. Mom says the same.'

Teresa bent to bolt the doors of the shop, the orange dress tight over her hips. I thought how grown up she was, now she was allowed to be.

'Genie —' She stood up, hesitating. 'It's just – we're all going to Mass now. Would you come?'

In all the time I'd known Teresa I'd never once been to Mass with her. In fact I'd not often been to church at all. Mom and Dad certainly weren't regular attenders, just went sometimes at Christmas. I had been on occasion with Nanny Rawson who barely ever missed a Sunday. Mom said she used to go to get an hour's peace from my grandad and his keeping on, but I reckon it was more than that. I don't know how you'd carry on the way Nanny Rawson did, keep steady, without faith in something or other flickering inside, and the religion she'd been given was Church of England. Sound and solid and no lurching from one extreme to the other. No fripperies, preferably no smells and bells, and what little I'd seen of church was along those sober lines.

The Catholic religion was seen by people like us as something very different from ours. Foreign, baffling, full of dread. The Pope and lots of what Nan called 'paraphernalia' like statues and incense and rosary beads. She'd been up in arms when Lil announced she was marrying Patsy, until she saw that even though he was a Catholic he was no more religious than she was and probably less so.

So it felt peculiar to be walking across towards Digbeth to Mass with the Spinis.

'Are you sure they won't mind?' I whispered to Teresa. Vera was beside us carrying Luke, and Teresa was leading Giovanna by the hand.

'Course not. People'll be pleased.'

Vera's face was drawn and stony and none of us had said much on the way across town except Luke who kept chattering, and we took it in turns to answer. All Teresa said to me on the way was, 'Now I know what it must be like for you.'

St Michael's was in Bartholomew Street, near the railway. Inside it seemed very dark after the bright afternoon and I liked the strange smell in there, the whiffs of wax and incense and floor polish. It was stuffy and cosy and the candles made me think of Christmas.

A row in front of us sat the little stooping figure of Nonna Amelia, Vera's mom, and beside her Vera's other two brothers, Marco, with his pretty wife and two children, and Paolo who wasn't married. Their hair was black as crows' feathers and clipped very neatly round their ears. Nonna Amelia had a black lace mantilla over her white hair and when I looked round I saw Vera, Teresa and Francesca were wearing them too and they looked pretty. Nonna Amelia turned and nodded at me, a warm expression in her eyes. A moment later she swung round, passing me a dark green handkerchief embroidered with white at the edges. As I took it from her gnarled hand, Teresa whispered, 'Put it on your head.' Nonna Amelia nodded as I laid it softly over my hair.

Most of the women I could see were kneeling down holding rosary beads and the Hail Marys were rattling out at top speed. I was surprised how quiet and well-behaved the kids were. Luke sat wide-eyed next to Vera, sucking his thumb.

A bell rang and the priest suddenly started speaking from absolutely miles away down the front somewhere and I wondered why they didn't get him to shift forwards a bit so we could all see him. '*In nomine Patris* . . .' Everyone was crossing themselves and I was completely lost after that. Couldn't understand one word of it. And it looked to me as if he'd lost quite a few of them there because they just carried on all the way through with those rosary beads as if nothing was happening at all, not seeming to take the blindest bit of notice. I mean in my nan's church people tried at least to look as if they were listening.

But I started to feel really grateful for being there. Normally at this time of night I'd be pelting about at home cooking tea with people on at me. My heart was so heavy and at least here I had some time to think. All these people came to my mind, Micky and Stevie and Uncle Matteo, and my own dad, and my mom too, until I thought I'd burst with sadness there in that church. Vera's face looked so grieved, and I thought about Mom struggling on at work and all that had happened to us. I'd wanted to believe that if I tried really hard I could somehow make things right. Make my family all right. Now though, I saw there wasn't much I could do about anything except to hope and pray.

After lighting candles at the end of Mass the family gathered outside the square-fronted church. Nonna Amelia shuffled out on her little bowed legs, supported by the arms of her two sons, the mantilla pulled softly back to lie on her shoulders. She wore little black mules on her feet and a black shawl, and rosary beads the colour of gunmetal hung from her waist. She had not put on mourning clothes for her son or her son-in-law. Mourning colours were her permanent state, her every-day clothes since the death of her husband, Papà Scattoli, eight years earlier. With her hunched shoulders it was hard for her to raise her head completely straight and she looked more at home in a chair than standing.

I'd always liked Nonna Amelia, even though I could barely understand a word she said. This was partly with it being in Italian, but also because she had no teeth. Her lips had shrunk into a web of deep wrinkles all pointing inwards round the little dot which was all you could see of her mouth, like water being sucked down a plughole. She was all there, Nonna Amelia, even though she didn't sound it, because the words came out all soggy, as if she had a mouthful of sawdust. Her eyes were sunken and brown like a little monkey's but glowing with life. There was a slight tremor to her neck which made it look as if she was nodding wisely at whatever was being said.

All of us went ceremonially to kiss her velvety cheeks and she nodded at me kindly and mumbled a greeting as I handed back her hanky, just as if I was one of the family. Her son Marco stayed with her while his wife and Paolo distracted the kids, Paolo throwing Luke high in the air so he gurgled, and tickling Giovanna and teasing her by untying the bow in her hair.

The rest of them gathered round Vera. Marco put his spare arm tightly round her and for a moment she said something to him in a low voice and leaned gratefully against him, closing her eyes. Her two sisters embraced her as well, their eyes full of concern, of fear.

There were similar groups along the pavement. The attendance at Mass was far higher than usual that evening. The priest came out and mingled among the crowd. He was Irish, not Italian. A priest would visit once a year or so from Italy and preach a sermon in Italian and this was always an occasion. But this priest was able to give them his sympathy none the less. A lot of the people there were still in their work clothes, the men in boots and caps, women in old everyday frocks, not like their Sunday best. I stood by Teresa as people milled back and forth, all talking in Italian. I didn't need to ask Teresa what they were talking about.

You could see the shock and worry that the sinking of the *Arandora Star* was causing in the Quarter. Some of the internees, especially the younger ones, had been released and sent home not long after they were arrested. Some families had heard from their relatives that they were safe in transit camps, but there were a few others in the same position as the Spinis, who had seen and heard nothing of their men since their last hurried visits in Steelhouse Lane police station, and they all knew that the very worst outcome, the news they most dreaded, was far from out of the question.

People kept coming to talk to Vera and Teresa, nodding to Nonna Amelia who had earned a lot of respect and liking in the district. She barely spoke, her eyes moving from face to face from the support of her son's arm, but her silence seemed to speak of their pain more than the words of those around her.

A young man came up to Teresa and put his arms round her shoulders for a minute. He looked older than us, had a head of black, curling hair. Immediately the two of them were off, gassing away, and I watched, puzzled. Teresa seemed to know him well, was at ease with him. There was none of the dizziness I'd seen in her over Jack and Clem. She talked to him as she would

238

have done Stevie or Tony. He did a lot of the talking, seemed worried.

Teresa interrupted him. 'Carlo – this is my friend Genie. I s'pect she's had enough of hearing all this Italian.'

'Sorry.' He smiled, held out his hand. Two blazing blue eyes looked into mine. He was so handsome, even dressed in his old work clothes. 'Nice to meet you, Genie.' He frowned at Teresa. 'I've heard of Genie, haven't I? How come we never met before?'

Teresa shrugged. 'She doesn't come to Mass. We've been pals for years. Her nan lives up the road from us. Hey, look—' She nudged Carlo and pointed.

Three men were standing together, one of them, the oldest of the three, talking loudly at the others, arms moving back and forth, touching the fingers of one hand against his forehead then beating the air.

'Fausto Pirelli's uncle,' Teresa explained. 'Sparks flying there all right. They think Fausto's being moved to Brixton. They send the real naughties there.'

'All this fuss about Fausto,' Carlo said scornfully, 'He knows nothing about politics. He's all hot air. Come to think of it.' He nodded his head towards the uncle. 'How did he slip through the net himself? If they took your dad?'

Teresa shrugged, eyes still on Fausto's aerated uncle. 'What's the matter with the stupid bugger?' she snapped suddenly. 'I'd rather know Dad and Stevie were in Brixton than—' She stopped, struggling to control herself. I squeezed her hand.

Carlo looked round at her and said softly, 'You all right, Teresa?'

She nodded hard. 'Have to be.'

Carlo suddenly pulled her close to him, his arm round her shoulder.

The air was cooling, the street full of shadow now. People were starting to drift hungrily home. There were cooking smells in the air from houses near by.

'*Ciao*, Carlo,' Teresa said, pulling away rather carelessly from him.

'*Ciao*.' He raised his hand, watching her. Suddenly it was as clear as day to me. Any idiot could have seen from the smile he gave her what he felt for her except, quite obviously, Teresa herself.

I don't remember you talking about him before,' I said as we began the walk back with the family.

'Carlo? I've known him years. I must've mentioned him, haven't I? The family are always there at Mass. He works in the terrazzo trade with his dad – laying floors and that. We used to do Italian classes at the church as well. I s'pose he was just part of the furniture.'

'He looks absolutely gorgeous,' I said, trying to raise a laugh in her.

'I s'pose he is.' Teresa sounded offhand, her mind elsewhere. 'Says he wants to join up but he's not sure how they'll treat him in the British army.'

Giovanna was chatting away on the other side of her, getting no reply. 'Uncle Marco says I can go to the park on Sunday with Adelina and Maria.' She gave a little skip. 'Just girls. Just me. Not Tony or Luke!'

I tried to answer Giovanna's babble since Teresa so obviously wasn't paying any attention. When we got to Gooch Street the shops had long closed, the blinds wound in, and the air was full of the smell from the brewery.

'I've been so stupid,' Teresa suddenly burst out, making me jump. Her face was fierce. 'All that matters is my family. I'm going to do everything, *everything* I can for them.'

'D'you know I've always envied you your family?'

'Have you?'

She'd never seen it up till now. They'd always just been there too, like air.

The days passed still bringing no news for any of us, not of my father, nor Micky Spini. Since there was no choice in the matter we kept on doing what we had to do, day in, day out.

Very early one morning when I was barely out of bed and Mom certainly wasn't, there was a great banging on the front door. Still in my nightdress I snatched up the crocheted blanket from a chair and flung it round me as I sped into the hall. Dad! was my first illogical thought.

Gladys was talking before I'd got the door properly open.

'You'd better get yourselves ready for a shock!' she informed the street at the top of her voice.

I was confronted by her and Molly, both already dressed in enormous frocks, baggy as potato sacks and covered with splodges of coloured flowers. Gladys was holding Molly tightly by the arm as if she might be of a mind to take off.

'Come in,' I said as they steamed past me though the hall, Gladys flicking the blackout curtain by the door out of the way as if it'd personally insulted her. She was off again before I'd got the door shut.

'Right goings on.' She dragged poor Molly along with her. 'And then what do I find?'

'Sit down,' I said. 'I'll get Mom.'

'You'd better do that,' Gladys called after me sanctimoniously.

Mom was no longer sick nowadays, but she still found it devilishly hard to shift herself out of bed of a morning and I had trouble rousing her. She rolled over and looked blearily at me. 'Gladys Bender? What the heck does she want this time of day?'

'She says we're in for a shock.'

Her face tightened immediately. Victor. News about Victor, and already she was half out of bed, twisted round too quickly and winced. Then she tutted, relaxed. What did Gladys Bender know about anything?

When we got down Gladys didn't even give her a chance to open her mouth. She propelled herself out of her chair and pointed at Molly, who was sitting hanging her head.

'It's not you should be coming down, it's that brother of yours!'

'Sssh,' Mom said tiredly, flapping a hand as if to shoo away the noise.

'This one 'ere's in the family way and your Len's the Jack Rabbit that got 'er that way. So what've you got to say about that then?' She just managed to fold her arms over her mountainous bosoms. In the light from the window I could see her specs were all smears.

We hadn't got anything at all to say. Not a thing for quite a few seconds.

'No,' Mom got out eventually, any wind she'd had in her own sails expelled completely. 'That can't be right. Molly, that's not true, is it?'

'Days it's been going on now. She's off her food, sick every morning. She's 'ad a go already today, isn't that right, Moll?' Gladys leaned over her, shouting.

Molly lifted her head and you could see from her face

she wasn't feeling any too well. Her normally pink cheeks were white and her hair was hanging lank and straight.

'But it can't be Lenny,' Mom stuttered, blushing heavily. 'Surely he hasn't been . . .?' She was looking at me and the blood rose in my cheeks. 'Genie?'

I didn't say anything.

'Genie – you knew all about this, didn't you?'

'I never! I never knew Molly was expecting!'

'What's been going on?' Mom was shrieking at me.

'What d'you think's been going on?' Gladys retorted. 'My Molly's got a bun in the oven that's what—' She tapped Molly heavily on the shoulder. 'And it didn't get there by itself.'

'Well it's not my fault, I wasn't even here,' Mom said. 'How was I supposed to know what they've been up to? You should keep your daughter under control. I can't be watching Len every moment of the day. There's a war on – I've got a job to do!'

'Oh, and you don't think I 'ave?' Gladys was hands on hips, cheeks plum red.

It was turning into quite a shouting match and no one was taking any notice of poor old Molly, as if she was a sack of turnips they were haggling over, so I went and sat down by her. 'You all right, Molly? Feeling bad, are you?'

'I want Lenny,' she said tearfully. Poor old Molly, I'd never seen her miserable like that before, with everyone shouting about her head and not really knowing what was happening to her.

Just then, woken by the racket, Len appeared, shirt hanging out, hair standing on end, only half awake.

'Ah,' Gladys said accusingly. ''Ere 'e is.'

It all went quiet suddenly. Len stared round at us,

243

rubbed his eyes like a little kid, then looked at me as if I should explain everything. Then Mom was looking at me too. So it was up to me again was it, to take responsibility? I was damned if it was.

''E's got to know,' Gladys said, back in the arms-folded-over bosoms position. 'So you'd better get on with it.'

I stared hard at Mom. This isn't my job. Not this.

'Len . . .' Horribly embarrassed, she took Len's arm and he turned his great head and frowned at her, struggling to get every word. 'You know you and Molly—'

'Molly!' Len pointed suddenly as if he'd only just seen she was there. ''Ullo Molly!'

'Len, listen. You and Molly like each other a lot, don't you?'

Len nodded very hard.

'Well, Molly's having your babby, Lenny. It is his, isn't it?' she hissed at Molly who stared back, then nodded.

Len still looked as if he'd got caught fast in a monkey puzzle tree and couldn't get out.

'Molly's got a babby in her tummy,' Mom spelt out slowly. 'And it was you that put it there, see?'

'And don't try saying it weren't,' Gladys threatened.

Len moved a few steps closer to Molly. 'You got a babby, Molly?'

Molly nodded again looking scared, poor child that she was. The two of them seemed stuck, Len standing there, Molly in the chair, not knowing what to do.

'Well, there's nothing for it,' Mom said. 'We're going to have to get this sorted out one way or another. I s'pose the next thing is to fix a wedding day.'

Molly gazed across at us as if she just couldn't believe what she'd heard.

'Wedding day, Molly? How would you and Len like to get married?'

The light dawned. Slowly, bit by tiny bit, Molly's mouth turned up into a whopping great banana of a smile.

The factory was abuzz with excitement. Doris was full of organizing a lunchtime show and trying to bludgeon as many as possible into a performance of a sort. It was amazing how much work they could get done while their minds were on other things.

'Come on, Agatha,' Doris wheedled. 'You've got a few rhymes up your sleeve. And Joan – you can do your trick with the bottle and string.'

'Oh not again!' Joan groaned. 'Everyone'll be sick to the back teeth of that.'

'No – you can't see that one too many times.' Doris was writing her down in a little notebook regardless.

'Don't know why you're bothering,' one woman said. 'More trouble than it's worth.'

'You old misery.' Doris's cackling laugh rang round the warehouse. 'Got to 'ave some fun from somewhere. What with tea going on the ration as well, there won't be any pleasures left at all soon!'

Her laughter moved closer to my ear. 'Right, Genie – put you down for a song, shall I?'

'I've got no voice!'

'Oh you 'ave, bab, I've 'eard you singing round the place – when you 'ad more to be cheerful about any rate. Sweet little voice you've got. From your nan I expect. It is 'er I've heard up the Eagle, isn't it? And your auntie – oi—' She held on to my arm and called out to the others for agreement. ''Ow about Genie gets 'er nan and 'er auntie and your mom is it? – over 'ere? The Andrews Sisters of Balsall 'Eath!' She laughed again. 'That'd liven us all up.'

'They couldn't – they're all at work,' I said, not sure they'd agree even if they hadn't been.

'I could sing with 'er,' Nancy butted in, jealous of the attention I was getting.

'Sorry, Nance,' Joan said. 'Not meaning to be rude or nothing but you've got a voice on you like a pair of clapped out bellows. I should stick to the day job if I was you.'

Nancy scowled viciously.

'Eh – I tell you what, girls,' Doris said, clasping my arm even harder. 'Let's make a real go of it and 'ave it of an evening. Get Genie's nan along with 'er squeeze box, 'ave a bit of a drink and that – what d'you reckon?'

There were cheers and a few scattered handclaps.

'Go on – we could do with a bit of a laugh.'

'It'd get me away from the old man for a night any rate!'

'You could bring 'im along.'

'Not on your life I won't!'

'But there's no room for a proper concert here,' someone pointed out.

Someone suggested the yard at the back and they were chewing over how it could be cleaned up when Doris cut in with, 'I know – the roof!'

Broadbent's had a flat roof with a parapet running round it.

'But we'll never get a piano up there – it's four floors!'

'Oh yes we will,' Doris said comfortably. 'Course we will.'

There was a hubbub as everyone started making plans and picking the day, which was quickly chosen as the Friday, giving us two days. Doris with her little notebook, was jotting down names before they could even volunteer.

While this was all going on, out of the corner of my eye I saw someone come in through the door from the factory at the front and stand quietly waiting, watching what was going on with a smile on his lips. I half guessed immediately who he was, and it was only seconds before his presence was noticed by the others, and Nancy in particular, who let out a shrill, excited screech, 'Look,' She pointed. ''E's back!'

Instant excitement to top up what was already there. Joe Broadbent was surrounded by a bunch of chattering women, the older, more motherly ones kissing him, and more forward ones making smart-alec comments and others just standing round chatting and giggling, demanding why he wasn't in his uniform. A few of us carried on with our work, listening to the others.

Nancy, of all of them, was by far the most forward. God Almighty, I'd never seen anyone behave like quite such a tit. Blushing, leering, simpering, she hung round him as he tried to make his way into the factory. It was sick-making. She was throwing questions at him like confetti and tagging his name on to each of them in such a syrupy way that I saw some of the other women grimacing.

'How've you been, Joe? How's it feel to be a pilot, Joe? Have you flown lots of planes? Have you got your wings yet, Joe?'

On and on until someone else said, 'Oh leave off, Nancy – you're enough to give anyone a headache.'

I'd heard more than a bit about the famous Joe while I was at Broadbent's and I was curious too, thinking he probably wasn't all he was cracked up to be, because they hardly ever are, are they? Tucked away in the background I had a chance of a good look at him.

He was tall, a head at least above most of the women, and the first thing I noticed was the way he had of tilting his head forward when he spoke to them, fixing everyone's face with his eyes, their questions holding his attention. Even Nancy's, for a while anyway. He didn't talk down to them as if they weren't worth the trouble, just like his dad didn't, and his manner was easy, standing with his hands in the pockets of his brown, worn-looking jacket. He had fair hair, half way between blond and brown, cut very short of course, forces standard, which looked a bit strange on anyone in civvies. His long, thin face was pale, tired I thought. But smiling out of it were dark brown eyes, the liveliest and kindest I'd ever seen.

I was affected by Joe immediately. He was a clever person, I knew. He'd been to grammar school and before the war had been due to go on to technical college, even university. This was an awesome thought for all of us because opportunities like that were way off the edge of our horizon. He seemed so grown up at nineteen, so admirable, yet for all that, so far as I could see, so very approachable. I'd never come across anyone like him before.

Nancy was proving difficult for him to shake off as he did his round of the warehouse, stopping to have a word with everyone on the way. He seemed to remember everyone's name, their family, their circumstances.

It really was a family firm and some of those women had been there years. Broadbent's was known as a good employer – fair, kind and reasonable.

'Nancy – get back and get on with your work,' Doris ordered her eventually. They were all browned off with her by now. Nancy pulled herself away with enormous effort as if she was strung to Joe by a piece of elastic and went pouting back to her place. With great ostentation she took the snood from her hair, which she proceeded to shake out, a long auburn mass of it, wavy down her back. She pulled her fingers through it, looking to see if Joe was watching her, and once she'd seen his glance turn her way she began coiling it briskly round her hand and put the covering back on it, patting it to make sure little wisps of her fringe were peeping out at the front.

'Quite finished, 'ave you?' Agatha said, sarky.

'Now here's someone I don't know,' I heard Joe say. 'Who's this then, Doris?'

My heart was beating so fast when he came up to me.

'This is Genie, the new checker,' Doris told him. 'Been here a few weeks. She's a good'un she is – Genie, Joe Broadbent. He's home on a week's leave, from the RAF,' she explained carefully, as if I was deaf and hadn't heard anything that had gone before.

'Nice to meet you, Genie.' I realized suddenly that he was holding out his hand to me. I wiped my left hand on my overall and held it out and then of course remembered it was the wrong one and had to start all over again. I felt such a scruffy little mouse in my overall and snood with draggly bits of hair falling out of it and my dirty hands, but I managed to look up at him. The smile that met me in his eyes gave me a feeling I'd never forget. Something that dug so deep in me I didn't understand what had happened except I felt dizzy suddenly and new. Those dark eyes, striking against the light hair, held an expression that was so open, so sympathetic. After a few seconds I was able to smile back with all the warmth I felt.

'How d'you do, Joe,' I said, taking his hand. My heart was going so, I thought it must be showing, rattling my body.

'You getting on all right here, are you?'

'Very nice, thanks. It's by far the best place I've ever worked.'

My hand was still in his and slowly he released me. I noticed the rubbed look of his jacket. It was old, a favourite probably.

'Course, a lot of things have changed here since the war. They'll have told you that?' He glanced round at the others. Nancy was watching us, hard.

'Oh yes,' I said eagerly. 'You used to take maps.' Flustered, I lowered my eyes. 'I mean make taps.'

When I looked up he let out a loud laugh which after a moment I joined in.

'You're not scared of me, are you? Good heavens, there's no need to be.' With the laugh still in his eyes he leaned forward, resting his hands on the table. 'If it's so good here, tell me where else you've worked then.'

'You got half the afternoon to spare, have you? The worst place I ever worked was a meat factory ...' I found myself babbling on, telling him about the pork pies and the bloke's nose and the woman whose finger got grated in with it too. And I told him about the taxi firm and the pawn shop and a couple of the others, although I kept some of the list back so's he didn't think I was a complete waster.

He laughed a lot at what I was saying which gave me

courage and I relaxed and was able to talk more like my normal self.

'Why so many?' he asked.

'I get bored easily. Not here though,' I added quickly. 'I like it here.'

Still chuckling, he said, 'Seems I've led a very sheltered existence! You've managed to put me off pork pies for the rest of my life any rate.'

'I never said what they did to the sausage—'

'No, please!' He held up one hand to stop me. 'I'm surprised you lasted as long as a week there. Half an hour and I'd've been hanging up my overall I should think.'

After a bit more chatter Joe said, 'Well I'd better let you get on, or Doris'll never let me hear the end of it.'

He hesitated. 'See you around, Genie.'

When I looked across at the clock I saw with disbelief that we'd been talking for twenty minutes. It felt more like two.

He stayed a bit longer, exchanging pleasantries with a few people. I could tell he was pleased to be back. Two or three times I felt his gaze on me, and I couldn't stop myself watching him, following him with my eyes. I knew exactly where he was all the time he was in there. I watched the way he walked, his long straight back, his gestures, the way he moved his head.

As he left, going out again through the factory, letting in the clunking noises of the machines, his eyes found me again. Feeling the blush rise in my cheeks, I thought, it had to be a coincidence: he couldn't really have been seeking me out.

But as soon as the door shut, Agatha said, 'Ooh Genie!' Whatever else she might've said was interrupted by Nancy who was round to my position in seconds and grabbing me by the throat.

'Just you keep off 'im!' Her face was all screwed up. ''E's mine,' she hissed, silly little cow that she was. 'Mine, OK?'

I seized her hand and jerked it away from my throat which was sore where she'd clawed at me. 'What'd you do then, eh? Buy 'im at the Co-op?'

'Get back to your place, Nance,' Agatha ordered her. 'And keep your catty mitts off Genie. What the 'ell d'you think you're playing at?'

For the rest of the afternoon Nancy gave me looks of such poisonous hatred along the table that I began to wonder if she was a bit barmy. But it didn't touch me. Nancy Hogan could go take a running jump.

'Will he be coming to the show on Friday?' I asked Doris.

She grinned at me. 'Who would that be, Genie?' She relented quickly. 'As he's home I'd be very surprised if he doesn't.'

'I'm working Friday,' Mom said when she got home that night, unsteady with exhaustion.

'Can't you swap?' I called through from the kitchen. 'Everyone else's going.'

Nanny Rawson never took much persuasion to play and sing. It was her one escape from the house, the endless work. And Lil said she'd come and bring the kids.

Mom sat in an armchair, leaning down, rubbing her ankles. 'No, don't think so,' she said listlessly.

I heard her get up and pour herself a drink. Suddenly I was full of angry determination. I wanted this so badly, wanted us all singing there together on Friday, and I wanted Joe Broadbent to see us. Without Mom's high-reaching voice which complemented Lil's deeper one, it wouldn't be the same.

Standing by the kitchen door I watched her sit down with a glass half full of gin.

'You managed to sort your shifts out all right when it suited you to see Bob.'

She hesitated, looking round at me, the glass to her lips.

I held her gaze, stared back. 'Do this for me, Mom. Just for once, do something for me.'

She took two gulps, shuddering slightly at the strength of it. At last she said, 'Oh well – all right then.'

I'd never been on the roof at Broadbent's before, but anyone could see it'd been transformed. A group of volunteers had stayed on after work the night before to make the place ready, and considering the drabness of a smoke-stained factory roof, they'd performed a miracle. It was surrounded on three sides by a brick parapet, and the fourth abutted a tall, thin building, higher than Broadbent's, occupied by Cobham's, a firm of tool-makers. So there was a blank wall facing us, only broken by a couple of filthy air vents. Across that they'd fixed old sheets made into a banner, painted in red and blue letters on the white, which read 'Showtime at Broad-bent's – 1940'.

There were already a good number gathering up there. I looked round with our nan, Lil and Mom (no Len – the pull of Molly was even stronger than that of a sing-song) and the kids, who thought being right up there was the best thing ever. I lifted Cathleen up and we looked across at the roofs of factories and houses, some below so we could see all their loose tiles, others on the same sort of level. You could see the spire at St Martin's in the Bull Ring, and Cathleen pointed at the shining barrage balloons which seemed so much nearer from up here.

'Don't think I've ever been this high up before,' Nan said, still breathless from all the stairs.

Mom looked over the edge, dreamily. She was wearing a loose dress, sensitive about being seen to be pregnant, and she'd evidently decided to join in tonight, to play along.

They'd swept the tarred roof, which still felt spongy underfoot from the warm day, carried up trestle tables and what chairs and stools could be begged or borrowed, and arranged them in rows facing the wall and banner. Wonder of wonders, to one side, stood a piano.

'We borrowed some muscles,' Doris said, coming up to us. She said how excited she was to meet the family, Nan especially. 'This is my 'usband, Ray.' She indicated a massive bloke next to her, built like an all-in wrestler with the broken nose to match. In fact he was a boxer in his spare time. I had a strong feeling I'd seen him somewhere before. 'Knew 'e'd come in 'andy some time,' Doris laughed, and I could see our nan warming to her.

Doris admired Lil's kids, picked up Cathleen and cuddled her as everyone did, with her pretty looks.

'She'll be another like Genie,' she said. 'Bet she gets away with murder with them big eyes.' Cathleen stole the show at this point by putting her arms round Doris's neck and squeezing her face against hers.

'When're we on then?' Nan asked. She'd put her squeeze box down at the side of the piano.

'You'll be called,' Doris said. 'Ray 'ere's our master of ceremonies for the evening. 'Ere Ray – get Mrs Rawson and 'er family a drink, will you?'

There were a couple of barrels of beer, courtesy of Mr Broadbent, and a whole assortment of cups and glasses on the table. We'd brought a few ourselves, as well as sandwiches to add to the collection.

'Tizer for you kids?' Ray said. As he was opening the bottle with a 'swoosh' noise, I couldn't help myself keep looking round at the stairs, every time there was the movement of someone arriving. I knew that until the Broadbents were here the place wouldn't feel complete.

Nancy came up with another girl who I thought looked like her sister. She was wearing a black dress with huge pink roses on and dashes of white in it, with a nipped waist. I saw Nan stare at her. 'Is that that Nancy you were on about? Looks a bit of a hussy to me. And that's a lower neckline than's good for 'er – she could catch a cold down there.'

Some people had already sat down on the chairs and boxes and a few other kids had arrived, so Tom and Patsy were chasing round with them and Lil just let them get on with it. She'd gone over to the piano where Tony, one of the lads from the main factory, was tuning up on it, improvising, feeling his way into songs. He was good, had the touch, and Lil leaned with one arm against the top of the upright humming bits she recognized, winking down at him. He was such a young feller I could see he was dazzled by her, this gorgeous woman with red lips, raven hair and sequins on her dress. He stopped for a minute and they talked, then tried out the openings of some songs together. Not to be outdone, Mom went over with her tumbler of ale and joined in. I was proud of them both.

Please Mom, I thought, don't drink too much tonight. Just don't let me down.

I stood beside Nan, who'd taken a seat to rest her knee. A cheer went up as a trail of coloured bulbs which'd been strung across the top of the banner lit up, bright as boiled sweets although it was still golden daylight.

'This is one show'll have to be over by blackout time!' Ray announced.

'Let's get on with it then!' another voice shouted. 'What's all the hanging about for?'

More claps and cheers. The place was filling up and they were getting impatient. We all wanted to break the hard lines of ordinary days. We wanted to laugh, to sing and forget.

Mom and Lil came over, gathering up the kids, and stood by me and Nan, leaving the seats for other people. As the piano struck up again Nan turned to me. 'You look very nice tonight, Genie.'

I had to bend my head to hear her and smile. 'Ta Nan.' I had on the polka dot dress Mom'd put together, with its little scarf and I'd curled the ends of my hair and pinned it so it hung nicely round my ears.

Ray, Doris's husband, looked more the type to be handy with his fists than his wit but he stepped forward to do his bit as Master of Ceremonies and erupted into a patter that took us all by surprise and soon had everyone laughing and cheering.

Nan leaned over to me. 'I knew I knew that feller's face. Used to work the Bull Ring, selling crocks or summat. Haven't seen him in a while.'

When she said that, I remembered him too. 'He's on munitions now.'

'And our first number tonight,' he was shouting in

his gravelly voice, trying to beat the catcalls and whistles. 'I tell yer, if yer don't settle down you lot, there won't be time for any bleeding show!'

More cheers and raucous laughter but the message seemed to have sunk in. Gradually they got settled down. But when I looked round I saw Mr Broadbent arrive at the top of the stairs, a woman behind him I'd never seen before, blonde, with sharp, rather haughty features.

'That them?' Mom whispered to me.

I nodded. 'She must be one of the daughters.'

Behind me I heard a voice say, 'I s'pect Mrs B's got the other sister at her beck and call at home.'

In the front row people were standing and shuffling along as Ray commanded, 'Make room now, ladies and gents, make room there.'

As they moved to the front I saw the one thing that I needed to see before whipping my head round to the front so it wouldn't be obvious I was staring. Joe was following behind them. He was here. My heart answered, speeding up.

Mr Broadbent senior and the daughter accepted seats in the front row, she looking like a chilly-eyed cat and Mr B with smiles to each side.

'Another space here!' someone called in a voice that sounded decidedly like Nancy's.

'That's all right,' Joe's voice came from close behind me. 'I'm happy to stand, thanks.'

My skin was up in goosepimples, knowing how close he was to me. As Tony struck up on the piano again I found courage and turned round.

'Hello again, Genie. OK if I stand here?'

'Course. Can you see over my head?'

He gave a laugh. 'With plenty to spare.'

The first person on stage was one of the main factory workers called Dick. 'This is Dick Busby,' he kicked off, 'talking to you from a munitions factory somewhere in the Midlands,' which earned him a clap before he'd even got started on his string of corny jokes, trying to sound like Arthur Askey. He told them pretty well in fact and bowed himself off.

Then it was Joan's turn. She was plump, middle aged, apple cheeked, and waddled forward with a length of white string, an empty milk bottle and a deadpan face, and proceeded to perform a series of antics. After a few minutes of this there wasn't a person in the audience who wasn't laughing until they ached and not one of us could have explained why. I could hear Joe behind me and after a few more manoeuvres from Joan we were all helpless with it. Eventually she gave a sniff as if we were all completely beyond her in our stupidity, wound up the string, picked up the bottle and marched off to the loudest possible applause.

'By special request from our pianist here, we're now going to 'ave a song. I'd like to call upon Mrs Lilian Heaney!'

Lil went up to the front wearing a blush that only made her look more ravishing than ever. The silky green dress she wore hugged her lithe figure, its sequins winking in the sunlight. She'd pinned a dark crimson rose behind her left ear and stood swaying to the rhythm of the piano. She sang a couple of Cole Porter numbers. After the first one, into which she poured all the longing of her own sad heart, because that was the gift she had, I felt Joe's breath on my ear.

'She's a real find, isn't she? Who is it?'

As I was turning to answer he moved forwards into Lil's place.

'That's my auntie Lil.'

'Your aunt?' He looked at me, then back at her. 'She's got real talent.'

I smiled, pleased for Lil as her rich voice poured out over the Birmingham rooftops and her fairytale face to go with it cast spells in people's mind. The clapping was at least as loud as for Joan with her bottle and string. Joe moved respectfully out of the way when she came back to us. I saw Mom whisper something to Lil.

There were more jokes, some told to laughs, others to groans, while helpings of ale were passed round and we polished off the last of the sandwiches. Poems, some politer than others. The pianist played dance music on his own. Nancy got up, eyes fixed on Joe, to do a gypsy dance which went off a bit half cock but could've been worse. Just about. She gave me a filthy scowl as she flounced back to her seat to not exactly rapturous applause.

'We 'ave some guest performers here tonight. We can't give you the Andrews Sisters from Hollywood but we do 'ave our very own Andrews Sisters of Balsall Heath! Let's hear it for Doreen, Lil and Genie and their accompanist, the much esteemed Edith Rawson!' He put his hands together and led the applause and we went to the front, Nan carrying her stool. She settled herself on it with the accordion, arms through the straps.

Lil, Mom and I arranged ourselves round behind her and Lil did the introductions.

'We've got a number of songs for you tonight—' This was interrupted by clapping. They were all getting pretty merry out there, and this was a special night. They were going to milk every second of enjoyment out of it before the dreary return to the factory.

We started off with sing-along numbers like 'Knees

259

up Mother Brown' and 'The Lambeth Walk' and everyone joined in at the top of their voices, stamping and clapping. We spun 'The Lambeth Walk' on faster and faster until we were all falling over ourselves with the words and laughing and Nanny Rawson's fingers were a blur on the keys of the squeeze box, her right foot madly tapping the rhythm. It was going fine. The whole evening had gone well and I knew I had wings, lifting me specially, because Joe Broadbent had stood behind me all the way through. He'd sought me out. I saw him watching the four of us, all so colourful – Mom in red, Lil sea green, me blue and Nan also in a royal blue dress, all so different but with our voices blending. I saw Joe was smiling, singing along with everyone else. Please God, I thought, don't let anything go wrong tonight . . . just this once.

After the rapturous end of the song Lil held up her hand to quieten them. 'Right, you've had your fun. Now it's time to settle down for summat more serious.' There was a good-natured groan from out front. 'We're going to turn the tempo down now and turn our thoughts to –' she drew the word out to raise a laugh, 'lu-u-urve.'

'Oooh!' everyone responded.

Nan struck up and Lil sang the verse of 'The Very Thought of You', her voice rising to bring the rest of us in for the chorus, and then our voices chimed in, harmonizing, Mom quite in control tonight, her voice high and lovely.

I'd barely ever sung with them in public before, although at home we sang together in the normal course of things. We hadn't practised, there was no time for any of that, but I found I could move easily in time to the music and the songs were so familiar it came as naturally as singing in a bath tub.

When that was finished Lil stepped forward again. 'And now, since she's our excuse for being here at all, we're going to hear from the little 'un.'

With a huge jolt I realized it was me she was on about.

'She don't usually sing with us, this one. Says she hasn't got a voice.' There was a pleased laugh from in front of us, although the only face I fixed on at that point was Nancy's and hers was full of spite.

'We think it's about time she joined the troupe. So, judge for yourselves, ladies and gentlemen. We'll help her along from the back of course, but now I give you my lovely niece – we're all very proud of her – Eugenie Watkins. Step forward, Genie!'

Heck, I hadn't been expecting this! But I couldn't exactly let them down now, could I? Even Mom was smiling. I moved nearer the front of the stage, my suddenly damp hands smoothing the front of my dress, but I hoped, looking more composed than I felt.

'Let's hear yer, Genie!' someone shouted.

I gave a little bow and turned to Lil with a grin. 'I'll get you for this afterwards.' Everyone laughed. More quietly I gave her a choice of song.

It went almost silent then, and into the quiet Nan struck up on the accordion. The sun was setting, had sunk behind the factory walls and the air was smoky. The faces in front of me had fallen into shadow.

I sang an old song, a beautiful song, 'I'll Be with You in Apple Blossom Time', and when I'd gone through a few of the lines I heard Nan, Mom and Lil join in with me and felt them hold me up, give strength to my voice, which was tuneful enough, but weaker and smaller than theirs. I've no idea how I sang, how it sounded, but I know I tried to do it the way Lil did, pouring everything

I could into it. That song promised things would turn out happily in a time of flowers and it was something all of us ached for. Things had to get better. And while I stood out there I thought my family should spend all their time singing because the songs went through and out the far side of everything else and let everyone be happy together.

I sang the final notes of the song and bent over in a bow. When I stood up I caught Joe's gaze fixed on me. His eyes were full of a quiet seriousness, but when he saw me looking he smiled back at me and raised his hands to show how hard he was clapping.

'Wasn't she lovely?' Lil quizzed the audience, and they roared back. 'Shouldn't she sing with us all the time, eh?' Another outburst of agreement. My cheeks were on fire. So was my heart, to tell the truth. 'For anyone who doesn't already know it, Genie's a great kid. And I'm going to give her the choice of our last song tonight.'

'Make it something jolly!' someone shouted. They wanted something to jump around to. OK, we'd let them have it. 'What about "Run Rabbit"?'

And so it was, and we went back to our places still singing. I felt proud to bursting. Joe's obviously admiring expression had given me a rare pride in who I was and my family. We may have been a complete mess in every other way but this was something we could do. It was us at our finest and I'd been included too. As I moved to my place I saw Joe's sister, Marjorie, lean towards her father and make some comment. Joe was still clapping.

'That was so good,' he said as I reached my place. This time it was he who seemed more shy of me.

Mom touched my shoulder as she passed me and found me a smile. 'That was lovely, Genie.'

'Have you really never sung like that before?' Joe asked, lips close to my ear.

'Only at home. I leave the performing to the others usually.'

'It was tremendous – listen, you can hear everyone loved it!' Only now were they winding down the clapping.

Joe made sure he stayed next to me this time and Mom and Lil squeezed in closer to the wall. The sun was going down fast now and very soon the coloured bulbs glowing there against the brickwork would have to be switched off.

After a couple more numbers, both saying we were a hard act to follow, Tony played 'God Save the King' and everyone stood and blasted it out, loud as they could.

'Come on you lot,' Ray shouted. 'Once more – and make it so that bleeder Adolf can 'ear it this time!'

When it was over everyone was suddenly milling about picking up chairs and clearing the trestle tables or trying to get to the stairs. A few were detailed to stay on and finish off after the rest had gone. The light was dying and there was a rush to get it finished, make the place dark.

Mr Broadbent and his daughter came up to us as we were shuffling towards the stairs.

'That was a real treat,' Mr B said kindly. He was a smaller man than his son, with his hair now steely grey but the same very dark brown eyes. His face always looked lined and tired. 'I'm glad you could all come. I didn't know we had such a budding little talent in the warehouse.'

'It were a pleasure,' Nanny Rawson said.

Even the sister smiled. She didn't seem all that bad up close. Probably just shy. 'It was really nice,' she managed to say.

And then they were gone, carried along in the tide moving into the stairwell, and Joe turned to say a quick goodbye which felt snatched and unfinished. Fittingly, as they vanished, the necklace of coloured lights went off, leaving us with only a shred of moon to see by.

At the top of the stairs I felt someone push up next to me and grab my arm, pinching it. 'Proper little bitch of a show off, aren't you, Genie Watkins?' Nancy dug her nails into my wrist. 'You've spoilt everything, you 'ave. I 'ate you.'

'Get off!' I yanked my arm away. 'You're hurting me, you barmy cow you. Why don't you just get home and hang up that chest of yours, Nance, before it falls out the front of your dress?'

'What was all that about?' Lil asked when I'd shaken Nancy off.

'Nothing,' I said. 'Nothing that matters anyhow.'

People didn't hang about outside. We all had homes to get to and work to do and the street was dark and deserted now except for us.

'We'll come down your way,' Mom was saying to Nan. 'It's not the quickest, but we might as well all stick together.'

'Coming for a cuppa?'

'Nah – best get back to Len,' Mom said. I guessed it wasn't tea she was interested in either.

We'd only got to the end of the road when we heard footsteps running up behind us.

'Someone's in a rush,' Nan said. We all pressed into the side.

The running slowed.

'Hello? Is that the Watkins family?' His voice. 'I wanted a quick word with Genie.'

We wouldn't be a minute, I told the others. I persuaded them I'd catch them up, and we were left alone. I could barely see his face in the moon's tiny threads of light.

'I couldn't go just like that. I told them I'd left something—' I could hear his quick breathing. He was nervous. 'Would you think of coming out with me, Genie? Say tomorrow night?'

Mom was sitting there staring at nothing, miles away.

'How do I look? Mom?'

'Very nice.' Sounded as if it was all too much effort for her to speak.

'The dress is smashing. Thanks again for making it.' It was the blue and white one again. I had nothing newer.

No answer.

'Look, Mom—' I went and squatted by her chair. 'I'm sorry to go out and leave you tonight, but Lenny'll be home soon. And you have said you could do with a quiet rest.' Umpteen times in fact.

She nodded but I could tell there were tears not far away. We'd already been through how it wasn't all bad, what good form she'd been in at the show.

'But I'm cut off from everyone – everything,' she moaned. 'I feel as if I'm locked in a cage . . .'

Now she was getting worked up. 'It's all right for you,' she said, jerking her head from side to side against the back of the chair in frustration. 'It's all bloody right for you, isn't it? Even that fathead Len has someone . . .'

I stood up, backing away from her. 'I've got to go. I'll be late. I promised . . .'

'He won't want you!' she shrieked after me. 'What would he want you for? He'll think he's too good for you, you wait and see!'

I started off along the Moseley Road before realizing I'd forgotten the little scarf that went with my dress, and by the time I'd torn back to get it I was in a proper lather. Joe and I had arranged to meet in Moseley Village, about midway between where we each lived, and I ended up running half the distance as I was so afraid of being late.

That mile and a half or so was torture for me. I was already in a state of nerves and Mom's kind sentiments ringing after me pulled me right down. At the concert everything had felt right and full of promise. Joe's smile, his eyes so obviously finding me, those short hours of forgetting all the grief happening to us. A dream world. Now all I could think of were bad things. Mistakes and hurts like Walt and Jimmy. The way they'd taken my hope and need and crushed them without a thought. Maybe I was all wrong again, clutching the end of a rainbow which would melt in my hand? There were all these differences between us: Joe was a grammar-school boy, older, his mom and dad had a nice house in Hall Green, and I was just a very junior pair of hands in his dad's factory.

But I had enough hope left to keep my feet, in their white buttoned shoes, trotting up the hill into Moseley, panting.

I'll know this time, I thought. When I see him again I'll be able to tell whether I've got this all wrong.

After all my running and fussing I got there early. It wasn't yet six. But when I turned up towards the gates of the church I saw Joe was already waiting for me. He'd come. That at least. He had his hands in his jacket pocket and was leaning against the wall, but when he saw me coming he straightened up and freed his hands quickly in a way that made me see he was just as nervous as I was and it gave me courage.

He smiled. 'Began to think you weren't coming.'

'But I'm early,' I protested, pointing up at the hands of the clock. 'Look, it's only five to!'

'I suppose I just hoped you wouldn't stand me up.'

'Not if I said I'd come.'

'You sound out of breath.'

I joked. 'Didn't dare be late, did I?'

We were at a loss then and stood looking at each other, and it seemed Joe's eyes penetrated deeper than the surface of my face. It was like someone stroking me, trying to know me. The feel of someone looking at me like that suddenly made me want to cry.

So's not to, I grinned at him and said, 'So – we going to stand 'ere all night then or what?'

Joe looked at me steadily. 'We could go to the pictures if you like. Or as it's a nice night, how about a walk?'

'Oh yes, a walk.' After all, what was the point in sitting staring at a silver screen? That was for escape from life, and now we had life spread in front of us to move about in.

'There's a private park.' Joe pointed across the Moseley Road. 'My mom knows someone down there'd lend us a key.'

'Is there? I never knew.'

We borrowed a key from a thin, weary-looking

woman called Mrs Munro who lived at one of the grand houses in Chantry Road, promising to drop it in on the way back, and she let us walk through a well-organized looking garden. At the bottom was a little wooden gate, and then the sloping edge of the park.

'Isn't it lovely?' I said as we walked down together under the trees. 'Fancy this being here all the time and me not knowing.'

'It's certainly tucked away,' Joe agreed. 'Seems a shame it's private really, but then that's why it's so quiet. It's not all that big though. We could go on somewhere else if you like.'

In the dip at the bottom was a little lake. There were trails of white, cottony seeds on the grass and birds chattered loudly in the trees around us.

'Loud, aren't they?' I laughed. 'Sound like my nan's neighbours gossiping.'

'Jackdaws I expect.'

'They the ones that pinch things?'

Joe laughed. 'They're the ones.'

At the bottom a path ran round the water and in the middle of it was a tree, its roots forming a tiny island. Water birds bobbed and skimmed around it.

'Those are ducks,' I pointed. That was about the limit of my knowledge. 'What about them then?'

'Moorhens.' Joe squatted down near the edge, watching another group of nervous brown birds. 'Nice little things them. Always look a bit worried. Specially when they're out of the water walking about.' He watched them for a few moments, smiling, then straightened up. 'Shall we go round?'

The path followed the curves of the lake, shady with trees on one side, more open the other. At the top of the hill you could see the enormous, elegant houses, with

268

their balconies and fancy woodwork and ornate trees growing around them. I wondered what they did with all the space they had in there.

Joe started asking me about myself, my family.

'I still can't believe that was the first time you'd sung with them. You looked such a natural. And what a family!'

Yes, what a family, I thought.

'First time properly in front of an audience, but I've sung with them all my life. Lil dropped me in it as a matter of fact. But we sing at home all the time, or at least we did before . . .'

'Before what? The war?'

'Mainly.' I didn't want to tell him too much. The less the better for now.

Joe was silent for a moment. 'Doris told me – I hope you don't mind, Genie – that your father's missing.'

'Yep. Missing. Maybe. Or dead.'

'Sorry. I shouldn't have asked.'

'No, it's OK. Not a secret, is it? We don't know, that's all, one way or another. Be easier if we did 'cause then at least we could adjust to it. We're not the only ones though.' I told him about the *Arandora Star* and the Spinis.

'God, how appalling! Yes, I remember hearing about that. But they still don't know where they are?'

'No. It's killing Mrs Spini, Teresa's mom. Very family minded they are. She can't sleep. Teresa's the one holding them all together.'

'What about you?'

I wasn't sure what he meant by this, what he'd seen in Mom. He was sharp, Joe was, even though Mom'd put on a pretty good act that night.

'Someone's got to be in the house,' I said stiffly.

'Mom's got her problems.' I told him about Lenny, risked telling about Molly, and his reaction wasn't shocked like I feared. 'And I've got a brother, Eric – he went with the evacuation. But he's eight years younger anyway so he's a bit young to take on much even if he was here.'

'That's not so young. That'd make him what? Ten?'

'No, he's only eight.'

'But that means – you can't be only sixteen! I thought you were nearly my age, specially with all those jobs you reeled off to me.'

'That was only some of 'em too!' But I was anxious now. 'Does it matter?'

'No, of course not. I'm just – crikey, that means you're younger than that dreadful Nancy!'

We both laughed then, easier together. 'In years anyway,' Joe added.

We talked a lot about our families that night, and never did move on anywhere else. We walked carefully, side by side, round and round that lake I don't know how many times and for all we noticed we could've been in the Bull Ring.

It seemed the factory's version of Joe's family was exaggerated to say the least. Joe sounded surprised when I asked about his mother's illness.

'She's not an invalid or anything. What gave you that idea? She just suffers from terrible headaches rather often. So the house has to be quiet and she just lies in the dark until it's over.'

He told me the younger of his two sisters, Louise, was still at school, and the older one, Marjorie, worked for a machine tools firm over in Witton, secretarial, and they thought, was on the verge of getting engaged.

'She's such a dark horse it's impossible to know what's going on with her.' Didn't sound as if they were close, but there was nothing in his voice to say she or her sister were the whinging vixens that Nancy and the others had made out.

'And you're set to take over the family firm?'

'Eventually. Dad's got a lot of go in him yet. But yes, I like it. Good enough way of earning a living. That's if things turn out.'

We both knew what things turning out meant. Joe went quiet and the silence stood out after we'd been talk, talk, talk all this time. I'd told him far more than I'd expected, stopping short only at Mom's pregnancy because it seemed too much to load on him, for him to have to accept. I was afraid of what he'd think. And, while it would seem disloyal to Mom as well, I also couldn't help thinking how like her it would be to come between us and spoil things. We talked so long it was almost dark, and the birds on the water were faint shadows, making plopping or quacking sounds somewhere to the side of us.

Joe put his hand on my arm for a second to stop me after these moments of quiet. 'Genie – look, I've only got a week at home. Less now in fact. I'll have to go on Wednesday night to be there for reveille Thursday morning.'

'What's revalley?'

'Oh – when they get us all up, reporting for duty. It's just I'd like so much – would you feel able to spend some more time with me? I don't want to seem pushy, but after this week I don't know when I'll be home again, or where I'm going next now I'm a flyer—'

I almost needed to laugh again, cover how much I

was feeling for him, because I wanted to say, 'I'd go anywhere with you, do anything,' and I was afraid. But I managed not to fall into joking.

'Course I'd like to.'

Joe nodded and I saw he was relieved. 'Would tomorrow be too soon?'

'It's my day off.'

'So have you got time, or . . .?'

'I can't think of a single other thing I'd rather do instead.' I still wasn't joking.

In what was left of the light I saw a smile spread across Joe's face. He had such a giving smile, with no falseness in it, and I knew I wanted to see it directed at me for the rest of my life.

'Good,' Joe said. 'Excellent. Neither can I.'

For once I put aside all that was happening at home. I was going out and that was that. This was more or less what I told Mom. They wouldn't starve, that was for sure, one way or another.

Joe suggested we hire bicycles. He'd given his away earlier in the war and I'd never had one, so we went to the Ladypool Road, and set off on two enormous pushbikes with saddles it would've been difficult to match for hardness and lack of comfort.

'I thought we could go along the canals,' Joe suggested as we set off. The canal system criss-crosses Birmingham and you could get on the paths and go for miles. Personally I didn't care whether we cycled round the Midland Red bus depot all day so long as it was with Joe.

The pushbikes turned out to be a disaster.

'Blimey,' Joe said after only about twenty yards, 'this

one's a boneshaker all right. Shan't have any teeth left by the time we get back.'

The chain soon came loose on mine and did it so regularly after that that I was soon spending more time off the bike than on it, and both our hands were black with grease.

'It would've been better just to walk, wouldn't it?' Joe said, exasperated as we had to stop and fix the chain on my tricky mount for the umpteenth time. He seemed flustered. 'I'm sorry, Genie – this isn't turning out to be much fun, is it?' He ran his hand through his hair in annoyance and left grease on its pale strands. 'It was a daft idea.'

I looked up at him from where I was bent over the bike, as I seemed to be able to fix the thing more easily than he could. 'What you on about? It doesn't matter, we'll get there. Bikes are always like this, aren't they?'

'Well, mine wasn't. Look, let's not let them ruin the day. Shall we take them back and walk instead? I wanted to see you, not deal with these blasted things all day long.'

So we walked the bikes back the scant mile we'd gone out of town to the bike shop, got cleaned up and went to join the canal in town. Joe gave a sigh of relief as we went and I realized he'd got himself more het up than I realized about the bikes, it not working. I suppose he wanted me to think well of him, and couldn't get it into his head that these sort of hitches were just normal life to me. The few days out I'd ever had with Mom, Dad and Eric had always been full of disasters great and small. These ranged from falling in rivers or cowpats to losing Eric or forgetting the food, and everyone moaning and being evilly bad-tempered because we all wanted to do different things and couldn't agree or afford to do any of them. This was nothing in comparison. And the company was the best.

Despite all the factories along the canal, stretches of it were very pretty, with grass and buttercups along the path, and bindweed, keck, mauve fireweed edging the railway tracks. Joe was much better on the names than me, liked to name flowers, birds, animals and seemed to know them all.

'I haven't done this for years and years,' I said, dimly remembering it from a time when the grass came almost up to my waist. 'There's never enough time for anything like this, that's our trouble.'

We walked along all morning, talking easily, pointing out the barges in all their bright colours, painted with roses and castles, jugs of flowers and birdcages, and the canal women in their bonnets.

'I wonder what it'd be like living on here,' Joe said. 'Seems very romantic but I'm not sure I'd like it for long.'

'Oh, I would. Nice little space, no one bothering you. I've always fancied living by a river, seeing trees every day and fields.'

'None too many fields round here!' Joe laughed.

We settled to eat our lunch in a pretty spot, smelling the canal water and hearing trains thundering past somewhere behind us, though not exactly sure any longer where we were.

We ate our sandwiches and some cake Joe's mom had sent along, swishing away the odd wasp, playing with strands of grass, shedding seeds.

'I'm ever so sorry about the bikes,' Joe said.

'You're not still on about those flaming bikes!' I gave him a playful nudge.

'You really didn't mind, did you?'

'No, I didn't. I couldn't care less as long as . . . Look, it's been smashing so far, OK?'

Joe reached out suddenly and stroked my cheek with the palm of his hand. 'I wish we had more time . . .' He looked away from me, at the rippling colours of the water. 'Then maybe I could be more sure of not making a fool of myself.'

'You won't do that.'

He heard the solemn tone of my voice and looked back at me. 'Won't I?'

As I shook my head he reached out and touched my face again. 'Don't look so sad.'

'I'm not sad, Joe. I'm anything but sad.'

His arms came round me and gently pulled me against him. 'After I met you, that first day, remember? I couldn't stop thinking about you. That was why I asked Doris about you. Genie—' He moved his arm up, rested his hand on my head so I could feel the warmth of it through my hair. 'You're lovely, d'you know that?'

I turned my head and looked at him deep into his eyes, making sure, quite sure, although really I already was, that he was speaking the truth, not giving me flannel, not teasing. And then I pulled him to me, this man, the one person in my life who really wanted me. I felt the beat of his heart against me and I knew I was safe with him.

When he said my name again, making me look up, we kissed, and my arms slid up round his neck. And for the first time I answered that kiss and loved it, and not once did I find myself thinking about groceries. At last I began to get an inkling of what it was Lil had been going on about all this time.

*

I stopped being the one who was responsible that week and spent every possible moment with Joe. He managed to get round his father, who had a soft spot for me already, and talked him into giving me a day off the day before Joe had to go back, though I didn't tell Mom about that. We took a tram out to the Lickeys. It was a beautiful day and we had the place more or less to ourselves. And blimey, wasn't it different from the last time!

This time I had a day of wonder, seeing all the lovely parts I'd missed when dragged along by Jimmy. We walked arm in arm round the green water of the lake.

'That's my dream,' Joe said. 'To have my own lake so I could keep birds. Imagine having something like this in your back garden!'

We wandered through the woods, smelling the pines, and found a warm patch of grass between sun and shade where we had our picnic and stayed on and on afterwards in each other's arms.

Joe lay back against a tree trunk and I lay on my front, half across him, looking and looking at him. He closed his eyes for a few minutes, face turned up into a little pool of sun. I watched him, holding on tight to every moment, trying to remember every line of his face, his slim, pointed nose, the dark eyebrows, his lips . . .

I moved up and kissed him. 'You comfy?'

'Not very.' He straightened his head, opening his eyes.

'Well, move then!'

'I might if it wasn't for this sack of potatoes slumped across me!'

'Charming!' I shifted myself over to lie on the grass

and Joe lay down and settled next to me, pulling my head onto his chest.

'I was trying to memorize everything about you,' he said. 'For when I go back. Big blue eyes—'

'They're grey!'

'Are they?' He leaned round and looked. 'No – blue! Well, somewhere in between. Long brown hair, high cheekbones, sweet face . . . But none of that's you, is it? I could describe you, but it wouldn't be you.'

'I was doing the same. I don't want you to go.'

'Why don't you want me to come to your house?' Joe asked suddenly. He'd offered to pick me up from home that morning and Mom would've been in.

'No,' I'd said, quick as a flash. 'I'll meet you in Navigation Street and then we can just get straight on the tram.'

I didn't want her anywhere near him this week, spoiling things. I wanted to keep this just for me. Ever since she'd known I was going out with Joe, that I'd found something of my own, she'd been poisonous with self-pity.

'Don't know how you can go gadding about like you do with your dad missing. You ought to be ashamed of yourself.' She was worried and frightened about everything I knew, but she wasn't taking this away from me.

'My mom's not always the easiest. Specially not that time of a morning. I just thought it'd be better if I came out on my own.'

Joe leaned up on one elbow. 'But I must meet her properly some time. It doesn't seem right.'

'There's plenty of time for that. Can't we just enjoy today without bringing her into it?'

'It's just, the way I feel about you I want everything to be right – with everyone. My mom and dad are happy we're walking out together and I'd like yours – your mom that is – to be as well. See?'

'I don't think my mom's got much idea how to be happy about anything.'

I must've said this in a bleaker voice than I intended because Joe rolled over and took me in his arms. He kissed my face then drew back, eyes searching me. 'I wish I didn't keep seeing you look so sad.'

'But I've told you, I'm not sad. I'm happier than I've ever been in my whole life before and that's thanks to you, Joe.'

He carried on looking at me for a time and then spoke the words his eyes were already telling me. 'I really love you, Genie.'

'And I love you more than anyone ever.'

We held each other so close. All the love I had ready to pour out on someone had found a place to settle.

'I never knew it could be anything like as nice as this,' I said. Joe's face looked happy. We kissed again, feeling the sun through closed eyelids.

That day drifted past in a haze. I had no idea at any point what time it was and I couldn't have cared less anyway.

But we couldn't shut everything out. Late in the afternoon we sat high on the hills looking back towards Birmingham. We had heard planes on and off that afternoon and there were ragged vapour trails across the blue. We had no idea then, but that very day as we sat there, Hitler was giving orders for the invasion of Britain. The first knocks of the Battle of Britain had already begun but it felt far away and unreal then. Gloria had given us news of dogfights over the Channel, the reporter making it all sound like an afternoon's football match.

'So don't you know where you're going next?' I asked Joe. I sat with my hand on the hard muscle of his thigh. I wanted never not to be touching him.

'I'm not certain. Down south I'd imagine – things are looking bad.' He never talked very much about the RAF or what it was like. 'I'd rather forget it all when I'm home with you,' he said. 'It's all too uncertain. Your mind can't quite take it in.'

'This is the best day of my life.'

Joe turned to me. 'So far. Think of it that way.'

'No. The very best ever.'

'Teresa was here,' Mom said when I got back late. She was drunk as a lord, only less gracious, her voice slurred.

'When – this morning? What'd she want?'

'I don't know. Didn't let her in.'

'You *what*? Why not?'

'Couldn't face it.'

I stared at her in disgust, hands on my hips. I could see she was barely awake now.

'Didn't feel like entertaining your friends at ten o'clock in the morning, if that's all right with you.'

Ten o'clock? It must've been something urgent for Teresa to have left the shop. I had to go to her, late as it was.

'Where's Len?'

Mom gave a nasty laugh, slumped back in the chair, her hair hanging loose. 'Where d'you think? Over at Molly's getting his leg over with never a thought.'

'You make me sick,' I said, heading for the door. 'Don't you ever think about anyone except yourself?'

'You're a fine one to talk,' she shrieked after me childishly. 'Takes one to know one!'

Despite the dark I ran most of the way to the Spinis. I felt I'd been woken up roughly from a dream, real life battering its way in at the door again. It was nearly eleven, but I had to see them and there'd be no time the next morning. I ran down the entry and saw there was still light showing downstairs in their house.

Teresa opened the door cautiously. When she saw it was me she stepped straight out and flung her arms round me.

'They're safe!' She was all aquiver with joy even now. Loosing me, she pulled me into the house and it was then I saw she wasn't alone. Carlo was sitting there with her.

'Mom's asleep,' Teresa explained. 'It was all too much for 'er – she's hardly had a wink since the ship went down. It all caught up with 'er tonight. Carlo's stayed on to give me a bit of company.'

Teresa laid a letter in front of me. 'Look – from Dad. They've been in Sutton Coldfield all this time if you please!' She laughed and I could hear a touch of hysteria in her voice, the days of pent-up tension only releasing themselves now.

Micky's letter was short. It said he and Stevie were in a transit camp which was 'not very comfortable' and that he'd been 'a bit unwell', whatever that meant. Uncle Matt had been moved on somewhere else a couple of days ago but Micky and Stevie were still waiting. Micky made a joke about holiday camps and sent his love. I felt my eyes prickle with tears when at the end of this short letter, after messages of love to his family, he'd written, 'and to little Genie'.

I looked up at Teresa. 'Oh, thank God.'

*

I went to the station with Joe on the Wednesday night, holding tight to every last second with him. Walking tall in his uniform, kitbags on his shoulders, he looked older, and I suddenly felt shy. In such a public spot for farewells as New Street Station it was still possible to find privacy because the place was so crowded, so full of traffic and clamour that it made you feel alone. Service people and their loved ones, people just travelling in civvy street, all of them were wrapped up in their own rush for a train or struggle with an awkward piece of luggage, with their goodbyes.

Holding Joe's arm, I passed through the crowds with him, banging against bags and haversacks, arms and shoulders clad in blues and khaki, through the cigarette smoke and shouting, the Tannoyed announcements and the hissing and chunking of other trains moving out, until we found Joe's. We'd cut it rather fine and Joe looked relieved he hadn't missed it.

Saying goodbye was awful. I couldn't stand it, felt I had to pull back, close in everything I was feeling, not let it wash over me so that it didn't hurt so much. I found suddenly I had nothing to say, and stood there next to Joe as minutes tore past, desperate for him to stay but incapable of even speaking to him.

Joe put his bags down and took me by the shoulders. At first I couldn't look at him.

'Genie – tell me you'll wait for me? You'll be here?'

I shrugged. 'Course I will. Don't be so daft.' I was awkward, angry almost, fighting back tears. All I really cared about would get on that train any minute and disappear to God knows where.

Poor Joe tried again. 'I love you, Genie. You do know that, don't you?'

I glanced into his eyes, then down at his boots, nodding. The whistle shrieked along the platform.

'This is it then.' He couldn't seem to let go of me. 'I'll have to get on . . .'

He bent to pick up his bags and move off. Turning, he said, 'See you then.'

The hurt in his eyes sliced through me but I couldn't seem to move. People were pushing past, scrambling for the carriages, shouting, snatching hurried kisses.

Joe was throwing his bags through the door, leaving them to the risk of being trampled on by all the boots clattering up and down.

Straightening up, he turned and his eyes found me again, me standing there all knotted up inside with my arms crossed tightly over my chest.

'Genie!'

He was going, really going. Another whistle cut the air like a scream.

'Joe. *Joe!*'

I tore to him, shoving and fighting past people, not caring, and pulled him into my arms, covering his face with kisses, frantic to tell him, to show him. 'I love you, I love you – I don't want you to go . . .'

Joe gave a shuddering laugh of relief, holding me so tight, kissing me back. 'Thank goodness. My love,' he called me. His love.

As the train moved off, I, like lots of other people, ran a few yards with it, kissing his hand through the window, hearing his laughter. My last sights of him were his dark eyes meeting mine, lips blowing a kiss, then his arm with all the other arms like bristles waving out along the train, until I wasn't sure any more which one was his.

August 1940

Joe, my Joe as I thought of him now, was posted up north, while every day the news from Gloria was full of the Battle of Britain. But at the moment, Joe was safe. And as the days went by I discovered he was a letter writer, and he wrote to me as often as he could, every two or three days.

'My dear sweet Genie . . .' He'd tell me a bit about the routine of the squadron – what he was allowed to tell without too much of the censor's blue pencil butting in. All day-to-day things. But by the end he always found something else to say – something specially for me. Things he might have been too shy to say to my face. And those bits I'd read again and again until I could remember every word. I'd recite them to myself in my head in the factory or in bed at night, trying to remember his face properly, the feel of him close.

'I never knew what it was to be truly happy until I met you . . . Every day I think of that night I heard you sing . . . I'll be home to you on the first train when they'll let me . . . You have taken a piece of my heart from me . . .'

And I wrote back and found it easier to say on paper what you really think because you don't feel such a tit doing it. It was just hard to find words for it all, when I wanted to fill the letters with 'I love you. I love you. Thank you for loving me . . .'

'When I used to work at the pawn shop,' I wrote to him once, 'this lady came in one day and passed away in the shop, right in front of me. And there've been all the other bad things that've happened, like Big Patsy taking his own life, my Dad going missing and my Mom never being happy. And now I've got you. I can't explain this properly – it'll come out all wrong. But things feel different. It's not that everything's all right suddenly of course. But it's as if before, there were all these bits hanging off. Like a tatty old mop. But now I've found the bit that holds them all together, the handle, sort of thing. Are you laughing reading this? I'm just trying to tell you that knowing you're there makes everything feel hundreds, thousands of times better than all my favourite dreams.'

Most of the news I told him would be about the factory because they were the people he knew. 'Nancy knows about us,' I wrote soon after he'd gone. 'She's really got it in for me, but I don't care.'

That's how it was then. Nothing seemed to get through to me, yet at the same time I could afford to be kinder somehow. Which was a good job, because if I hadn't had the protection of Joe's love my poor mom would've driven me completely round the bend.

Her emotions were like a big dipper ride, only the dips were a hell of a lot longer and wider than the heights. She was drinking of course. The first drink mellowed her and she could be almost pleasant. Then the slide began. Mainly she was sorry for herself. And angry – with anyone and everyone. Everyone's life looked rosier than hers.

One day the post brought a letter from Joe for me that set me singing inside (I didn't dare sing out loud in front of Mom) and one of the much rarer ones we had from Eric.

Dear Mom,
    I hope this letter finds you well? I am in good health thank you. I am doing well at school and making progress on the piano. Mrs Spenser says I may be able to start on the violin. Her cat Lucy has had kittens and one is going to be mine.
    Are you and Dad and Genie and Len all keeping well?
    With regards from Eric.

This made her cry like anything. 'He didn't write that himself. She's just told him what to say – to his own mom! "Regards" – to us! He's not my little Eric any more. He doesn't even know about his own dad, but what use is it me telling him anyway?'

Eric did seem such a long way off, and not just in miles. Mrs Spenser had no kids of her own and was lavishing what she had in the way of middle-class comfort and opportunity on this kid she'd had foisted on her. I suppose we should've felt grateful really. But it was nearly a year now, a long time in a lad's life, and he seemed like a stranger to us.

But it was Joe's letters, the smiles they brought to my face, that Mom could stand least of all. She was used to me courting her, needing her to love me and hungering after it, and now I'd turned to someone else.

That night her despair was terrible. Len sat watching her, his big eyes frightened as Mom got more and more drunk and her tears drew lines of black mascara down her face, which she smudged with her fists. She sat on the edge of her chair, hands clenching and unclenching, crying, sometimes flinging herself back in the chair, jerking about like a child in a tantrum, only much more pitiful for the age of her. I just didn't know what to do.

'It's all right for you!' she yelled at me. She kept saying that, accusing me.

'Why is it all right for me?' I didn't dare touch her and I didn't get any answer. She just mewled and sobbed.

'Wasser matter with 'er, Genie?' Len said.

'Lenny—' I spoke as calmly as I could manage. 'Go and get our Lil, will you?'

It was late, and I knew as Len plodded off that Lil was going to be anything but pleased, but I was scared of Mom. I couldn't cope with all this on my own.

'Mom—' I sat down by her when he'd gone. 'Look, why don't you ask to give up work? You're getting too tired all the time.'

'Oh yes,' she snapped at me, voice thick with drink. 'Then what'll I do? Sit here all day?'

'There's loads to do here. If there was someone at home it'd make things a lot easier. There's the house, and I've no time to shop. The off-ration stuff is all queues and Saturdays're terrible for that now. It'd be a help to all of us – we mightn't all be so tired all the time.'

'Huh,' was all she said, but I did at least feel she was listening. There was a lull, before she started getting all in a state again.

'Where's your dad? I want him. When're we ever going to know if he's coming home or not? You tell me that. I can't go on like this . . .'

Wearily I went and set a kettle to boil in the kitchen,

partly to get out of her way. When Lil arrived she wasn't nearly as mardy about it as I'd expected, and she was all dolled up.

'S'all right,' she said cheerfully. 'I'd only just got in anyhow.'

'Where've you been then?'

Lil took me by surprise by giving me a wink and putting a finger to her lips. 'That'd be telling. Anyhow, sssh for now.' She went to Mom. 'Oh Dor – you can't go on getting yourself all in a state like this. It's no good for you or for the babby.'

Mom cried exhaustedly. 'I can't go on,' she murmured into Lil's shoulder. 'I just can't.'

Lil looked at me over her head, her eyes troubled. Len stood by the door.

'Ta, Lenny,' I said. 'Tell you what, you could take Gloria into the front for a bit, how about that?'

Relieved, and hugging his beloved wireless to his chest, he escaped, and we heard music drifting through from the other room.

Lil prised Mom off her and tried to look into her face, though her head was lolling.

'Look, Dor.' Her voice was sharp now. 'You've got to pull yourself together. You can't go on like this. You're making yourself ill.'

'I can't,' Mom groaned. 'Just can't.'

'You've got to. You don't have a choice. What about the babby? And Genie here?'

'But what about me?' Mom was wailing.

'You're supposed to be their mom. And there's Len's wedding. You can't just cave in now!'

The kettle was gushing steam. By the time I'd made tea things'd gone quiet and I went back in to find my mom falling asleep across Lil's lap, her breath jerky as a sobbing child's.

Molly and Len's wedding arrangements were causing quite a kerfuffle. This was partly because Gladys Bender was making sure they did, quite apart from everything having to be done at such short notice because of it being a wedding with a shotgun pointing at its head.

Gladys pestered us from morning till night, whenever anyone was in. She'd never in her dreams expected her enormous, not quite all there daughter to find a mate, and now she'd got the chance, Molly was going to be MARRIED, and married with bells on.

'Oh-oh, here she comes again,' we'd say, seeing Gladys steaming across in her slippers. A door slamming somewhere across the street was enough to send us scuttling to the window to see if we were about to have another lethal dose of her.

Then she'd be hammering at the door as if we were all deaf, and when we let her in, would often be as red in the face and beady with perspiration as if she'd run a couple of miles to get there. In she'd come, us grimacing at the smells of sweat and disinfectant. We put up with her self-righteous tyranny day after day because we had to: we were Len's family and he'd got Molly into trouble.

'I thought it'd be right for you to see to all the food afterwards,' she announced. This was half past seven one morning. 'Since I've got my hands full and there are more of you with a wage coming in like. And I've got all the trouble of the dress and Molly to look after in her condition . . .'

'Well, she is your daughter,' Mom snapped. 'And it takes two, doesn't it?'

There's the pot calling the kettle black, I thought. Felt like saying to Gladys, I've got one to look after an' all.

Gladys folded her arms, pulling herself upright so that a good inch of greyish petticoat showed from under her stained red dress and pinner.

'It's snowing in France,' Mom murmured, but this was completely lost on Gladys.

'You saying you're not happy with all I'm doing?' she bawled at us. 'D'you want to give Molly and your Len a good send off, eh? Or don't you think they're worth it?'

'We can do some food, can't we, Mom?' I looked nervously at her. Even as I said it I already had a feeling 'we' was going to mean 'me'.

Mom nodded, yawning at the same time. This was a bit early for her to start a slanging match. 'Lil'll give us a hand. Not as if there'll be crowds, is it?'

'There might be quite a number actually,' Gladys announced, now we'd safely volunteered. 'After all, I'm one of fifteen and there's no one'll want to miss seeing our Molly tie the knot.'

On the Saturday I went to Nan's for a conflab. The kids were at the table filling their faces with liver and onions and spuds and Lil was cooking more for her and Nan. The kids were staring at her and I stared too. What'd come over her? She was by the range, stirring gravy with a metal spoon and humming, actually humming.

'You swallowed a budgie or summat?' I asked her.

Lil turned, laughing, and gave me another wink.

'No, that'd be the sensible thing to do,' Nan remarked, limping in with a bucket of slack. The coal hole was in action again since there'd been so many months of not having to shelter in it after all.

I looked from one to the other of them. Only one thing would put that glowing pink in Lil's cheeks which had been pale and tired for so long.

'Who is he then?'

Lil laughed like I hadn't heard her laugh in years. 'Can tell you're in love all right. Takes one to know one, doesn't it? How is Joe, Genie?'

'All right.' I blushed as Lil came closer to look in my eyes, teasing. 'He's doing fine.'

Suddenly she stooped towards me and kissed my cheek, her dark hair brushing my face. 'I'm glad for you. Really glad. He's very nice. I'd soon tell you if I didn't think so.'

'You've hardly met him!'

'I met him at the show that night. His eyes hardly left your face.'

'Who's this feller of yours then?'

Lil went back to the gravy. 'His name's Frank. Met him when we were playing at the pub down Bissell Street.'

'Proper charmer 'e is,' Nan said drily, stoking the range. She didn't like men to be charming. Charm to her meant snakes in the grass, blarney and insincerity.

'He's not!' Lil said. 'Well I mean, yes, he is – but not how she means.'

I was sitting by Cathleen who was idly letting me feed her little squares of liver. 'What's he do?'

'He's a mechanic. Got a garage out in Kings Heath.

And he's part-time ARP. But there're a couple of little things he does on the side.'

'Yes, I bet there are.' Nanny Rawson straightened up, holding her back. 'No one's shoes should be as shiny as them 'e turns up in.'

Lil laughed in exasperation. 'Oh Mom! Frank's all right. He's not selling anything – not as such. He's interested in fortune telling, tarot, that sort of thing.'

I frowned. 'I thought it's only women do things like that?'

'Oh, he doesn't actually do it himself. He's got a room – lets it to this woman. He knows all about it himself though, how it's done—'

'I wonder what else she's selling while she's at it,' Nan retorted.

Lil started to get a bit shirty. 'I've had enough of this. You've condemned the man when you don't even know him. And he's very good to me.'

'Well, that's all very nice,' Nanny said. 'But you find out what 'e's after before you get in any deeper, because you can be sure there'll be summat. Now that's quite enough of this in front of the kiddies. Want some jam on that, Genie?' she said, seeing me eating bread and scrape.

'No ta. Let Tom have it.'

Tom gave me his handsome smile, gappy with missing teeth. There came a banging on the door of the shop. Nan's face turned thunderous. 'It'd better not be,' she growled.

'I'll go.'

Morgan. As I slipped into the shop I could see him through the glass, and the outline of the girl with him. When I opened up the door I saw she was a lot older

291

than she appeared from inside, in her little girly clothes, and she looked browned off with the whole set up before she'd even started.

'Forgot my key,' Morgan said in his castor-oil voice. 'Sorry to disturb you.'

'Not half as much as you'll disturb us in a few minutes no doubt,' I said, standing well back as they went in as if they were a passing stink bomb. They disappeared quickly up the stairs.

'Was that that bastard Morgan?' Cathleen lisped in an interested sort of way when I went back to them.

'Cathleen!' Lil exploded, although neither of us could help a smile.

Nan leaned over to her. 'It'll be mustard on your tongue next time if I 'ear any more language like that. Now off to bed with you all if you're finished.'

Nan had made sure, since Lil came back, that the kids slept in the back bedroom away from the dividing wall with Morgan's part of the house at the front. They were such tiny houses and the noises travelled with barely an obstacle through the walls and floors.

Cathleen was still up in the attic in a cot with Lil.

I changed her – the kids had nightclothes now Lil was earning better – and took her down for a drop of milk which she sat on my lap to drink, next to the range, quiet now with heavy eyes and suddenly sweeter. I kissed her soft cheek and stroked the fine blond curls. 'You sleep now, Cathleen. You're a tired little girl, aren't you?'

Once I'd carried her up to bed I went to see the boys, and read from an old book of ghost stories, Tom's hand resting on my arm.

'Now I've scared you witless you can get some sleep,'

I said when I'd finished. The springs creaked loudly as they climbed into bed. 'Night night.'

Downstairs, before the kids had even settled, we were soon aware of another set of bedsprings under strain on the floor above.

'How many's up there?' Lil hissed to me while Nan was upstairs. She didn't like any mention of them up there, any admission they existed.

'Only one.'

'Makes a change. Usually takes two to get him going nowadays.'

We heard Nan's slow tread at the top of the stairs and Lil made a face. 'You coming singing with us now you've got the courage? You enjoyed it, didn't you?'

'I can't leave Mom.'

'You've left her tonight. Anyroad, you don't need to leave her, she can come.'

'She won't though. And I haven't left her at home. She's at work.'

'Genie – look, Dor's in trouble, there's no doubt, and we're all sorry for her, the babby and that. But if your dad's not coming back she's just going to have to knuckle down and get on with it. It's terrible – I know 'cause I've done it. But she can't expect you to take over the running of her life for her. Because if you'll do it, she'll let you. That's what she's like, always has been. One for sitting back and letting everyone else do it all. But you've got your life to lead as well, so don't let her take it away from you. She's already wrecked Len's—' She stopped abruptly as Nanny Rawson walked in.

'But I still don't think I should leave her. Not when she keeps getting in such a state.'

'She may be in a state,' Lil said drily, 'but she's just going to have to get out of it.'

Nan was dishing up liver and spuds for us. 'Let's get going on Len's wedding,' she said. 'After all it's not just Molly's wedding, it's his too, and he deserves the very best we can give him.' I saw her eyes meet Lil's, and there was a hard look in them I didn't understand. 'He's owed that much.'

So, with years of practice, we ignored the thumps and squeaks from upstairs. The wedding was booked for a Monday, ten days away, and everyone was arranging the day off. Gladys had said, 'Molly can't possibly be showing if we do it that soon.'

Lil had snorted at this. 'She's such a size she could get to nine months without anyone being the wiser.'

Although Lil had pledged to do anything she could to help, she was full of doubts about this marriage. First of all was the fact that Len and Molly were, for the time being, going to carry on living where they were, in their separate homes.

'Don't seem right,' she said.

'Lenny seemed well put out at the idea of moving in with Molly somewhere,' I told her. 'Don't think it'd crossed his mind that anything might actually change. He wants to stop at home with us.'

'There's no houses to be had,' Nan said.

'What's Dor got to say about it?' Lil asked, grimacing at the colour of the tea. 'Proper maid's water this is.'

'Not much.'

Lil was still looking disbelieving. 'What about – where're they going to sleep and that?'

Nan gave her one of her looks.

'Search me,' I said. 'All they talk about at the moment is clothes – Molly's dress.'

'Who's this woman who's making it then?'

'A Mrs Van der Meyer.'

Lil frowned. 'That a Kraut name?'

'No, Dutch, and anyhow he's dead. She's a widow. Anyroad, Molly's not going to let any of us within a mile of that dress before the day.'

'Course not. Bad luck else, isn't it?'

'If you ask me,' Lil said, 'the whole thing's bad luck.'

For the time being Vera Spini was like a person reborn. When I came to the shop that Saturday after the good news I heard her singing. She looked younger suddenly. There was colour in her cheeks, she'd touched up her hair again and it was twisted into a straw-coloured knot behind her head.

'That's a happy sound,' I said. 'Nice to hear you. More like before the war.'

She was bustling around the shop with a broom and turned to smile at me.

'I can't say I'm not worried. It's all wrong what they've done – he shouldn't be there. There's no trial or nothing, so what are we supposed to do? I get so angry thinking about it. But for now—' She stopped and leaned on the broom. 'They're all alive. That's all I can think about.' Her expression turned bleak for a second. 'I don't know what I'd have done ... This is daft thinking about something that hasn't even happened.' She carried on sweeping. 'D'you want Teresa? She's round the back.'

'Is Carlo there?'

Vera looked round at me with a mischievous smile. 'You've noticed then?'

'He seems to be round a lot.'

'Well, he's not here now. Lovely boy he is. I just wish Teresa would open her eyes and see the lad's crazy about her. But that's Teresa for you, always facing the wrong way when it matters. He'll be gone and she still won't get the message.'

'Gone?'

'He's joining up.'

Teresa was washing the floor in the house so I climbed on a chair to talk to her, watching her egg-timer shape from behind as she knelt, circling the scrubbing brush on the tiles.

She looked up and grinned through black curtains of hair. 'Thought you were up to your eyes in wedding dresses.'

'Oh no – Gladys is in charge of all that. We know every stitch and tuck of it, except for the fact we've never seen it!'

'She wearing white?'

'Oh, I don't know about that!' Both of us laughed. 'Can't really, can she, in her position. You are coming, aren't you?'

'I wouldn't miss it for anything.'

'We're decorating the church tomorrow night – me and Lil. I've been down the Bull Ring buying up the flowers.'

Teresa asked cautiously, 'How's your mom?'

It was such a relief to have someone I could tell the whole truth to. 'She's bad. In a right state most of the time, Teresa. I can't get through to her at all since Joe and me . . .'

Teresa stopped scrubbing and sat back on her heels, pushing her hair out of the way with her arm. 'You really serious about him?'

I nodded.

'I can see you are. You're different. How does it feel, Genie?'

'What?'

'Loving someone – really.'

How to tell her? The very best best. 'What about Carlo?'

'I've always liked Carlo – a real lot actually. It's just I've known him so long. He's always just been there, like Stevie—'

'Up till now,' I interrupted.

She looked into my face. 'I'm very fond of him. He loves me, has for a long time, so he says. I suppose I thought it'd be more dramatic. Like in the pictures. He's always so polite. He hardly touches me—'

'A gent?'

'I s'pose. Shy of changing things, I think. I know I don't want him to go. I do know that much. By the way—' She stood up and lifted the bucket. 'Have you heard about Walt?'

'No,' I said stiffly. 'What?'

'He's got a girl into trouble. Run off to join up and left her instead of facing the music.'

'But he's too young to join up! He's only seventeen.'

Teresa put her head on one side. 'D'you know, since they took Stevie, and all the trouble we've been through with it, he never once came in to see us. No "How are you, Mrs Spini, any news about Stevie?" Nothing. Some friend he turned out to be. That girl's better off without him. So I don't s'pose lying about his age'll come too hard to him, do you?'

Lil and I did our best with the church. The flowers I bought were a whole mix of colours, and as well as those, Mr Tailor from down the road let us have some out of his garden which was decked out like a flower show every summer. It was from him we had a bundle of wheat which he grew because he liked the look of it and tight yellow rosebuds which made Lil say wistfully, 'Aren't they lovely? They're my favourites, they are.'

Mom half-heartedly offered to help, but she still had sewing jobs to do on Len's suit for the next day so we left her to it. Lil and I carried our buckets and ribbon and scissors down the road and let ourselves into the church in the evening light. Peach-coloured rays were shafting in through the west window. The atmosphere was stuffy and filled with the smell of floor polish.

Lil eyed up the wrought-iron flower stand. 'I'm not sure I'm very good at this. We'll have to hope for the best.' She turned to me. 'I want Len to have the best. Have we got hymns and that?'

'Mom's sorted it with the vicar. She wanted "Lead Us, Heavenly Father, Lead Us". She said that's a good one for a wedding.'

We managed, after a few false starts, to cut and arrange the flowers in a magnificent spray on the stand, and put vases of flowers round to decorate the altar and sidetables. We tied sprays of wheat ears with yellow ribbon and attached them to the ends of the pews.

'Looks like a harvest festival,' I said, tying bows and flattening them the best I could.

'No it doesn't.' Lil backed down the church, surveying what we'd done. 'It looks beautiful. Molly'll love it, bless her. Time something nice happened to her.' Lil was coming round much more to the idea of the wedding now she'd got caught up in the spirit of it.

'You've changed your tune.'

'It's just – seeing it all, like this . . . D'you remember my wedding – Patsy's and mine?'

'Course I do.' I was seven when they married. 'Wouldn't forget being a bridesmaid, would I?'

Lil shook her head. 'I was so happy that day. It really was the best day of my life – well, maybe except the ones the babbies were born. Not even a wedding beats that. My poor Patsy. I hope he don't mind me going about with Frank.'

'D'you really like Frank, Lil?' I asked shyly. Now I was with Joe it seemed we could talk woman to woman.

Lil picked up a long curl of leftover ribbon and started winding it round her fingers. 'I do, yes. At first – well, still really, because it's only been a few weeks – I couldn't stop thinking about Patsy. Comparing them, and feeling bad at being with someone else. As if Patsy was watching, talking to me in my head. I've felt that on and off since he died. At first he was always saying, "Why didn't you stop me? Why did you let me do it?" My own guilt talking, I s'pose. But I know really it wasn't my fault, wasn't anyone's. It was all an accident. Anyhow, after a bit I'd hear him saying more ordinary things, just like chat. That was nice, for a bit.' She gave a little laugh. 'Now though, it's more as if – how can I say it? – he's still there and I love him, but he's not part of now. I can see Frank without being ashamed. I can love both of them.'

'Our nan doesn't take to him, does she? I'd've thought she was a pretty good judge.'

Lil gave a snort. 'Mom? Are you kidding? She may be a good judge of some things, like how much stew a bag of scrag end'll run to. But when it comes to men . . . I mean look who she married! And she was wrong about Patsy, wasn't she? Had him down as a navvy and a waster. No, if you want advice about men, Genie, come to me, not my mom – and not your mom neither, come to that!'

We both laughed, but Lil with an edge of tears. 'Sometimes I just want to feel someone's arms around me so bad I ache with it.' She caught hold of the broom. 'Best get on. Be dark soon.' I followed her round with a dustpan and brush, and we went to search for a dustbin out the back of the church.

'Your Joe now,' Lil said, shooting flower stalks into the bin. I felt myself blush. My Joe! 'He's a good'un I reckon. You could do a lot worse than him, and you deserve to be happy, Genie. God knows, you do.'

The wedding morning dawned bright and we were all up and running like headless chickens before we were half awake. Our nan was down by half six carrying plates of stuff already cut with muttoncloth over them, I was brewing up tea for everyone and there were eggs on the go in a pan. Mom and Nan started laying up the table at the front, talking about beef and chicken sandwiches. We'd saved everything we could for that wedding, and lots of people had chipped in. We'd already done a trifle of sorts and there was tinned fruit, and Gladys was being very mysterious about the wedding cake, which was another aspect of things she'd taken on herself.

She soon made an appearance of course.

Mom rolled her eyes to the ceiling. 'Go and answer the door before she knocks it down, Genie.'

Gladys sailed in with a tray of little cakes. 'Straight out of the oven,' she boomed. 'I've been up since four.'

The smell of them drifted in after her, sweet and delicious, and they looked soft and golden. Good job our mom didn't volunteer for that bit.

'How's Molly?' Nan asked.

'Got her 'ead over a pail at the moment,' Gladys reported to anyone in the whole neighbourhood who might happen to be listening. 'She'll be awright with summat on her stomach though.' She wiped her hands on her pinner and lowered her voice, which was a relief. Looking round at us in grand triumph she said, 'We've got the dress. You're in for a surprise.'

We all stared at her. Were we supposed to ask questions?

'Can't wait,' I said since no one else opened their mouth.

'Anyroad, this won't get the babby a new coat,' Gladys said as if we were all in a plot to waylay her. 'We'll see you later.'

'Gladys,' Mom called across after her. 'Any idea how many you've got coming?'

Disappearing into her house, she called, 'Oh, quite a few . . .'

We had to get Lenny out of bed and get some breakfast down him. Nan had starched him a collar and she fixed it all for him, pushing in the studs. 'Chin up, Len. It's a bit tight,' she said, struggling. Len's huge face loomed over the tight collar which was biting into the side of his neck. 'How d's it feel?'

'Awright.' He was grinning, which was more or less what he'd been doing non-stop ever since we first got him up. She helped him into his trousers and jacket, fastened his tie for him, soaped his hair flat and combed it. 'Now – let's have a look at you.'

My nan stood there in front of her enormous,

damaged son, looking him over from his plastered down hair to his newly blacked shoes. I saw a nerve in her face twitch. I bet she never thought she'd see this day. Her Len getting married. She licked her lips to bring the tremble in them under control and, pulling out a hanky from the front of her dress, she looked down so her eyes were hidden.

Finally she said, 'You'll do.'

The wedding was at eleven. At the last minute I was still putting whitener on my shoes and searching for gloves. But we walked down to St Paul's in good time, Mom with her arm through Len's, explaining to him for the umpteenth time that when the service started he was to wait at the front for Molly to walk up to him, and then the vicar would do all the other things they'd practised.

'Remember what you have to say when he asks you the questions, Len?'

'I—'

'Do. I *do*, Len. That's all you have to remember.' She made him repeat it over. 'Anyway, Mom and I'll be sitting right at the front so if you need any help you just look at us, right?'

'Church looks very nice,' Nan said approvingly as we walked in, and it was true. The blaze of colour from the spray at the front, edged with the half-open yellow roses, looked beautiful, though Mom didn't bother to say so to us. Everything had to be perfect for her precious Lenny's wedding day but she wasn't going to hand out any credit for it. The only thing she said to me on the way in, in a melancholy voice, was, 'I wish Victor was here.'

Our side of the church was empty until we arrived. Nanny Rawson's sister over in Aldridge said she might get there but we never saw any sign of her and no one else knew it was happening. But over on Molly's side there were quite a few there already, all dolled up.

After a few minutes the lady organist started up and we saw more and more trickle in on the Benders' side. Nan, next to me, was watching them from under the same hat she'd worn to Lola's funeral, only this time she had on a flowery frock instead of the mourning-coloured coat. I knew she was sizing up the numbers, wondering if they were all coming back to the house and if we'd got enough food.

There was a tap on my shoulder. 'Genie!' It was Tom, all scrubbed and in his school shorts and jumper. 'Can I sit with you?' He didn't need to ask. As he squeezed into the pew he opened one hand and showed me a shiny shilling.

'Look what Frank gave us. Patsy's got one too, and he gave a tanner to our Cathleen.'

'Blimey, lucky you!'

I turned round full of curiosity. Lil was coming down the aisle towards us with Patsy and Cathleen. She looked marvellous, in a sunny yellow dress which matched the roses, her lips glossy red and her hair swept up with a few curling tendrils hanging down, and I was struck again by just how beautiful she was. It was so hard to believe Nanny Rawson had looked similar in her youth. Cathleen was holding Lil's hand, wearing a little pale blue pinafore dress with white rabbits appliqued on, which I knew Lil had stitched herself. But my glance soon shifted from her to the man whose face I could see over Lil's left shoulder. I saw immaculate, shiny black hair, a thin black moustache, and as they came nearer, a sharply pressed suit. He was following Lil closely, looking coolly down at the rest of us.

'Crikey!' I whipped round to my nan. 'Is that Frank? 'E looks just like Clark Gable!'

'That,' Nan said, thumbing determinedly through *Hymns Ancient and Modern*, 'is what I'm worried about.'

Lil, Frank and the other two children settled in the pew behind us and after a moment I turned timidly to have a peep. Lil gave me a gorgeous smile and a surreptitious wink. Frank was looking at me and Lil leaned over and touched his hand. 'This is my little sister, Eugenie.'

He held out his hand to shake mine. 'Very pleased to meet you.' And he smiled.

I felt rather wobbly. The resemblance was so striking I thought any moment he'd say, 'Frankly my dear, I don't give a damn.' But instead he said, 'I'm Frank.' I stared back at him hard and couldn't see anything in his eyes to make me suspicious so I smiled back and said hello.

Just then, behind them, Teresa came in and, to my surprise, I saw Carlo was with her. She gave me a little wave and they sat in the third row. I couldn't help wondering how things were going with Carlo.

The organ struck up louder and everyone stood. Mom pushed Len out to the front where he waited, lost looking for a moment and then, as he caught sight of Molly, beaming like a sunflower opening out. Everyone on both sides swivelled to see the bride.

There was a gasp from all round. We couldn't help it. All of us watched, riveted, as she swayed along the aisle on the arm of one of her uncles, since her dad had been dead years.

As they came closer I heard Nan mutter, 'God Almighty.' Afterwards Lil said Molly was the nearest thing to a jam roly-poly on legs she'd ever set eyes on. The dress was simply enormous. It had every possible combination of frills and leg-of-mutton sleeves and bows and flounces that you could ever imagine all crammed into the same space together. The sleeves made Molly look as if she'd been blown up with a bicycle pump, the layered skirts flounced hugely over her backside and the neck, cleavage, sleeves and skirt were all trimmed with huge floppy bows. Not only that, although the dress was white – a bit cheeky of Gladys, considering – the edges were piped with a bright rasp-berry-coloured material and half the bows were made of the same colour. On her head she wore a little white cloche hat with a long gauze veil trailing from it which was, at the moment, down over her face. Actually she looked more like an enormous summer pudding with only some of the juice soaked through the bread.

But she was Len's Molly, and his face was brimful of delight. The fact she looked good enough to eat would be a bonus in Len's list of priorities.

The uncle was quite a size as well, and the two of them had rather a squeeze to fit along. It was only once they'd passed we saw the bridesmaid behind, a girl of about nine, in a dress of a terrible bright acid blue. Nan looked at me and I could hear her thoughts: What could have possessed them? But the child, unlike every other member of Molly's family, was extraordinarily pretty, with long, wavy chestnut hair, striking light blue eyes and the longest eyelashes I'd ever seen. A real beauty. It was like seeing Snow White with all the dwarfs around her.

The service sped past. I could tell Mom was on edge, sober as a judge today, afraid of Len putting a foot wrong. But he said his 'I do's' with such feeling that there was a ripple of laughter from behind him. He fed the ring on to Molly's pudgy finger and was allowed to lift the veil and kiss her. Molly turned, smiling coyly. They were married. I wanted to clap.

Outside we deluged them with rice and confetti and they looked like the happiest pair of people I'd ever seen.

'Heaven help us if all that lot come back,' Mom panted as she and I sped down the road ahead of everyone else. The few photographs had already been done. 'We'd better keep some of the sandwiches back so they don't all go at once.'

The minute we were back in the house she was swigging at the gin bottle.

'Mom!'

'What? God, I needed that. What're you staring at?'

'Don't get drunk, Mom. Not today – please.'

'Don't be silly – course I shan't.' She let out a titter, putting the top back on the bottle. 'I just wanted a little pick-me-up. I don't get drunk, do I?'

'Not half,' I muttered, checking the things laid out on the lacy cloth.

'Think of our Len, married!' Mom's voice was high with nerves and excitement. Suddenly she burst into hysterical-sounding giggles, hand over her mouth. 'Oh, that dress – have you ever seen anything like it?'

I had to laugh with her then. 'It was a bit loud, wasn't it?'

Tears of laughter trickled down our faces. 'How're we going to cope with her here?' Mom spluttered. 'It'll be like having a minesweeper in the house—'

'And that bridesmaid – talk about Reckitt's blue!'

Mom wiped her eyes, trying to calm down. 'Pretty little thing though, wasn't she? Oh dear, it's good to have a laugh. Come on though, Genie.' She started flapping again. 'They'll all be here in a minute. How on earth're we going to manage for glasses?'

'Someone'll have to go round the pubs, see if they can spare us any.'

Soon we heard the first knock on the door, but it was only Nanny Rawson and Lil with the kids. Lil went off round to the neighbours and pubs begging use of more glasses, plates and cups. Mom was spreading more bread and Nanny Rawson took over the sandwich factory so by the time Molly got there we were as ready as we'd ever be.

Molly filled up most of the hall and with Gladys and Len trying to squeeze in too there wasn't a hope, so Mom shifted them all through into the garden. Then there followed a thick stream of Gladys and Molly's relatives and it looked as if every last one of her fourteen brothers and sisters had turned up, along with bits and bobs of family and children, so the place was soon heaving with them all. When Frank arrived I was impressed to find he'd stayed back to show people the way. He looked even more like a film star when set against Gladys's clan.

Looking at Frank carefully, I could see he was quite a bit older than Lil – forty-something probably. The suit was smart and you could have looked in the black toe-caps of his two-tone shoes to put your lipstick on. How Nanny Rawson was going to loathe those shiny shoes!

'How's it going, Genie?' He pushed in through the throng of the front room where they were already lighting fags and drinking beer. I had a good look at his face again. I felt protective of Lil. She'd had enough on her plate. He was gorgeous, but was he a chancer? The smile in those steely grey eyes was warm enough, so I gave him the benefit of the doubt.

'All right.' I smiled. 'Lil's still rounding up glasses somewhere.'

'Anything I can do?'

'Beers?' We'd got a couple of barrels in.

'Right you are, Genie. And anything else you want – just give me the word.' And he really did knuckle down and help, seemed like a worker all right.

Nanny Rawson came in holding two plates of sandwiches high so they didn't get knocked. 'Right!' she boomed, and everyone went quiet. 'There's more of you than we bargained for today which is awright. It's very nice. But you'll have to go easy on the grub and make sure everyone gets a share, awright?'

After that the party got into full swing and I went round offering food to a large number of people who looked very like Gladys and others of her relatives who looked totally different. Molly and Len stayed in the garden with a crowd, including the blue bridesmaid who was dashing about playing tig with Patsy, Tom and some other kids. Molly looked very hot in all her finery. Seeing me, she swooped down and clasped me in her arms so I was buried in bows, frills, bosoms and cheap scent. Up close I felt the dress was made of cotton.

'So you're my little niece now, Genie!'

I smiled. 'S'pose I am. You look lovely, Molly.'

Lenny and I had a big hug too. 'You did well, Len. We could all hear you.'

'I'm married now,' he announced.

'You are. And soon to be a dad,' I added more quietly.

'Never thought I'd be the one getting married.'

I squeezed his hand. 'I'll get you some grub.'

Inside, the house was full of chatter and smoke. Teresa and Carlo were there and I realized I hadn't had time to see them, but I caught Teresa's eye and grinned and waved as I went through the back room. In the front, Frank was still in charge of the beer and I heard him say to Nan, 'I hope you're going to give us a tune later, Mrs Rawson.'

'We'll 'ave to see.' Nan gave him a look as if to say when she did it wouldn't be as any kind of favour to him.

And then a noise broke through all the celebrating, a high, rising and falling whine.

'God Almighty!' Lil cried, 'It's an air raid!'

No one knew what to do. We weren't in practice for this. A bomb had come down last week across town but we had no routine.

'Well we won't all fit in the Anderson,' I said. Found I was giggling and didn't know why.

'Get Len and Molly in there, and the kids,' Nan said. 'The rest of us'll just 'ave to make do.'

For the next few minutes there was a low-level panic. Some of the guests went off saying they'd find a public shelter and Gladys pointed out that she had a cellar, so a few of her kin went across with her. Mom made sure she got into the shelter outside saying she was going to keep an eye on Molly and Len.

'Now isn't that just typical,' Lil hissed down my ear. 'I mean it's not as if she's got to worry about Molly getting pregnant now, is it?'

But in the end they found room for Nan as well. The rest of us sheltered in the little cupboard under the stairs – where I found myself with Lil and Frank – and under the tables front and back.

The raid went on for three and a half hours, and if it hadn't been for the absurdity of the situation and us all being together it would've been absolutely terrifying. The planes sounded so loud and close and when they were really overhead we all stopped talking and held our breath. We heard the crash of explosions in the distance.

'So it's really happening, isn't it?' Lil said as we crouched, ears straining, in the tiny space where there was barely room for the three of us.

'If I'd stayed out you could've had a lot more fun, couldn't you?' I said to them and Lil gave me a pretend slap on the cheek. 'Hey girl – what d'you take us for?'

When there was more of a lull we'd poke our heads out and call to the others under the tables. At the front were some of Gladys's family, who kept climbing in and out, polishing off the remains of the food, and Lil said it was a good job we'd still got the cake, 'if we ever get out of here.'

In the back room, under the smaller table, were Teresa and Carlo, and after the first time I popped in and found them wrapped tight in each other's arms, I thought I'd better just leave them to it. We heard their voices now and then, talking Italian mostly, and Lil winked at me. 'Lovely language, isn't it? Makes everything they say sound romantic.'

'Don't think they need the Italian for that by the look of things,' I said.

'Really?' Lil stretched out, put her head round the door, then drew back grinning. 'Ooh, I see what you mean!'

Frank told us jokes and stories to take our minds off it all, making us laugh. I was still trying to work him out, wasn't sure. He looked such a spiv, but at the same time in his face there was something worn and vulnerable that you didn't expect. And he did seem genuinely to care for Lil. By the end of the raids, what with all the laughs he gave us, I was more or less convinced.

The sun was low in the sky by the time the All Clear went, and we all crawled out to find the table empty.

'Greedy sods,' Lil said. 'Honestly.'

Gladys came back with her little band, although the lot who'd gone to find another shelter never reappeared and must've gone to the pub. Everyone was in a mad mood after the hours cooped up and we had a lot of laughs, ate trifle and evap and little cakes, then Gladys trotted back over to get The Cake.

When she stood it on the table everyone clapped and laughed. There were two tiers and on the top, moulded out of icing, was a little figure obviously meant to be Molly, with pink colouring piped round it something like her dress, and silver horseshoes at her feet.

'Where's the one of Len?' someone asked.

'You didn't want to crush the cake, did you?' another voice shouted. And amid the laughter and the cheers that everyone truly meant for them, Len and Molly cut the cake, each of them holding the knife with one of their enormous hands, both smiling madly and Molly's glasses misting up.

We hadn't got to the stage in the war when people were reduced to icing cardboard cakes. This was a real one with fruit and candied peel and it tasted delicious.

As the evening wore on, those who were left sang, led by Nan and Lil who dragged me in with them as well. Mom managed to get through the evening with barely a sniff at a bottle. Len and Molly were the picture of young love on chairs in front of me, Molly still in her amazing frock. And I don't know exactly what changes took place under the table in our back room that afternoon, but as we were singing, Teresa and Carlo sat smiling and holding hands, their shoulders touching like a couple of budgies. Life would have been perfect, really perfect, if my dad and Joe could have been there too.

Later that week my mental peace was blasted right apart by a letter from Joe telling me he was being re-posted down south, which could mean only one thing. He was going to join the fighters over the south coast and I could not rest easy again. The day I got his letter Gloria reported the RAF as having lost thirty-four planes that day. There was more bombing to the east of Birmingham. The war was real now, and drawing closer. We were on the alert for raids. When the sirens went the tradesmen harnessed their horses to the back of the carts to stop them bolting. Nanny Rawson had cleared the coal hole and started to get back into the shelter mentality. But I wasn't really worried about the raids. My own safety didn't feel all that important. It was Joe I worried about, day and night. Gloria was on overtime and one night when the accumulator went in the middle of the news I found myself screaming at her.

And there was Nancy carrying on. She was as nasty to me as she knew how, and had been ever since she found out for sure I'd 'stolen' Joe from her. She tried to turn the other women in the place against me by telling malicious tales.

The others knew where Joe was and gave me a lot of sympathy, which drove Nancy into even sorer vexation.

'What're you asking 'er for?' she snapped one day when someone enquired about him.

'Because she's the one Joe's writing letters to,' Doris said, 'whether you like it or not, Nance.'

''E's not!'

'Course he is,' Agnes said. 'Ain't 'e, Genie?'

I nodded. 'A couple of times a week.'

Nancy suddenly came at me round the table, hands like claws. 'It was all right before you came along. 'E liked me best!'

She was held back by two other women, both telling her to pack it in.

'I'm going to give 'er one, the sly bitch!' she shouted, struggling.

I was wound up tight with worry as it was, and sick to death of her stupidity and all the spite I'd had off her.

'Joe doesn't even like you, Nance,' I shouted at her. 'And I'll tell you another thing. You don't care about Joe. You don't care about anyone except your pathetic little self, and while you're here having a go at me he could be out there getting killed. That's what I'm carrying with me day after day, because I love Joe and he loves me and there's nothing you can do about it.'

313

I'd hoped my voice would come out strong, but instead it sounded as desperate as I felt.

'Shame,' someone said. 'Poor kid.'

Doris took a firm hold on Nancy. 'One more spat like that my girl, and you'll be looking for a new place to work, make no mistake. I'll not 'ave it in 'ere.'

Nancy walked out of that factory at the end of the day and Doris never had to send her packing. We never saw her again.

The Blitz began for us at the end of August. The Luftwaffe shifted from the daylight raids to night bombing. They bombed the Market Hall in town, leaving desolate, smoking rafters and a terrible mess in the place where we loved to go shopping. I felt as if this must be a film or a dream and I would soon step out of it. But there wasn't a way out.

The next night we spent mostly in the Anderson: Mom, Len and me. As they came over they felt very close, and I can't say the shelter made you feel all that much safer. Less, if anything. What if there was a direct hit? For hours we listened to the drone of the planes, the whistles and bangs of the bombs and our ack-ack guns firing now and then.

I'd thought Lenny might go to pieces. We all jumped at every explosion at first. But Len just perched there with us as if this was normal. He'd always loved fireworks. It was Mom's nerves that took it badly. As we sat there in the light of the hissing Tilley lamp she kept digging her nails into my arm and sometimes, when something landed close, she let out a squeak or a cry. 'Oh, I can't stand it in here,' she cried. 'Can't stand it another minute. I'll go mad.'

I didn't choose to remind her of a time when she'd stood it in the shelter very well of her own accord.

In the middle of it all she said suddenly, 'I can feel it – the babby! I just felt it move.' She put her hand to her stomach and stared at the little dancing flame. 'What on earth sort of life am I bringing this child into?'

September 1940

'It's a year today since war broke out,' Mom said gloomily into her morning cuppa.

I was at the table with Len, both getting breakfast down us quick so's to get off to work, though I hardly felt like eating. Mom didn't seem too bad this morning though. I thought maybe she was trying to take Lil's advice and pull herself together.

There was a rattle at the front door which set my heart pounding. Post. Joe. Would there be a letter for me today? My first and last thoughts of the day were of him, and so many in between. Every day Gloria gave us a reckoning of the number of planes lost and pilots missing. I was constantly worried.

Mom was already out of her chair. 'I'll go. You get on with it.'

She padded off into the hall in her slippers and I heard her give a little grunt as she bent down. She moaned as if in pain. When I got there she was sliding down the wall on to the green lino in a faint, the letters slipping from her hand. In those seconds relief spread through me like warmth: Joe's writing on one of the envelopes.

'Mom?' I sat her up with Len's help and we propped her with her knees apart, head between them. She groaned again, her face white.

I picked up the other letter. A card in fact. *Recovering*

from wounds. Prisoner of War. France. Alive! My father was alive!

'Len, it's from Dad!' I shrieked.

'Victor?' A slow grin spread across Len's face.

'Yes, of course Victor. Mom – he's alive!'

She was going into shock. 'Oh God,' she kept saying in a distraught voice. 'Oh my God.'

We got her into a chair and I squeezed more tea out of the pot but her hands were trembling too much to take the cup. I told Len to get off to work and cooled a helping of the tea for her on a saucer and she finally got some down her.

'Go back to bed for a bit,' I told her. 'Give it a chance to sink in.'

Her mind was jittering, racing. She grabbed my hand. 'I'd just got used to the idea of having my babby. Of keeping it ... I'll have to have it adopted now.' She stared hard into my face, wanting an answer from me. 'Won't I?'

'My sweet Genie,' Joe's letter said. It was written, I could see, in a very great hurry. 'The pace of life is very different here at ——. This'll have to be quick I'm afraid. Scarcely time to eat or sleep. Can't go into detail. Enough to say I'm on a crash course – but not literally so far!

'Just to let you know all's well. Longing to see you – you've no idea how much. Keep safe and well my sweetheart, until I see you.

'All my love, as ever, Joe.'

This short letter, tucked in the pocket of my dress, seemed to glow against my thigh all day and sometimes I took it out to read if I had a spare moment. I was loved, really loved by someone, and it was the best feeling in the world.

I was so excited that day I could barely keep still. 'My dad's alive!' I told everyone. At the factory they shared it all with me as if they were part of my own family. In fact with a lot more enthusiasm come to think of it.

Nanny Rawson scarcely said a word to start with, just carried on serving out the kids' tea.

'Uncle Victor?' Patsy said. 'He's been taken prisoner? By the Germans? Blimey!'

'Sit down,' Nan said sternly. 'Just get to the table.' She lifted Cathleen on to a chair, handed her bread and a bowl of soup and started absent-mindedly spooning it into the child's mouth.

'It's hot, Nan.' Cathleen spat it out. 'And I can feed myself.'

I could tell Nanny Rawson was turning things over in her mind but there was no use hurrying her. She poured me a cup of tea, then sat on the sofa in her pinner, thoughtfully rubbing her bandaged leg.

'I had a letter from Joe today too.'

'Oh ah.' She got up and beckoned me into the scullery. 'Eat up, you three.'

'Your mother all right?' We were squeezed in between the stone sink and the wall.

'She passed out. The shock. Said she'd have to get the babby adopted. She won't, will she Nan?'

Nan rolled her eyes to the ceiling. 'Daft mare she is.'

'D'you think it'd be for the best?'

'No. I don't. That's my grandchild she's casting off. Parting with your own flesh and blood – most un-natural. I'll 'ave to talk to 'er. Victor's a reasonable man, not like some.'

Lil burst in through the back door, face alight with smiles.

'All right, Genie!' she half sang. The kids looked round, mouths hanging open in amazement. ''Allo kids, what's up?'

'Victor's alive,' Nan said.

Lil flung her bag down, the smile wiped off. 'Oh dear.' Then she saw my face. 'Sorry, Genie. Good news really, in't it?'

'Yes, it is,' I said crossly. Teresa had flung her arms round me with joy as soon as I'd told her. There was a chance for us all now, that's how I saw it.

'How's Doreen taken it?'

We went through it all again in the scullery, the ifs and buts. Lil thought like Nan. Adoption was right out.

'How can she even think of it? Giving away a babby you've carried in you? Two wrongs like that aren't going to make a right whichever way you look at it.'

When this had been chewed over Lil whispered to me, 'Can you stay and give your nan a hand with the kids? I'm off out.'

I grinned. 'Course. Len'll slope over to Molly's if he gets hungry.'

After a quick bite Lil prettified herself, not that she needed to, being gorgeous already. She changed into the shimmery green dress, put her hair up and her lipstick on and she looked like a Persian queen. Although her life was as exhausting as ever, the colour had come back to her cheeks and her hair was glossy.

'You look really pretty, Mom,' Tom said, watching her with admiring eyes. 'You going out with Frank?'

'How did you guess?' Lil smiled into the glass by the door. 'That OK with you?'

'Yeah – 'e's awright Frank is.' He'd long bought the kids' affection with pieces of silver.

''E gave me a spinning top,' Cathleen piped up, enthroned on her potty in the corner by the stairs.

''E said 'e'd play football with me!' Patsy cried.

Lil laughed happily, kissing each of them, which was an unusual occurrence at the best of times. Indignantly Patsy wiped lipstick off his cheek. 'I'm glad you all like him 'cause I think we'll all be seeing a lot more of him.'

'What I want to know,' Nanny Rawson said, 'is where 'e gets 'is money from. I mean mending cars and the ARP – not places where you find a crock of gold, are they?'

Lil turned. 'What money?'

'Well it's obvious 'e's got money – the way 'e's dressed and that—'

'Mom,' Lil said patiently. 'Frank hasn't got that much money. What've you got that into your head for?'

'It's 'cause he looks like Clark Gable,' I teased. 'Nan thinks he's a film star.'

'Oh Mom.' Lil gathered up her coat. 'I thought you was the one who didn't hold with judging a book by its cover?'

I was alone in the house when Mom came in that night. Len had decided to stop over at Molly's. Her eyes were circled like a panda's from exhaustion.

Instead of heading straight for something alcoholic as she did every other night, she sat down on the edge of a chair in the back room, stone cold sober.

'What's up, Mom?'

'I've got to think,' she said in a far-away voice. 'Think things out.'

I wished I could tell her it'd be all right. That Dad wouldn't mind. But he would. Course he would.

'I went to the Welfare this morning. The woman said I couldn't give up a babby for adoption without my husband's consent. I didn't know what to do. I couldn't say, "He's in France", because I knew how she'd look at me and I couldn't tell her about its real father.'

There was a long silence before she said, 'It felt such a little thing I did, going with Bob. And it's turned into all this.' Bitterly, she added, 'Hasn't given him much trouble though, has it?'

On 7 September London had its first big air raid. Four hundred and thirty people died in London that night, so many we could barely take it in.

But the Battle of Britain wasn't over yet and Joe was still flying while those Germans were making up their mind exactly what it was they were playing at. Were they going to invade or not?

I had a letter from Joe sounding tired out, but full of affection. This affection that felt like a miracle, still unbelievable. Then nothing. Every day I rushed to the front door, waited, heart going like mad. Got to the point of crying with fear and worry when there was nothing. He'd been writing every other day when he could. Something had to be wrong. Of course it had to be. Things didn't go right for me.

'Joe – oh Joe, where are you? Write to me and make it all right again!'

I was choked with emotion but like everyone else, tried to keep it down. Always waiting, things out of our control.

' 'Eard from Joe?' the women asked.

'No,' I snapped, not meaning to turn on them. But they understood, kept quiet then, with knowing looks at each other.

On the Tuesday Mr Broadbent came in, so everyone suddenly put on that extra-busy look like they did whenever he put in an appearance. He took no notice, headed straight for me.

'Could I have a word a minute, out there?' He jerked his head at the back door, face terribly solemn.

The other women's eyes followed me out and they all had disaster written in them. He'd heard something, I knew it. The kind of telegram only moms and dads or wives are sent. I didn't want to follow him, didn't want to hear it.

We went out into the yard at the back and closed the door on the warehouse. I couldn't control myself any longer.

'Joe's dead, isn't he? You've had a telegram?' I couldn't help it. My heart felt swollen fit to burst.

'No, Genie love!' Mr B was overcome. 'It's all right – we haven't.' He put an arm round my shoulders as if he was my own dad. He wasn't that much bigger than me, smaller than Joe by nearly a head.

'I was only going to ask you if you'd heard from 'im, that's all. He's a good lad for letter writing but I'm sure 'e'd write to his young lass more than to us.' He was trying to sound light-hearted, make a bit of a joke of it, but I could hear the worry in his voice and this didn't help me, though I was grateful for his kindness.

I shook my head, tears pouring down my face. 'I haven't had a letter since Friday.'

'Oh,' Mr Broadbent said soberly. 'I see.'

Words were swirling round in my head. Where are you Joe? I can't bear it, I just can't bear it.

'Look.' Mr B rallied himself. 'They're very busy, under a lot of pressure. He'll get in touch when he can, love. I'm sure there's an explanation.'

The explanation, the only one possible it seemed, hung in the air between us like a cloud of flies and Mr Broadbent looked sorry he'd spoken.

'Just hold on, Genie. The moment I hear anything I'll let you know, all right? And you do the same, eh?' He patted my back. 'You take your time now, as much as you need, before you go back in there.'

The endless, gnawing worry took away most of my happiness in knowing Dad was alive. Nothing compared with the way I felt about Joe, how we'd had this bit of time together that was almost too good to be true. I couldn't talk to Mom about it, she was too wrapped up in herself. Only Teresa knew how sick with worry I was. Carlo had left for his army training and she came round to see me of an evening sometimes, knowing I'd just sit and fret.

'I know now,' Teresa said to me as we sat together that evening. 'Seeing the way you're feeling. If I thought something'd happened to Carlo I'd be exactly the same. Funny how I never saw him before, right there under my nose. Always trying to get away from the Italians and be different. This lot has made me see us all properly, the good that's there. I was such a stupid little cow, wasn't I?'

I managed a grin. 'I wouldn't put it quite that strong.'

'Hear that?' Teresa said. 'Wasn't that your door?'

There was another, louder knock.

Mr Broadbent was outside in the dusk, face all smiles, handing me a folded piece of paper.

'You'd never believe it – blooming postman delivered this wrong. It came two days ago and they put it through at 87.'

I must've just gawped at him.

'We're number 37,' Mr Broadbent explained. 'Joe didn't write it any too clear. He must've been in a rush. We've not been living there long, so they didn't know to pass it on to us. It's OK, Genie. Joe's all right.'

When he'd gone I opened it.

I'll write properly when I can. I love you. I love you. I love you.
Joe.

I sat down opposite Teresa and burst into tears.

The daylight air battles petered out in the middle of the month. The Germans had worked their way through attacking the coastal convoys, the airfields, the control centres, and now they turned their attention on the cities. London was getting it every night. Churchill made his famous speech about 'Never in the field of human conflict was so much owed by so many to so few.' They were heroes of the age, those flyers.

I was so proud of Joe, but I never had a minute's peace. His letter was like having him back from the dead, but I was sure that would never happen again. I knew he was alive and safe each time he wrote, but by the time it reached me? And the next day, and the next? I felt so unworthy of him I just could not believe he'd survive and come back to me.

This was different from anything I'd felt before. Frightening, because I couldn't just brush it off like I could with Walt or Jimmy. Joe had marked my heart and I couldn't get away from it.

That week Mom handed in her notice at work and a day or two later she was summoned to the Labour Exchange. She came back fuming with humiliation.

'D'you know what that hoity-toity little bit said to me? Cut-glass accent she had, can't have been much older than you. "Well, Mrs Watkins."' Mom was pretty good at taking off other people's voices. '"Are you quait sure you heven't got yourself in the femily way in order to get orf war work? Surely at your age you wouldn't normally be plenning to enlorge your femily?" Stuck up little bitch. What's she doing in a soft job like that anyhow? She could be in the army or summat.

'Anyhow, I told her she could keep her airs and graces and not talk to her elders and betters like that. She didn't like that, I can tell you.' Mom was roving round the room tidying, slamming things down on the table.

'Did they say you could give up war work though?'

'Yes, in the end,' she admitted grudgingly. 'Bugger this cowing war. Your life's not your own any more, is it?'

Music while you Work was blaring out as usual. 'We'll Meet Again . . .' and 'Bless 'em All' – thank goodness for the jolly ones because they didn't touch me. Horrible, being wrung out by music all day long. I wished they'd switch the flaming thing off half the time. My eyes and hands worked automatically, head down, not joining in with the jokes. They kept trying to cheer me up, bless them, but even though I tried to put on a brave face, nothing worked. I'd had one more very short note from Joe, but I'd got myself in such a state I was always consumed by worry.

'Genie!' A call passed along the warehouse. I hadn't seen the yard door open wide enough for his head to poke round. 'Mr B wants you out the back.'

All those eyes watching and my legs watery, nearly letting me down. If it was good news about Joe he'd have come right in. Run and told everyone, because after all everyone loved him, not just me.

By the time I reached that door I was trembling so much I could barely get it open. Someone helped, twisted the handle, shut it behind me.

My first breath on the other side of that door I gasped in so hard you could hear it. He was standing waiting for me across the yard, half smiling, uncertain. The time he'd been away felt so long.

'Oh—' I gasped again, grinding my fist into the middle of my chest. For a moment I couldn't speak. Breath came in jerks and pants.

'Genie . . .?'

I didn't remember crossing the yard. I might've flown for all I know. I was holding him, squeezing his arms, pressing his cheeks between my hands, pulling him to me tight, kissing and kissing his lovely face.

He didn't speak at first, calmed me with his hands, taking me by the shoulders to hold me at arm's length, and we looked at each other. His face was thinner, cheeks covered with a day's growth of stubble, dark eyes full of emotion. He pulled me to him and held me so tight.

'Joe, Joe—' My tears flowed, like fear dissolving down my face. 'Oh my God, are you all right?'

326

He nodded. 'I'm fine. On top.'

'You're here.' I couldn't let go of him, couldn't stop saying it again and again. 'You're here – really here . . .'

'Yes—' He sounded as if he couldn't believe it himself. 'Finally made it.'

'Don't ever, ever go away again,' I demanded.

Joe was holding me, laughing as Mr Broadbent came back out smiling, the worry lifted from him. He even looked taller. I mopped my eyes.

'Thought I'd leave you both for a bit,' he said. 'Betty, my wife, telephoned to say Joe'd got home and I said she'd better send him up here quick because there was someone losing a lot of sleep over 'im.'

Joe smiled properly for the first time. 'Thanks, Dad. But I was coming anyway.'

He only had four days and we spent every possible moment we could together. At the end of the week, while I was at work he stayed at home with his mom and sisters, catching up on sleep after the punishing weeks he'd been through. But he was young and very fit and he bounced back.

His first evening home Mr Broadbent asked me to come over and spend some time with them.

'Are you sure you don't just want him to yourselves?' I asked, uncertain about being included in the family like this. I knew Mr B was OK with me but I wasn't sure about the rest of them.

'Course not. And anyhow, if we don't get you along we shan't be able to tie Joe into his seat long enough to get anything out of 'im!'

I was nervous about meeting Joe's mom and his sisters. What on earth were they going to think of me?

327

Marjorie, the sister who'd been at Broadbent's show, opened the door of their recently built house in Hall Green with its fresh-looking white window-frames.

'We were just finishing off tea,' she said. I saw she had Joe's dark eyes and the same pale hair and skin. She did have an aloof manner but I think it was shyness, and she was trying to be nice to me.

'Sorry. Am I too early? I could go and walk round for a bit . . .'

'No!' She thawed further and laughed. 'We're expecting you. I'll never hear the end of it from Joe if I send you off again. Come and join us.'

Joe was coming out to meet me and introduced me to everyone – his mom and Marjorie and Louise. And he made it very clear I was someone special, brought me in as if I were royalty.

Marjorie was soon to be twenty-one, according to Joe, though as we sat round that evening I kept looking at her, trying to take this in. I couldn't help feeling I was older than her. There was something cardboard about her. Amiable enough, but with a bit missing somehow. She seemed like someone who was afraid of life, even her own shadow.

Joe sat beside me on their sofa and I basked in being close to him. Mr and Mrs Broadbent were in chairs on either side of the little tiled fireplace. Mrs Broadbent was, over all, a very pale woman. Looked as if she'd had a bad shock, the colour of her. Her hair was white-blond and her skin ashen and thin-looking so that you could see the veins in her neck. I was trying to puzzle out how she'd managed to build up the vile reputation she had round the factory. I came to the conclusion that because she was beautiful and fragile-looking she was like a red rag to a bull for some of those women. They were expected to be tough, coping, hard-working, whatever time of the month, stage of pregnancy or chronic illness they were suffering. Mrs B looked like one of those Victorian women who might get the 'vapours'. Actually her health seemed quite all right. Her manipulative illnesses must have been a factory legend that started small and swelled into something much bigger.

The fact was she was quiet and shy and pleasant and I was grateful to her that she didn't seem to mind me. After all, if she'd been half the snob she was painted as being she'd've objected to her son courting a factory lass. Maybe she thought it'd all blow over and he'd grow out of me, but either way, she was kind to me.

'I hear your father's been in contact,' she said, passing me an oatmeal biscuit. 'What a relief that must be.'

'Oh it is. Couldn't believe it when we heard. It's been so long, and no one telling us either way.'

'Like someone else we could mention.' Louise, Joe's younger sister, nudged him with her foot. She wasn't much older than me, with jet-black hair, Joe's cocoa-brown eyes and a lot of spark to her. She was in her last year at the grammar school. Her hair was cut in a pageboy with her fringe long and dead straight, level with her eyebrows. 'Next time just send us a piece of paper every day with a cross on or something, and then at least we'll know the Jerries haven't had you for breakfast.'

'Sorry,' Joe said, for what was obviously far from the first time. 'I did my best. It's not my fault if the postman can't read . . .'

'You've always had illegible handwriting,' Louise retorted, slouching back in her chair. 'Why *do* boys always write so much worse than girls?'

I wanted to tell her to shut up and leave Joe alone but

fortunately his dad did it for me. 'Leave 'im, Louise,' he said. 'Anyway, I thought you were off out?'

'I am.' She pushed the last piece of biscuit into her mouth and got up. 'The pictures with Laurie. Won't be late.' She nodded at me. 'Cheerio, Genie, nice to meet you.'

Marjorie drifted off as well, leaving the four of us sat round on their coffee-coloured furniture. They didn't make me feel awkward and I liked the way Joe and his dad talked to each other, man to man. Joe often turned to smile at me as we talked. I was still reeling from him coming home, didn't care where I was or what we did as long as I could be with him. Mrs Broadbent asked me about my family and later she made drinks of Bournvita.

As it grew late Mr B said, 'Are you going to run Genie home?'

'Can you drive?' I was impressed with that. No one else we knew had a car except the doctor.

'I'll give you a demonstration, shall I?' Joe took my hand to pull me up.

When we'd climbed into his father's Austin, me looking round the inside in amazement, he said, 'It's good to be home, but I've been dying to have you to myself.'

We waited while his dad gave us a wave and closed the front door, then Joe took me in his arms and I rested against him, smelling his familiar smell mixed with the leather of the seats. Our lips found each other's.

'I thought so much about what it would have been like if you hadn't come back,' I said, looking up at him. 'It felt as if anything good in my life had ended.'

Joe stroked my head against his chest. 'I thought about it too – about losing you. You've had raids here already, haven't you? And there'll be more if London's anything to go by.'

'Didn't you think about yourself – what danger you were in?'

'Only when I let myself. You can't too much. Hardly ever at Tangmere – otherwise I wouldn't be able to do the job. You don't think about dying. You get through every day, somehow. You have to be nearly as much of a machine as the planes.'

I didn't want to press Joe too much on the subject. Wasn't even sure how much I wanted to know anyhow. He'd said he was in an air crew at Tangmere and that towards the end of it all, Tangmere and Kenley had been the only sector airfields left to handle the defence.

'It's over anyway, that part,' Joe said. 'Let's think about the future.'

He started the car and drove across to the Stratford Road.

'How d'you fancy a day out tomorrow?'

'With you? Nah, don't think so.' I grinned at him as we pulled up outside our house.

'Cheeky hoyden!' He leaned over and tickled me until I was begging him to stop. 'Dad might lend us the car.'

'The car!' I sat up straight. A car to drive anywhere we wanted! 'Pick me up as early as you can,' I ordered him. 'I don't want to miss a single moment.'

Apart from the Lickey Hills, which just about counted, I'd never been out of Birmingham before. Joe drove us out to Kenilworth, me in a state of high excitement.

'There's a castle,' Joe told me as I was bouncing up

and down on the seat next to him. 'And lots of country round to walk in. That's if the car's still in one piece to get us there by the time you've finished.'

'I can't believe this, Joe,' I kept saying as we drove out along the Coventry Road, and Joe laughed again at my fidgety happiness as the edges of Brum faded behind us.

'It's not a very marvellous day,' he said, leaning forward to look up through the windscreen. 'Doesn't look as if it'll rain though.'

'I don't care if it does.' We laughed. Laughed a lot that day.

Now we were out of town I was full of exclamations about the fields, the fresh smell of the air, old cottages in the villages, cows and sheep, and the fresh hay bales spilling out of barns. All of it was exciting to me, like travelling into a story book.

'Oh Joe, I want to live in the country,' I said, overcome by all I could see and how lovely it all looked, even under a cloudy sky. 'I know it seems strange, no pavements and chimneys and shops and that, but I wouldn't miss them. Not if I could have all this.'

Warwickshire seemed at least as good as heaven that day.

Joe parked up the car in a narrow side street in Kenilworth and we walked through the little town with its pretty houses and generous green space in the middle. In the gardens there were still roses, beds of marigolds, golden rod.

'It all looks so small, doesn't it?' Joe said.

'It's beautiful,' I sighed, and Joe laughed.

'You're nice and easy to please.' He put his hand in the pocket of his jacket, and with his spare one, drew my hand through the crook of his arm. He leaned round and kissed me. I didn't care that it was in the street where people could see. I was proud to be there on his arm and I didn't give a monkey's who was watching.

We walked around, close together and very leisurely all morning, talking and laughing. We had a fish dinner in the Queen and Castle (a big treat), before going to see the real castle, not far away, at the edge of the town.

As we walked round inside the shell of the castle walls, where it felt very quiet suddenly, or set out along a path into the fields, I held my hand in Joe's, or sometimes slipped it into the pocket of his coat where his change rattled against the silky lining.

'I don't even know why you're wearing a coat this time of year – must be a born pessimist!'

We walked across the fields, climbing stiles, as the sky turned to lead, and watched the cows grazing, wondering when the rain was going to come. It wasn't long before enormous drops started to fall. Right away everything smelt lovely in the wet.

'Oh no!' Joe groaned, getting all bothered like he had over the bikes. 'Here, Genie. You have my coat.'

'No, I'm all right. I don't mind!' The rain made me feel wildly happy and reckless. It was heavy but warm, and the sound of it was all around us like a loud rustling. I turned my face up and held my arms to the sky, half dancing along the path.

'It's raining, it's pouring, the old man is snoring—'

I didn't care if I got drenched to the skin. I tore along, feeling it dash on my face and sink into my scalp through my hair.

Seeing me, Joe must have decided there was no point being worried, and he ran behind me and took my hand.

'Look!' he called out. 'Over the other side – we can shelter.'

The field we were running across was pasture for cows. It had clumps of enormous thistles with purple tops and there were cowpats all over the place. I was glad to see the black and white cows were all huddling right at the other end. Joe and I ran together, careful where we put our feet, laughing and whooping as the rain streamed down our faces.

'Crikey, what a downpour!' Joe shouted.

He felt very strong and fast but I kept up easily, even though it was all uphill, feeling as if I had an iron body and could have just gone on and on running.

The barn at the border of the fields was almost full. Joe picked me up and lifted me on to the ledge of straw bales which was about up to my chest, then climbed up himself and at last we were under cover. The rain was still coming down like mad, sweeping sideways across the slope of the field. We looked round, then at each other, and laughed again.

It was perfect. The stack was packed like a staircase, the bales at the back and sides piled right to the roof of the barn, but with a wide-stepped gap up the middle presumably designed so you could climb up to reach the ones at the back. It might have been made for us. The light was dim as we climbed further towards the top of the stack and the rain thundered on the roof. We settled down together surrounded by the fresh, prickly bales of straw, water seeping from the ends of our hair.

Still getting my breath back, I lay and looked up at the darkness. 'This is the most wonderful, exciting thing I've ever done.'

Joe turned and smiled at me, shouldering his coat off.

'I suppose you think that doesn't say much for the rest of my life? And that'd be about right. But it's doing this with you. That's the thing.'

He leaned over and wiped my face with his handkerchief, his own still shiny with water, eyes on mine. 'Some people would have let it spoil the whole day. Not you though.' Teasing, he pressed his little finger into my cheek as I smiled. 'Dimples.'

He mopped his own face, then absent-mindedly opened up the white square and laid it out flat on the other side of him, although there wasn't much hope of it drying. I think he was looking for something to do. Neither of us spoke for a time.

Things changed in those moments. I went from wild, crazy happiness to feeling solemn suddenly, affected by Joe's closeness to me. I watched him, wondering what he was thinking.

Joe had never said or done anything to offend me in any way. We'd kissed of course, touched outside our clothes, but he was always considerate and tactful. He'd never pushed me to do anything more than I wanted. I suppose he thought I was more innocent than I actually was, coming from households like ours and Nan's. I knew promiscuity led to punishment, like it had for my mom. That it was cheap and wrong to think of going with a man before you were married and that he'd probably think so badly of me if he knew what I was thinking . . .

Yet as I lay looking at him my whole body was full of longing. I found I was trembling with love for him and with need. I knew that at my age I shouldn't be wanting what I did then, from Joe. And as he turned and lay beside me all this desire and confusion must have shown in my eyes because I couldn't hide it. He leaned over me and in his eyes I saw the same struggle between thought and emotion, the same overwhelming longing.

I reached up and put my arms round his neck, shaking.

'Are you cold?'

I shook my head. 'No. Not cold.'

He understood me and half sat up again. 'Genie, the way I feel about you, I'd give anything, anything – But you're so young. I keep forgetting that. I don't want us – you especially – to do anything we'll regret.'

I sat up and put my arms round him again. Here he was. Now, in my arms. 'We could be dead soon. Either of us.'

Joe looked down at me, eyes full of emotion. 'I didn't know this feeling could be so strong. Wanting you all the time. I know I couldn't write, but you were in my mind so much. I kept thinking of you – your body.'

'And I did. I remember thinking I don't know you – all of you – what your shoulders are like. Your legs. And you might never come back and I'd never know. It's like a dream all this, Joe, to me. You've got to believe me – nothing anything like as good as this has ever happened to me before.'

Joe held me close. 'I love you, Genie. More than I can – anything I say never feels enough.'

'Joe—' My cheeks were burning suddenly. 'I'm only afraid of having a babby.'

He blushed then, fiddled with a wisp of straw. 'I can prevent it. Forces issue.'

'I want to tell you something.' Heart beating hard, I spoke all in a rush. 'Now, so I'm never hiding anything from you. It's my mom. She's having a babby and it's not my dad's. I need you to know, that's all. That's one of the reasons things are difficult at home. I never told you before because I was ashamed and scared of what you'd think.'

He let this sink in. 'Well, whose . . .? No, it doesn't matter whose, I suppose.' He kissed my hair. 'But it's not your fault. It's nothing for you to be ashamed of.'

'But when it's your own mom—'

'Look, you've nothing to worry about with me. It's not for me to judge her.'

'People will though. They do.'

We lay kissing and touching, both of us trembling, pressed tight together as if we could each slide under the other's skin. The hard, pummelling downpour had eased but it was still raining steadily and the light came to us as if through cobwebs. I could sense Joe's excitement and I sat up in our little half-lit funnel between the bales and undid the buttons of his shirt. His shoulders were slim, pale and strong as I'd known they would be. He sat up to pull off the shirt and I put my face to his chest, soft with hairs, and breathed in the smell of him, felt the pulse of his blood.

He undressed me with shaking fingers and his shaking made me love him more. I thought how I would never in a million years let Jimmy do this, see any of me, let alone down there, the private place between my legs, and I felt very shy even with Joe. But I trusted him as he peeled off my blouse, then my damp little camisole, hesitating before touching my tiny bosoms as if he hardly dared.

When we were both fully undressed we touched each other's bodies. I felt his warm breath on my skin. Our eyes kept finding each other's, talking with no words. When Joe's hands moved between my thighs I heard his breath catch and this desire, his need to keep control, made me lift myself to him, legs widening.

We lay there afterwards on the scratchy straw, warming each other. 'Joe, my Joe,' I said again and again, my arm tight over him. 'You're all I've ever wanted.' The small amount of light cast deep shadows on the dips and hollows of our bodies. Joe pulled the dry side of his coat over us.

'Has its uses, you see.' Then he said. 'My love. My love.'

There was silence, except for the rain.

'When I was a kid,' I said, 'and it was raining outside – at night like – I used to lie there and think of all the people out in it. Not just people. Cats and dogs, anything that had nowhere to go. And I used to wish I could bring them all in, know that everything was safe inside under shelter. I had this doll, Janet. I've still got her – she looks pretty rough now – and I'd cuddle Janet and talk to her and pretend we could rescue everyone. We had soup made, the lot, in our game!'

Joe squeezed me. 'Be nice if everything could always be safe.'

'I feel safe with you.'

Talking and staying silent in snatches we held each other until we heard the rain stop, then dressed, shivering, back in our wet clothes. When we climbed down from the barn on the sodden grass mingled with loose straw, a movement caught Joe's eye.

'Look, Genie!'

From across the field a long, ungainly bird pulled itself into flight, huge wings beating with what looked like an enormous effort, and long, thin legs trailing. It looked like an old man in a panic.

'Heron,' Joe said, eyes following the slow path of its flight until it disappeared over the bushes into another field. 'Wasn't it lovely? Marvellous they are, I think. What bit of luck spotting one today.'

I put my hand in his, sighing. 'I don't know about so many things. You'll have to teach me.'

Joe turned and took me in his arms again. 'With pleasure. Genie?' His face was serious. 'What we just did. I wouldn't want you to think it didn't mean anything more to me. One day I want to be able to wake up with you in a bed in our own home. Our marriage bed.'

On his last day, I asked Joe to come to my nan's. It was Sunday afternoon and everyone was there: Nan, Lil and the kids, Frank, Mom, Len and Molly. Mom was deadpan but in control, although I kept eyeing her to make sure. I wanted Joe to meet my family properly now because I trusted he'd accept us for what we were, even though going there meant taking him to a slum house, however clean.

'Hope you'll take us as you find us,' were Nan's first words to him when we arrived. She was smiling, had met him before of course, and was impressed. And he did just what she asked.

One thing was worrying me though. I didn't want Joe having too many shocks at once. In a moment's opportunity I took Lil aside. 'Any sign of him up there?' I rolled my eyes at Morgan's ceiling.

'No, and there shouldn't be with any luck. I hear he's got back trouble.'

'Ah, now I wonder why.'

'Cheeky girl,' Lil dimpled at me. 'But it's all right. I think you're safe.'

With everyone there it was a tight squeeze of course, but we all fitted in. Joe talked to Mom and managed to get some joy in reply and he seemed to cheer her up a bit.

It was a wonderful afternoon. Cups of tea and cake, sing-songs led by Nan which had Molly and Len rocking from side to side putting the chairs in danger, Len yelling out bits of song. Lil made me sing solo, and Joe, who was obviously thoroughly enjoying himself, egged me on too.

'You know you can do it – and I want to hear you.'

I liked the old songs – 'Apple Blossom Time' again and 'Maid of the Mountains', and Joe led everyone clapping me.

'Come on, let's hear you now!' I challenged him, and after protesting he couldn't sing, in the end he and Frank clowned about together singing 'Some Day I'll Find You' and 'The Little Dutch Mill'.

Seeing the two of them together, Frank with his dark Hollywood looks and Joe's fair, handsome face, Lil linked her arm through mine and squeezed it, giving me a wink as if to say, 'We've done all right there, kid.'

The two of them finished, bowing from side to side as if they were in the Albert Hall, then Frank snuck up behind Lil. 'Here, I want to show you summat.'

He stood at the back of her and laid his hands on her head, feeling around.

Lil squealed. 'What the hell are you playing at? That feels really funny. Eh, pack it in!'

'You can tell a lot from feeling the shape of someone's head,' Frank said, kneading Lil's skull. 'I've learned a bit about it from a pal. It's a branch of science, you know.'

'Oh ah,' Nan said, rubbing her bandage. 'So's flying to the moon on a magic carpet.'

'Gerroff will you!' Lil stood up, poking him in the tummy.

'Awright.' Frank gave in. 'C'mere Joe, boys. Who knows some tricks?'

Patsy and Tom crowded round, keen, and Joe sat watching Frank dealing cards with a flourish, a fag hanging jauntily from the side of his mouth. Even Mom laughed at his antics and Lil stood at his shoulder. Only Nanny Rawson was giving him sceptical looks and sniffing over her teacup as if to say 'Huh!'

Some time in the afternoon we heard planes, and we all stiffened and went quiet except for Joe and Frank, who rushed out to see, looking for the formation, but they'd already passed.

'No siren anyhow,' Lil said. 'Must've been ours.'

But it seemed to remind Frank of something. He looked at his watch. 'Got to go.'

Lil frowned. 'Where're you off to?'

'Couple of things to see to, that's all.' He gathered up his cards, then leaned forward and kissed her. Our nan scowled so you could almost hear it. 'See you tomorrow.'

Lil looked disappointed, but there wasn't a lot she could do about it. I suppose she wanted things settled, wanted married life again.

Later in the afternoon we had a visitor. A little black and white terrier with tan eyebrows and bright liquid eyes was peeping in at us. Joe, sat by the open door, was the first to notice.

'Who's this then?' he said. 'Hello Mister!'

'Never seen him before.' Lil snapped her fingers at him. 'C'm'ere!'

The small, wiry body came in, wagging a stump of black tail so hard its whole body snaked from side to side, face turning fast from one to the other of us. Then it launched itself into Len's lap.

341

'Oi!' Len laughed as the terrier pushed its wet nose against his ear and Molly leaned over and rubbed at him roughly with her big meaty hands.

'Well where did he come from?' Lil said, bending over to stroke the rough, fidgeting back. 'Not from round here, is he, Mom?'

'Not as I know of,' Nan said. ''Ere – get 'im off the table!'

There were shrieks of laughter as the dog leapt skidding off the table and went round the room sniffing at everyone's legs.

'Ooh, he's tickling me!' Mom giggled. 'He's a proper livewire, ain't he?'

Then he was in my lap, scratchy tongue on my face, and I cuddled him. He felt warm and comforting. Joe reached round and stroked him and looked into the dog's face and I saw a kind of communication there that he seemed to have with all creatures. Patsy, Tom and Cathleen gathered round, squabbling about who could stroke him next.

'Wish we could keep him,' I said.

'I s'pect he belongs to someone,' Lil said. 'But he's nice, isn't he?'

'Could be a stray.' Joe was still making a fuss of him. 'If you haven't seen him before.'

Our nan got up to put another kettle on. 'Looks well enough fed, doesn't 'e? We'll just 'ave to see. Really and truly we need 'im round here like an 'ole in the 'ead.'

I didn't want that afternoon to finish. I kept shutting my mind to the terrible thought that not only would it have to end but that Joe was leaving today. We'd come so close and now we'd have to be torn apart again. All afternoon we were close to each other, nearly always touching, legs, shoulders, hands, or Joe's arm round me.

As we all left Nan's, the dog followed.

'He likes you, Genie!' Lil called from the door.

'He's got good taste,' Joe whispered.

'You're not going to get rid of him in a hurry.'

'Go on – go home!' Mom turned and swished at him with her hand. He stopped for a moment, puzzled, then followed again as soon as we started walking. 'Shoo!' she tried again, but it was pretty half-hearted. I could see she'd taken a shine to him. And there was no stopping Molly turning round, chuckling and calling to him, giving him every encouragement.

When we got to Brunswick Road he was still there like our shadow.

'Oh, can we keep him, Mom? Please? He'd be company.'

'Well . . . I s'pose if he belongs to someone he'll take off home later.'

But he ran into our garden at the back, sniffed around and cocked his leg as if he owned the place.

'He staying then?' Len asked.

'Dunno.' Mom's eyes followed him as he did a tour of the Anderson's roof. 'But he looks as if he might have it in mind.'

I couldn't face the railway station with Joe this time, so we said our goodbyes more privately, on the way to his house, where he had to go and change and get his kit. But it was even more terrible than before. Hard as I tried not to I cried this time, just wanted to hold on to him and drink him in, make up for all the time I

343

wouldn't be able to touch him or have him close. The nearer the moment came for us to part the less we spoke, but this time it was not fraught and unsure, just full of longing for things to be different. And I still had my feeling of not deserving him, a sense of doom, that this was too good to last.

When we said goodbye Joe held me close, chin resting on my head, and my arms were tight round his waist. He kissed the top of my head, and I could tell from his silence he was as emotional as I was.

'Ssh,' he said after a while. 'Don't cry, Genie. I'll be back soon, you'll see. We'll be together. And one day we'll be able just to stay together without all this.'

I reached up and put my arms round his neck so our cheeks were pressed together. Then we kissed as if it was the last kiss in the world.

'You're everything to me, Joe.'

He smiled down at me and I loved that smile so much my tears started falling again. 'You're part of me, Genie, you always will be. I love you.'

When at last I had to watch him walk off it was with a terrible tearing feeling, as if a piece of me was being snatched away and taken into the hands of an evil force that might not let me have him back.

October 1940

The leaves started to crisp and fall and Mister was still with us. From the day he followed us home he was a fixture. Now and then he used to wander off and we thought we'd lost him, but sooner or later we'd hear him bark out the front and Mom'd say, 'Oh-oh, here comes trouble,' and she was nearly as glad as I was to see him back.

I called him Mister because that was the way Joe greeted him that day and when I thought of Joe holding and stroking him it was like some contact with him apart from his letters, which were what I lived for these days.

Whenever I got home from work, Mister was there, jumping to greet me like a mad thing, panting and licking, on the teeter for food. I'd try and find him some scraps, telling him about my day almost as if he was Joe.

The bombing started gradually at first. They were taking more of an interest in us up in the Midlands, but it was like the lull, that early part of October. Mom was calm for a bit then. It was as if she'd put herself through so much agonizing and worry that her mind had blanked out. She was quiet, moved round the house doing odd jobs, went shopping in a loose dress she'd knocked up, slept and wrote letters to Eric. She smoked and drank, but for the moment, not as much as she'd done before.

She knew there was talk about her, bitching on the street, and they didn't trouble themselves to keep their voices down either. Mrs Marshall, Mrs Terry, Mrs Smith. You'd've thought they had enough to do with themselves without poking their noses into other people's lives. They got a thrill out of calculating the length of a pregnancy and talking about it loudly as we went past. We just looked hard faced and ignored them. But it was horrible, and you got to dread going out.

Teresa's Carlo came home on leave and one Saturday night they came over to see us. I liked Carlo, warmed to him. He was a year younger than Joe. His wiry black hair was cut shorter now, he had those striking blue eyes and a loud infectious laugh. He told us about some of the ragging he'd had as an Eyetie in the British army, though he seemed to be able to throw it off. Teresa, who was looking as beautiful as I'd ever seen her, sat close to him, and it was obvious she was just plain crazy about him. She kept turning, smiling into his eyes, and there were moments when the rest of us might as well not have been there. I was so happy for her, for them both.

Len and Molly were with us, Molly looking even more enormous already, although she still had four months or so to go with the pregnancy. Len sat between her chair and Gloria on the table, alternating between fondling each of them.

'Ssh!' Mom said, holding a hand up. 'Listen!'

A tiny, nervous voice was coming out of Gloria.

'It's Princess Elizabeth!' Teresa said. 'Ah – listen to that.'

We listened in wonder. We'd never heard her voice before. She was broadcasting a message to the evacuees.

'My sister Margaret Rose and I feel so much for you,' the high, cut-glass little voice was saying.

Mom scowled heavily as the Princess talked about the 'kind people who have welcomed you to their homes in the country'. By the end, as the little girls said their goodnights, she was dabbing her eyes with a hanky. 'Oh my poor Eric!'

'Oh, don't upset yourself, Mrs Watkins.' Teresa leaned forward and took her hand. 'Eric's safe as houses, ain't he? And it looks as if they were right about the bombing now, don't it? So he's probably well out of it.'

Mom tried to smile back. It was hard to resist Teresa. She could deal with my mom far better than I ever could.

'I know,' she sniffed. 'It's just hard to feel someone else's bringing up your son.' She rallied herself. 'Any more news of your dad, Teresa? And Stevie?'

Teresa's face fell. 'They've been moved, we think. There was a lad came home not long back – lived up by my nan. He's only fifteen, should never've been taken in the first place. Says they're moving them but he doesn't know where. Mom's ever so worried about him again now, because of his chest. I mean we don't know what conditions they'll be in – sleeping out and that.'

Carlo stroked his hand down Teresa's back, trying to reassure her.

'If only we knew more. We've had no letters for ages and we don't know what's going on or where they are. Sorry.' She tried to smile. 'I don't want to put a damper on the evening. We've all got our worries, haven't we?'

I put my hand down and stroked Mister's black and white back, remembering Joe's hand doing the same. We

347

certainly did all have our worries. But for those brief hours, things were as OK as they could be.

Our days had already been broken into by the chilling rise and fall moan of the air raid siren. But none of those interruptions – the scramble we made to the cellar at Broadbent's, smoke canisters going off outside to screen the factories, the singing to pass the time – compared with the night raids.

Birmingham's Blitz began at full strength in mid-October. There was a raid every night after that for the next two weeks.

We weren't ready for the first raid. At the sound of the siren, Mister put his head back and set up a shrill howling. Maybe it hurt his ears – it certainly jarred ours – but his high yowl made it all even more nerve-racking.

'Can't you shut 'im up?' Mom snapped. She couldn't seem to think what to do, just kept picking things up and putting them down again. 'Give him summat to eat – anything so's he'll pack that racket in.'

Not having a routine for this yet, we grabbed hold of things we thought might be useful – a lamp, Thermos, rugs, coats – and struggled down the garden into the shelter, seeing the searchlights criss-crossing in the sky. We had no idea how long it might go on for.

Len sat perched for a while on one of the shelves that made thin bunks on each side as the planes droned closer and closer overhead, then lay down and went to sleep, his bent knees hanging over the edge because the bunk wasn't long enough for him.

Mom and I sat side by side on the other bunk facing him across the narrow gap. The planes came over in waves, the noise growing louder, our hearts beating faster. It was like standing on a railway track, knowing there's a train coming. With every explosion outside, our heads ducked. If it was close enough you felt the impact under your feet. And all you could do was sit there, waiting.

It took me a little while to notice what a state Mom was in. That first night as they came over she was feverishly smoking and biting her nails but she was quiet. She'd lit the lamp and her eyes, stretched with fright, reflected back the flame. When it'd gone on for a time she said, 'Jesus – I wish I had something to drink.'

I reached down for the flask. 'There's some tea—'

'A proper drink!' she half yelled at me. 'It's bloody horrible in here. They're going to hit us, I know they are.'

'It'll be all right,' I said, though my legs were rubbery with fright. I cuddled Mister, who was more scared than I was, to steady myself. 'We're supposed to be safe in here.'

Mom gave a harsh laugh. ''Bout as safe as an empty peach tin.'

'Why don't you try and get some sleep?'

'Sleep? You barmy? How the hell's anyone s'posed to sleep through this lot? Well, 'cept him of course.' She jabbed a finger resentfully at Len.

It was terribly frightening. More than I could've imagined. My hands were sweaty, stomach all churned up. It was like being alone in all the world with the bombs. The rest of the city might as well not have existed.

I was exhausted too. To the extent that it was beginning to fight with the fear and to win. Mom could sleep this off tomorrow but I had to be at work. Tiredness could make you fatalistic. Whatever would happen would happen. You had to sleep, just had to. That was my first taste of the half-awake, half-asleep state you found yourself in during the raids. Asleep and yet not. Still half aware of the planes, the screams and thuds of the bombs in the soapy haze that your over-stretched mind had become. And whenever Mom thought I was nodding off she poked me awake. 'Don't leave me alone in this, Genie. I can't stand it.'

When it stopped and the sky went quiet, the All Clear finally sounded its two minute relief and we crawled up out of that damp hell-hole feeling as if we'd come out again into a different, miraculous world where there were stars in the sky, the shapes of houses round us, still standing, and fresh air. We were not just alive, but reborn.

'Oh, I can't go back in there again,' Mom said, stretching her arms to the sky. 'Never again.'

But we were back in there that night and for many nights after. This was the striped existence of the bombing raids. The days full of brightness, sunshine and fading leaves on the trees casting yellow light. After sitting there in the dark of the night, terrified and weary, the possibility of death coming at you all the time, the light of day was like an enormous cheer breaking out. We're alive. ALIVE. Everything felt bigger and more vivid than usual, the sky close and blue, our house bolder and more solid, the colours of flowers a cause of wonder and every building in the city, however functional, a great work of art. Every day we came out into the rank smell of smoke across Birmingham, looking round to see what had been destroyed in a city that until then we hadn't realized we loved with a passion.

From the second night Mom made sure she had a bottle of the kind she preferred with her. Len tried bringing Gloria in but she crackled and beeped and didn't seem at all happy in the shelter, and what with all the racket outside we couldn't have heard her anyway. So he stowed her under the stairs in the house after that.

The strain began to tell on us. Even in the daytime there were enough hazards. Dread of daytime raids, though they'd mostly stopped them now, unexploded bombs left over from the nights and glass blown out by the blast, the checking and rechecking that everyone was all right, had survived the night.

But it was the nights, those hellish nights. Mister, made distraught by all the noise, would burrow as deep as he could into my lap. Len sucked barley sugars, or hummed to himself, which drove Mom round the bend. She spent the time swigging gin, trying to drink herself into oblivion. And I sat in there with them all, so glad of Mister to cuddle, thinking of how it must have been for Joe up in those planes, holding on to the thought of him and trying to swallow the panic which rose in me like bile.

'Can I have some?' I asked Mom one night as she held tight to the neck of the bottle. No messing with glasses for her now.

'Go on then, have a sip. It'll make you feel better.'

I took a mouthful, felt it burn down inside me and gagged. 'Ugh – it's horrible.' My stomach was already to pot from fear and lack of sleep.

More than once Mom drank until she passed out and I was left alone, as Len could sleep through anything. I sat holding my dog, counting the seconds between each whistle of a bomb and the crunch of the impact, trying to keep a hold on my mind out there in the dark garden, with only this tiny metal hub between me and death.

When it was time to crawl out, blinking and squinting

as the door opened, I had to shake and shake Mom, and more than once just had to leave her there to sleep it off.

Another time she woke wild and hysterical, as if her dreams were a worse hell than the raids themselves.

'No,' she screamed at me, 'I can't go on – can't stand it—' clawing at me in a crazy way, and I was frightened. Her hair was loose and her face crumpled with drink and tiredness. I wasn't sure she was even really awake.

'Look,' I said desperately. 'Why don't you just go back to sleep for a bit?'

To my surprise she did lie down again and close her eyes. I think she spent most of the day asleep now, because there wasn't much sign of anything getting done except her managing to get to the Outdoor for more drink. We were lucky if we got a meal down us before the sirens went off again. Sometimes we ran down with steaming plates and ate in there off our laps.

One night, when we got to the shelter, she found that the gin supplies were disastrously low. There were only a couple of fingers left in the bottle.

'Christ – I can't get through it with only that.' The skin of her face looked thicker nowadays. She was puffing out with the pregnancy, but the boozing can't have helped. 'I'm going to have to get some more.'

'You can't,' I begged her. 'You'll just have to make it last.'

She looked at me as if I was a prison guard. 'You're getting a bit of a bossy miss round here nowadays, ain't you? Don't leave much room for me, does it?'

'I'm not!' I said, hurt. 'And anyhow, there'll be plenty to do when that one arrives.' I nodded towards her bump.

'Oh yes, that one.' She drank from the bottle, then gave a crooked smile. 'D'you think it'll be a boy or a girl? I bet it's a boy, don't you? And what do I call him then? Bob? Or Victor? Bictor, or Vob?' She laughed her stupid drinking laugh.

I thought, Lil wouldn't have been like this. Lil would've coped. But then Lil wouldn't have got herself in this mess in the first place.

'Do us a favour, Genie?' She had to speak loudly now, over the noise outside.

'What?'

'Go down the Outdoor for me and get some more?'

There were planes overhead. I stared at her in disbelief.

'I'll go for you,' Len said.

'No you won't, Len,' I snapped at him. 'They'll be in the cellar anyhow. They don't just stand there selling gin day and night in this lot. None of us is going anywhere.'

Mom pouted like a child. There was a long silence then, except for Mister's frightened whimpering and a tired moth battering against the lamp. Mom was sulking and I was too furious with her to speak.

With every wave of planes passing over I felt my heart bang harder until it was almost a pain. You couldn't move, you couldn't do anything about it – you just had to wait it out. Sometimes I wished I was old enough to be a warden, so's to get out there and do something.

It was a heavy raid that night. The first wave brought incendiary bombs, 'breadbaskets' of them rattling down to set the city alight, turn it into a beacon for the heavy high explosive bombs following close behind. The smell of smoke found its way to us. What was burning tonight? What would be left when – *if* – we got out of here in the morning?

Mom didn't have enough drink to knock herself out. She sat slumped on the bunk, leaning against the crimpy wall near the front of the shelter, staring at Len who was now sleeping like a princess in a fairy story.

I was so stung, so angry at what she'd asked me to do, I couldn't let it go. In the end I burst out, 'So you think more of a bottle of booze than you do me?'

She frowned, focusing on me slowly. 'What?'

'You'd send me out in this – just to get booze for you?'

She nodded in a befuddled sort of way and for a moment I thought she was too far gone to answer me. But eventually she said, 'Well that's me for you all over, ain't it?'

There was a sudden escalation of noise outside and both of us ducked, cringing, protecting our heads with our arms. The impact was loud and horribly near, shaking the ground, and the crashing and whooshing outside seemed to go on for ever.

'God, that was close,' I said as it started to die away. It was hard to straighten up. You got stiff and crumpled with fear.

In the lull that followed Mom nodded across at Len. 'I suppose you know why he's like he is?'

'Like what?'

'Like he is.' Her voice was harsh. 'Soft in the bleeding head, what d'you think? Thought your nan might've let on to you.'

'No. I always thought he was just born that way—'

'Nah, he wasn't born like it.' She shook her head as

354

hard as a Punch and Judy puppet. 'It was me did that. Ain't it always?'

She talked with her eyes fixed on Lenny's face.

'When he was born I was two – two and a half more like. He was a big babby, always was huge right from the start. And he was like six Christmases rolled into one for me. He was my dolly, my babby, he was going to be my best friend. And he was. I was all over him, all the time. Mom didn't mind. I took him off her hands and that suited her. She needed a hand, she was that pushed, what with the house and all the extra work she took in and our dad being the way he was. So Len was as much mine as he was hers really.

'Anyroad, he grew. I'd cart him about – course, he was heavy and I was a skinny little thing. Then one day when I was turned four Mom said she was going out to take some things up for a Mrs Brigham who lived in another yard up the road. The lady'd just had a babby and she wasn't any too good, so Mom was helping her out, the way she always has. She said to me – I can still hear her – "I'll only be a few minutes. Don't come up. You stay with Len."

' "But Mom—" I started arguing with her. "I want to see the new babby. Can't I come with you?"

' "No," she said. "You stay put. You'll only be in the way. Mrs B's not herself and she won't want me carting you two up there as well."

'And off she went. I was furious. I remember punching the couch downstairs with my fists, shouting, I was that cross. Don't know why I wanted to go so much really – there were always babbies about. But I s'pose I saw myself as a kid who was good with them and I wanted to be counted in.

'So in the end I wrapped my arms round Lenny, sort of in a hug, and picked him up. And I ran up the road after Mom. With his big head in the way I couldn't see where I was going and he was such a weight. I tripped and fell down right on top of him. His head went down with a bang on the pavement. Knocked him out. He wasn't quite two then, and he'd been starting to chatter on, but he never said another word after that – not for about five years, and he was never the same again. The doctors said he had brain damage . . .'

I could see it all, the little girl hoiking her baby brother along the road. Nan's face, the anger that even now she couldn't help spilling out on occasion when she spoke of her eldest daughter.

'You didn't mean it though, did you Mom?'

She shook her head, crying now, like the frightened child who'd done the deed. 'Course not. I wouldn't have hurt him for the world.'

I crept closer and sat by her, not quite daring to take her hand.

'Look at him.' Her cheeks were wet. I wondered if her tears tasted of gin. 'He's going to be a father and he's still only a kid himself. Thanks to me.' She looked at me. 'I deserve them hitting me after all the things I've done. One of these nights they'll get me.'

'Mom, no,' I said, frightened. 'Of course not. You didn't do anything on purpose. You're just . . .' I trailed off. Just what? Unlucky? Careless? Foolish? 'You've just had some accidents, that's all. You've had enough punishment.'

Later in the night, when she'd quietened, we felt sleep coming over us even though the raid wasn't finished. It was more distant and I found I'd blanked out for a time, I didn't know how long. It could have been seconds or

356

hours. But then they were hard over us again and I was suddenly awake. The battering of noise was back, the planes, ack-ack guns with their tennis-like rhythm, the whining and crashing. I sat up, wide awake. The lamp had gone out.

Mister was still lying beside me, but I stretched out on the bunk. Mom wasn't there.

'Lenny?' I shouted across to him. 'Where's Mom? Where's Doreen?'

'She's your side.' He must have been awake already because he sounded alert.

'She's not.' I wondered if she'd tumbled on the floor. 'Mom? Where are you?' I felt around in the dark. Nothing.

'Len, take Mister. I'm going to see out there.'

I wrenched the door open and stepped up into the crazed, coloured world outside. The sky was copper streaked with yellow and red, and puffs of white from the ack-ack fire. Fires across the city – beacons to guide the bombers – were filling the air with acrid smoke and the searchlights scratched at the sky with their cold beams. The explosions of light now were from the foul-smelling high explosive bombs.

But my eyes were fixed on Mom. She was standing with her back to me half way down the garden in her nightclothes, staring up at the glowing sky, her arms stretched out in front of her, open, as if she was in the act of embracing someone. Just standing there, quite still.

'Mom – for God's sake!' I ran to her, wondering if she was asleep or awake. Her pale nightdress stuck out at the front over her belly and I realized she'd taken off her coat. She must have been frozen. Her eyes were open.

'What're you doing?' I bawled at her. 'Come back in for Christ's sake.'

'I thought I'd just get it over with,' she murmured, so I could only just hear.

There came the most massive bang from very close by that snatched the ground from under us and we curled on the ground like babbies, our hands over our heads. I squeezed my eyes tight shut. The noise seemed to go on for ages and ages, the crashing and splintering and explosions of glass. When we stood up, instinct guiding our hands to our bodies to check everything was there, tongues of fire were shooting up from the street behind our house. There was already the sound of fire-engine bells somewhere near.

Mom and I dashed into our dark house. There was glass everywhere, front and back, strewn like a hard, crunchy icing on every surface we touched as we groped our way through to the front. I heard Mom gasp, cutting herself. The blackout blinds at the front were in tatters and through them we could see that a great swathe of the opposite side of the road was gone. Just matchwood and rubble, burning, and more to see than usual of the sky.

Mom's hands went to her cheeks, breath sucking in. 'Oh, look!' She was gulping breath in and out and couldn't speak for a moment. 'They got it – not me ... Someone else got it!'

When the light came we could see it all. The three of us walked out dumbly into the dawn, only half dressed, to see our familiar street changed utterly. We stepped over fat hoses squiggling along the road, leaking feeble arcs of water and lying in a mouse-brown mess of wet plaster and brick dust, and more glass crunched under our feet.

'Lord above, look at it.' Mom stood with her arms folded, a rough dressing on her cut finger. 'God in Heaven.'

Gladys and Molly's house was still standing, as were those on each side of it, but not much further along a great block had been blasted out of the terrace, the inside walls of some still left standing pointing jaggedly up, with their pathetic strips of wallpaper, their picture hooks and damp stains, and the rest of the houses smashed to charred rubble, bits poking out at all angles like spillikins.

There were people out all along the street. Len rushed across and banged on Molly's door and after a time Gladys opened it and the two of them came out, already dressed as they'd most likely been all night. The pair of them looked as tired and dishevelled as we must have done. In the quietest ever voice Gladys said, 'Wasn't it awful? Just a few more yards this way ...' and she looked along at the shattered houses, her eyes filling.

Len put his arm round Molly, who huddled close to him. Along the street a vicar, shabby old mac flung over his cassock, stood comforting a man who was watching the rescue squad, his face full of fear and desolation. They'd already been working out there for several hours, and the flames had all been put out. We could hear sawing and drilling and the men calling to each other. A team was waiting with stretchers. Other neighbours were gathering round. Mr Tailor from our side of the road stood out in his braces, and everyone was squinting in the shocking sunlight, no one saying, but all of us thinking, as we stared glumly at the houses opposite, 'Who's in there still? Who's dead?' A horrible, dank smell hung over everything, of wet, charred wood and plaster, wisps of grey smoke still floating in the air like the ghosts of those already dead. And mixed with this, the sickening smell of gas seeping from broken pipes in the houses.

One of the gossips I recognized from down the road was standing in front of what had been her house, two toddlers clinging dumbly to her coat and a baby yawling in her arms.

'Look,' Mom said. 'Mrs Terry.'

We went to her, seeing her shivering, the shock on her face.

'We was in the Anderson,' she said. 'In the Anderson. The Anderson at the back.' Their faces were brown with grime like panto gypsies but they all seemed unhurt. There was a mobile canteen at the end of the road handing out tea and we led her down, handing her carefully over the rubble because she didn't seem able to look out for herself. As we waited for our turn they carried a stretcher past to a grey ambulance, the face covered by a sheet. We all watched, no one speaking, but somehow we couldn't take our eyes off it.

Those who could go had already been taken to first aid posts, but the workers were still having to follow the trail of the buried or dead, listening for moans, tiny gasps, any flicker of life entombed under the houses. I heard a voice somewhere saying loudly over and over that we had to boil all our water. The bombing cracked and destroyed water pipes and the water wasn't safe.

As Mrs Terry sipped her tea, handed out by the cheerful woman in the mobile canteen, we stood trying to offer her comfort by our presence, not knowing what else to say. Mom held the babby for her, trying to quiet it.

'You can come back to ours and rest for a bit,' she said. 'They'll find you a place to go after, won't they?' None of us was sure. We couldn't think straight and it was all too new. Later we'd be able to gather our wits and ask one of the wardens where she could go.

Mrs Terry shook her head. She didn't know anything. She was in a state of paralysis. But she did hold out her arms to have her babby back. The two kids were chewing on the canteen's stale buns, both of them unnaturally silent.

A shout went up from amongst the wreckage. 'Here! There's someone under this lot!' There was urgent activity, equipment carried over at a jerking run, men sawing, lifting chunks of masonry, throwing out objects here and there when they got further down, a clock, a clothes-horse, a skein of baby-pink wool. It seemed to take so long. After a time they called a nurse through to give an injection.

'Morphine I s'pect.' Mom shuddered violently, arms folded tight. 'Christ, imagine being under there.'

As we watched, a man appeared in the street in trousers but bare at the top, blood dark on his head and stains of it on the shoulder underneath. His feet were bare as well and he was turning his head frantically from side to side as if looking for someone. One of the ambulance crew led him gently away.

'I've got to get over to your nan,' Mom said. 'See if they're OK.' She was agitated suddenly, pulled her fags out and was about to light up, hands shaking.

'No!' The warden almost flung himself at her, knocking it from her hand. 'Can't you smell the gas? You'll have the whole bloody street going up!'

'Sorry,' Mom said. 'Oh I'm sorry, I never . . .'

But he was too busy to listen to apologies and had already gone.

We were leading Mrs Terry and her children down towards our house when a murmur rippled through the straggling group of neighbours, a low moaning sound of everyone breathing out together. The rescuers were now pulling a body from the house where they'd heard the tiny sounds. It was a woman, and at the sight of her I saw Molly turn and bury her face in Len's chest with a whimper of distress. So slowly and tenderly they lifted her out, as if they were handling some treasure precious to their own lives. She was unconscious now, drugged out of her agony by the morphine, but how and what she had suffered these hours was more than any of us could bear to imagine. Her face was almost untouched except for a few small cuts, and the upper part of her body appeared unscathed, though it was hard to tell as she'd been trapped down there and could be crushed. But when the bomb came down she'd fallen, and been trapped by the weight of her house, next to where the fire burned in her little grate. For these past hours the heat of it had smouldered along the lower portion of her body so that all that remained of her feet were gnarled things like charred twigs which crumbled, dropping in small bits as they moved her, despite all their carefulness. The clothes on the lower part of her seemed melted round her like black tissue paper. Her head lolled to one side.

She can't live. Everyone must've thought the same. Not after that. I knew her face. Mrs Deakin, a widow in her late sixties who'd always been kind. I saw the nurse who'd given her the injection turn from the sight of that

362

grilled body on the stretcher and take deep controlling breaths. She was young, with light freckles on her nose.

Silently we led Mrs Terry to our house, where yellowed leaves piled gently against the door as they would on any October morning, except that today they were mixed with ash and glass.

After work that day I hurried across to Belgrave Road. There was a lot of damage in the area, gaps and mess where before it'd been whole. Life itself was wobbling. I had to rush because sometimes they came over as early as six and the sirens'd be off, barely giving you time even to get home.

Teresa and Vera had volunteered their house to the WVS as a respite point where people could be taken temporarily for rest and help.

'Otherwise we're no use to anyone, are we?' Vera said. 'It's the least we can do.' It gave them a sense of purpose, and they both seemed lifted by it.

At Nan's they were already preparing for the raid. Lil had made a makeshift bed for herself and Cathleen under the table. The others would go down the coal cellar and they had coats and shoes rowed up and blankets ready.

Lil, cooking chops, was in a state about Frank. 'He was on yesterday and he's on tonight. Thinks he's got a charmed life. God, I do hope he's careful with himself after that lot last night.'

Mom'd told them about our street, but the other news on everyone's lips that day was the Carlton Cinema. A bomb had come down in front of the screen when the place was packed. Killed nineteen.

'They say they were just sat there as if they were still watching the film,' Lil said.

'That'll be the blast.' Nan was filling a flask with cocoa. 'Does odd things. D'you know, Genie – when we came up this morning every window in the house was open?'

I looked round. 'All the glass is in.'

'No breakages. But they were all open. Wouldn't credit it, would you?'

I only stopped there a few minutes, but in that time it would've taken an idiot not to notice there was something wrong with Tom. He wasn't himself at all. I tried talking to him, making jokes, but he was pale and very jumpy, poor kid, very sunk into himself.

'This is all making him bad,' Lil whispered to me. 'I don't know what I can do for him.'

I could do no more either, except give him a cuddle and say goodnight to go and face the next round. The days which had seemed such hard work before now seemed like a rest cure compared with the nights.

And then it stopped. After two weeks of raids every night, suddenly there were days of no siren, no Mister howling, no shelter. It felt really peculiar. The bombing had so quickly become a way of life. But all the same you couldn't relax because there was no guarantee it was over. They might go and bomb somewhere else but they'd be back, and we never knew when. The siren could go off any time. So throughout those days there was still the same fluttering heart and acid stomach. A couple of times during the raids I'd been woken suddenly from a quick snatch of sleep and been sick, such was the shock to my system. Even on those nights of quiet I kept waking, blood rushing, ears straining, not being used to a full sleep.

One morning Mom came down, grey faced with tiredness and nerves. 'I've decided. I'm never going out in that shelter again.'

I gave a sarky laugh, readying myself for work. 'Not till the next time.'

'No. Never.'

'Mom?' I walked round and peered into her face but she was looking out somewhere way beyond me, one hand absent-mindedly stroking her big belly as if it was too tight and she needed to ease it. 'You all right?'

There was a long silence and I nearly asked again. But then, more firmly than I'd expected, she said, 'I'll be all right.'

Something about her bothered me, though I couldn't say what. It wasn't as if I wasn't used to her being lost to me, depressed or drunk, but she was stone cold sober this morning and she frightened me, nearly as much as she did when I'd found her standing out in the garden holding out her arms to embrace the bombs.

I put tea in her hands. 'Why don't you go over to Nan's today? Have a bit of company.'

'Don't fuss, Genie.' She spoke dreamily. 'Just get off to work.'

To start with she was on my mind that day. I couldn't get Mrs Deakin out of my head either, the horrible thing that had happened to her. I tried to think, Mom'll be better once the babby's over with and born. Give her something else to fix her mind on. I was beginning to look forward to that, a babby in the house, whoever its father was.

It was a busy day at the factory with all the work and talk and the women asking me if I'd heard from Joe.

Yesterday's letter from him, safe for the moment with his squadron, was folded close to me in my pocket. I thought of us making love and blushed, blushed even more when they noticed and teased me. It had brought us even closer. I had no shame, no sense of wrong. Not with Joe. And not now during this war when you couldn't take anything for granted. You took what you could and were grateful.

I wanted to go round to Nan's at the end of the day and look in on Tom, talk more to Lil about him. But by the time work finished I felt I ought to get home to Mom. Some instinct I had, that made me run half the way there in a cold sweat, not stopping to queue for any food. I don't know what I was afraid of. I suppose I expected her to get drunk and have an accident one day. Fall when there was no one in.

When I clattered in through the front door, Mister came at me like a cannon ball, yapping and jumping round my legs in ecstasy, licking whatever bits of me he could reach.

'Mom, where are you?' I needed to hear her voice.

There was no answer, but then she hardly ever did bother to answer when I called.

To my surprise she was in the kitchen standing by the stove. Cooking of all things. And the place looked as if she'd had a tidy up too.

'Thought it was high time I did a meal,' she said.

I was all smiles of relief. 'You feeling better?'

'I'll be OK.'

I picked up Mister who was still frantic for attention beside me. 'D'you go to Nan's today?'

'I popped over. Picked up a few things on the way

back.' She was stirring the pot, looking so frail standing there in the gaslight, pregnant, her hair loose, seeming younger than her years.

'We'll wait for Len,' she said. 'He can eat with us tonight, not at Molly's.'

She'd done stew and spuds, even a kind of egg custard for pudding, and the three of us sat together round the table, Gloria playing to us. Mom didn't drink. Not a drop all evening.

'Quiet without Jerry, isn't it?' I said. We were still waiting, could hardly believe it was another night free.

'When all this is over,' Mom said to Len all of a sudden, 'you and Molly'll have to get yourselves a little house somewhere.'

'If there's any left standing,' I joked.

She looked solemnly at me. 'And you and Joe. He's a very nice boy, Genie. The sort who'll really look after you.'

'And we'll look after you too, Mom. Don't you worry. And little'un in there.'

She just gave a bit of a smile at that, as if to say it wasn't her that mattered. She was so calm. Perhaps I should have seen that as odd but I was just glad. Things felt normal, whatever that was nowadays.

We sat listening to Gloria and then Mom took herself off to bed. As she passed by my chair she rested her hand on top of my head. 'Goodnight, Genie.'

I was the last up. I switched the lights off and left Mister snoozing by the remains of the fire.

The high wailing sound woke me and I was out of bed, completely awake, pulling on the coat I'd left at the foot of my bed. It stopped. Started again. It was only then I

367

realized it wasn't the siren but the other noise we normally heard along with it. Mister was howling, somewhere outside. I went and opened my window over the garden.

It was very dark and I could only hear, not see him, howling and whimpering under my window.

'Mister? How d'you get out there, boy?'

There were more yowls as he heard my voice and the rasp of his claws scratching against the back door.

'OK. I'm coming.'

Going to the door, I wondered whether I'd dreamed him being by the fire when I came up, or whether Mom'd been down, put him out and forgotten him. But as soon as I was on the landing I smelt it, that stink of the mornings after the raids, the mean, seeping smell of gas. I tore down the dark stairs.

When I opened the kitchen door the rush of it set me coughing and gasping. I could hear it hissing in the dark and the thoughts going round in my head were, who the hell, who'd been so stupid as to come down and leave the gas on in the middle of the night? I groped towards the back door and heard my feet knock into glass, bottles crashing together. Then I tripped over her legs and fell across the floor, banging my head and side. I got up and struggled with the back door key knowing now, knowing what was happening, taking gasps of air as I got the door open, sick with the gas. Mister tore inside and disappeared somewhere into the front of the house yelping and howling.

Everything was automatic now, with a kind of perfection born of instinct. My steps across the kitchen, one hand over my nose and mouth, the other going to exactly the right dial on the cooker to shut it off.

The hissing stopped. With more strength than I

knew I had, I bent and pulled out the dead weight of my mother's body from where she was lying, head resting on her crossed arms in the greasy base of the oven.

November 1940

Mr Tailor was the one I went to for help, after I'd knelt in the black kitchen, feeling along her wrist. My fingertips found the veins slanting across her bones and a tiny pulse like a bird's.

I was retching from the gas and sobbing out all sorts of stuff to her. 'Don't die. Don't do this ... Don't you bloody well go and die on me ...'

The smell was still awful in there – there wasn't much of a breeze coming in – so I lifted her under her flopping arms, her feet bumping down the step into the garden and the cold air. I found the crocheted blanket and laid it over her. Mister was running in circles in the garden, barking.

I went and picked him up, so glad he was there. 'We've got to get help, boy.' I ran down the road with his soft head pressed to my face.

Mr Tailor was marvellous. Didn't make a fuss. He found a working phone box and dealt with the ambulance, while Mrs Tailor was kindness itself in the face of my shaking. She made me sweet tea. I clung to my little dog and couldn't stop my teeth chattering. They asked no questions. Most likely guessed most of it in any case. They took me to my nan's, said they'd go round to Len first thing. It was three in the morning and I had to tell Nan what had happened. Nan sat down and stared ahead of her. It was Lil who did the crying for all of us.

She was a long time in hospital. At first I was just scared she'd die, and she came very close. Death's door, that's what they say, and she was on the step, hand raised, knocking. She lost the babby. The labour came on with the shock and was born dead, much too small for this world. They said it was another little girl, although she'd thought it was a boy. She haemorrhaged badly and had to have a blood transfusion. For days she lay barely conscious and we'd sit with her in that ward at the Queen Elizabeth. Dots of light flashed round my eyes from exhaustion and I couldn't keep my food down. They were bombing every night again now and we crouched in Nan's house thinking 'What if they hit the hospital?'

But Mom didn't know about these worries. I'd sit watching her white, sunken face, wondering what I was going to say to her when we could talk again. Nan kept bringing in things for her to eat, bits of fruit, little custards or junket she'd made. But she never even had a response from Mom, let alone got her to eat anything. I'd grip her hand but got no squeeze from her in return. Only later we found out why. As she regained consciousness the doctors said she'd lost the use of the right side of her body – the right arm completely, the leg showing little flickers of life.

The first time she came round while I was there, her eyelids seemed so heavy she could barely prise them open as she bubbled slowly back up to us. Her right eye wouldn't open.

'Mom.' She croaked the word, coughed, tried again. Only half her mouth was working. 'Oh, God, Mom – Genie—' She couldn't say any more. Tears seeped down her face.

'Mom, oh Mom . . .' I could only bow my head,

resting it on her, and cry too, overcome by her misery and my own shame.

There was Mom and there were the raids. That was what made up our lives. Nan and I went to the hospital every day, Lil when she could. I told Mr Broadbent my mother was ill. He told me to have days off, take my time. 'The others'll rally round,' he said.

I was staying at Nan's and Len was at Molly's. All other aspects of life faded into the background. Something happened to me during those days. Everything had changed from my life before, like a coin flipping over. The thought of seeing Joe appalled me, revolted me even. No, never again. Such things were not meant for me. This was family, and only family. And not even my family knew the depth of pain I was carrying in me over what had happened.

I couldn't look my nan in the eye. I'd let her down. Let us all down. I hadn't looked after Mom properly. That had always been my job. I was the one who saw her out there, arms out, calling to the bombs, and I should have known how near the edge she was. I should have been able to save her.

Nan did what had to be done, though she'd aged in a week. I thought she was angry with me. I couldn't stomach food, kept being sick at odd times. I wished I could be like Lil and let it all out. Lil could say all the things she needed to say, 'Poor, poor Doreen – fancy us not knowing she was that bad. Was she bad, Genie? And the poor little babby . . .'

But it was my nan I couldn't stand to be near. I couldn't bear the grief pushed down in her as she ran the shop still, day after day, in her pinner, her jawline held proud, listening to the grievances of her customers. She didn't let on about her own.

By the early evening the sirens were screaming and it was a terrible rush to get some food, get organized. The minute it started Mister was howling and Tom would be curled up under the table quivering and refusing to move.

'I ain't going in that coal 'ole – I'm never going down there again!'

The poor kid. When he was awake he was terrified and when he was asleep he was thrashing about screaming with nightmares and wetting the bed. He nearly jumped out of his skin at the slightest sound.

So we arranged it that I'd stay up with Mister and Tom under the table. I was happier up there in any case, what with my sudden bouts of sickness, and because I was happier away from Nan, couldn't face her. I also wanted to do the best I could for Tom. I told him stories and we both looked after Mister, who was just as scared as he was, or we lay curled up together, the darkness in the house made even thicker by the heavy table above our heads, while the sky was set on fire outside.

This particular night as we lay there I said to him, 'D'you know what day it is today, Tom? It's fireworks night!'

We both managed a bit of a laugh at that. 'Don't exactly need to bother with it this year, do we?'

Tom clung to me, shaking, as the noise escalated outside.

'I wish it'd stop,' he said. 'Stop and never come back.'

'So do I.' All the time I was thinking about the hospital, what a big target it was. At least Nan's house was small.

When the All Clear went, some time late in the night,

my muddled brain didn't know how much time had passed. Tom had finally fallen asleep, his arm across me, and I lay there listening to his breathing, his restless muttering. Poor kid.

There was light moving in the room and I heard Lil taking Patsy and Cathleen up to bed. It went dark again. After a time Nan's slow tread came up the steps and through from the scullery. She went to the range and struck a match to light a candle. Her shadow moved nearer the table and I shut my eyes, sensing her bending to look under at us, taking it that we were both asleep. After a moment I heard a spoon chink against a cup and knew she was taking Turley's Saline to settle her stomach. I waited for her to move the candle and find her own way to bed, but instead of that she went and opened the door. Picking up a chair she carried it outside, came back in to put her coat on and blow out the candle, then disappeared again, quietly latching the door.

When she didn't come back in I moved Tom's arm off me and crawled out from under the table. My insides churned and I stopped, wondering if I was going to retch, but it passed. I felt my way to the window and moved the blackout curtain. There was a tiny piece of moon in the sky and I could see stars. And right the other side of the glass criss-crossed with tape I could see the back of Nan's head. She was sitting out there, quite still.

It took me quite some minutes to pluck up the courage to go out to her. But I couldn't go on living with her the way I was. Not with the shame I felt. She didn't turn her head when she heard the door open, was looking up at the moon, her hands folded in her lap, and I stood there by her shoulder.

'Can't you sleep, Genie?' She spoke very quietly.

'No. Tom's gone off, though.'

She nodded slowly.

'Nan—' My heart was like a throbbing pain. I needed her forgiveness, for her to say it was all right, although it wasn't, none of it.

She waited.

'Nan, I'm sorry. I'm so sorry – I know it was my fault.'

She seemed really startled and looked right round at me. 'Genie love? What've you got to be sorry for?'

I wished so much that I could cry. I tried to make the tears come, to ease it, but they wouldn't. 'I let you down. I was supposed to be looking after her. It was my job. I should've been able to save her.'

'But bab, you were the one that *did* save 'er.'

'But before – I should've known . . . I should've woken up. But the day before she seemed better than she'd been—'

Nan gave a sigh then, the great breath of someone pressed by a heavy burden.

'There's no blame on you, Genie love. She's been a poor mother to you in many ways and you've been better to 'er than she ever deserved. It's a hard thing to 'ave to say about your own daughter but it's the truth. When I think back, 'ow things might've been different, what I could've done . . .' She shook her head and brought up one hand, clenched in a fist, to her lips, the elbow resting on her other arm.

I thought of Lil's saying, 'Kids – when they're young they break your arms, and when they're grown up they break your heart.'

I saw that all this time she'd been blaming herself as well. I don't know if Nan's heart was broken. She'd had enough in life to chip it all right, from her dead babies and my rotten grandad right the way through to this, and it all sank somewhere deep in her like a stone so the world never saw what she was feeling. I'd have done anything, anything to make her feel better.

After a week at Nan's I went back to work. There was nothing much I could do at home and I felt I owed Mr Broadbent, but I was nervous about facing them all, or disgracing myself if I was sick without expecting it. It didn't happen all that often, maybe once every day or two, but it was always very sudden. Just happened, not much warning. Put me right off eating.

'How's your mom?' they all asked, and I made up something about how she was poorly and getting better.

'You awright, Genie?' Agnes asked me. 'You're looking terrible. You're all skin and bone.'

The others agreed. 'You want to get some flesh on them bones, girl. Joe'll think we're overworking you when 'e comes back!'

Course, everyone was tired and jumpy, not just me. The sound of a car engine in the road'd make you start violently. Every noise felt like a bomb coming to get you, even in the daytime. I just tried to smile at them through it all, praying my innards would behave themselves, at least while I was here.

I went back to our road, dreading the house. I called in on Len, told him Mom was OK. At home there was a letter from Joe. I picked it up and stared at it. His writing seemed like something so foreign to who I was now. I couldn't open it, couldn't stand to read his words of love when I felt so hateful. I knew how terrible it was not hearing, that I owed it to him to write back straight away, but I couldn't. There was nothing in my head except the bombing and what had happened to Mom. I had nothing to give Joe in a letter. Nothing to give him full stop. And I'd been a silly little fool, living in a dream world to think I could be with someone like him. I may have had Nan's forgiveness, even if she thought none was needed, but I couldn't forgive myself.

I put the letter in a drawer up in my room, still unopened.

It came on when I got to the front door, a sudden rush so I only just made it back into the kitchen, retching over the bucket, nose and eyes running, until I was empty and wrung out. I sat on my heels on the floor after, too weak for a while to get up. If only I could cry instead of this. Stop feeling so numb. This was my punishment. I didn't deserve Joe and now I'd lose him. If he wanted to know how I was he'd have to ask his dad. He wouldn't get an answer from me. Not from someone who'd died inside.

On 13 November there was a daylight raid on the Austin Aero factory, but thank God, Lenny was safe. On the night of the 14th the Luftwaffe flattened Coventry, bombed and burned it to the ground. Nowhere else disappeared as thoroughly as Coventry. As Teresa said to me after one of the endless, terrifying nights when they'd been over us, 'What the hell will there be left when they've finished?'

The night they bombed Coventry was a rest for us, but they were soon back. I was at Nan's all the time. That day it was her and me went up the hospital. Mom just lay there, face white as the sheets, her one open eye blank and empty. She had no energy to give it any expression. But the blankness looked like an everlasting sadness that no one would be able to take away.

We always tried not to look at the women in the other beds round us, with their rasping lungs or odd swellings. Sometimes you just couldn't stop yourself looking round, your eyes pulled by a noise or a smell, but we'd try to fix everything on Mom. We never knew what to say to her though. Nan put her coat on to go up there like a suit of armour, always as smart as she could manage, hat on too.

That day, nestling in the bag she always carried, was a carefully wrapped little cup of egg custard, carried delicately as if it were the actual shell of the egg. She fed it to Mom with a teaspoon, Mom half sitting up, bending her head forward, bits of custard slipping back out of the right side of her mouth.

'This'll 'elp get your strength back, Dor,' Nan kept saying. 'We'll soon 'ave you out of 'ere and back 'ome where you belong.'

Mom's good eye looked at her. 'I want to go home,' she whispered, mouth twisting against her will.

'Soon, Mom.' I took her hand, my heart thumping. I was almost afraid of her. 'They say a bit longer – maybe next week.'

'When you're a bit more yourself,' Nan said, stowing the little cup from the custard back in her bag.

What was 'a bit more herself' going to mean now?

'I've brought you a drop of beef tea. Will you have some?'

Mom closed her eyes as if in revulsion. Nan's face twitched. She put the bottle back in her bag and sat turning her wedding ring round and round on her finger, cuddling the bag on her knees as if she thought some-one'd nick it if she put it down for a second.

I picked up Mom's brush and stroked it over the hair round her face. She hated to be a mess. Her eye flickered open and closed. She was falling asleep.

On the bus home, full of smoke and the smell of stale old coats, Nan and I sat without talking. Nan's hands were clasped tight round the handles of the bag. The lights were very dim in the bus, and when tears started rolling down my face I didn't think anyone would see. Just a few tears I was going to allow myself, but something caved in in me on that bus ride when I thought of my mom so far away from us and so sunk in despair she might as well have been dead. I even wondered whether stopping her when I did had been the right thing. I'd kept her alive into something worse. I started sobbing and couldn't stop. I was too far gone to control myself, just pushed my face into my hands, trying not to make too much noise. All the fear and guilt and worry of the past fortnight came over me and I couldn't help myself. I was only sorry for embarrassing Nan.

''Ere, bab.' She didn't tick me off like she might have had things been different, just leaned over and gave me her hanky and that made me cry even more. She took one of my hands and hers kept clenching and unclench-ing on mine. When we were nearly back into town she led me off the bus and crossed over to the bottom of our road where she stopped me, took the hanky and mopped my face.

With no warning I was heaving, sick in the street. I rushed to the gutter, so glad it was dark, and stood there gulping in misery when it was over.

Nan led me by the arm. 'There now. You shouldn't

be in a state like this, that you shouldn't. Let's get you 'ome—'

Next thing, the air raid warning was cutting her sentence in half and everything was forgotten in the fear that noise brought up in you. I took Nan's bag off her to carry – it was hard for her to hurry with her bad legs – and as fast as we could we raced up the hill, terrified of being caught out in the road. The last tears dried on my face.

'Thank God,' Lil said as we came in. The room smelt of stew. Tom was curled up under the table and Lil, in a tizzy, was trying to persuade Patsy to take Cathleen down the coal hole, and dishing up plates of food.

Coat off, Nan started sorting out saucers and stubs of candles for the cellar.

'Fetch me a couple from out the front, will you Genie? We shan't get far with these bits.'

The sirens had stopped by now and although we were all doing things we were straining our ears to hear the planes coming, those minutes between the two usually one mad rush of getting ready.

I ducked under the counter into the shop, holding up one lighted candle stub, fumbling for new ones on the crowded shelves. It didn't take me long to realize there was an argument going on outside. Morgan's voice and no mistake, right outside the shop door, and a girl, pleading with him, it sounded like.

Pulling back the bolts I opened up to the moonlit night.

'Ah,' Morgan said, seeing me. 'Course, you've closed early tonight. I couldn't get in.' We weren't supposed to bolt him out but Lil had shut the shop right up without giving it a thought.

'Course we're closed – there's a flaming raid on in case you hadn't noticed.'

As I appeared, the girl made to take to her heels but Morgan grabbed her by the arm, and although she couldn't get away she wrenched round away from us, hiding her face. Seemed a bit timid this one, not like some of the brazen hussies he brought along.

'Don't be silly now,' Morgan said to her. 'You can't go rushing 'ome – as Miss, er . . . Miss Genie 'ere says, they'll be over any moment.'

The planes moved into the range of our hearing as he spoke.

'Get in then.' I stood back to let them past, making sure he didn't so much as brush against me. He kept hold of the girl, who from what I could see was plump and quite young, and she kept her face pushed down in her coat collar.

'What the hell're you doing here tonight?'

'Thought there wouldn't be a raid.' Morgan let go of the girl now I'd shut the door and rubbed his hands together.

'Course there wouldn't be a raid. Why should there be a raid? I mean they only smashed the living daylights out of Coventry yesterday.' Must admit, I was rather enjoying myself. 'I don't know how we're going to fit you in. You can't go up there, can you? Mrs Rawson's really going to love you turning up.'

As I turned to lock the door, the girl gave out a noise like a whimper and moved over to me, speaking with her head still right down. I thought she seemed a bit odd. 'Let me go,' she whispered. I could hardly hear her. 'I'll just go 'ome.'

'You mad? Hark at them out there! It's the daft

bugger you came with wants his head looking at. See – he don't care about you. He's in there saving his own skin already. You come on in. I dunno what you've heard about my nan but I s'pect even she'll call a truce in this.'

'I can't.' This time it was almost a sob. I picked up the stub of candle on the saucer and held it by her face.

She cringed away from me. 'Don't.'

'Shirl?'

Turning away, she put her hands over her face. 'I'd no idea in the world 'e was going to bring me 'ere, Genie, honest I didn't. He just said it was somewhere in Highgate. I couldn't believe my eyes when it was your nan's . . .'

The first bombs were falling and I rushed her through the back and under the table with Tom. Shirl sat crying and I put my arm round her. Nan must've told Morgan he could shelter under the stairs if he was prepared to clear himself a space, because we could hear him banging about, moving out Nan's enamel wash pot, the bucket of sand and stirrup pump, some old crocks and something that fell over with a crash which might've been a clothes-horse.

From feeling so down before, my emotions swung right the other way and I suddenly got the giggles, hearing Morgan's muffled cursing from under our stairs.

'Hark at him,' I spluttered to Shirl, who actually managed to look me in the face for the first time and mopped her eyes, seeing I wasn't about to have a go at her. Some other hard object came flying out with a clatter, we heard Morgan say, 'Bugger it,' and I was in stitches as the planes came over, Tom clinging to my legs, still holding on to Shirl, the old wood smell coming from the worm-eaten table.

There was a bang from upstairs, no explosion, just a real big thump from the roof and the planes passed over, followed by more.

'Mrs Rawson—'

I half crawled out from under the table and saw Morgan's scrawny figure standing over the entrance to the coal hole, his shadow enormous on the wall behind him.

'I think you've 'ad one of them incendiaries come through your attic . . .'

'What do you mean *my* attic?' Nan's voice came back loud and clear. 'This is your 'ouse, Morgan, not mine – you'd better get up there with that bucket of sand mighty bloody quick.'

So there was Morgan forced into being the big man, creeping off up with the bucket. We didn't know where it'd come down but he went to look up on his side. I imagined his gloomy attic with the white light of an incendiary up there sputtering like a firework.

'Just hope he knows what he's doing,' I said to Shirl. I kept trying to be light and cheerful because I was embarrassed for her, but I didn't want her to think I was going to hold anything against her, even though it wasn't exactly normal behaviour to turn up at my nan's as one of Morgan's trollops. But now wasn't the moment for explanations. We were all too busy listening to the movement of the planes. Keep going, you found yourself thinking. Just keep on going. Go somewhere else . . .

Next thing was, Morgan came crashing down the attic stairs, first the bucket, him following, effing and blinding his way down making a hell of a racket until he landed with a groan in the shop.

Shirl looked at me. 'D'you think we'd better look?'

'Not cowing likely. Not with this lot.' Bombs were falling, proper explosives. 'He'll be all right.'

He came through a minute later, groaning and cradling his right arm with his left. I peered out from under the oilcloth.

'I think I've bust my arm,' he moaned.

'For God's sake get under the stairs!' I yelled to him and retreated back in to save my own head. Shirl had her arm round Tom.

'D'you put it out?' Nan's voice boomed up from the coal hole. 'Or couldn't you even manage that?'

'Heartless bitch,' Morgan mumbled, backing into the stair cupboard. 'Oh Christ, my arm!'

The house shook, the windows rattled and a lump of something fell from the ceiling.

I saw the gaslight flicker. 'Blimey, this is a bad one.'

Even with all the noise, we could hear Morgan groaning and carrying on. 'Serves him right,' I said. 'Oversexed little bugger.'

Shirl turned away, embarrassed again. I thought how different she looked tonight – hair all fluffed up, heavy eye make up and lipstick.

It didn't suit her. She had a sweet face normally.

'What the hell're you playing at, going with him of all people?' I suddenly found myself shouting at her.

Shirl shrugged sulkily, still holding on to Tom who trusted her instinctively, despite the tart disguise she was wearing. 'He was nice to me.'

'*Nice* to you!'

When there was a lull, she said, 'There's only me and Dad at home, see, and he's never had any time for me, even before Mom died. My life with him's like a servant's – nothing else. He isn't even there at nights most of the time because he works a night shift now. But even when 'e is ... 'E hardly treats me as if I'm human, Genie. Never a word except "Get this – fetch me that. Sit down and fucking shut up." He kicks me out of the way as if I'm a dog. On my life, Genie. I wouldn't lie to you. I've been so lonely, specially since you went. It was so nice with you at the factory, and I used to love coming 'ere.'

I swallowed. All along I'd thought she was doing me a favour.

'I met Eric down the pub—'

That knocked me back a bit. All this time I'd never known Morgan had the same name as my brother.

'I know he's not God's gift, 'ow 'e looks and that. But 'e'll spend time with you. Say nice things—'

'To get what he wants.'

'He comments on how I'm looking and that. No one's ever done that before. Dad never even looks at me. I'm sort of invisible so far as 'e's concerned. Anyhow, after a bit Morgan started asking me to dress up for him a certain way – like this – because you know I don't as a rule. Next thing was coming out 'ere. I knew what 'e was after and I'd have given it 'im. I was that lonely and that grateful.' She looked at me with her huge eyes. I remembered they were china blue in proper light.

'I've never done it before, I swear to you. I s'pose you haven't the faintest what I'm on about, 'ave you Genie? What with all your family round you.'

'I had no idea things were so bad for you. I do know what you're on about, sort of. But Shirl, *Morgan*. I mean, he's vile.'

'Beggars can't be choosers.'

'But why should you be a beggar? You're so pretty and kind – I bet loads of blokes'd give their right arm to go out with you—'

Another moan came from the stairs cupboard. Shirl rolled her eyes. 'Sounds as if someone already 'as.'

That really set us off then, even Tom too, watching us, and Shirl and I were helpless with laughter and for a time the stupidest little thing set us off.

'Oh, I'm glad you're here,' I said to her, wiping my eyes.

It was a long, long raid that night, nearly ten hours of it until we heard the All Clear. There were some lulls when we crawled out and had a drink. Nan managed to fix up a makeshift sling for Morgan using an old strip of sheet, with a look on her face when she had to touch him like someone clearing a dead frog out of a drain. Morgan had to put up with whatever treatment he got and sat quietly sipping Bournvita. Seeing her with him then it dawned on me why she'd put up with him all these years. Amid all the hurts and setbacks of her hard life, which had, I think, cast her lower than any of us had guessed, Morgan was the one person she could always guarantee feeling superior to.

'Much damage up there?' Nan asked him.

Nose pointing into his cup, he nodded, swallowing.

'Your side?'

'Yep. Great 'ole in the roof. Room's in a hell of a state.'

'Shame,' Nan said. 'Well, that'll cramp your style for a bit, won't it?' And sparks of triumph glinted in her eyes.

*

386

We were all exhausted next morning as much from tension as lack of sleep. Morgan drifted off saying he was going to get himself seen to, which Nan shouted after him was not before time. We sat round trying to rouse ourselves with weak cups of tea, because sleep or no sleep, there was work waiting.

Of course Nan would normally have blown a gasket at the first sight of Shirl in Morgan's thrall, but what with all the goings on in the night she'd had time to calm down. We'd spent most of the hours talking, Shirl and me, and it'd been a huge relief for me so that once again I felt it was her doing me a favour. I told her about Mom, about how I felt. Swapped my shame for hers. I didn't talk about Joe though, couldn't even speak his name.

Between us we'd come up with a kind of plan.

'Nan – Shirl's not happy at home with her dad hardly being there nights and that and I've said she can come and live with us, back home, when Mom comes out of hospital. I could do with the extra help.'

Nan considered this, looking sternly at Shirl. 'You know what I think of the company you're keeping. You'd better mend your ways. For your own sake as much as anything.'

Shirl blushed a heavy pink and looked down at the floor. 'It was the first time, Mrs Rawson. And the last. You can be sure of that.'

Nan kept the kids home from school and they were already back in their beds sleeping the morning away. We heard Tom crying out in his sleep.

Lil tutted, leaning towards the mirror to put her

lipstick on. 'I ought to get him away from here. It's making him really ill.'

The three of us, Lil, Shirl and I, set out for our different factories in the morning's custard-coloured light. It was raining, but even in a downpour you'd have that new-born feel of it being a miracle after the long, threatening night. Even in all my sadness and worry I felt my spirits lift. This was now, today, and I was alive.

But there was so much devastation outside. Houses down along the road and all the morning shock and horror of it, the way everything looked squalid, and stank even worse. The wardens were on the street with the rescue squads, helping and reassuring. Someone said they'd hit the BSA over at Small Heath and a lot had been killed.

'I hope Frank's all right,' Lil said.

Vera and Teresa were out too, Vera helping a woman along the road with cuts on her face, taking her to their house. Teresa came over to me, hair scraped up in a hurried ponytail.

'How's your mom?'

'Same really. They're talking about her coming out next week.'

'How're you going to manage? You handing in your notice?'

'I might,' I said.

I hadn't decided until then, but even as she asked I knew that's what I was going to do. Mom needed me and I found seeing Mr Broadbent very awkward now. Sooner or later he was going to ask why I wasn't writing to Joe and I couldn't answer. If I was going to be unhappy it was no more than I deserved, but I didn't want to have to explain to him. Or to the other women who kept asking about Mom.

'You all right, Genie?' She touched my shoulder.

I turned away. 'Yeah. Better get on.'

'Genie?'

I looked round at her again, noticing properly the strain in her face. 'Nonna Amelia's very bad. They don't think she's got long. I thought you'd want to know.'

'Oh Teresa,' I said helplessly. Because that was the only way we seemed to be able to feel now about anything. Helpless.

The next heavy raid on Birmingham wrecked a lot of the water mains. Instead of us boiling water after the raids there was now none at all for a period and they were having to send water wagons round. Without a hot cuppa first thing in the morning after a raid you felt hopeless. Couldn't cope with the exhaustion, the jangled nerves and all the awful and weird goings on in the Blitz. The way everything was turned inside out, terraces ripped open like dolls' houses, showing everyone's private rooms. You heard stories about people caught on the toilet by a bomb, tales of relatives who'd died years ago appearing out of the dark, rumours of Fifth Columnists. All this was a bit much without Brooke Bond in the morning.

In the middle of all this chaos, Lil dropped her own bombshell. She was leaving her well-paid job at Parkinson Cowan, and Frank, who so far had survived the raids like a cat with nine lives, was going to 'set her up.'

'He's got me a little place in Hurst Street,' she told

us, aglow with excitement. 'The rent's a pound a week and he's going to pay it for me to start with. Till I get going.'

'Setting you up as what, in 'igh 'eaven?' Nan hadn't really got started on her yet but you could see it was coming. The world had truly gone mad.

'A phrenologist and clairvoyant.'

Nan opened and shut her mouth quite a few times before she could get going, like an old pair of bellows. 'You *what*?'

'He's been teaching me.'

'But he's a mechanic!'

Patiently, and with what seemed an astonishing steady sureness given the barminess of it, Lil explained. All this feeling of our heads that had gone on lately was practice for the real thing. Add to that knowledge of tarot cards and palm lines, throw in a crystal ball, and Lil was in business.

But this was only part one of the grand explosion. Parts two and three were to follow swiftly on. Two: there was another wave of evacuation from Birmingham and she'd decided to send Patsy and Tom.

'Look at the state of Tom,' she said. 'He can't sleep without screaming, can hardly talk to you without twitching. He's as thin as a rake and it can't be doing him any good at school. Patsy can go and keep him company. And I'm not just sending him anywhere. Frank's got an auntie lives over in Stoke and she says she'll have 'em while things are bad.'

Before Nan had had a chance to field that one, we were on to part three. 'And I'm moving in with Frank over the garage. Me and Cathleen. It's not far, and Kings Heath's not getting bombed anything like as much as over 'ere. Don't worry, Mom. I'm not going to be leaving you on your own all the time. Frank'll be out so much with the ARP anyway we'll probably be here as much as we ever are now!'

I went back to our house to pick up letters. I never opened the ones from Joe. I gave Mr Broadbent my notice, speaking to him formally, not meeting his eyes. He was my employer, nothing more.

'But why, Genie?' He ran his hand through the white-streaked hair, absent-mindedly smoothing it down.

'It's Mom. I've got to look after her. There's no one else.'

'I'm sorry, love – serious as that, is it?'

I nodded, looking down at the floorboards.

'That'd explain it. Joe said in his last letter he hadn't heard from you. If you'd said, we could've arranged more leave for you.'

'It's all right, thanks. I'll need to be at home for good now.'

Mr Broadbent came round from behind his desk towards me and I felt myself cringing. I set my face, chin out. Don't be nice to me, I shrieked inside. Don't give me sympathy or try to soften my feelings, because if I let myself go under any of this I shan't be able to bear it.

'Genie? You don't look at all well yourself, love. You've got so thin.'

It was true. There were pits under my eyes you could crawl into. 'Everyone's tired, aren't they?' I still couldn't look at him. 'You can't be anything else with the nights the way they are.'

I think he was probably a bit hurt, certainly puzzled, by the way I was behaving. But he was too nice a man,

Mr B, to try and force his way past my wooden determination.

'You're sure this is the right decision? Everyone'll miss you.'

'I'm quite sure.'

They had to carry Mom into the house that Friday when they brought her back. Two plump women were in charge of the ambulance and they laced their frozen hands together, gripping each other's wrists, and made a kind of chair to lift her between them. I had a fire going inside and offered them tea but they said no, they had to go. Seemed to be relieved to be out of there. I didn't blame them.

Lil, who'd already given up work too, was with me, though Shirl hadn't moved in yet. I couldn't have stood it on my own. Lil was in enough of a state about the boys going off the next Monday, and seeing Mom there with her arm hanging all floppy by her side, and that dead half of her face, she started crying all over again.

'Oh Dor – Dor.' She knelt down and put her arms round Mom's waist, resting her face in her lap, shoulders shaking.

Mom looked down at Lil's sleek head, and after a moment she brought up her good hand and started stroking Lil's hair.

She looked across at me as I stood watching, torn up inside, wishing I could cry as easily as Lil.

Mom's lips were moving. 'I'm sorry,' she whispered, then managed it louder, her own tears falling now. 'I'm so useless to everyone. I'm sorry . . . sorry . . .'

*

Shirl moved in over the weekend. Just packed her bags and never told the old man where she was going.

'Teach 'im a lesson,' she said. ''E'll be round to fetch me back else. 'E can learn to fend for 'isself for a bit.'

I was so glad she'd come I hugged her. Even though I'd given up my job and could manage the house I was scared to be alone with Mom. Even Nan visiting when she could and Len popping in to escape from Gladys carrying on at him were not enough. Mom was like someone who'd been trapped in a dark well full of icy water and the coldness of it still billowed out from her. I was scared of catching her chill.

Shirl was one of those people who's happiest looking after others. Even with her doom-laden voice she could give off cheer like catkins shedding pollen. She was still working of course, but come the evening she'd be rattling the front door to be let in and I'd feel relief rush through me.

''Ere y'are.' Most days she'd thrust something into my hands, flowers or cheap meat. 'Been over the Bull Ring. Thought these'd 'elp.' It was her way of showing gratitude even though there was no need. My thankfulness was a giant compared with hers. I'd just about stopped being sick now Mom was home.

Shirl and I'd cook together, chat. She'd tell me about her day. She brought news to us, what buildings were down across town. And she stopped me brooding as much as I'd have done left to myself. I never mentioned Joe to her. I thought I could cope, just about, with these other things. With Mom. But I couldn't talk about Joe. Couldn't allow myself to think about him. I thought of Mister as my dog now, shut the memory of Joe's hands stroking him out of my mind. His letters were in a drawer, unopened. Soon he must stop writing and then that would be that. I could forget those kind of hopes, thinking I could have love like that. I didn't know the state I was in, couldn't see it for myself.

I had a job to do here, that's what I thought. And it was going to take everything I'd got. The doctor said that in time, Mom could recover. Perhaps not completely, maybe not the arm which was too dead. But she could learn to walk and probably to talk properly again. Only time would tell. She could get about on one leg holding the furniture with her good arm, steadying herself with the other foot. It wouldn't take the full weight, but she had some feeling in it. She had to arrange the position of her right arm with the left one, bending it to rest in her lap when she sat down. And she sat for hours, not even trying to talk, listening to Gloria.

If it was the last thing I did, I was going to make sure she got better. Looking after her was my job, and up to now what a miserable mess I'd made of it. But this time I was going to give it everything. I had to save her.

Saying goodbye to the boys, Tom especially, was terrible. I couldn't bear the thought of losing him as we seemed to have lost Eric.

'Soon as it stops we'll come and get you,' I told him, hugging him tight. Tom nuzzled his face against me, seeming younger than eight.

'Promise, Genie?' He looked up at me, those melting brown eyes full of tears. He was trying so hard not to let them fall.

'I promise.' I was struggling too, holding back my own tears. I may have longed for the release of it on lots of occasions but this was no time to start blarting. 'It'll be an adventure. You know, when I went out of Birmingham—' I came out with that without thinking and stopped short. My day out with Joe in Kenilworth. How long ago that seemed! It had happened to someone else. I couldn't think about that now. 'It was beautiful. You'll see. And you'll be able to write and tell me all about it and I'll write back.'

Lil and I went to put them on the train and waved them off, their little faces at the window, Tom's glum, Patsy full of bravado.

'So like his dad, our Patsy,' Lil said.

I comforted Lil. Nanny Rawson was livid with her and had been since she'd announced her intention, as Nan put it, 'to pack your kids off so you can play about with That Chancer of yours.'

'But Mom,' Lil had said to her, 'things are so different now. If you find a bit of happiness why not hold on to it and bugger the rules?'

'That's all very well,' Nan retorted. 'But whose rules are you living by now, eh?'

'It's not like that, Genie,' Lil sniffed as we walked through town on the way back. 'I'd have sent Tom anyhow, the way he was. And Frank says he wouldn't have minded them living with us. He likes kids. Wants some of his own.' Lil blushed, looking away.

'Nan knows really that they're better off out of it,' I told her. 'It's you living in sin she can't stand. You'll never see eye to eye on that in a million years. She's waiting for lightning to strike you.'

Lil looked sober. 'Like Doreen.'

When I got home I found Mom had got up and moved. In the still, silent way she had about her now, she was standing with her back to me, leaning on the doorframe which led out of the back room, staring across the kitchen.

'Mom?' I hurried to her.

Her eyes were fixed on the cooker and I felt terror rise in me. She was thinking about it. She's going to do it again! Jesus Christ, no.

'I can't remember.' She brought out the words, turning to look at me. Her face was so thin now, her open eye looked enormous. It was terrible seeing her face in that state. The worst part. 'Don't remember doing it.'

'Mom, come and sit down.' I helped her to the chair, her leaning on my shoulder, hopping and shuffling. 'I'll make a cup of tea.' She seemed glad to sit down and as I filled the kettle I told her the boys had gone.

'Poor Lil,' she said.

When I brought her the tea she whispered, 'This is no life, Genie.' I thought she meant her own reduced, miscarried, crawling-about existence, and I opened my mouth to tell her again how much better she was going to get, when she added, 'Not for you.'

I knelt down and took her hand. 'I don't mind, Mom. I just want to help you get better. You're my mom, and that's all that matters, honest it is.'

She shook her head, wouldn't believe it. 'How's your Joe?'

I managed to bring a smile to my face. 'He's all right, Mom. Things are fine. Really they are.'

December 1940

Shirl and I stood outside Lil's shop in Hurst Street. It was a narrow, scruffy frontage, squeezed between other shops, with filthy maroon paint flaking off the wood-work and its old sign, saying 'Stubb's Pawnbrokers', roughly whitewashed over. The golden balls had gone from outside though. Lil had evidently given the win-dows a going over but it still looked seedy and depressing.

'Bit of a dump, innit?' Shirl pulled the ends of her mouth down comically. 'I thought this was supposed to be 'er big break?'

'Well, give her a chance. She's only been here a week.' I was trying to be brave on Lil's behalf. She deserved some sort of new start, even if it did feel she was leaving the rest of us in the lurch.

On the pavement in front of the shop an old piece of blackboard had been leant up under the window. Chalked on it in swirly writing were the words: 'Liliana – Professional Phrenologist – 2/6d, 5/-, 7/6d.'

'Flipping 'eck, not cheap, is it?' Shirl exclaimed.

Underneath in smaller letters it read, 'Tarot, For-tunes, Palm Readings.'

''Allo girls, come on in!' Frank stood in the doorway in his shirtsleeves, although it was freezing, looking miraculously handsome. 'Lil!' he shouted into the shop. 'Your Genie's 'ere!'

'Cor, look at 'im!' Shirl hissed at me. ''E's a bit good to be true, ain't 'e? Can see why she'd risk 'er everything for that.'

I nudged Shirl hard with my elbow to shut her up and Frank stood back to let us in. It was dark inside and made even more gloomy by the winter day outside.

Lil, though, was looking anything but gloomy.

'Blimey, Lil. What do you look like?' I stood back staring at her, laughing. My auntie had been transformed into a gypsy. She had on a very full skirt in blues, reds, orange and green and a blouse which was just as bright with pink, orange and black flowers. She had her hair pinned up and a red silk rose, which matched her red lips, fastened over her left ear, and there were big gold earrings clipped to her earlobes. She pulled the skirt out at each side, curtsied, then twirled round on the wooden floor so it billowed out like a parachute.

'What d'you think of 'er?' Frank said, sounding like someone who'd just bought a new motorcycle. 'Looks right for the part, don't she?'

She did look gorgeous of course, but so strange and different I wasn't sure what to make of it. Was this Frank's influence, changing her, making her into someone else? And was what they were doing all a con anyway?

'This is it,' Lil said, turning round to look at the room. 'What d'you think?'

Course the place was very like Mr Palmer's shop in a way, only a bit bigger. The room was painted the colour of milky tea and there were long, filthy marks along the walls where shelves must've been taken down, and damp stains on the ceiling, which was flaking. There was still a counter at the back with oddments of clothes and crocks left by the previous owner, and Lil and Frank had put a table and two chairs in the middle of the room. On the table was a tiny vase with another silk flower stuck in it, and a crystal ball.

'Ooh,' Shirl said. 'Can I 'ave a look in?'

'You can look, but you won't see much,' Lil said.

Shirl bent over the table squinting into it. 'Well what d'you see then?'

'Oh, you'd be surprised.' Lil laughed mischievously. 'I had this woman in yesterday, said she could see mountains in the crystal ball. Convinced, she was. Said she'd always had this dream of going to Switzerland. "I'm going to go!" she said. "After the war's over." So there's one very happy lady thinking she's going to see the Alps. D'you know what it was?' She pointed over the counter. 'See them egg-holders?' Upside down on the counter was a white china holder for a half dozen eggs. 'It was them she could see reflected in the glass!'

We all laughed, Frank loudest of all. I mean it was funny after all, but I couldn't help wondering about it. 'Well, is any of it true then, what you tell 'em?'

'Course,' Frank said, through a fag he was lighting. The cigarette hissed and crackled between his lips and he pulled it out and glared at it. 'Christ! What are these things they're passing off for fags nowadays? It's a proper profession. And it'll be a good little earner. She's got quite a talent for it your auntie 'as.' He winked at Lil. Shirl was poking around in the leftovers from the pawn shop.

'Has Nan been to see you?' I talked to Lil. Wasn't any too sure about Frank these days. He was taking over a bit much for my liking.

'Nah, not on your life.'

'Well she wants to see you.'

Frank tutted. 'Never lets up, does she?'

I turned on him. 'She's Lil's mom. And she was looking after her long before you came on the scene.'

'Oi, Genie, no need for that,' Lil said. I saw Shirl look round at me. 'Frank didn't mean anything, did you?'

Frank gave me his most charming grin. 'Course not, no offence, Genie. She's a great old stager your nan.'

I stared hard at him. Cracks were showing here. No one, as Nan kept pointing out, should have a smile so bewitching or shoes you could see to powder your nose in.

Some woman came in then with an anxious face wanting her palm read, and Shirl and I took off to do our shopping.

'Go and see Nan,' I said to Lil before I went.

She touched my arm. 'Don't fret. It's all right, Genie – things are OK. I'll go tonight.'

'I just hope she knows what she's doing,' I said to Shirl. 'Our Lil thinks she's the world expert on men, but I can't say I'm any too sure about that one she's got there!'

The other person in our family who was happy as Larry was Len. Molly was coming up to seven months pregnant and was like the side of a house. Her big belly fascinated Len. Actually it fascinated Shirl too and she was forever leaning over Molly, asking questions about how it felt, was it kicking and all that. Len was a funny mixture of behaviour with Molly. He could ignore her for ages at a time while he fiddled about with Gloria, chuckled away at wireless programmes and forgot even to answer her as if she plain didn't exist. Other times he was all over her, feeling the babby moving whoever else was about, and stroking and kissing her as if she was a dolly or a pet dog until sometimes she got a bit sharp with him.

'Aw leave off, Lenny, will yer?'

Mister loved Molly and had been in the habit of curling up on her enormous cushions of thighs when she was around.

'Ooh!' Molly cried, shaking with laughter one evening when Mister leapt up in a great hurry and shot off her lap. 'The babby's kicked 'im off of me! 'E's going to be a footballer 'e is!'

The two of them often came over and sat with us, eating anything in sight, Gloria on, completely comfortable with everything in a way I never saw in anyone else. No restlessness, no question about Mom or worry about the way she was. No discontent. Nothing. That was Len and Molly – happy in chairs, for ever.

They were there when the siren went early on that month and Mister leapt up – this time off me – and howled, head back, the black and white fur across his throat stretched tight.

'Oh Lor,' Molly grunted, struggling to get out of her chair and not managing. 'Pull me up, Lenny. I'll 'ave to get over to Mom's.'

As she went, Lenny taking her along, Shirl and I started organizing. Tea in a flask. No booze. Light, coats, rugs.

'Len,' I called, hearing him come back in. 'Come and help with Mom.' But he lumbered in, picked up Gloria before anything else and stowed her under the stairs.

'My God,' I said to Shirl. 'What happened to women and children first?'

'No—' Mom was struggling to speak. 'I'm not going. Not out there.'

'Please, Mom, come on. We've got to.'

'NO.' She pulled her bad arm in close with the other one and leaned forward, curling in on herself.

What with the siren going and Mister howling and my nerves already in shreds before all that, I felt as if I was going to explode.

'What the hell am I s'posed to do?' I raged at Shirl. 'I can't force her, can I? What does it matter if we go out there anyway? We could all get killed whatever we do.'

Shirl took over, squeezed my arm. 'You're awright, Genie,' she said, sounding like Mr Tailor. She bent over Mom. 'Mrs Watkins, we're going to take you to the shelter. You can't stay 'ere.'

Mom hadn't the strength to resist us for long but I could feel the distress coming from her and I felt terrible. But I couldn't help thinking about Mrs Deakin and we struggled down the garden and got her inside. I put the Tilley lamp down on the floor and we laid Mom on one of the bunks, covering her up well. She turned her face away towards the corrugated wall.

Len brought Mister and closed us in. As the door shut I thought about tombs. Mister whimpered and came over to me.

'I'm so glad you're here,' I said to Shirl for the umpteenth time.

Her big eyes shone in the lamplight. 'Not 'alf as glad as I am, I can tell you.'

'What does your dad do – in the raids I mean?'

'Oh, 'e'll be all right. The factory's over Duddesdon – they've got a shelter there.'

'What, so you was on your own of a night?'

'Went round the neighbours – they've got a cellar. But I'd much rather be 'ere with you, Genie.' She turned her head. 'We're OK, aren't we Len?' she said, squeezing his arm. She nodded across at Mom and mouthed at me. 'She awright?'

I reached round, took Mom's good hand and held it. 'You asleep, Mom?'

She made a little noise so I knew she wasn't.

'You warm enough?'

'I'm OK.' It was a hoarse whisper.

When I turned back to Shirl I could see the pity in her eyes and I didn't know if it was for Mom or me. But seeing someone else looking in on my life made me feel so terrible about everything, the way it'd been broken and changed. First Big Patsy, Dad and Eric – even Lola, I felt sad about her – Mom and Bob and the dead babby, and Joe. But no, not Joe. I wasn't even going to let myself think about him . . .

Shirl made jokes to try and keep us going and I tried to laugh, thankful to her because it wasn't as if she had a lot to laugh about either. We talked in short bursts, going quiet when the planes came over, shrinking our heads down into our necks and cringing until they passed. A couple of times as it was going quiet Len put his arm round Shirl, and she said, 'Oh, you're a devil, you are.'

And I held Mom's hand and felt her silence like a leaden weight behind me.

I found Nan alone in her house the next day, down on her hands and her one good knee, the other bent up in front, blackleading the range.

'Here, let me do that.' I took the cloth and polish off her and tried to rub off some of my outrage at Lil on to its black surface.

'She said she was going to come back. Sod her! I

mean it's not as if Frank would even have been in with a raid on!'

'It would've been too late for 'er to come with the raid already started.' Nan had managed to pull herself stiffly to her feet. 'And anyroad, I'm awright. Take more than a load of Jerries to frighten me, I can tell you.'

She looked tired though. 'It's just not right you being on your own. Lil should know better.' I found I was shaking with anger, wanting to scream with it. There was never anything you could do about anything. I wanted to come and keep my nan company of a night, but how could I with Mom the way she was? And going into her house felt awful – no Lil, no kids running round.

Nan waved a hand at me to shut me up. 'How's your mother?'

'Same.' I was scrubbing like mad at the range.

'You're all skin and bone. You still being sick?'

'No.'

She absorbed this, then said. 'Morgan was bombed out last night – 'is place over in Aston.'

I stopped and looked round. 'D'he get out?'

'Oh, that sort always do. Rat out of a sewer. 'E was in the cellar, not a scratch on 'im. 'E was over earlier to see what state the room up 'ere's in again.'

'He's never thinking of moving in here?'

'Not unless he wants rain on his face every night. D'you know what 'e 'ad the nerve to ask me?' She didn't sound all that outraged, just exhausted. '"You being on your own now, Mrs Rawson, I was wondering if you could spare me one of your rooms for a bit?" Rubbing 'is hands together how 'e does.'

'Nan, you never . . .?'

A wicked twinkle came into her eyes. 'I told him I only ever live with men if I'm married to 'em, ta very much. That drained the colour out of 'im I can tell you.' She let out a big laugh and it was good to hear her. ''E says 'e's lost his business and 'e can't do any repairs till 'e gets the insurance and there's no telling 'ow long that'll take. So that'll keep 'im out of action for a bit!'

'Nan!' I laughed with her.

Wiping her eyes, she said, ''E's 'aving to find somewhere else to move in with his Mom!'

'God, you can't imagine him being anyone's son, can you?' Remembering, I pulled a letter from my pocket. 'This came today. I haven't shown it her.'

Eric's letter contained the usual wooden scraps of news that we'd had to get used to, but in the middle he wrote, 'Mummy says I can stay here for good if I want to.' Mrs Spenser had let him leave it in. She'd obviously wanted us to see it.

'Mummy?' Nan flared. She stared in disbelief. It wasn't just Eric thinking of Mrs S as his mom, it was him sounding like a toffy-nosed twit into the bargain.

'She can't do that, can she? She can't just keep him?' I was tearful all of a sudden. 'Soon there'll be nothing left.'

Nan gave my shoulder a pat. 'She can't just keep 'im, not unless—' She broke off and I knew she was thinking of Mom, of what sort of life Eric was going to come back to here. He wouldn't be getting piano lessons, that was for certain. I could see the grief in Nan's face, just for a quick flash. 'No. She can't just do as she likes.'

Teresa and her mom were spending as much time as they could over in the Quarter because it was obvious

Nonna Amelia was dying. But Teresa found time to call in and visit us and ask if I wanted to go and see the old lady for what would surely be the last time.

Teresa hadn't seen Mom since she'd come home. Mom hated anyone in the house, couldn't stand to be seen in her state. And Teresa couldn't keep the shock out of her face.

'It's terrible, Genie,' she said as we set off towards town. 'Is she going to get any better?'

I told her the little bit of hope we had. Even talking to Teresa I felt at a distance from her, and fiercely protective of Mom. I was almost sorry I'd let Teresa see her. Mom wouldn't go out at all, didn't want the neighbours' tongues wagging any more than they had already. Teresa was an outsider in this. It was Shirl who'd come in and got involved and I felt closer to her nowadays, and somehow that was another sad thing. I could tell Teresa didn't know what to say to me and I couldn't speak to her. If I asked about Carlo she'd be bound to bring up the subject of Joe, so I said nothing and walked along with my old friend feeling distant and tense.

Vera was already at Nonna Amelia's house with her sister and the youngest of the children. They greeted me warmly, but whether in Italian or English, everyone was speaking in hushed voices, as if Death was already in a conversation with the old lady that they were afraid to interrupt.

'You want to see her?' Vera led me upstairs, treading very quietly on the staircase. Teresa stayed down. Vera showed me into the room and then, to my surprise, left me and went down again. Soon I knew why. Communing with the dying's best done on your own.

There was no light in the room. It was a grey, overcast

406

day, and the curtains had been half drawn, leaving a gap of only about eighteen inches between them. Nonna Amelia was lying in her enormous bed with its high wooden bedstead in such deep brown wood it looked black. The only part of her to be seen was her face because the rest of her was well covered up with sheets and blankets, an eiderdown and a brocade coverlet. They seemed to have piled everything possible on top of her to try and keep the warmth in her tiny, shrunken body.

I could barely even see her face in the dim light and I moved closer to the bed. Her white hair was swept back behind her head which was resting on a white pillow slip embroidered with green leaves at one edge. I licked my dry lips and went to stand right by her. I didn't feel frightened or sad, just awed. Like a tiny, new-born babby, she was already half somewhere else that the rest of us have forgotten, with this life we know still just clinging to her. Now those wise, dancing eyes were closed there was only a shrunken, bony face, the skin yellow, the Nonna Amelia we knew blown out like a match. But she was still there. I could hear her breathing.

'Nonna Amelia?' I whispered, putting my face close to hers. 'It's Genie – Watkins. Teresa's friend. I don't know if you can hear me. I just wanted to say—' What the hell did I want to say? What do you say to someone when you know it's the last thing you'll ever say to them? And if she could hear me she most likely wouldn't understand a word.

I pulled up a chair and sat leaning forward towards her. For quite a time I didn't say anything and that was OK. But then in a funny sort of way I felt as if she was listening to me, not like her, the old her, but just a sort of presence there to listen, like a priest or a statue.

'I wanted to say—' I hesitated, then looked away from her face and kept talking. 'I've always looked up to you, Nonna Amelia, because you're the sort of person who everyone loves. D'you know that? You might not have noticed, like Teresa hadn't until the war came – I expect you have though, because so many things have happened to you, haven't they, to make you wise?' I talked in fits and starts, not sure half the time whether I'd said something or just thought it. 'All I can say is I envy you your life because you've made a lovely family who all respect and love you. That's all I've ever wanted really, to have a family who are happy and who love me. But I can't seem to make it happen however hard I try. I thought, just for a little time – the best time of my life—' As I said this my throat started aching and I had to stop and swallow hard. 'I thought I might be able to have it with Joe. I tasted what it might be like . . . But now I know that was only a dream . . . I've wrecked everything and I know things don't happen for me like that, and it's all falling apart round me and I can't keep it together . . .'

Words kept coming out of my mouth, about Mom and Joe and how bad I was feeling. Words I couldn't have said to anyone else. I felt she was listening, but maybe that was because I wanted someone to. After, I leaned down and kissed those cheeks, soft as flower petals, staring into the shadowy face of this old lady whose life was laid out in front of me.

A light sigh came from the bed, a lift in the breathing, little shudders in the rhythm as she breathed out. I stood up and managed to smile at her. 'Thanks, Nonna Amelia.'

It was a moment before I saw that had been her final breath. No, it couldn't be! I lifted the covers and felt around in a panic for a pulse in her frail wrist. Nothing. I hardly remembered getting downstairs.

'She's gone, Mrs Spini,' I said. 'I was just standing there, and—'

It was expected, but still a shock. Vera's face tightened and she gave out a long breath almost as her mother had done. I was upset and embarrassed. I wasn't family. I was the wrong person to have been there. Why did old women have to keep choosing to die suddenly when I was around?

But Vera stepped forward and embraced me, kissing my face on each cheek before she went upstairs. 'I think it was a compliment to you.'

Thick clouds and foul weather saved us from bombing that week but also meant that the day of Nonna Amelia's funeral was cold and wet. Whatever the weather the Italians were going to send Nonna Amelia off with all the pomp and splendour they could gather together.

I paid my respects to her again once the women had laid out and clothed her in a stiff black dress. Now she was dead her face looked like someone else.

They carried her to the Requiem Mass at St Michael's in a horse-drawn hearse. The six black horses, blinkered and adorned with noble black plumes, gleamed in the rain, their breath snorting out jets of steam around them, and walked with high steps as if they sensed the honour of the occasion.

Vera's brothers and other friends of the family carried wreaths to the church, the biggest taller than they were themselves, and there was an enormous crowd inside. She had been very much loved, that old lady, for her kindness, and very much respected.

Teresa walked in with Vera and the other girls, all in their black lace, and Nanny Rawson limped beside me. Nan could swallow her misgivings about Catholics generally for the sake of this family in particular.

The strain was showing on Vera's face. As we settled in our pews, Nan steadfastly refusing to bob up and down to the High Altar or any of that, I whispered, 'If only Mr Spini was here. It's so hard on her, in't it?'

After the solemn Mass Nonna Amelia was taken off to Witton Cemetery with the closest of the family. But we called round later to join in the wake, the men and bottles ensconced in the front room, the women in the back, some of them crying as if they were there with the job of letting out grief on everyone's behalf.

We sat with the women for a time, everyone in black, accepting food and drink. Teresa came and sat by us in her black crêpe dress, looking worn out.

'You all right, love?' Nan said to her.

'I'm OK, ta. Thanks for coming both of you.' She seemed a bit distracted I thought, in a bit of an odd mood, because through all the tiredness and formalities she looked somehow excited. While the other women were talking loudly she moved closer to me. 'I've got summat to tell you.'

I looked round at her.

'Carlo's asked me to marry him.' I hadn't imagined it then, that light in her eyes. He'd written to her, couldn't even wait to come home and ask.

'He's such a hothead,' Teresa said affectionately. 'Not quite the same as going down on one knee, is it!'

I didn't have to ask what the reply was going to be.

'But at your age – what does your mom say?'

'I'll be seventeen soon and she adores Carlo. Always has. I s'pose if it wasn't for the war she'd tell us to wait,

410

but she was so scared I'd go off and marry a Prot and leave her, she's quite happy. A good Italian Catholic boy with his family in the Quarter, she's not going to let that one slip past!'

I flung my arms round her. 'I'm really happy for you, Teresa. Nice to have some good news for once.'

'Well, good luck to you both,' Nan said when we told her, though we had to keep our congratulations low as no one else was to know yet. Even despite the sadness of that day Teresa did look happy and settled in herself.

As we left she kissed me extravagantly and hung on to my arm, hugging it. 'Maybe you and I should make a double wedding?'

Gently I pulled away. No one was going to see the ache in my heart, not now. I covered it with a laugh. 'Bit tricky that one, ain't it, since neither of us are Catholics!'

That Sunday afternoon I answered a knock on our door to find Mr Broadbent standing there. His car was parked across the road. My knees went weak.

'Genie?' He looked ever so uncomfortable having turned up like that. I couldn't ask him in. There was Mom asleep in a chair and out of pride I didn't want him seeing her. And I guessed why he was here. I just couldn't let him near me because if he said too much I knew I'd cave in completely. I stood stiffly in the doorway, my expression closed tight as an iron door.

'Sorry to bother you, love,' he said. 'I know it's a bit funny me calling. But Joe's very anxious about you. Said he hasn't heard a thing from you for ages and he asked me to check and see if you were all right.'

I swallowed, looked past him seeing the ground was

wet outside and it was filthy still, mess from the street's wreckage continually trodden back and forth. 'I'm awright.'

Mr Broadbent seemed so embarrassed I felt guilty, but I couldn't help him.

'He keeps hearing about the raids of course. It's not as bad where they are, nothing like.' He paused. 'Are you sure everything's all right, Genie? Only Joe's wondering why he hasn't heard. He's upset and worried. You mean a lot to 'im.'

I shifted my weight from one foot to the other, arms folded tight, stared over Mr Broadbent's head across our smashed-up street.

'I can't write,' I said, holding on tight to myself inside and out. 'Just can't. You'd better tell Joe he's made a mistake. Tell him to forget me.'

'Oh.' He stroked his hand back over his hair. 'I didn't know it was like that.'

I was moving back into the house.

'But Genie – wait, love . . .'

'Love' undid me. 'Got to go. Mom's calling.' And I shut the door. Leaned on it, gulping, and closed my eyes.

Tuesday. And there was Lil at Nan's, sobbing her heart out, and Nan's face clenched like a rat trap with 'What did I tell you?' written all over it. It took me quite a time to get the whole sorry story. Nanny Rawson, it seemed, had been right about Frank with a vengeance.

'That didn't take long, did it?' Nan said. 'Talk about living in Cloud Cuckoo Land – people like that believe their own lies.'

Lil sobbed even harder.

'So you mean he's got another woman?' I said, trying to put together the bits of information dribbling out between Lil's snuffles and sobs.

'I – I was so sure about him,' she wailed. 'How could I have got it all so wrong? How could he tell me so many lies?' She had no make up on and her lids looked naked, pink and puffy. She put her head in her hands, so betrayed and dejected. I looked at Nan, framed in the window's dying light. She folded her arms, glanced at Cathleen who was on the floor with a rag doll.

'Not only is lover boy already married with a kid, 'e's got this other trollop set up across town – where is it? Hockley or somewhere – doing all this fortune telling and that . . . Only she's a bit more to 'im than 'e was letting on before!'

'And there's a flat over the top of that one,' Lil wailed. 'I reckon she sees more of him than I do!'

'Christ,' I said, 'how does he manage it?'

Nan frowned at my blaspheming.

I didn't know whether I was surprised or not. I mean I was, by the facts, by Frank's cunning, his sheer energy. But somehow not by the actual truth of it. He was much too good to be real, too charming, too slippery.

'So how did you find out, Lil?'

'Oh—' She waved a hand tiredly, as if that hardly mattered any more. 'He didn't come home.' She gave a harsh laugh. 'Not that that should surprise me, by all accounts. Anyway, he'd been on duty, or so he said. So I went up to the ARP post. I mean it's not as if we've had any raids, is it? They were ever so funny with me at first, wouldn't say a thing. Didn't know where he was. So I was going, then one of them came after me and said Frank'd been in an accident. They'd gone into a bombed out warehouse and Frank'd had a load of stuff come down on him and done his neck in bad. So I go carting up the General to find 'im ...' She sat twisting her hanky round and round. 'I'm sat there by the bed when this bird walks in, looks at me as if I stink and says, "Who the hell are you?" So I say, "Well, who are you?" And she says—' Lil's voice broke again. '"I'm his wife." They've got a little lad an' all, six years old, called Bertie.'

'Well, what about the other woman?' I could feel rage rise in me for my poor auntie Lil. What I wouldn't do to that smarmy ...

'She, his wife, knew about her. Suspected anyway. Didn't know about me.'

Did now though.

'The raids gave him the perfect excuse,' Lil sobbed. 'He was always telling us he had to be somewhere else. And the flat over the garage was a bit bare, but I thought it was just his bachelor way of life.'

Nan's fury twitched in her cheeks. She sliced bread for Cathleen, loaf under one arm, with a look of it being Frank's neck.

'Oh Lil,' I said. We put our arms round each other and I stroked her back. Sweet, loving Lil. It knifed me through to see her so hurt and destroyed, so alone all over again.

'How could he do it?' she sobbed, shaking. 'How could he? What have I done to deserve this? How could he lie to me and me not know – and to her? Poor cow's got a kid and she's saddled with him. The worst of it is ...' She pulled away from me and sat up wiping her eyes with the wet hanky. 'I really loved him. I still do. I mean if he walked in here and spun me some tale about it was all a mistake and none of it was true I'd have him back, I would.'

Nan yanked the blackout viciously across the window. 'Then you're a bigger fool than you look.'

'Can't all be like you, can we, Mom?' Lil said, without aggression. 'Some of us have to believe you can have something better.'

Nan didn't rise to that, just slopped tinned pears in Cathleen's bowl.

'What're you going to do, Lil?' I said softly.

She sat very still, staring into the fire. 'I dunno. Oh God. I suppose I'll have to come back here – if Mom'll have me.' She didn't look at Nan. 'Go back to Parkinson Cowan or somewhere. The factory. Right back to square one.'

When I left them, feeling guilty that I'd be so late home, I was bursting inside. I had a tight feeling in me from pent up emotion about everything that had happened, and seeing Lil in that state of betrayal and lost hope had brought it all to the surface. We were all so stuck, waiting, and not knowing whether what we were waiting for was going to bring more pain and more disaster into our lives. We could lose the war, my mom was stuck in a mockery of what was once her body, I'd rejected a good man who loved me because of my anger with myself – and now this. Now I'd seen Lil fall victim to Frank's self-obsessed greed and lust.

It was already dark as I stormed along the Moseley Road, trying to release some of the feelings. If it was light I'd have run. This time of the evening there was too much danger of colliding with someone or knocking myself out on a lamp-post. But the sky was clear and there was a moon. Bomber's moon, I thought. *God.*

It was as if my thoughts set it off. The sirens wailed

round me so loud and horrible I wanted to scream myself. People out on the street started rushing and I could see threads of light from torches moving fast, combing the pavement.

I needed to get home quick. At least Shirl was there. Wonderful Shirl. She'd get Mom and Len organized. But the thought of the shelter, of sitting still in there when I was so frantic with anger and frustration was hateful.

Turning the corner of St Paul's Road I could just make out that someone was standing there, and as I passed, in the quick yellow flare as a match was struck, lighting the end of a fag into a glowing orange bead, I knew those features. Dark brows, heavy-set face. Bob. My rage boiled over.

'You bastard! You shit-faced bastard!'

With all the fury of my compressed emotion I flung myself at him, taking him completely by surprise, yelling and screaming against the noise of the siren. I tore my nails down his face with every bit of my strength, kicked at him, grabbed something, his hand, took the fleshy bit above the thumb knuckle in my mouth and bit right into it until I felt it crunch.

'Aaagh – what the *fuck* . . .?'

He caught hold of me, easily stronger now he'd got his act together and was furious and in pain, pinned my two hands together, pulled out a torch and shone it in my face.

'You! You little bitch!'

With pleasure I saw blood on his cheeks. I drew up a big gob of spit and let him have it in one eye.

'Christ.' He had to wipe it with his shoulder, moving his grip to the tops of my arms, pinning them to me hard.

416

'Get off me.' I struggled, fighting him. 'Don't you touch me.'

'You evil little bitch, you—'

'My mom nearly died because of you. She was having your babby, the one you ran off and left her with, you lump of dog muck. She put her head in the gas oven and now she's a cripple thanks to you. I hate you! I hate you ... Get your fucking hands off of me. I've got to get her into the shelter – she can't walk properly. Let me go ...' I was sobbing and cursing, beside myself, and Bob relaxed his grip on me. I twisted free and started running.

'I hope they get you—' Through my tears I screamed at the sky. 'Come on you stupid Jerry bastards – come and get this one!'

They were overhead, the planes, but I just kept running. This area was a favourite of theirs of course. They thought a lot of the factories were here instead of on 'shadow' sites like Castle Bromwich. They were after the BSA – Birmingham Small Arms – the big munitions factory which made motorbikes in peacetime. They'd already hit it but they were back for more. Looking up through my tears, I saw planes pass black in front of the moon. That wave of bombs fell over to my left, further north. It sounded as if there were a lot of them out tonight.

I tore along Brunswick Road. Thank God for Shirl, I thought again. If she'd not been there I'd have been too late. I dragged my hands impatiently across my wet eyes. There was no more time for emotion.

The house was dark of course, like all the others. There was no point in banging on the door so I ran to the side gate, struggling with the latch, caught my sleeve on the fence and then stumbled down the garden. There were more planes and the whistle and crunching boom of the explosions. Even before I got to the shelter one came down very near and I threw myself down, curled up. The ground snatched under me and the sky lit up. I heard glass breaking.

'Shirl. Shirl!' I yelled. 'Get the door open for me!'

She couldn't hear me over the racket. They'd be worried about me. Head down I covered the last few yards, pulled the front off the Anderson and flung myself in. To find it empty and dark.

There should have been matches but nothing was there. I felt around every inch of the floor but couldn't find them. It was pitch black.

'Damn! Damn you, Shirl. Where are you? Why aren't you all out here?'

I felt my way up on to one of the seats and perched on the edge, once more boiling over with anger and frustration. Did I have to do everything? And I wanted Mister, the distraction of comforting him in my lap and being able to think about him and Mom instead of my own skin.

The shelter seemed to close in round me. I had a picture of it in my mind as a flimsy bubble, thin enough to give off rainbows in the sun, out here under all the bombs. I didn't like being alone in the dark. I pulled my legs up, resting my heels on the edge of the berth and curled tight, hugging my knees.

When it lets up a bit I'm going in, I thought. Couldn't do it now, it'd take too long to move Mom. She couldn't just run down the garden like the rest of us. I wondered where Len was. Maybe he was at Molly's and Shirl hadn't been able to manage on her own?

I lost track of time. I wasn't sure exactly when I'd left Nan's – I guessed it had been about half six – or

418

how long I'd been in the shelter. Seemed like hours. I couldn't keep my mind on anything but how scared I was, because it was all too much, much worse on your own. My mind did something it'd done before during the worst raids, it sort of closed down until I was repeating just one word: Please, please, please . . .

One came down very near. The ground shook and I pulled my head tight on to my knees, hearing myself moan with fright. Clifton Road at the back, it sounded like, though the noise could mislead you. I was thinking who did we know, did we know anyone in Clifton . . .?

I didn't hear it coming, not that one. Just knew one minute I was sat there, the next I was choking, buried, my mouth and nose full of soil, earth over me, terrible the close fit of it, buried alive. Every muscle of my body was clenched in a mad, fighting panic, wrenching and twisting, spitting, coughing, savage with desperation for a clear unclogged breath. In a second I found I could move, so it wasn't a deep cover. Clawing with my hands, I felt air above and I fought my way out, hawking and spitting, feeling the soil crunch between my teeth, the horrible thick plugs of it in my nose and its tightness on my face, weighing down my lashes.

The door of the shelter had been blown right inside and was jammed in at a tilt, so I had to crawl past it to get out, forcing my shoulders out into the garden.

The next thing I remember was running up and down the street under an orange sky, not knowing what I was doing. A warden loomed from the shadows yelling at me, 'Get under cover! For God's sake get in!'

'Our house—' I stood pointing, lost. It only took one look from him. He steered me to a doorway. 'You can't hang about. Got anywhere to go?'

And then I was tearing along the Moseley Road

again, a road that had seen so many ordinary days, ducking in and out of doorways as the sky seemed to tear apart above me.

We were down there as soon as the All Clear sounded, even though it was still dark, holding on to each other, Nan, Lil and me, braced for the sight.

They were working on our house. The air was full of dust which coated the inside of your mouth and once more there was the queasy-making smell of gas, but today we noticed these things only in the very far back of our minds. Morning dawned slowly, the colour of an old net curtain, and with the light more and more people came out into the road, watching and murmuring to each other. An ambulance waited near by.

We stood in silence. There was nothing to say. We had long ago done the things we could do: called at the Benders' house; no, no Len. He'd stayed home. Lil, the only one of us who could function at all, ran, jumping the hoses, to one of the wardens and grabbed at his sleeve. He listened, shaking his head. Couldn't tell her anything. Not yet.

As we stood there with Gladys and Molly a nurse with red hair came to us from the ambulance, seeing who we must be, and spoke to us in a reverent sort of voice. 'Maybe it's better if you don't watch. It can be distressing. Would you like to come and wait over here?'

But we couldn't move, shook our heads dumbly. Cups of tea were given us by people whose faces we didn't even see. I didn't remember drinking except suddenly I was holding an empty cup, until someone took it away. I heard Molly sobbing.

It took a long, long time, eyes straining, listening to the grunts and shouts of the rescuers, feet crunching on glass and rubble, sometimes the noise of a saw or drill on the cold morning air. And we could do nothing except stand and wait.

'Quiet!' The man who seemed to be in charge of the team eventually waved his hands. 'I need quiet. I can hear something.' Silence came down like a chopper. We all strained our ears and heard tiny mewling noises from somewhere in the wreckage. The men looked at each other. I knew as soon as they did that that wasn't a human sound. It was a dog – Mister, alive somewhere in all that. My spirits lifted for a second. But what about the others? What about Mom, Len, Shirl? What we all wanted to hear, what we yearned for from the depths of our being, was to hear their voices crying for help so we knew they were alive. But apart from Mister's frantic scratching and whining, there was nothing to hear from inside, just quiet. Deathly quiet.

They brought Shirl out first, covering her bloodied face with a sheet. We couldn't see the rest of her. I gripped Lil's hand. There was no need to ask if she was dead. With each body they brought out, so carefully, so painstakingly, a ripple, that low murmuring sound passed through the scattering of people, a sound of horror and sympathy, a long, wordless, human breath.

Mom was next. It took them some time to bring her out. They did their best for us, closing ranks, their backs to us as they arranged on the stretcher the parts of her they had salvaged, shielding her, and us, before they could decently cover her. They didn't look at us as they carried her away. Nan's hand came up and clasped over her mouth and stayed there, her eyes fixed on the house as they carried her children out. She didn't move. She was waiting for Len.

They had to move more rubble from the brown, crumbling heap that was our house. Mister didn't let up whining. Some of our things were scattered in the road, looking small, dirty and humiliating. Scattered bits of furniture, shreds of a chair cover, the mantel clock with its glass shattered rolled out into the road, pink-backed playing cards turning over in the breeze. Shirl's black bag. *Oh Shirl.*

Len's fleshy, schoolboy body was soaked in blood. When she saw them bring him, Molly threw herself forward, taking the rescue team by surprise, falling on him, a great howl coming from her that seemed to crack the air apart. 'Len – Lenny – my Len – no-o-o-o-o.' She kissed him again and again and came up with blood on her face as they prised her away, belly shaking with sobs. Gladys drew her into her arms, her child with child.

When they brought Len to the ambulance Nan walked forwards, pulling her coat round her. Lil and I followed.

'It's better if you don't—' the nurse started to say.

Nan held up a hand to stop her. 'It's awright, love, I'm not going to make any fuss. Just give me a minute – there's no harm.'

She pulled the sheet back and looked at him. Len's eyes were half open, his face cut by glass but not disfigured.

'Good lad.' She ran her rough hand over his matted hair. 'You've been a good'un, Len. A good son.' She gave him a last, long look, then covered his face again and started walking away.

'Mom.' Lil took her arm. Nan's eyes were glassy. She was in shock, we all were. 'Where're you going?'

'Home. There's nowt to stay 'ere for, is there?'

'I've got to stay,' I said. 'For the dog.'

Mister was freed shortly after from the cupboard under the stairs and he tore out still yapping hysterically. When I called to him he rushed into my arms in convulsions of quivering, and licked my face. It was only then my own legs started trembling, and it was all I could do to stay standing.

Later that day there was a knock at Nan's door. It was Mr Tailor. His house was still up.

'I'm sorry, love,' he said to Lil. 'Sorry what's happened, and for barging in on you like this. Only they found this – under the stairs, so it's kept safe. I thought you'd like to 'ave it before some bugger nicks it.'

In his arms was Gloria, plus accumulator, without a scratch on her.

'The King's 'ere,' Mr Tailor said as he went. 'Walking round town. Come to see the damage, I s'pose.'

We laid Gloria on the table. Nan sat by her, stroked her hand over the dusty veneer. Slowly, lovingly, she touched the knobs. Then she laid her head on her arms and wept.

I was ill after that and the days disappeared. My throat was so painful I could hardly even stand to swallow water. It must have been all the soil and muck I'd had in my mouth, and I had a very high temperature and delirium. A lot of the time I couldn't remember what had happened in a direct way, but all the sensations and dreams wrapped in that hot, twisting fever were threatening, sometimes shapeless, sometimes clear, always awful.

In one of my dreams Mom was back in our house as it had been. She was speaking to me and I knew what she was saying was the last thing I'd ever hear her say, but however much she strained and forced her slack mouth to shout, she couldn't make me hear her. I sweated with concentration trying to remember the last living thing my mother would say but I always failed.

There was another dream. Again I was in our house. Pieces of my mother were lying in a chaotic jigsaw puzzle round the rooms and I had to put them together before – before what I didn't know. Before it was too late – for something. I ran from room to room picking up an arm here, a hand or foot there. I had to save her. The horror of the dream was knowing all the time I wasn't going to make it. Once when I dreamed that dream it was Joe, not my mother, whose limbs were lying scattered.

Again and again I woke trying to scream, my throat a ring of fire, and Lil would come to me, trying to quiet me, her hand cool on my forehead. Day and night I couldn't stop my hands from shaking.

I don't know how my nan got through those days. I was so sick, and it was Lil who held on, who was strong for us all. She knew bereavement, perhaps knew how to survive.

'It's all right, Genie love.' She held me all the times as I mumbled out, feverish, all the things I blamed myself for. Kept going on about Shirl, Shirl's dad.

'None of this is your fault, love. None of it. The only person to blame for all this is Adolf bloody Hitler. That's who's the cause of all of it. You stop blaming yourself. You've been a really good kid and no one could've done more than you. You've just got to get yourself better now.'

The fever left me and I lay in bed weak and thin as tissue paper, looking round at the bare walls where Tom and Patsy slept when they were here. I barely had the strength to move and my throat still felt as if I'd been gargling with gravel.

'Look.' Lil came in one day carrying a card. 'From Victor – from your dad.'

She held it in front of my eyes. A card from a POW camp addressed to Mom. His health was good, it said. At the bottom he sent 'Best regards to yourself, Genie, Eric, Len, Edith, Lil and the rest. Happy Christmas. Yours ever, Victor.'

I looked up at Lil. 'Of course he doesn't know. We'll have to tell him.'

She looked away out of the window, her eyes very sad. 'Yes we will. Poor old Victor.'

Teresa came and her face in the doorway looked scooped out and deathly white.

'You better, Genie?'

'Think so, ta.' I hid my trembling hands under the covers. 'Bit wobbly still.'

'Your nan says d'you want a drink?'

'In a bit. What's up?' I pulled myself up on one elbow, disturbed by the way Teresa looked.

She sat on my bed. 'Stevie's home.' Her voice broke up and she spread her hands over her face, distraught. Only after a few moments she managed to say, 'Dad's dead.'

'Your dad – dead?'

She lowered her hands despairingly. 'They didn't even bother to let us know. Probably didn't think a wop traitor was worth it.' I'd never heard such hate in her voice before. 'They just sent Stevie out to do it for them.'

'When, Teresa? What happened?'

'Stevie says a fortnight ago. He caught pneumonia. No one'd do anything, although Stevie went on and on at them – said Dad's lungs were already bad and he needed attention. They didn't get him to hospital until it was already too late.' She thumped her fist on the bed, her face twisted with anger. 'No one was there when he died. None of us. Not even Stevie.'

'Oh God, Teresa. I'm so sorry.' I thought of Nonna Amelia's death, all the family waiting to hand her gently into it. And Micky so much younger, shouldn't have died at all. Micky who was told the Mother of God would catch him when he fell.

Teresa wiped her red eyes. 'I've been to see you before but you was too poorly. You looked really bad.'

'Felt it.'

'I'm sorry – your mom, Lenny ... It's terrible, Genie.'

I nodded. 'Your dad, Teresa – he was good to me.'

'I know. I knew when he'd gone – what I'd missed. And then when I got to know Carlo properly I started wanting to know all about his life over there, Dad's childhood, his mom and that. I used to get fed up with him trying to tell me – I was so arrogant. I thought, when he gets back I'll be able to ask him . . .' She trailed off, wiping her eyes. 'Oh, what's the use?'

She shifted closer and we put our arms round each other.

'God, Genie, you're skinny!'

'I can feel your bones too.'

We rested our cheeks together.

'When Carlo and I get married, will you be my bridesmaid?'

I squeezed her. 'Course I will.'

I stayed in just about all the time, mostly up in my room, often lying on the lumpy bed but not asleep, not exactly awake, but in a weak, dreamlike state brought on by my illness. When I thought about moving I had to concentrate hard to make an arm move or a leg. Mister often came and lay on my bed to keep me company and I liked his warm weight by my feet.

Now and then I found the strength to go down, even outside. But people stared, and once I had Clarys bitching at me in the yard. 'I hope you 'aven't brought your bombs with you.' People believed that, that the bombs followed you. Not that we were having much in the way of bombing at the moment anyhow. But I stayed in. It was freezing out. Now and then I sat down by the fire, Mister at my feet. I switched Gloria on, stroked her sometimes. She was all that was left of home as it had been.

Lil and Nan were just getting on with it. Keeping going. The shop opened, the jobs got done, Nan's hair was suddenly almost white, the skin looser on her face. Lil too looked very haggard, but everyone was gentle. We knew we were all we had.

Now I'd surfaced I started to remember other things. That it was nearly Christmas for one. And that Lil had lost Frank. She never mentioned him, just came and went, looking after me and Cathleen like an angel. She even tried to decorate the house up a bit for the season.

'What're you going to do, Lil?' I asked her, watching her hang snippets of holly on the mantel. I was huddled in my nightdress and a coat by the fire. 'You going back to the factory?'

She stood back to eye up her decoration. 'No.' I saw her chin come out, determined. 'I've been doing a lot of thinking. I may not be able to have Frank, but one thing I've got out of all this is that shop. I was doing well at it – got a bit of a flair for it.'

'But Lil, is it real? It looked like a big con, that lady thinking the egg-holders were the Alps and that?'

'Depends on your attitude,' Lil said seriously. 'Course you can trick people. Tell 'em any old rot. But there's a skill to the cards and the palm reading and the rest. You can use your instinct. Really try and feel your way into a person, who they are. I can do it – I know I can. People trust me. Sort of open up to me. I'm going to keep the lease and make a go of it. Make it nice inside with a little grotto for the crystal ball and the palm readings. I've coped on my own before and I can do it again.' She grinned at me suddenly. 'Not as if Frank's the only bloke in the world, is it?'

She frowned then. 'Why aren't you opening your letters, Genie?'

Our post came redirected now, from the old house.

'Letter. There's only been one.'

'Well – one then?'

I shrugged, looking down, pulling the old brown coat close over my knees. 'Don't, Lil.'

428

'Don't what?'

'I don't want to talk about it.' I'd thought he'd stopped writing. I was glad. It was over. But then this other one had come.

Lil knelt down in front of me, staring up into my face. 'You loved him, Genie. Don't shake your head at me. It was clear as anything.'

I stood up, pushing her away, my throat aching with tears.

'I told you, I don't want to talk about it. You don't know what you're on about. Just leave it.'

I went up to bed again, swallowing hard, Mister following me, his claws loud on the wood stairs.

We got ready for Christmas out of habit, even though there was nothing to celebrate except the lack of bombing. The night air had been a lot quieter lately. You could sleep right through if habit allowed you. Preparing for Christmas was a way of remaining steady, keeping some of the normal things going when the rest had been smashed apart.

Nan ran the shop, accepted people's condolences and put up with blokes coming and going to mend Morgan's roof. Morgan was desperate to get back his access to a private place away from his elderly mom as soon as possible and he kept coming and eyeing up the work, demanding to know how many days it would take. It was a sign of how things were that Nan made not a murmur. Even the thought of Morgan creeping back and forth had suddenly become a sign of longed for normality.

We didn't speak about Mom or Len much. We all knew what had happened to Mom and no one wanted to bring it out in the open. It was too terrible. Nan hadn't even been able to see her at the end. In secret shame I wondered how Mom's life would've gone on if she'd lived. Would I have kept finding her eyeing up the gas oven until one day she finished it that way for good?

Instead of talking about Len, we talked of Molly. She was heartbroken, poor thing.

'We'll have to give her any help we can,' Nan said. 'After all, I'm the babby's grandmother, aren't I?' It was clear to see that if there was ever a little babby going to be swamped with doting nans, this would be the one.

On Christmas Eve we sat round the fire, Nan and Lil drinking hot toddies. Cathleen, full of excitement, was allowed up late and the rest of us were doing our best for her, although I could tell Lil was low. She and Cathleen were missing the boys and it'd really hit home tonight. She'd sent parcels for them out to Leek and was toying with the idea of bringing them home.

'It's not over yet,' Nan said, swirling her drink round to cool it. 'Now you've sent them you might as well wait till it's safe for 'em – even if it is *his* aunt. She's good to them by all accounts, and you don't want Tom all worked up again.'

'So you don't think I was all wrong sending them?'

'No. Even if your reasons were dodgy at the time.'

'I do hope they're all right,' Lil fretted.

'They sound it. Sure you don't want a drop of this, Genie?' Nan offered.

'No ta.' I stuck to tea. Mom'd given me a horror of drink. I'd have signed the pledge the way I felt about it. And I still wasn't well. I felt feverish again tonight, turning hot and cold, my hands shaking so I could only just control the cup.

'Look at the state of her,' Lil said. 'You poor kid.'

I tried to give her a smile.

We had carol singers round, kids mostly, and stood outside the front door listening, door closed because of the blackout. Their feet crunched on the frost and I was shivering.

'Once in Royal David's City,' they sang, not quite in tune but well enough to make you fill up. Made me think of those stories of the last war – the Christmas truces, carols floating across the trenches. How blooming peculiar the world was.

The singing brought our emotions to the surface and we couldn't stand much of it. We gave them a couple of coppers to get rid of them. We hadn't sung together at all. Not without Mom and Len. Back inside we were all quiet, full of that swell of emotion that Christmas brings, but for each of us this time, an unbearable amount worse. It brought us up against all we'd lost. I knew everyone was thinking of it.

In the end Lil said, 'You're going to have to take her place now, Genie. Should we sing, Mom?'

We both looked at Nan. Her jaw tensed. 'No,' she said quietly. 'I don't think so. Not yet.'

We got Cathleen ready for bed, eyes still bright with excitement, like a Christmas angel herself in her little nightdress. I thought of how she used to sleep in her raggedy vest and bloomers before the war when times had been so hard for Lil.

'You get off to sleep now,' Lil and I told her. 'Or Father Christmas won't come.' Lil had bought her a puzzle and a cheap little ornament, a mermaid with a shiny blue tail. She was going to love it.

431

On the way down from saying goodnight to her I came over dizzy and had to sit down quick to stop myself falling downstairs. Lil looked at me anxiously.

'You're not right yet, are you? Nowhere near.'

'No. I feel pretty bad. I'm going to turn in too.'

I lay in the dark feeling the fever come over me in hot waves, shivering one minute, pushing the covers off the next, sea-tides of hot and cold pushing me back and to. Thoughts seemed to clang into my mind harder than usual, chopped up, distorted by fever. Thoughts of how this house felt like a home to me, always had, down-stairs, Nan's shop, how I'd once dropped a drawer full of reels of coloured cotton and they'd bounced and spun off all over the shop going 'plok-plok' on the floor and it seemed to take for ever to pick them up. The sound echoed loud now in my mind. Eric had been there, a babby then, crawling round the floor, and he stopped, mouth wide open, head turning this way and that and not knowing which one to watch. Everyone paraded through my mind – Dad, Len, Mom, Bob. That fantastic feel of Bob's thumb crunching between my teeth.

I was asleep yet not asleep. I knew Mister had jumped off my bed and pattered off downstairs. He was barking for a time. Gloria must've been on. Music, then voices talking on and on. I wasn't sure how much time had passed, and whether I'd slept in the middle of it.

There was a light in the room, the unsteady glow of a candle, very vivid. Not a dream. Lil come to look in on me. Very drowsy, my eyes kept opening and closing.

'Can I have some water?' I managed to say in a hoarse whisper.

I thought I heard her talking, low voices, and I said, 'What?' Then the cold cup came to my lips as I half sat up, cold suddenly, teeth knocking against it. I opened my eyes, sipped. 'Ta.'

Not Lil. Was this a dream? Joe sitting on my bed, face full of anxiety. I heard myself gasp.

'Genie?'

'Joe. Joe?' In my weakness I lay back in the bed and found I was already crying. The wave broke over me, a great wash of tears that I couldn't hurry or stop. I heard the forgiveness in his voice even when he'd said so little, I saw it in his face, and it began to release everything. The terrible loss, the pain and fear and guilt of these past weeks that had been locked down in me, keeping him out, punishing myself as unworthy of him.

He knelt by the bed and took me in his arms as I sobbed hoarsely. 'It's all right.' He held his cool cheek against my burning one. 'It's all right now, my love. Sssh, my sweet one.'

'I'm s-s-sorry, Joe. I'm sorry. I'm sorry.'

I felt him take in a deep, shuddering breath and I clung to him, this miracle of love and forgiveness who'd appeared out of my dreams.

'Mom's dead. And Len.'

'I know. Your auntie Lil told me.'

I frowned, all muddled up. 'When?'

'Just now. I've just got in. From the station. I wrote and said I was coming . . . I know, you've had a terrible time.'

'Did she tell you Mom tried to gas herself?'

His head jerked back, horrified. No, she wouldn't have done.

'I felt so bad. So ashamed. I let everyone down. I thought you were too good for me. That's why I didn't . . . couldn't . . .'

'Sssh, Genie. It's OK.' He soothed me like a little kid

and that was just how I felt. I wanted someone to be my mom, my dad, my love, all in one. He sat me up and held me on his lap, stroking my hair.

'I didn't write because I thought—' I was still sniffing and gulping. 'I don't know what I thought. I just hated myself and it made me think you couldn't want to see me again.'

'I was worried.' There was a flash of hurt, of anger. 'Your letters were what kept me going, see. But Dad said he'd been to see you and said something about your mom being bad so I thought maybe you were too busy to write.'

I looked up into Joe's face. Mr Broadbent hadn't passed on my message. Not what I'd really said. Maybe he hadn't wanted to hurt Joe. Or did he just plain not believe me?

'Soon as I got here I had to come and prove to myself things hadn't changed. And of course when I got to your house, I saw—' I could hear tears in his voice. 'Jesus, I thought you were dead, Genie. You were dead and that's why I hadn't heard anything. When I saw your house – smashed up, gone – I felt as if everything had been destroyed, everything I'd hoped for, all we talked about doing together. Torn apart. It was the worst moment I can remember, ever.'

Wretched, I stroked his face and he took my hand and kissed it hard, a lot of times.

'I'm sorry, Joe. I'm terribly sorry.'

'No – I just wish I'd known. All that's happened . . .'

'D'you really love me – still, after all this?'

'I could never not love you.'

I held on to him so tight. 'I thought I'd lost everything. Almost everything. And then suddenly, oh Joe, you're here.'

We kissed, his lips pouring new life into me. We sat there quietly in each other's arms. I didn't know it was possible to feel so happy while I was so sad.

'You're very hot,' Joe said, feeling my head and neck. 'Your nan said you've been really bad. She's been worried about you.'

'She must be,' I said, cuddling against him in a haze of joy. 'Otherwise she'd never've told a bloke to come up into my bedroom!'

After a time Joe tucked me back in bed and kissed me. I put my arms round his neck. 'Don't go,' I said sleepily. 'I might wake and find I dreamed you.'

'You didn't dream me. I'll be back, love, every minute I can be.' He watched my face. 'I can't believe my luck. Now we've just got to get you better.'

'Oh, I'll be better now. I'll be better tomorrow!'

My eyes followed him to the door, candle in his hand. He turned, his lovely smile across the room more powerful than any medicine. 'See you tomorrow. Good-night, sweetheart.'

On 1 January 1941 the BBC launched a new programme called *Any Questions* which became very popular and was later renamed *The Brains Trust*. That day, I spent in my nan's house, my home for now, with Nan, Lil and Cathleen, and Joe on the sofa by my side, my bony hand held in his. Gloria sat, newly polished and shiny on the table, the voices pouring out through her sunburst. Mister was on my lap, a fire in the grate, tea in our cups.

Joe's eyes met mine as we first heard the posh, chattering voices and we laughed. I leaned into his arms and felt his kiss on the top of my head.

'Hor hor hor' laughed the chappies on the wireless. Lil's eyes filled, although she was smiling. She looked round at us all. 'Wouldn't Len have loved this?'